I0760304

BRIDE OF THE MIDNIGHT PRINCE

BRIDE OF THE MIDNIGHT PRINCE

ANASTASIS BLYTHE

BRIDE OF THE MIDNIGHT PRINCE

www.AnastasisBlythe.com

Hardcover ISBN: 978-1-960606-12-9

Laminate cover and jacket design by Saint Jupiter.
Interior art by Trif Designs.
Interior formatting by Dragonpen Designs.

FOR MY SWEET LYDIA

CHAPTER 1
KAT

VINES TRACE THREATENING patterns around my ankles as I wiggle my shoulders into the laundry chute. Of all the Fae Courts, the Nothril Court has the narrowest chutes. I curse them—and myself, for not finding an alternative option—every time I break in.

Don't be claustrophobic, Kat. Don't be claustrophobic, I tell myself when my hips get momentarily stuck. *You're in an enormous tunnel. Definitely not inside a tiny tube where you could totally get stuck and die before anyone found you. Or maybe you would be found, and that would be even worse.*

"It's your fault, Tailor, for being the best tailor on this side of the Vale," I mutter almost silently, my mask keeping the air around my face too warm. He's the one who was supposed to get this last target out. I could be completing my final task of robbing the Nothril prince of his precious supply of *ollea* instead—or we could even be gone already. But Princess Pelarusa decided she needed several unnecessary alterations for the gown he'd brought her. Tailor said we should count the last target as lost and leave before we're caught.

ANASTASIS BLYTHE

No, I told him. I'm not leaving this place without *all* our targets.

Restraining my grunts to a minimum, I crawl on my elbows through the tight chute and slide down it half a dozen times before I grab the edges and haul myself up into open space. The vines are forced to release me as I tumble onto the dirty floor of the Nothril slaves' laundry room. It is, as expected at this hour, utterly abandoned.

"Thank the saints," I mutter as I peel off my cloak and hood and stuff them into the linen sack I brought. I hurry to one of the baskets of dirty clothes and hunt through as quickly as I can. *There.* A perfectly soiled maid's uniform. It's slate gray, formless, and a little too big for me—even more perfect. I pull it on over my tucked tunic and trousers. My shoes I trade for another dirty pair.

My disguise is almost complete. I cast around for something—anything. I find a roll of bandages. *Yes*. I unwind my braid quickly, letting my hair fall everywhere as I wrap the bandages around the back of my neck and cover as much of my face as possible. The Nothril Court abuse their slaves enough that this shouldn't pass as anything out of the ordinary. Then, I pull my hair in front of what isn't bandaged and hunch my shoulders to give the illusion of a terrified slave girl.

Tucking my bag under my arm, I shuffle out of the washroom and into the maze of dark, cave-like servants' tunnels. None of the slaves in their matching uniforms, be they fae or human, give me a second glance. The tailor's directions rattle around in my head until I reach the door into the main corridors, where I pause. There is a grate in the rock, giving me a view into the grand hallway beyond. Great pillars of carved obsidian line the ornate hall.

The echo of boots on the stone floor carries into my hiding spot. I wait until it passes, and all goes quiet.

I slip out of the door into the grand hallway, making sure to stay hunched and mousey. I come upon a table of refreshments near the wall. They seem to be remnants left from a recent celebration. The food has been picked over, leaving nothing but crumbs. There are still drinks, though. Different types of fae wine, strong enough to make a human go mad, and Faerieland's favorite golden nectar. I march over to the table, pick up a tray, and stack a few goblets on it. Not sure how fae like their drinks, I pour a mix of both the wine and nectar into the goblets—about half of each, because that feels like a good ratio at the moment—and dust the remaining food crumbs onto the floor.

Then I grab my tray and scurry down the hallway, keeping my senses sharp. Only once do I run into a pair of Nothril guards. Monstrously tall with gleaming black armor, wickedly curved blades, and smooth helmets, they are the stuff of children's nightmares.

They pay me no heed, and I make it to my destination with no delays.

The door is, to no one's surprise, locked. Thankfully, since fae consider humans so beneath their notice, they overlook one of our most powerful tools: our blood. The things I have been able to unlock with a simple drop of my blood! It's the work of a few seconds to prick my finger and unlock the door.

I'm standing in an opulent chamber. Only three sides are walled, with a grand and jagged arch carved into the fourth wall—opening out to a vast overlook of an underground black river. The furnishings are an elegant blend of raw stone and polished details. The light is a low, blue glow emanating from uncut precious stones embedded in the cave-like ceiling. I bring my lower lip between my teeth and hurry past the empty reception room into the bedchamber beyond.

There, waiting on her knees, with her head bowed, is my target.

She's very young. Younger than me. Hair the color of raven's feathers falls around her beautiful face. Her dress is sheer, clinging to her form. She doesn't even look up when I enter.

My gut burns. *This* is why I wasn't about to leave a target behind.

"What's your name?" I whisper.

The girl's head whips up, her startlingly vibrant green eyes meeting mine in shock before they run over my attire and the bandages covering most of my face. "Elizabeth."

"It's a pleasure to meet you, Elizabeth. I've come to get you out of here."

Her mouth falls open. "Ivy Mask?"

My hands are occupied with the tray, so I jerk my head for her to follow me. "We've got to move fast."

She gets to her feet and we hurry back to the main chamber. I leave first, glancing around before I signal for her to follow me. We dive into the nearest entrance to the servants' tunnels. When the door shuts and darkness envelopes us, her knees wobble. I set down the tray quickly, looping my arm in hers, and whisper, "Have courage. You will be free of the Nothril Court within the hour. Forever."

She lets out a shaky breath, nodding, and firms her chin. Determination overtakes her features. I leave my tray behind, and we move quickly through the tunnels.

"Elizabeth!" hisses a woman's voice when we are halfway to the escape.

The girl beside me flinches. I spin around to face the voice.

It's a middle-aged woman in the same gray, shapeless servant's clothes I wear. Her features are slightly sunken and pale from lack of sunlight, and yet there is something instantly warm about her. Perhaps it is the way color still lingers in the apples of her cheeks, or her slightly heavy-set frame. Her hair is a light chestnut brown, but she still reminds me of my mother. Both relief and pain unfurl from my heart at the thought.

"You're supposed to be in Lord Nothril's chambers," the woman hisses at Elizabeth.

"He sent me to get her," I reply quickly.

The woman regards me. "Who are you?"

"I have no idea," I say, hoping to alchemize her suspicion into sympathy. "I only remember waking up in these clothes and being told to obey the orders of the people with the long ears and the wings."

The woman turns her frown from me to Elizabeth. "Go back to Lord Nothril's chambers. This girl doesn't know what she's talking about."

Excellent. I've undermined my own sanity. I snatch Elizabeth's arm before she can move. "No. She has to come with me. The one with the crown that looks like it would be very painful to sit on told me to get her. He wants her in the throne room."

"Lord Nothril will kill us all if she goes missing," the woman says fiercely, pointing at Elizabeth. "I won't have the lives of my other servants jeopardized because orders have been misunderstood. It's my job to make sure everyone stays beneath notice so that none of us incur wrath. And with what has happened to little Princess Pavi today, Lord and Lady Nothril are going to be extra furious if something goes wrong."

Elizabeth's jaw slackens. That movement is enough for me to grit my teeth. This girl doesn't deserve to be tortured any more than she already has been. I'll see if I can figure out a way to redirect the fury at her disappearance from the other human servants.

"Yes ma'am," I reply, dragging Elizabeth away before she can tuck her chin and return to her post. "I'll make sure none of us incur wrath."

The woman looks like she wants to protest, and I hate the fear shining in her eyes. I wish I could bring her with me. But I've got to get Elizabeth out of here. I must. I've never had a failed raid before—and this one isn't going to be my first.

"I should stay," Elizabeth whispers as we turn the corner. "I don't want the others to be hurt because of me."

"If others are hurt, it is *not* because of you," I reply fiercely. "I'm getting you out of here, and you are going to be safe. I will come back for the others."

I will come back for that woman, and she, too, will be safe.

Elizabeth doesn't reply, her courage waning with a guilt that I cannot assuage. She leans on me heavily as I navigate the darkness. My shoes make soft sounds but soon, light begins filtering from ahead. Her weight against me isn't much, weak as she is from malnourishment and ill treatment. This day will begin life anew for her. It will take time, but she will heal.

Most wounds heal, after all, if given enough time.

I grind my jaw and push onward.

When we spill out into the fading light, clogged with mist, someone is waiting for us.

The Valehaven tailor immediately rises from his hiding place behind one of the few shrubs that grow in this festering hole of a court. His spectacles are in disarray, his waistcoat smeared with dirt, and his eyes, normally glazed, flash with adrenaline. Elizabeth lurches in shock, huddling closer to me.

"It's alright," I say, still whispering. "Go with him now. He'll get you to safety."

Alarm turns the tailor's voice thin. "You're not coming?"

"I still need to get the prince's *ollea*," I reply, disentangling myself from the girl and prodding her forward. "This is my last chance before our big raid to get it."

And I need to make sure Lord Nothril gets mad at me, and not his other servants.

"You cannot go back in. You'll be caught. We've delayed long enough as it is!"

"Please don't go back in. I couldn't bear it if something happened to you!" Elizabeth cries.

The only bad that would come of something happening to me would be my work being halted.

"You can't go back in," the tailor repeats.

I flash a grin. "Watch me."

The tailor sighs deeply, rolling his eyes to the tops of the scraggly tress. The girl's brows pinch together nervously. He takes her by the shoulders and guides her away as I duck back into the tunnels. I check the bandages over my face and set a vigorous pace.

I shuffle through the bag slung over my shoulder and pull out my mask. It covers the full face, with tiny ivy leaves stitched over its entirety. I've been successful this long because I don't leave anything behind.

Now it's time to see just how much I can get away with.

"You've just got to rob a vicious Nothril prince, announce to the entire Court that wants you dead that you're the one who freed their slaves, and not get caught," I mutter to myself, and grin. "Easy."

CHAPTER 2

RAHK

I SLAM THE unseelie's body into the cliffside, the roots protruding from his scalp shaking with the impact. "I'm going to ask you again. Where is my sister?"

The creature's eyes roll back and turn glassy. I sigh as I release my grip. He falls to the ground in a lifeless heap, the back of his head caved in. I forget how delicate their skulls are.

It doesn't matter. I can track my sister without him, and he deserved far worse than what he got.

The air around me tingles with a symphony of scents. I inhale deeply, sorting through the sweetness of evergreen, the heaviness of earth, the dusty tang from the sedimentary cliffside, and the distinct spice of rot coming from beneath the fingernails of the dead unseelie. *There*. Among those scents, I catch what I'm looking for: the bright zest of lemon mixed with blooming jasmine.

Don't worry, Pavi, I'm coming to get you.

I follow her scent, running along the cliff's base, staying near the boundary between Caphryl Wood and the Star City. When the scent grows from a tiny thread to a river, I leap into the air, letting my wings carry me faster than my feet can. The scent takes me higher, higher, until I've reached the top of the cliff. The city sprawls below in the valley, its tall spires piercing the evening and rising even above this cliff.

I land on the waving grass beneath the setting sun.

There, a stone's throw away, is a line of Star City warriors. They wear violet armor imprinted with glowing rings of star-like gems. I cannot see past them, but Pavi's scent is so strong that she must be here. My blood runs hot. I brace my feet wide as I draw my two broadswords.

So it *was* the Star City that captured Pavi. It is a bold move for a vulnerable city not associated with a Court.

"Caspar!" I shout. "I know you're behind this. Don't make me slaughter all your good men."

Pavi's high-pitched voice comes from behind the line of warriors. "Rahk! You've come too early!"

So Caspar has her at knife point. *Cowardly snake*. "If negotiations are what you want, then say so. The Nothril Court doesn't deal kindly with those who harm their heirs," I shout. I size up the warriors between my sister and me, landing on the one with a misbalanced stance as the target of my attack.

Abruptly, they fall back, parting like a curtain to reveal Pavi.

She's sitting at a table set with a white tablecloth, a tiered tower of sweet refreshments, and a very human set of china for tea. Caspar, with his long, purple robes and tied back golden hair, sits on the opposite side of the table. He doesn't hold a knife to Pavi's throat, and though I search his person, I find no sign of a single weapon. Knowing his magic, however, that doesn't mean he isn't threatening her. I scan the area beyond them, looking for archers. The cliff is rocky and grassy, with no visible hiding places.

"Rahk!" Pavi cries, clapping her hands together after popping a tiny pink cake into her rosy mouth. Her white hair blows in the wind, her pale complexion brighter than normal. "Look—I'm winning!"

I frown, not lowering my swords as I tentatively step closer. Caspar doesn't turn toward me, but instead keeps his attention fixed on . . . a game board?

"We're playing Fool's Circle and he's very good, but I've practiced so much against you that I caught him off-guard with the Seizer's Strategy!" Pavi laughs, before turning to Caspar. "You should be ashamed of yourself, Starborn Prince. Maybe I'm more fit to rule your city than you are."

"It's true," Caspar says to me, leaning back in his chair. "She's outwitted me with her Nothril strategy. I'm taking notes."

My mind flips through a dozen possibilities of what is happening. Has Caspar threatened that if Pavi doesn't act happy, he'll kill her? Or does he hold a shadow hand at her throat? Surely, he isn't trying to charm my sister into an illicit relationship that he intends to leverage against the Nothril Court? She is beautiful, but she is far from marrying age. That would be greatly lower than I anticipated him stooping—and if it's true, he will pay for it with more than his life and his precious city.

"Come here, Pavi," I say as a test, aware of the warriors flanking us.

Her bottom lip protrudes in a pout. "Can't I finish the game? I'm so close to beating him!"

The next instant, my blade rests against Caspar's throat. He doesn't move, only shifts his gaze from the board to me with one lifted eyebrow.

"Finish the game," I growl, a dark threat in my voice.

"Rahk!" Pavi whines. "Don't you dare hurt him! He's been very nice to me this entire time."

"I should clarify that I was also not *too nice* to her," Caspar adds, only flinching slightly when I press the blade harder against him. He waves one hand for his warriors to stay back.

"He was a very normal and decent level of nice," agrees Pavi, nodding. "So put away your sword and let us finish our game. Then I'll come home."

"The sword stays where it is," I reply. "Finish your game quickly."

She huffs irritably, but makes her moves. Caspar uses his turn to put himself at a disadvantage. A wise choice. Pavi claims her win in triumph, none the wiser.

"I told you I'd beat you," she croons at Caspar.

I nod. "Time to go."

She sighs as though I am asking a great deal to remove her from her kidnapper. She pops one more little cake into her mouth before I can stop her and hops to her feet. "Thank you, Caspar, for the lovely afternoon."

He smiles, not moving because I keep my sword at his throat. "I'd offer again, but your brother might not approve."

"You are not going near her," I say coolly.

"Then don't touch my city." Caspar's teeth flash in a smile. "I know the Nothril Court has been sending spies. I know you want to claim it as part of your Court."

There is the reason for this kidnapping then. He's making a statement to Lord and Lady Nothril—and the rulers of any other Court that tries to annex his city—that he isn't to be trifled with.

I ease my sword away from Caspar. "I do not care who rules your city. You leave Pavi out of your threats, or I will personally ensure there is no city for anyone to rule."

His eyes flash with anger, but beneath it is a tinge of fear he tries to bury. His posture may be casual, but the salty drift of his sweaty hands gave him away from the beginning. He wonders if he has miscalculated in the statement he made by stealing Pavi.

If he had laid a hand on her, that would have been a grave miscalculation. As it stands, he might just get away with his city's continued independence.

It'll all depend on Lord and Lady Nothril's moods when I return home.

"Come, Pavi." I sheathe one sword and place my empty hand between her shoulder blades, keeping my other armed and ready.

She gives one last wave at Caspar, and then surrenders to being rescued. Her wings are not deep blue like mine, but gleam like the moon in the last light of day as we leave the cliff and the Star City behind us, flying toward the Path that will take us home.

"How did he capture you?" I ask, once we're on the Path. I'll need to inspect our fortifications when we arrive back at the Nothril Court.

"He just knocked on my door and asked me if I wanted to visit the Star City and play Fool's Circle with him. Of course, I said yes. You cannot imagine that I would turn down such an opportunity when Mama and Father keep us so confined at home!" *Us*—even though Pelarusa and I are hardly confined anywhere. Our third sister, recently bonded with another Court's heir, almost never returns to Nothril these days. Only Pavi is *confined at home*, and for good reason.

I restrain my groan. She just *went* with him? I've always known Pavi's personality is not suited to the Nothril Court, but the older she gets and the more she refuses to conform to the expectations placed on her, the more certain I become that she will get herself killed.

Not by outside forces—but by Lord and Lady Nothril.

"If you must temporarily escape the Nothril Court, then do so with me or Pelarusa, not strangers." I try to keep my irritation and fear out of my voice, but I don't fully succeed. "We will ensure you won't get caught."

She isn't satisfied, her little brow puckered, and her chin lifted in that characteristic stubbornness that always makes me anxious for her. Very early on, I ascertained what was expected of me, observed the consequences of failing to meet those expectations, and arranged my life accordingly. Pavi has no interest in doing the same.

"You wouldn't want Caspar's entrails to decorate the throne room, would you?" I ask darkly.

She turns such a look of disgusted horror up at me. "Why must you be so *morbid*?"

"That is what will happen," I say, forcing home my point. "You know it as well as I do. If he had hurt you, every single Nothril warrior would have been sent to rip apart the Star City. All because you didn't slam your door in his face and scream for your guards. Would your few hours of fun be worth it then?"

"I hate you," she growls, and then spits as iron fills her mouth and my nose.

I wince, the stench so strong it pulses through my brain, almost blinding me with its intensity. "You are cruel to speak lies in my presence."

"It's the only vengeance I can have for you ruining my conscience and making me now feel guilty for enjoying even the smallest moment of fun."

The smell of her lie fades from the air, and I take a deep inhale. I look down grimly at the top of her white head. There is only so much Pelarusa and I can do to protect her.

In the darkest, quietest parts of my heart, sometimes I wish I didn't care about her so much. I wish her goodness and innocence were blackened like mine and Pelarusa's. Maybe, if she was hardened like us, I wouldn't feel the need to protect her. Maybe then, I wouldn't feel this creeping sense of vulnerability that always follows me when she enters the picture.

An army of guards meets us at the grand iron gates leading into the palace set into the side of Nothril's great cave. I hold up a hand and nod toward Pavi beside me. "She's unharmed. Stay at your posts." We pass them, the air turning damp the deeper we take the hallways into the cavern, and I say to Pavi, "Don't say a word. I will speak for you."

"You never let me talk," she grumbles.

If she learned the art of politics and placation, I would. "Do you want Caspar to stay alive and keep his city?"

She tosses back her head and groans irritably.

"Do *you* want to stay alive?" I ask, nodding to the runner quickly approaching us, giving her permission to announce Pavi's recovery to Lord and Lady Nothril. The runner turns on her heel and vanishes. "Unless you have a plan to maintain both of those things, you will stay silent."

She stops fighting me, biting back her tongue, and I do not know if it is because she has accepted defeat, or because there is an unexpected figure lounging by the doors to the throne room. He wears fine robes of gold, the crest of Valehaven, and his crown rests slightly lopsided on his brow.

"Rahk!" cries Trenian Ashrift—Ash, as he is known to me and others close to him—as he straightens and flashes a bright grin at us. "There you are. I've been waiting so patiently for you. Hello Pavi."

She gives a little wave but doesn't answer back.

"What are you doing here?" I ask in a low voice. "Why aren't you in Valehaven with Stella?"

He twirls one finger in the air. "I need you to run a little errand for me."

"For *you*?" I lift my eyebrow.

He gives a dramatic sigh. "For your High King and Queen of Faerieland."

I nod my head toward the doors of the throne room. "I'm in the middle of something. I have a kidnapping victim to restore to her parents, and a city to discuss destroying."

"He didn't kidnap me!" Pavi protests.

Ash smirks before returning his attention to me. "The borders of Caphryl Wood have begun receding, returning what my father stole from the human lands. I need you to go to the human lands and act as emissary for the High Throne of Faerie during this time of transition. I anticipate it getting messy."

I frown. "Why?"

Ash scratches the back of his head. "Well, Ymer the Indefatigable is squatting on the edge of the Wood, and when the border recedes . . ."

"You're not serious."

"Unfortunately, I am."

"You want me to kill the troll, so he doesn't terrorize the humans?" I ask blandly. It won't be easy, but I've succeeded against greater foes.

"Ah, no, I would not prefer that. Stella and I are still working to settle any unrest after my father's death, and you know how the trolls can be."

I shift my weight to one leg. "Old Ymer won't move under my persuasion. He follows the ancient ways."

"Yes, exactly, so you must persuade the human queen to come down to the border, once it has receded, and politely ask Ymer to return to the Wood."

I hesitate, reading the lines of Ash's expression. "And why, pray, would you send me to do such a simple task?"

Ash snorts. "Well, unfortunately, the queen is Stella's eldest sister. We don't anticipate her being cooperative. And Ymer will hardly be cooperative either. That is why I am sending my best man."

It makes sense that he would ask me, considering that I am the only person besides his wife that he trusts. Lord and Lady Nothril might be pleased that I receive this *important commission* from the highest power in our land—or, more likely, they will be put out that it takes me away from their service.

"Do I have a choice in the matter?" I ask, laying a hand on Pavi's shoulder to keep her from barging into the throne room without me because she's bored of this conversation.

Ash shrugs, tilting his head from one side to the other.

Ah—it's not an order if I don't want the assignment, but it is an order if Lord and Lady Nothril object. "I understand. As long as you're not sending me to get embroiled in some political marriage with a human."

Ash grins. "You might find a political marriage to a human to be exactly what you enjoy most." He pushes off the wall, smirking at my unamused face, and begins marching away. "Give my best wishes to your parents. I'll send over details of the post immediately."

With that, the High King of Faerieland saunters off, ignoring the guards and servants dropping to their knees in obeisance.

This night grows more complicated by the moment.

"Mama and Father aren't going to want you to go," Pavi says. "And they won't want you to get married."

The last thing I would ever do in the human lands is get married. I give her a stern look. "Not a word out of you when we go in."

She rolls her eyes as I shove open the doors to the throne room.

Lady Nothril sits quietly on her throne of carved obsidian, her white hair contrasting sharply with her dark skin and the shining silver dress she wears. She doesn't move a single muscle. Unlike Lord Nothril, who has abandoned his throne and paces across the dais, his hands in a knot behind his back.

At our entrance, Lord Nothril stops pacing. Lady Nothril's eyes shoot to us.

Pelarusa, who sits second in the line of three smaller thrones to the right of the dais, is the one who cries, "Pavi! You're safe!"

I nudge Pavi toward Pelarusa, and she hurries over to embrace our sister and then take her seat. Out of Lord and Lady Nothril's line of vision—just where she needs to stay.

"You have done well, my son," Lady Nothril says with a lift of her chin.

I bow before them both, silently accepting the praise.

"Who was it?" Lord Nothril demands. "Who dared to take our daughter?"

I rise, fixing my gaze on the wall just above their thrones, where the Nothril crest hangs. "The Starborn Prince took her—not by force, but by coercion—as a statement he will do worse if the Nothril Court continues to make efforts to claim his city."

Pavi's desire to defend Caspar emanates from where she sits. I will her to keep her mouth shut.

"Did he, now?" Lord Nothril growls. "Does he truly think his city can stand against the force of Nothril?"

Lady Nothril's gaze is heavy on me. I keep my face blank, and my eyes fixed on the crest. "He does not think his city will survive an attack by the Nothril Court, but he makes it clear that he will fight hard to maintain his city's independence, and that such attacks will prove costly for the Nothril Court."

That is all I can do for Caspar and his city.

"Interesting," muses Lady Nothril, tapping one finger lightly on the armrest of her throne.

"I will investigate any breaches in our defenses at once," I say.

Brow furrowed, Lord Nothril shakes his head. "Pelarusa will handle that."

I mask my surprise.

In my periphery, Pelarusa blinks twice. "Me? Why?"

The doors burst open behind us. All eyes—save mine—swivel toward the loud bang of thick doors against cold stone walls.

"Lord and Lady Nothril! It has been far too long since you visited Valehaven!" cries a bright, golden voice.

I stifle my groan.

"High King Trenian," replies Lady Nothril with snakelike calm. "What brings you to our Court?"

I was going to handle this. He didn't need to announce his presence.

But of course, he did anyways. He's Ash.

His hand lands in a smack of comradery on my shoulder, his wide grin a sunny contrast to the blacks and grays of the throne room. "I am here for the services of my most trusted warrior."

"He is busy," Lord Nothril growls.

"I'm afraid my errand is too important. He will go at once to the human lands and act as my emissary while the High Queen and I adjust Faerieland's border."

Lord and Lady Nothril both go quiet, which is typical for the latter—not so much the former. Ash stays at my side, facing them both, the cunning light in his eye sparking. Lord and Lady Nothril may be the rulers of this Court, but Ash and Stella are the rulers of Faerieland. My parents may not like this assignment, but try as they might, there is nothing they can do to fight it.

"Please do not keep him too long," Lady Nothril says with a smile. "We do not like being parted from our heir."

Ash offers another bright grin. "Noted. Your service to the Crown will be rewarded." He squeezes my shoulder and gives me a look that seems to say: *"Enjoy your time away from home, my friend."*

Normally, I'd return the gesture.

He strides out of the hall, whistling as he goes. The doors shut with a *thud* that resounds through the entire space. I keep my gaze fixed above the thrones, not moving an inch.

Nothing I do or say, however, will overcome the suspicion now lingering in Lady Nothril's eyes as she regards me. It is like my friendship with Ash, and all I did to put him on the throne of Faerie—even aiding his overthrow of the last High King—suddenly come crashing back to the forefront of our relationship. No matter how unshakeable I have always proved my loyalty to be, no matter that overthrowing the last High King directly strengthened the Nothril Court, I am forever tainted in their eyes.

They wonder if I entertain notions of working with Ash to overthrow *them* too.

"As I was saying, I have a different assignment for you," says Lord Nothril irritably. "One that you can tend *while* you are in the human lands on business for the High King."

I breathe out slowly through my nose.

He flings something to the ground at my feet. Something he had crumpled in his fist this entire time. I watch it skitter to a halt. My pulse leaps with recognition.

A mask covered in ivy.

I lift my head. "The Ivy Mask struck while I was gone?"

The vigilante is not well known, but I am familiar with how he sneaks into the Fae Courts and breaks human slaves free. Because of his neglect of fae slaves, it's assumed that he is a human too, though his proficient navigation of Faerieland has always struck me as a curiosity.

"His mask was found in Lord Nothril's chambers. He stole several of our slaves, including your father's favorite," Lady Nothril says. "He has trifled with our Court long enough."

"I will apprehend him," I say.

Lord Nothril sits back on his throne, his perpetual frown deeper than normal. Caspar better be glad that the Ivy Mask infuriated him so much tonight—otherwise the Star City might have become a desolation within a fortnight.

"You will apprehend him under blood oath," says Lord Nothril.

A chill races through my blood, followed by a thick cord of irritation. Must they always be so paranoid? I keep my gaze from straying to Pavi. "Have I displeased you, Lord Nothril, that you would require such a guarantee on my word?"

I do not ask the question because I do not know the answer, but to remind them of my proven loyalty.

"It is nothing that you have done," Lady Nothril says with another light tapping of her fingers. "But your association with High King Trenian and his hideous human wife poses a conflict of interest. We wouldn't want anything to . . . *distract* you from your mission."

I translate this to mean: *We don't trust you unless you have collateral at stake.*

"You will swear the blood oath," says Lady Nothril firmly.

"Very well." I take a knife from my belt and hold out my wrist, pretending to be oblivious to what they intend. "What are the terms of the bargain?"

"We will not swear on your blood." Lady Nothril's gaze trails away from me and lands on Pavi, who hasn't stopped fidgeting in her chair since she sat down.

And this is why I wish I didn't have any collateral at all.

I briefly close my eyes, and that is all the vent I give my frustration. Pavi hasn't been safe for even an hour, and now she is at risk again.

No one is allowed to hurt a Nothril heir . . . except Lord and Lady Nothril themselves, I think derisively, but I bite my tongue.

This is punishment for Pavi, too, for her reckless behavior and continued refusal to fall in line. I'll just have to fulfill the terms of this bargain to the letter—something I would have done without the blood oath anyway.

"Come to your mother, Pavi," says Lady Nothril.

Pelarusa doesn't move a muscle, despite the weighty gaze she levels at me. Pavi obeys at once, coming to kneel before Lady Nothril. Without a word, she offers her palm.

She winces at the pain of Lady Nothril's long, taloned nail raking across her palm and drawing a line of blood. If she is afraid of the instant death, the consequence of this bargain not being upheld, she doesn't show it.

Lady Nothril drags the pad of her finger across Pavi's cut and paints a rune across the back of her own left hand. Pavi gets up and, without looking at me, offers me her bloody palm. I am careful not to aggravate the wound as I take the blood I need to paint a matching rune on my skin.

"You will bring the Ivy Mask to us for rendered judgment within three moons, measured by the human lands," says Lady Nothril.

Lord Nothril motions for Pavi to go to Pelarusa. I drag in a shallow breath through my teeth as Pelarusa's face shifts in alarm.

"And if you do not return with the Ivy Mask by the second moon, Pelarusa will join you on the hunt, and she will not be allowed to leave the human lands until the task is finished."

"Me?" Pelarusa cries. "Stuck in the human world?"

"Do you object?" Lord Nothril asks in a cold, weighty voice.

Pelarusa's pale skin goes ashen. She shakes her head quickly. She accepts Pavi's blood and writes the rune on her hand. The magic locks into place, searing a tattoo into my skin at the back of my neck. I shove away the instinctual trepidation that always floods me when blood oaths are invoked.

They've given me three months, two on my own. It's a very generous allotment of time. It only took me a few hours to hunt down Pavi. This tells me that they don't want to risk the bargain being broken.

It won't be broken. I will hunt down the Ivy Mask, hand him over, and wash my hands of the matter before the week is out.

"That is enough," Lord Nothril declares, rising from his throne. "The wrongs of this day will all be righted. Our Pavi is back to us safely, and the Ivy Mask will be brought to justice."

"You were in need of a new slave girl anyway," Lady Nothril says.

"I did have her longer than usual," Lord Nothril agrees.

"You'd better catch the Ivy Mask quickly," Pelarusa growls irritably, getting to her feet. "I think I will *die* if I have to go to the human lands. I can barely put up with the human stink of the Valehaven Tailor."

I can think of fewer things worse than Pelarusa stuck in the human lands. I give her a nod, acknowledging her concern and offering my promise to avoid the situation she fears. She scowls at me—apparently having decided it is my fault that we're now bound by a blood oath with Pavi's life in the balance, even though *I* was the one who hunted down Pavi while she did nothing.

When I've left the throne room, I finally let myself breathe. I go straight to my chambers, craving peace and quiet. The problem of Pavi's behavior returns to haunt me. Pelarusa will do her best to keep Pavi in line while I'm gone, but Pavi trusts me more and follows my bidding readily.

She doesn't realize how precariously her life hangs in the balance. She doesn't believe Lord and Lady Nothril would kill her if they knew she'd walked out of this palace with one of our enemies. She doesn't know, because they haven't grabbed her by the throat and threatened to squeeze the life out of her if she didn't obey.

But I know.

And I need to get her out of here before she finally finds out.

An idea occurs to me. What if I caught the Ivy Mask, temporarily allied with him and made him get Pavi out of Nothril—so I could not be implicated with her disappearance—and then double-crossed him? That would fulfill the terms of the blood oath. It would also ensure Pavi's life is never again at risk.

And also that Pavi is not used to control me anymore.

I place my hand on the smooth, cold surface of my door. The wards unlock, and I push it open.

Immediately, the air is different.

I shut the door behind me and grab one sword hilt, ready to draw it. I take a deep breath, filling my lungs with the familiar scents—and the one unfamiliar one. One that smells very sooty . . . and very human.

Moving silently past my wall of weapons, I follow the scent. It's a slave's scent. Which one, I'm not sure, but I've smelled it before. What is a human slave doing in my rooms? I have given strict orders that only fae slaves are to service my rooms; the human stench is too unpleasant. It lingers and clings like a rotting carcass.

I reach the bedchamber, still not making a sound. At last, I find the culprit.

A young woman in an ill-fitting slave's uniform is on her knees, half of her torso stuck under my bed.

I let go of my sword's hilt. "What are you doing?"

CHAPTER 3
KAT

THAT LOW, RUMBLING voice nearly sends me flying out of my skin. Who is in the room? I swear it was empty only a minute ago!

The small jar of *ollea* I found—and promptly dropped—rattles against something as I grab it. In a moment of pure desperation, I shove the jar into my mouth and clamp my jaws shut. The tiny object it rattled against remains in my palm. *A lost button*. Irrelevant, but I clutch it until it bites into my skin. I shove out from under the bed.

A face towers over me. At first, his sheer size is the most terrifying thing about him. He has both brawn and height, strength emanating from the way he stands in the doorway. Then I lift my gaze past his dark, blood-streaked armor to his silvery-white hair, a hard brow hewn as though from granite, and a pair of black eyes colder than a frozen lake.

Those eyes, I decide, are by far the most terrifying thing about him.

It seems I am going to die.

I know who he is. I've never been this close to him, but anytime I come to the Nothril Court, he is my biggest fear. It is because of him that I covered myself in soot to hide my true scent. It is because of his piercing gaze, now, that I am endlessly relieved that my face is almost entirely covered in bandages.

Prince Rahk.

I stare up at him, frozen.

The tailor was right. Going back in, even for something as valuable as the *ollea* that clinks against my teeth, was a stupid decision.

I've always known I would die at the hand of a fae. I deserve to. One doesn't run raids of Fae Courts for years and get away with it forever. I just didn't want to die *today*.

"What are you doing?" Prince Rahk demands again.

Wait—does he buy my disguise? I fling myself to the ground in a prostrated bow. The *ollea* in my mouth prevents me from speaking.

"Answer me."

My hand trembles as I point to my mouth and shake my head.

"You cannot speak?"

I nod quickly, keeping my head bowed.

"Do you know you're not supposed to be here? Human slaves aren't to be in my chambers."

He thinks we're so far beneath him that we cannot even have the honor of scrubbing his floors? I rein in the sudden flare of my temper. I shake my head in answer to his question—and then point at the tray of goblets I brought. Can I make him believe I've made a mistake, and that I thought I was supposed to deliver drinks to him?

Prince Rahk sniffs in the direction of the goblets. He winces. "Great Kings, what possessed you to bring such a violation to me? What is that, a mix of nectar and wine?"

I give him my best doe-eyed look of innocence and confusion.

"Did someone tell you to bring me that?" he asks.

I nod eagerly.

"A human slave?"

I shake my head. If wrath must fall, it will not be on one of my fellow humans.

"A fae?"

I nod.

"Slave or master?"

I lift my shoulders in a simple *I don't know*. Maybe I will survive this. Maybe he will forget that I was under his bed and let me leave.

Maybe I won't die today, after all.

He shifts his weight to one foot and narrows his frosty eyes in suspicion. "Show me what you were doing under my bed."

Curse it all.

I cast desperately for an excuse. The goblets are all infuriatingly upright and unspilled, so I cannot use that as an excuse. That is when I become aware of the lost button that was under the bed next to the *ollea*. Slowly, I lift my hand and uncurl my fingers, holding up the button to him.

"You were getting this," he states in a monotone of pure skepticism.

I nod. Bile builds up in my mouth from the jar I conceal.

He regards me dubiously. He doesn't look like he is about to let me get off without a rational explanation of all this. Maybe I *won't* make it out of here alive.

"Are you new?" he asks, his frown so deep it looks cut from marble.

I nod quickly and prostrate myself once more.

"Then take your tray and get out. You are not supposed to be in this room. If you ever return, the punishment will be severe. Understand?"

I nod, barely breathing for fear that if I make a single sound, he will change his mind and take one of those great swords—and lop off my head.

I sweep up the tray and scurry to the servant's door. Prince Rahk remains standing, not moving a single muscle until I enter the tunnel and shut the door behind me. Even then, through the grate, his cold gaze remains fixed on me.

I turn on my tail and run as fast as I can. I spit out the jar, cradling it to my chest, expecting sudden pain to burst through my chest at any moment.

Proof that the prince only meant to make me *think* I was safe, when in truth he just wanted to play with his quarry before striking with the killing blow.

But nothing happens.

No one stops me as I make my escape from the Nothril Court.

I catch up to the tailor just as the sun dips below the horizon, back in my own clothes. "I'm so late!" I whisper to him as I rush to my brown mare. She is hitched to the cart loaded with precious human cargo. To the horse, I give half a carrot wrapped in a calming herb and say, "You're doing so well, baby girl. We'll get you out of this wretched fae forest in no time."

She nuzzles into my hand, her ears cupping forward at my voice. She eats the carrot and tries to spit out the herb, but she ingests enough for it to be effective.

"That's it. Good girl."

"You've got them now?" the tailor asks, glancing around the darkening forest.

I swing up into the driver's seat of the cart and salute him. "Don't give us a single thought. We'll be safe from here."

The tailor presses folded parchment into my hand. "These are the dates I will be delivering wardrobes around Faerieland. I've also included the details for our big raid. I am working to get you a liquid glamour to make things easier."

I tuck the paper into my breast pocket and give it a pat. "Excellent. Be safe."

"You, too, Kat."

I hold his hard gaze for one second. Then I turn to the four people huddled in the back and grin. "Hold on! We move fast. Legend says the longer you're in the Wood, the more of your soul it steals. We're not about to give it any more than a pinky toe's amount of soul!"

The girl sits closest to me, shrouded in the tailor's own cloak. The other three—a couple with a seven-year-old child—stay close together. The husband gives me a nod, holding his son close to his chest.

I click my tongue and give the reins a gentle slap to get the cart moving. I guide us onto the Path, picking it out by the very faint sparks on its edge. It's lethally dangerous to travel through Faerieland without a Path, as I learned very quickly when I was younger. But Paths don't show themselves easily to me, and if it weren't for the tailor teaching me the ones I needed, I'd be as useless as any other human out here.

I'm almost blind in the darkness, but I let the sparks and my horse guide us as I drive us faster through the depths of Caphryl Wood.

A soft touch on my elbow startles me out of my focus.

"Is everything alright?" I ask, twisting my head toward Elizabeth even as I keep my gaze focused ahead.

"Yes—I just . . . What's your horse's name?"

My eyebrows rise. I clamp my lips together before a chuckle escapes me at the sheer randomness of her question. "Her name is Bartholomew. Don't judge—I named her when I was a child and didn't know how to tell the difference between a boy horse and a girl horse."

She actually snorts, covering her mouth with her hand.

"Careful, you'll hurt her feelings," I say with a quick wink. "You'll not find an animal as perfect as her. Strong, smart as a whip, brave, with just enough quirks to keep things interesting. Now, make sure you hold onto that railing there. We're about to enter the willowwart stretch and I don't want anyone getting pulled out of the cart."

Willowwart cannot touch us while we're on the Path, but she doesn't know that and obediently ducks back down. Everyone stays low when the trees turn long and thin, their branches like whips that stir at our passing. Twice, one of those branches snaps overhead, and once they try to grab a cart wheel.

But we're safely on the Path, and we quickly move past them.

"What are those voices?" the man asks from behind me.

His question startles me. I've learned to thoroughly ignore the voices in the Wood. I don't even hear them anymore. Now that he mentions them, however, their whispers crawl up my spine.

"Come to me, my darling. I have loved none but you."

"He never forgives. He will require your blood for what you have done to him."

One quieter than the rest slides along my skin: *"I know what you did, Katherine Vandermore. It will catch up to you some day. You know it will."*

"Ignore those," I say briskly. "Some say they are the voices of those lost in the Wood. Others say it is the Wood itself, laying claim to the souls who traverse her Paths. Personally, I am convinced they are squirrels that have learned to talk for the sole purpose of spooking rational people like you and me. When you've been in the Wood as much as I have, you learn they cannot hurt you."

At my words, all four of my passengers visibly relax—only to stiffen as a loud voice roars: "Who over yonder doth pass into Ymer's dominion?"

I grin and wave. "Hullo Ymer!"

The old troll sits just off the Path, plopped on muddy ground. He is the size of a very large carriage and thrice as heavy, with thick, flabby arms, a rocklike hide, and tattered clothes that leave his rotund belly exposed. His face is gnarled, knobby, and arranged in a grumpy frown. In one hand, he grips a club bigger than me. "You again! You thin legged, disrespectful, toothy elf! Ymer has a boiling pot ready for you. Supper will be a delicious elf soup!"

Elizabeth draws back, a squeak escaping the hand she slaps over her mouth.

"You're right," I call back, keeping Bartholomew on the Path. "Ymer the Indefatigable, please pardon the disrespect. But you won't be boiling me today—and I'm not an elf. Sorry if that ruins your plans for the evening."

"Ymer will eat you raw instead!" roars the troll, surging upright and swinging his club.

It's the child who screams now, practically splitting my head open with the noise. Bartholomew whinnies nervously.

"He can't touch us," I say quickly to my passengers. "Not while we're on the Path. Go bother someone else, Ymer!"

"One of these days, you will be Ymer's dinner!" he roars as we pass him, heading toward the border.

"No, I won't!" I shout. "See you next time!"

We make good time, despite the dark, and the moment we spill out of the forest into an open field, my chest loosens a fraction. Enough that I can start to feel the exhaustion and weakness weighing down my muscles. But this night is far from over.

I pull the cart to a stop and motion for everyone to get out. I feed Bartholomew another carrot, rubbing her muzzle as I tell my charges climbing out of the cart: "This is as far as I can take you. There's a bag of provisions for each of you. We are in the kingdom of Harbright, west of Aursailles and south of Osremer. If you walk straight from here for a few miles over the rise, through these farm fields, you'll get to the city Ashbourne. You can go further west about fifteen miles to Shurtlon and the cheapest stages to the coast are there. I would recommend getting as far away from here as you can. Fae don't like being in the human world, so the deeper into it you can get, the less likely they'll follow."

When Elizabeth turns pale with alarm, I add quickly, "I've never had anyone be followed into the human world before. I simply say this in an overabundance of caution. In each of your sacks, there's enough food to last five days, if you ration it, and enough coin for one ticket for the stage. I wish I could do more, but—"

The older woman steps forward and immediately covers my fidgeting hand with hers. "You've done more than enough, dear. Thank you for giving us a future. You are a saint."

My lips tighten. I look away as I scratch the back of my neck.

The man helps me hide the cart beneath its customary pile of brush at the edge of the forest while his wife speaks to Elizabeth, who nods and tries to fight back tears. I force myself to ignore the stab of guilt that traces through my blood. If only I could have gotten them all out faster. If only I could carry more refugees with me each raid, instead of leaving so many behind!

My mind immediately goes to the slave woman who was so afraid of what would happen if Elizabeth disappeared. The woman who reminded me of Mama.

I'll get her out. I swear it.

I'm mounting up my horse, my usual hatred rising at leaving them here in this field with nothing but a little food and a shockingly pitiful amount of coin. If I had my inheritance, I could give them money enough for clothes, an inn, food, a comfortable journey to wherever they decide to go.

Instead, I lean in close to Bartholomew and kick her into a gallop.

This night is never going to be over.

I take my usual path to the city and then dismount to avoid straining my horse too much. "Good girl," I keep mumbling under my breath as she sniffs my coat for more treats. I give her every last carrot I have. "Such a good girl."

When I finally knock the special sequence on my home's backdoor after handing Bartholomew off to Charles, the stable hand who doesn't ask questions, it swings open so fast it nearly clonks me in the nose.

"Kat! Where have you *been*?" Mary hisses. Her usually pristine red bun has a few loose, frizzy curls, her pretty face flushed like she's been standing over a stove for the better part of the day. "Saints—look at you! You're disgusting!"

"I have every faith in you," I reply as she hauls me inside.

"Every faith in my ability to turn back time to avoid you being over an *hour* late to the ball? You're going to get me dismissed!"

"I had to steal the *ollea*! It was my one chance! I'm not going to be back at the Nothril Court for a month!"

"I should have known it would have been over something stupid." She shoos me up the stairs and into my room. "Hurry! We've got no time at all!"

"Stupid? *Ollea* will be invaluable. Ever since I learned fae with sensitive noses use it to dull their senses, I knew I needed to steal some for my raids. I'll be practically invisible with it. And besides, no one will care I'm late to the ball! I'm a walking fortune! I could come in a potato sack, and everyone would just say it adds to my *mystery*. I'll start a new fashion trend."

"You can think that."

I roll my eyes as she helps me strip and step into the tepid water of the tub set up in my washroom. "It would probably be in my best interest to wear a potato sack. Some of these men are so insistent I'm not sure what they wouldn't do for my fortune. And with Agatha working against me, I'm not sure I'll manage to stay unwed before my birthday!"

Mary scrubs my skin until it stings and clucks over the sorry state of my hair. "Maybe if you would actually *talk* to the young men, you would find someone you liked who could help you."

"Impossible."

"Kat."

"No, really!" I step into the towel she holds for me and dry off as fast as I can make my limbs work. Then it's time to pull on the undergarments and lace up the stays. "These men want my money, and they will pretend they care about me and act like they're in love with me until they have it."

"Then just explain to your favorites that you need their help staying single until you're twenty-one so you can claim the fortune for yourself and not have to hand it over to him. If he agrees and stays with you, you know he's here for you, not your money. But if he tries to persuade you away from that, you know he's only after your money."

"That sounds like the perfect way to get the provisions of my father's will into the paper's gossip columns. Then it'll be even worse as men flock to make their proposals before it's too late!"

"You could manage. You always find ways to get out of your responsibilities." She says this while shooting a dour look at me through the mirror as she picks dust and leaves out of my hair. "Your freckles are standing out especially stark today!"

I smile sheepishly at her. "I'm sorry I'm late, Mary."

She pauses her work long enough to whack me with my comb. "You should be glad that I'm very good at what I do."

"The very best."

She rolls her eyes, and I try to help by applying my own cosmetics, but she bats away my hand and bids me sit still. I watch her working hands, then frown.

"Did you burn yourself?" I ask.

She immediately hides the hand. "No."

"Mary! Let me see it!"

"It is *fine*. We have much more pressing things to worry about."

"Well, since Agatha is gone, I'll raid her creams before I leave. It will be healed by morning."

"I dare not touch the mistress's creams! She will have my head!"

"Yes, well, *I* dare," I say—and before she can stop me, I leap up and rush to Agatha's room. She keeps it locked, but I snuck a spare key years ago. It used to be my mother's room, after all.

I work fast, checking the full drawers of Agatha's vanity in the dark. I hate coming in here now and avoid it whenever possible. But I won't let Mary suffer when the remedy is within reach.

It is only a few minutes later before I return, a large dollop on one finger, holding it out to Mary. "Suffer no longer, my friend!"

Her mouth thins as she looks at the glob. Then she swipes it off my finger and rubs it into her burn. "I shouldn't let you do this, but thank you."

It is a record-breaking forty-six minutes of preparation before I'm ready. The gown Mary chose for me is pale green with elegant half-sleeves trimmed in long lace. I glance in the mirror at the towering updo strung with pearls she managed. What a feat! Mary is unstoppable. "Am I ready?"

"Just one moment," she replies, her lip caught between her teeth as she fusses with the back of my gown.

"I'm ready!" I declare and dash out the door.

"Kat!" she calls after me in pure frustration. But I don't have time for her perfectionism.

"You're incredible!" I shout from the stairs.

"I hate you!"

I'm still laughing when I climb into my waiting carriage and set off for the ball.

CHAPTER 4

KAT

"LADY VANDERMORE!"

My name, called so loudly into the ballroom of sparkling chandeliers and twirling gowns, draws a wave of attention I'm never prepared for. Practically every young man in the room whips his head in my direction. Their abandoned dance partners pout in frustration—or in some cases, sigh in relief. All the mothers of said ladies scowl darkly.

One particular set of eyes sears into me like fire, as though the potency of her hatred could simply burn away the fine gown I wear. My stepmother leaves her two daughters and hurries to join the throng of young men waiting at the bottom of the staircase.

"Forgive me for my tardiness, dear stepmother," I say with a little laugh. "My horse had a bad shoe, and I had to walk all the way back from the Biltwalls."

Her smile is all teeth. "You could have summoned the carriage, darling."

"I didn't want to trouble you! I didn't want to make you late too, after all." The lies come so easily, even though Agatha isn't fooled at all.

She believes I have tarried on purpose, to avoid the young men. Which, to be sure, is definitely something I would have done—if I hadn't been sneaking into Caphryl Wood and robbing fae princes and nearly getting myself killed instead.

"You are always so thoughtful of your stepfamily, Lady Vandermore," says one of the gentlemen with a kind face and slightly crooked cravat—bless him—as he reaches for my hand to bow over it. "Would you care for a dance? If I remember, the waltz was your favorite."

"Oh!" says Agatha, stepping forward to pat the young man's arm. "I'm afraid she's already promised the first few dances to Lord Boreham. But I'm sure she will have openings later in the evening for you."

Fabulous. Just fabulous.

I still don't know what Agatha's obsession with Lord Boreham is or why, of all the young men, the rather short and rotund one boasting allergies to everything outside the confines of his house was *the one* she decided I should wed and bestow my fortune upon.

"I believe the lady can answer for herself," says the gentleman, lifting his eyebrow at me.

How dare he give me an escape and put my stepmother in her place? Now I must begrudgingly like him, even though I *know* he only cares about my money.

This is why Mary's plan can never work. I'm much too eager to like these young men's attentions and if I am not careful, I will fall under the spell of so-called *love* and give my fortune away to someone who will squander it on foolish things.

I withdraw my hand with an apologetic wince. "I'm afraid my stepmother is right, and I am otherwise engaged for these next few dances." I force myself to smile and add, "But do find me later."

At least, with Lord Boreham, I am not at all at risk of falling for him.

The young man—the son of the Baron Cranswick—smiles politely as he accepts my dance card and scrawls his name. *Oliver.* When he looks up, he says, "I have some news for you. I'll tell you when we dance." He winks at me, then drops his tone so Agatha cannot hear him when he adds, "It's about the fae and the Long Lost Wood."

My attention whips to him as I'm passing my card along to the others waiting. He grins, happy to have my attention—though I am instantly terrified to know why he thinks *I* would be interested. Has rumor gotten out about my escapades as the Ivy Mask?

Surely not!

My full card is pressed back into my hand before I walk away. My stepmother's low voice tickles my ear with a tight, "I'm glad you made the right decision."

That only makes me want to retract my decision and snub her choice. If for no other reason than to prove I didn't do this for her.

I do *nothing* for her.

Instead, I hide my fists in my skirt and paste a smile on my face as I follow the bane of my existence to Lord Boreham.

The gentleman is nowhere near the dance floor, sprawled across a settee and laughing hysterically at something the group of men near him are saying. He clearly has no intent of dancing—least of all with me—and I have a particular dislike for the man gripping the back of the settee with one hand and holding his wine goblet the other. Sir Alsbee tried to seduce me when I was much younger, to force me via scandal into marriage with him.

I do not like any of them, but I will take the watery nose of Lord Boreham any day over one like Alsbee.

"I found her at last!" cries Agatha. "She was late because of that worthless horse of hers. But she is here now!"

The laughter quiets, and Lord Boreham grunts as he gets to his feet. He bows to me. "Lady Vandermore."

I curtsy. "Lord Boreham."

"I had to fight hordes of men to get her for you," says Agatha, patting Boreham's arm. "Use your time wisely."

Oh dear.

"Oh, you look lovely, Kat!" cries one of my stepsisters from behind us.

We're turning around when Agatha says, "It's *Katherine,* Bridget. Do be proper in public, my darling."

Bridget grins at me when I curtsy to her. She flaps her fan, making her golden ringlets flutter. She looks me up and down. "I like the pearls. Did they belong to your mother?"

I pretend I don't stiffen at the mention of Mama. "Mary found them at the market on a discount. It was a peddler trying to pawn off the last of his wares before he died or something. I cannot remember the story exactly." I shrug one shoulder.

Bridget chortles, glancing between me and Lord Boreham while Agatha sighs and closes her eyes.

"That," I say, glancing at my stepmother who looks like she is trying to restrain the urge to murder me, "was not very proper of me, now was it, Lord Boreham?"

"I'm afraid it wasn't," he agrees.

I smile. "But you don't mind too much, do you?"

"Um, well—" Lord Boreham starts to say.

Agatha interrupts him before he can say something too damaging. "He finds your liveliness charming, I am sure. I can see the way you look at her, Lord Boreham."

One look at the mottled color in the gentleman's cheeks and the way his eyes shift around uneasily, and *charmed* is definitely—*definitely*—the word that comes to mind.

"Where's Edith?" I ask, glancing around for my other stepsister to end this uncomfortable turn of conversation.

Bridget waves her fan, ruffling the lacy trimmings on the square neckline of her rose-colored bodice. "Oh, in some back room banging on an abandoned harpsichord. I think she feels sorry for any instrument that goes five minutes without being played."

"Darling," hisses Agatha under her breath, before smiling at Boreham and I. "The music is starting. Off you two go!"

As Boreham leads me to the dance floor, I cannot fathom for what possible reason Agatha has decided that he is the gentleman I ought to marry. She *is* from Aursailles originally, as is Lord Boreham, so perhaps she feels a kinship to him and thinks I ought to feel the same.

I glance at my partner, whose arms are not long enough to put a comfortable distance between us while we dance. It's just a waltz, yet he is breathing hard not even halfway into the dance. To be fair, my breath isn't even either—but that's because I was tearing around fae forests only an hour ago. A girl's legs can only take so much in one night.

What strikes me as strangest about this arrangement is that, of all the young men at this ball, Boreham seems the least interested in me. He doesn't even attempt to make conversation, and his eyes are dancing around over the top of my head, very occasionally flitting to mine and then away.

"Did you travel from Commington today for the ball?" I ask just before he sends me into a twirl.

"Yes."

"And how long are you staying in Ashbourne?"

"A few days."

"Ah! What is keeping you here? If I remember correctly, you usually return home very quickly."

His shifty gaze finds mine. He swallows and clears his throat. Then his gaze is back to staring at my forehead. "Well, your mother and I—"

My reply comes out far too vehemently than it should. "She is *not* my mother."

He nods in acquiescence. A bead of sweat slides down his temple. "Your stepmother and I have been in discussions of marriage."

I trip over my skirt. "Wh-what?"

"Marriage. Lady Agatha has agreed that a quiet ceremony—just family—in a fortnight's time would be splendid."

I stop dancing. In the middle of the ballroom. He flushes hot, glancing around as his hand tightens on my upper ribcage and tries to tug me back into the dance.

“Lady Vandermore,” he says with a strained chuckle. “Don’t embarrass yourself.”

Don’t embarrass *myself*? If I had the strength to do it, I would pick him up and hurl him across the ballroom.

“I’m not marrying you,” I snap, losing every shred of the persona I try so hard to paint at these balls. I lean closer to him, wrenching my hand from his grasp so I can shake my finger in his face. “If you wanted to marry me, you should have discussed such arrangements with *me*, not with my stepmother.”

He stares at me, baffled, before looking around at the people staring at us. He grabs my hand and pulls me off the dance floor, dodging the couples still dancing. Everyone is staring at us, and I do not care one tiny bit. He does, however, and his attention is wasted more on his friend group than on me. I catch Alsbee grinning wickedly at the two of us and our obvious irritation with each other.

“She is your guardian,” says Boreham, trying to keep his voice low and pretend everything is normal—even though all the mothers in the room have suddenly seemed to materialize within hearing range, eager for a scrap of gossip. “Of course I should discuss marriage with her. I am titled. I have land. I am respected. I am young. I have need of a wife, and you have need of a husband. Since Lady Agatha is your legal guardian, it is only proper that I discuss marriage with her.”

Stop trying to play the level-headed victim here! I barely keep those words from flying out of my mouth, and instead manage to say, “I don’t care that she’s my guardian. If I—”

“Katherine, dear!” Agatha’s voice rankles down my spine.

I clamp my lips tight, hide my fists in my skirts, and turn around with a forced smile. “Yes, Stepmother, dear?”

Agatha waves her fan as she approaches us. The beading of her gown catches the flickering light of the chandeliers. Her shadow slides along the golden paneled walls, larger than her figure, prowling ever closer. Then she stands in front of where Boreham and I have sequestered ourselves between two tall potted plants. "I do hope you are not creating any trouble for handsome Lord Boreham."

But Lord Boreham glares darkly at her before turning it on me. His face continues to redden. A muscle clenches in his rounded jaw. "I will be off. Lady Vandermore, you have three days to consider my proposal. I will call to receive your answer. Think it over."

He leaves us at once, storming through the milling crowd of curious onlookers. When he passes his group of friends, Alsbee tries to hail him with a wine goblet, but Boreham shoves past him, grabs his coat, and vanishes out the door.

Serves him *right* to be embarrassed and offended!

I fight the urge to cross my arms over my chest and stick out my tongue like a toddler. Instead, I accept a goblet from a passing servant in black livery and sip delicately. Whatever will be in the gossip column of the papers tomorrow? *Lady Vandermore has fought off another suitor, and all of Ashbourne is beginning to wonder if the lady's fortune isn't worth putting up with her boorish manners.*

Agatha sidles up next to me, the beading in her hair shaking as a vein stands out above her eyebrow. "If you just ruined—"

I swallow my wine and then pour the rest into the potted plant. The plant is probably jealous, after all, of watching the rest of us drink and dance without it. "Oh look!" I hold up my dance card. "I believe I have a prior engagement with one of these other fine gentlemen. Please excuse me."

Lord Oliver Cranswick with his crooked cravat is there immediately, as though I've summoned him from thin air, and I practically throw myself into his arms.

"You had news for me," I say, mustering a smile and endeavoring to put Lord Boreham behind me for the rest of the night. "Though I'm curious as to why you thought news of the fae concerned me."

The young man returns my smile with a conspiratorial one of his own, holding my hand more possessively than my last unwelcomed dance partner. "You'll see why. The news, Lady Vandermore, is that a fae is coming to town. Not many know this yet because it was only discovered an hour ago, but my father, Baron Cranswick, has the ear of the queen. Do you remember the tales of how a prince of the fae came to Aursailles and stole one of their princesses years ago? Queen Vivienne's younger sister?"

"Of course I remember."

"Yes, well, no one knows *who* this fae is—except that he is believed to be a warrior—but he sent his servants to purchase a house and property. Here, in Ashbourne."

"A fae? Come to live here, in this very city?" The gears in my mind are spinning at once, more from possibility and opportunity than danger. This is *very* interesting news indeed.

"Indeed! And after the last fae came to steal a bride, it begs the question: Is *this* one here for a bride too?"

"It hardly sounds like the same situation. The princess of Aursailles was taken back to the fae world." I catch myself before I name the fae Court of Valehaven and give away that I have a much deeper understanding of the fae and their ways than the rest of the Harbright people possess. "Why would one come to live here?"

Oliver shrugs. "Some rumors say he is here as an ambassador from the fae world, now that our peoples are no longer at war with each other. Regardless, I thought to warn you."

My eyebrows lift. "Warn me?"

His hand shifts on my shoulder blade slightly. "Forgive my boldness, but you are the rose of the city—of all Harbright. If this fae is seeking a wife, he will likely set his sights on you."

My mouth twists. "You're concerned about me? That is very sweet of you, Lord Oliver."

He blushes and doesn't seem to know what to say as the dance finishes. He escorts me off the dance floor, and we barely make it to the edge before the next gentleman comes to claim his dance with me.

Not once do I feel relief from Agatha's gaze searing into my back the entire rest of the night.

CHAPTER 5

KAT

MARY DRAGS ME out of bed the next morning at the ungodly hour of eleven o'clock.

"My eyes don't work anymore," I protest. "And neither do my legs. I'm stiff as a hairbrush after all that running and dancing and *ugh* my shoes were a torment! I still cannot believe the man proposed to me during a dance by casually suggesting we marry in a *fortnight*. Just in time to steal my fortune! The *nerve* of some men. At least pretend you're in love with me!"

"You'd better get downstairs," says Mary in a tone that shuts up my groaning immediately.

I sit upright, suddenly wide awake. "What's the matter?"

Mary helps me dress and pulls my dark hair back into a tight bun matching her own. "It's not good. I tried to stop it. The mistress is not pleased by your refusal of Lord Boreham."

Dread sinks into my stomach. "She's come up with another punishment, hasn't she? I don't see why she should care who I marry! It's not as though *she* is going to get any of the money."

Mary gives me a sharp look, and my stomach sinks even more. I shut my mouth, straighten my skirts, and pretend I'm oblivious as I march out of my bedroom, down the stairs, and to the dining room.

No one is seated at the long table spread with a fine, laced runner, a bowl of fruit, and steaming plates of biscuits, eggs, sausages, and porridge. My stepmother and two stepsisters are, instead, circled around the end of the table that isn't set for breakfast, exclaiming over something in a box. A box that looks . . . *familiar*.

"What's all the excitement for?" I ask uneasily, trying to sound natural.

"Kat! There you are!" cries Bridget. She is bright and golden and lovely—her hair coiffed and curled, her cosmetics perfectly applied, her gown fresh as though she wasn't up all night. "Look what one of the maids found!"

Edith traces the faded velvet of the box and the scalloped edges of its lid on the table. Eyebags hang from beneath her lower lashes, her hair slightly frizzed and her dress a simple mud brown frock. "I want the box."

Bridget slaps her hand with a laugh. "You selfish creature! I think it's Kat's."

I finally get close enough so I can see inside the box. A pair of perfect, gleaming slippers of cut glass rests in a bed of tissue and cloth. My heart drops all the way to the floor and pounds there like a drum. "Those are my mother's! They were her wedding slippers! Where did you find these?"

Every instinct in me demands to grab the box and run. So few pieces remain of my mother by now, and nothing like this. Nothing that carries the memory of both my parents in its shining, crystalline cut.

"A few servants were cleaning through the attic for things that might be sold. The upkeep of the house is expensive and the allowance your father left us is hardly enough," says Agatha, who holds the edge of the box as though prepared to wrench it away should I try to grab it.

"Things that might be sold?" I cry, fury rising like a tumultuous wave in my chest. "You sold *everything* of my mother's the moment you married Father! And now you would sell this too?"

"Would you have asked me to stand by and watch my newly married husband sigh over all the remnants of his first wife? Truly, Katherine, you would have had no such patience if you stood in my shoes. You act as though I did it to spite you! I have given no orders to sell the slippers."

I pause, suddenly wondering if I jumped to a wrongful accusation too quickly.

"Considering that you're not twenty-one yet," continues Agatha, "and the estate does not belong to you, these seem like just the thing I should keep safely for you until you come of age."

I stare—at first, dumbfounded, then a moment later, suspiciously. Is this a trick?

Bridget's face has gone pale. She laughs nervously, glancing between Agatha and me. "But Mother, my dowry! You just said—" She cuts herself off suddenly and turns her attention to me. "Kat, I know these slippers are special to you, but you know that I have practically nothing for a dowry! Your father has given his entire fortune to you and left nothing for us—"

"Because you aren't his daughters!" I cry back. The instant the words are out of my mouth, I can feel Mary's exasperated insistence of, *"Be a nice little stepdaughter and they won't torment you so! Your provocation makes everything worse!"*

A prickle of shame makes me wring my hands. My gaze turns back to the box. It's like my mother is locked away, imprisoned under the firm hand of Agatha. *Be nice, Kat, and maybe they will let you keep the slippers.*

"Yes, we aren't his daughters," Bridget says coolly, the laughter gone from her voice. "He had every right to give you his fortune. But it doesn't change the fact that Edith and I have no dowry. These shoes must be worth a small fortune and could give one of us a sizeable dowry, or the both of us a modest one. I know it's selfish of me to ask for anything of yours, but I don't want to be a spinster!"

Now I'm a selfish miser if I want to keep my dead mother's shoes.

Edith pops a grape into her mouth and says dryly, "You know no one will marry me without a dowry."

"Why do you keep saying you don't have dowries?" I demand instead of giving an answer to their requests of my generosity. "Your father left you each dowries! Unless Agatha spent them all—"

"I did not!" cries Agatha, indignant. "They are trite sums that would hardly tempt a man of consequence!"

"Why must they marry men of consequence? Why not marry a good man with a modest wage? You act as if it is some great trial to not be rich!"

"That is easy for you to say," says Bridget. "You are the wealthiest person at the court except Queen Vivienne herself! Why are you so desperate to not share an ounce of it? You could hardly spend it all in your lifetime!"

Because I have plans for it. There are hundreds—*thousands*—of human slaves in Faerieland I've yet to rescue. I need that money to help them build new lives for themselves. I'm sick of giving them a scant loaf or two of bread and just enough pence for a coach.

But . . . it *isn't* fair that my stepsisters have so little when I have so much.

I look at that box, the gray velvet only barely tinged the pink it once was. I open my mouth to make an offer: the price of the shoes contributed to their dowries in exchange for me getting to keep them.

"Girls, girls," chides Agatha, cutting me off before I can speak. "Bridget, it is not your place to ask such things of Katherine. Her dowry is hers and hers alone."

My shoulders sink in relief. Maybe Agatha doesn't intend to punish me after all.

"*But.*"

That single word slices through my thoughts. My gaze shoots up to find Agatha staring grimly down at the slipper box. She picks it up and tucks it carefully under her arm. My mouth drops open.

"Since Katherine is not yet of age, I am still mistress of this estate, and I decide what is done with its properties."

A rock lands in my stomach. "Agatha, please, I—"

She fixes a look of such finality upon me, I know there is no fighting her. "I will make a deal with you. I will give you the slippers—*if* you accept Lord Boreham's proposal and marry him before you turn twenty-one. If you do not, I will sell them."

I grind my teeth together, trying to quell the rising panic inside me. It feels like the moment I watched my mother's casket slam shut. I want her back. I want those slippers back.

But Agatha summons her servant Sylva—the only one Mary and I are not friends with—and gives her the box. Likely to go lock in the depths of Agatha's chambers where I can never find them.

I watch mutely as the servant disappears with the box, knowing I will never see that part of my mother again.

My stepsisters sit down at the table, their breakfast now cold, as I keep standing where I am. I am not hungry at all.

"By the way," says Agatha, taking her place at the head of the table and pouring herself a cup of tea. "You will take the carriage when Lord Boreham comes to call in three days to propose to you. The manservant—I always forget his name. Anthony?"

"Charles," I say.

"Charles, yes. He should be back any moment from the market. I told him to sell that horse of yours. It's better if you take the carriage from now on. The horse has served its purpose, and since it's the reason you keep being late for events, I figured it was best to move it along."

The horror, the sheer panic that descends upon me is *nothing* like what I experienced when I saw the slippers. "You sold Bartholomew? When?"

"Oh, early this morning. What? Don't tell me you're attached to the creature. It failed you over and over again! You told me so yourself! She had a bad shoe, she was sick, she wouldn't take her bridle suddenly, and so forth!"

I'm already running out the door. My chest burns, my throat tingling with thickness.

I find Charles coming into the kitchen, where the rest of the servants are cleaning up their breakfast work and preparing for the next meal. He is not in his usual livery, but trousers, suspenders, and a pair of worn boots.

"Where's Bartholomew?" I demand. "Where is she?"

He gives me a pitying look. "I'm so sorry."

Beatrice, the cook, shakes her head in sympathy. Viola looks up from scouring a pot in the sink, sadness etched across the worn lines of her face. Matthew has set down his mending.

This is what Mary warned me about. Not the blasted slippers. *This.*

I ignore all of them except Charles. "Who bought her? Tell me who bought her! We need to reverse the transaction. No one knows her like I do! No one is going to appreciate her! They'll think she bites because she loves rubbing her lips on flannel and if you happen to be wearing it, it seems like she's going to bite you! They'll think she's being rebellious when she throws her feed buckets in the air but it's just a game she plays! And they won't know that she absolutely *needs* her daily neck scratches—and she cannot *stand* having her tail messed with! What if they try to braid her tail? And, and—"

Charles's hand on my shoulder stops my stream of words as tears run down my face. "I'm so sorry."

"Sweet child," says Viola, coming at once to wrap me up in her soft, motherly embrace.

"All those times I blamed my tardiness on Bartholomew! I never thought she'd *sell* her!" I'm a bawling mess, burying my face in Viola's shoulder.

"You need breakfast, or you'll cry away all your strength," says Beatrice, pulling back a towel from a freshly baked tray of pastries. "And a cup of hot cocoa, I think."

They all know how much I love my horse. Father gave her to me when we were both young—we've grown up together, half-raised by this staff. Some of the staff have been with us since before my mother was lost to Caphryl Wood, and the rest since my father was alive.

When Mary enters the kitchen, she's the one who says, "Enough crying. Eat some food and then go upstairs and cry where the mistress won't see."

The words are barely spoken before the click of Agatha's heels warn all of us of her approach. I sit at a barstool with my back to the door, dragging my sleeve across my wet cheeks and taking numb bites of the food set before me. The servants snap back to their work, giving me a wide berth as the door swings open.

I don't turn.

I'm too afraid she'll see the murderous hatred in my face. Too afraid she'll see that I've been crying and know just how much power she has over my life.

"I didn't know the creature meant so much to you," Agatha says to my back. The servants are silent except for the clang of dishes, the shift of laundry being sorted through, and the ripping sounds coming from Beatrice removing the feathers from tonight's chicken.

At this point, I don't care to decipher if that is a lie or truth. If she hadn't thought it would hurt me, why did she sell Bartholomew early in the morning when she knew I'd be asleep and couldn't stop it?

Mary appears in my periphery, her pristine red bun a contrast with her starched white and black uniform. I dare not look at her for fear Agatha will take her away too. Just because she *can*.

"As already agreed upon, if you accept Lord Boreham's proposal, I'll give you the shoes. Perhaps we can even buy your horse back. If it means so much to you."

"I understand," I say, glad when my voice doesn't crack. I haven't agreed to *any* of this. I force myself to keep shoveling bites in my mouth, to keep chewing, but I taste dust instead of the buttery, flaky crust of the pastry I eat.

"He will be here in three days. You can let us know of your decision then."

I listen to the clicks of her heels as she leaves, and they seem to echo long after the collective sigh of relief goes up among the staff.

Three days to figure out how to get myself out of this mess. Three days to figure out how to break Agatha's control over me.

CHAPTER 6

KAT

"THE SLIPPERS—THE slippers don't matter," I tell myself, ignoring the pulsating longing of my own heart as I pace over the uneven floorboards of my room. "Bartholomew matters. I need to get her back. But I cannot marry Lord Boreham for multiple reasons." A shiver of disgust runs down my spine—one reason. For another, I couldn't look at myself in the mirror if I allowed such an excuse of a man to claim my fortune. And for a third, he's planning to marry me before our biggest fae raid! We'll be off at the coast for a dreadful honeymoon. Which means a dozen people won't be free of their abusive fae masters.

Mary sneaks in, carrying a basket of folded laundry that she takes to the wardrobe.

"I need to get out of this house," I say by way of greeting.

"Oh, Kat."

My throat thickens when she looks at me that way—with so much sorrow and compassion—but I swallow it away. "I need to run away, but I must stay in the city so I can keep doing my raids. Long enough that I can turn twenty-one before I wed and claim my money. I'll need to be in disguise, so no one recognizes me."

Mary raises one brow. "You're going to hide in the streets."

"No, no, that would be a terrible idea. I need to—"

I stop. It's like the plan just suddenly floats down from heaven in a glittering cloud, right into my open hands. My grin spreads across my face.

A fae come to live in Harbright . . .

"That face scares me," mumbles Mary.

I grin even wider. "Oh, it should."

"You do *not* look like a boy," says Mary as we stand before my bedroom mirror. I wear the clothes she fetched me: a pair of worn, baggy breeches, a dust-colored tunic, stockings, thick-soled shoes. "You can get away with it as the Ivy Mask when you have a cloak. But this is different."

"We can work with this," I say, looking at myself from all angles.

"Boys don't have hips. Or—"

"Yes, yes, but we'll figure out how to disguise that. I think I'm going to need a size larger of breeches to make this look convincing. And some sort of chest binding—"

"You think a few scraps of tightly bound fabric will suffice?" She points at my chest.

I wince. "I'll just . . . have to skip a few meals, wear baggy clothes . . ." My mind works as I keep surveying myself.

"You're going to cut your hair." Mary groans. "Saints preserve me."

"We've got to go all the way for this to be convincing! And it must be convincing by the time Lord Boreham comes to propose to me. I need to be gone by that morning."

We don't cut my hair just yet. I skip the noon meal with my stepfamily, claiming a headache, and only emerge from my room midafternoon to join them in the drawing room. I'm shaking so hard

I prick myself multiple times with my needle as I try to distract myself from my gnawing hunger with my embroidery. My stepfamily says nothing to me, and I say nothing to them. We sit in silence filled only by Edith drilling the same section of her piece on the harpsichord over and over again.

"Katherine," says Agatha, "you should be aware of a rumor that is circulating."

I tense. If she brings up Lord Boreham one more time—

"There are reports that a fae has moved to town and intends to marry."

Not Lord Boreham. I relax and wave my hand. "Baron Cranswick's son told me that at the ball."

Bridget looks up from her own needlework. "But did you hear that he arrived today? Mellie Thompson said one of her servants saw him—and he's terribly frightening. She said he's taller than any man she's seen, and he's got long, pointy ears. You know what they say about fae beauty, don't you? Apparently, it's true. Mellie said her servant said—or maybe it was a friend of the servant's—that he is tremendously beautiful and very strange."

Edith scoffs from her place at the harpsichord, mercilessly pounding out the section of the piece she's drilling. She shouts to be heard over the noise. "She also said he has white hair. Before you know, the reports will continue until he's over seven feet tall, with a nose the shape of a candlestick, bright purple skin, and biceps made of iron."

"Ladies!" Agatha chides. She closes her eyes briefly, in which Edith and Bridget exchange an amused look. I glance between them, hoping to be included, but they don't look at me. "Nothing has been confirmed except his arrival. His intent to marry is also uncertain, but it seems highly likely. You should be aware, Katherine, of his possible attentions."

Why does everyone think this fae is going to be interested in me? I doubt they would want my money; Faerieland runs a different currency.

"He's not going to take two looks at either of us, that's for sure!" Bridget says sourly.

Edith lifts her chin, never pausing her drilling. "I don't want to marry a seven-foot-tall monster with purple skin and a candlestick nose. Katherine can have him to herself."

"He's not seven feet tall, you imbecile! And are you a devil from hell sent to torment us with your music?" Bridget finally snaps, whirling on her sister. "The rest of your piece is getting lonely from your worship of those four measures!"

Edith bangs on the keys. "I don't enjoy it either! Botsov is a misery, and no one does his work justice, so the unfortunate duty falls upon me."

I've suffered in their presence long enough. It's time I do what I came to do. When no one is looking, I stick my finger in the back of my mouth. Then I heave, grabbing the nearby scrap basket.

"Kat!" shrieks Bridget, shooting up as I empty the meager contents of my stomach into the basket.

"Mary!" calls Agatha. "Take Katherine to her room at once. She is ill."

"No, I'm quite fine," I say, wiping my mouth and pressing a hand to my hollow middle. I've got to put up at least *some* struggle here. "I feel much—"

"You are ill. Go upstairs. Mary will tend your needs," orders Agatha sharply.

I nod and find myself actually needing to lean on Mary as we make our way up the stairs. "I feel so weak."

"It's your own fault for pursuing this harebrained idea."

"Do you have a better plan for getting me out from under Agatha's thumb?" I hiss. "While having the privilege of spying on someone who could give me the information I need to more effectively do . . . *business*?"

Silence is her only reply.

"I thought so," I mutter.

The moment we've entered the haven of my bedroom, I collapse beneath the sheer white canopy of my bed and lay with my arms and legs in every which direction.

"I'm so hungry I could eat this quilt," I groan. "Look at how shaky my hand is!"

"You cannot lose every ounce of curve in three days of fasting," Mary says.

"No, but I can become a little gaunter and paler."

"It'll be impossible for you to be hired if you're gaunt and pale. And shaking so much! Being a servant is hard work, and you must be able to manage it."

"I'll make it work."

Mary sighs, shaking her head. But then she pulls something out of the pocket of her petticoats. She holds it up to me. "I was up almost all night working to get it done."

I study the handstitched garment. "Is that . . . what I think it is?"

"A substitute to starving yourself? Yes, indeed. Try it on."

The chest binding is sturdy, yet thin and easy to fasten by myself—which is a very necessary feature. Mary pulls my ensemble out of the back of my wardrobe, hidden beneath my lacy stockings and drawers. I quickly don everything and stand before the mirror after Mary locks my door.

Her eyes widen. "Oh, saints have mercy."

"Flat as a board! Look at your stitching! This thing could flatten a pregnant belly!" I'm almost laughing, forgetting my starvation for the span of a few glorious seconds.

"Now you're flattering. But it'll work, you think?"

"Oh *yes*, this will more than work!" I sling my breeches a little lower, so they sag on my hips and belt them. "Add a little grime to the face and cut the hair—and I'll be the perfect—"

"Little boy of twelve."

I snap my fingers at her. "That's brilliant. Without the cloak I use for my raids, I cannot pass as a grown man, but perhaps a child? Especially with the dirt—"

"You cannot be completely caked in grime, or else no one will hire you. No one wants filthy urchins serving them."

"Maybe I should cut across my face and then I'll have a scar that—"

Mary's gaze turns fierce. "If you do that, I will take that chest binding and rip it to shreds."

"It's not like having a scarred face will ruin my marriage proposals," I say, laughing. "I could have a dozen extra toes in unfortunate places, and no one would care."

"Some men don't care about money," Mary says.

"When you find one," I call over my shoulder as I get back into my regular clothes, "introduce me."

CHAPTER 7

KAT

THE LAST NIGHT before Lord Boreham comes to propose, I'm quiet when I come down to dinner, claiming well from my *illness*.

Just play the submissive, dutiful stepdaughter, I tell myself. *This is the last time you have to see them.*

"Reuse the lace?" Bridget is saying, aghast, to Edith. "Maybe *you* are fine looking like a pauper, but if there is *one thing* to spend money on, it is always fresh lace. That design screams last year. I could never—"

The conversation between my stepfamily dies when I enter the dining room. I don't want to look at any of them, but I want them to believe all is forgiven and that it is highly likely I intend to accept Lord Boreham's proposal. So I glance at each and muster what I can of a smile.

"You look gaunt and pale," says Edith.

"Is that any way to greet someone who has been ill?" says Bridget.

"Ladies." Agatha massages the space between her eyes. Then she smiles up at me. "Katherine. I'm glad to see that you are feeling better. Come, eat with us."

Since Mary sewed me that chest binding, I haven't been starving myself as much, but I still force myself to eat little tonight. And because I don't trust my tongue, I occupy it with food instead of conversation.

"I've news to share of your horse," says Agatha.

I sit up straighter. "Have you found Bartholomew? Are we buying her back?"

She doesn't look up as she cuts into her meat with a sharp knife. "No."

My composure fractures. I sink lower into my chair.

"I truly thought you'd want one that was more reliable. But have no fear. I've spoken to Lord Boreham, and he's promised to locate the horse for you and buy it back once you are wed. The two of you made such a handsome pair at the ball. You were exquisite in that gown."

Once you are wed. It's another part of her *deal.*

I force a smile and a bland, "Thank you," out of my mouth.

Bridget leans forward, a bright grin overtaking her features like I haven't seen in days. "Kat, you should have seen Malcolm's face when Mother asked him about the horse!" She bursts into a fit of laughter. "He was so confused!"

"Malcolm?" I repeat, brows lifting with my curiosity. "You and Lord Boreham are on intimate terms, I see."

Agatha shoots such a look of venom at her oldest daughter, I startle and instinctively brace for her wrath. But it's not directed at me.

"Bridget Duxbury, what have I said about calling young men by their first names? It wouldn't matter if Katherine gave you half her dowry—you'd be scandalizing yourself out of husbands!"

Bridget's face turns scarlet. She's shockingly penitent. She bows her head, her golden curls shaking from the movement. "Forgive me, Mother. I am far too presumptuous. It shall never happen again."

"See that it doesn't."

I move a small bite very slowly to my mouth, glancing between the two of them. Edith catches my eye, and when I expect her to make a silly face mocking the exchange, she immediately looks away.

The three of them know something. Something I don't know.

"Did Lord Boreham call earlier today, while I was indisposed?" I ask, concerned the answer might be yes even though I didn't hear a peep of it from Mary.

Bridget shakes her head. "Oh no, we ran into him when we were calling on the Cromptons." She looks at me and offers a wiggly-eyebrowed smile. "He looked so handsome today."

Do Bridget and Lord Boreham have a secret understanding between them? Why would Agatha have me marry the man if her daughter loved him? Unless she has some objection to the man and is using my fortune to lure him away from Bridget.

"If you think he's so handsome, why don't you just marry him?" I say, before I can think better of it.

All three of them blurt a stunned, "What?"

Edith covers her mouth with a napkin, trying to smother a burst of laughter. "*Bridget*? And *Lord Boreham*?" She fails, and her chortle rings out against the paneled walls and their intricate trim.

"Oh, please, Kat! I could never try to steal your intended!" Bridget rushes to insist. "Lord Boreham and I are not suited *at all*."

She's still talking as Agatha says, "Bridget is not going to marry Lord Boreham."

"Why are you all acting like this is a preposterous idea?" I demand. And why, if he is so vastly unsuited to Bridget and Edith, am I the one required to marry him? "There are three of us. He could have married any of us. Why is this so strange a concept?"

Agatha's face freezes for a split second, so fast I almost think I imagined it, but then she smiles. "My dear, it is because you are the one he is interested in."

"He's never seemed all *that* interested in me," I retort.

Edith and Bridget are sitting uncomfortably across from me, but Agatha continues placidly, having successfully pulled her composure back under her tight rein. "Lord Boreham is not an expressive man, but he has always spoken very highly of you in our conversations. He may not show it to you, but he is quite smitten. He would never have proposed otherwise."

Why does it still feel like there is some crucial piece of information being withheld from me?

"Speaking of his proposal"—Agatha lifts her napkin and daintily wipes her mouth—"have you thought of your answer?"

I push back my chair, leaving my unfinished meal. "I have."

Then I make my escape, having successfully survived the last dinner I ever plan to have with these women.

I didn't tell Mary when I was leaving. She needs to give an honest answer in the morning when Agatha demands to know where I have gone, and why I am refusing to give an answer to Lord Boreham's proposals.

By the light of a gibbous moon, I pull on my trousers and belt them. The chest binding goes on next, covered by the collared white shirt that buttons down the front. I yank on the boots with worn soles and lace them up. Mary cut my hair last night, saying that if someone was going to, it had better be her and not me—else her reputation as a servant would be tarnished. I tie the short strands in a little queue at the nape of my neck.

I stand in front of my mirror, regarding my disguise. It's good. I look unfamiliar and wide-eyed to even my own gaze. Mary has always bemoaned my freckles, but they add to the disguise very nicely, lending me youth. I sling my satchel with an extra change of clothes and a few necessities over my shoulder.

My excitement propels me to the window, which I open silently with years of practice. The night air has a bite to it. It'll go away after a few minutes of brisk walking.

The latticework is familiar beneath my hands and feet. I climb down it quickly, taking care as always when I get near the window to Agatha's study. She usually isn't awake at this early hour, but soft candle glow reflects out the window. I peer inside and find her in a robe, her hair pinned up in curlers, as she reads a letter.

My foot slips on the lattice. I catch myself, but not before I see Agatha's head whip toward me. I plaster myself against the wall and hold my breath.

Nothing happens.

I don't dare glance through the window to see if she's watching. I shimmy gingerly the rest of the way down the lattice until the ground is solid beneath my feet. Then I break into a run, making for the hedge. There's one spot I always squeeze out of, and it's worn through with use. I get on my belly and pull myself through.

It feels wrong not to head toward the stables now and get Bartholomew.

"You're doing this to get her back," I remind myself firmly. I'll stay unwed until my birthday, claim my fortune, and then I will go reclaim my horse.

For now, I'm free of Agatha.

"Now to get to this fae ambassador's house," I murmur under my breath. I take out the scrawled map from my pocket, and hurry down the street.

The night is quiet and full. I dodge the shadiest parts of the city and stay out of the way of city guards—*mostly*. Half an hour into my trek, I come upon two quite suddenly. They stride down the street where the moon doesn't shine and it's only just before they step into the light that I catch the glint of a sheathed sword.

I try not to flinch like I've been caught doing something wrong. I put my head down and make to walk past him.

"What are you doing out so early, lad?"

Curse it all. "I don't want to be late for my new job, sir!" I call, pitching my voice just slightly deeper.

"Is your job all the way in Aursailles?" the second one teases, and they both break into laughter.

"No, sir," I say, and hurry past their laughter. *Be meek. Be small and inconspicuous.*

I allow myself to eat the small snack I packed just before sunrise, to ease the shaking of my limbs. "You hate this," I tell myself, "but not nearly as much as marrying Lord Boreham and watching him spend all your money."

That is what keeps me going.

And the certainty that I *cannot* get married before my raid in two months. I need—*need*—to pull this off. I'm not sure how I'll manage it while being a servant, but I'll find a way. It'll be easier than if I was married, for sure! If I must give up sleeping as well as eating, I'll do it.

The sky turns gray before dawn when I arrive.

It's a large manor, positioned on the edge of town, with what seems to be acres of green forest behind it. A row of neat hedges line the path to the entrance. There is a grand circle after the hedges, perfect for receiving carriages for a ball. Tall evergreens rise on the edges of the circle, giving the manor a sense of secluded grandeur.

My own home, the Vandermore Manor, is larger than this, but there is an elegance to its structure, to the scrollwork above the windows and along the edges of the roof.

I keep away from the grand entrance and skirt around the back, reading Mary's directions again to ensure I've got it right.

I land on one particular doorstep, my knuckles raised to knock.

There's no going back once you knock, I tell myself.

I hesitate, running over my plan in my head. I've just got to keep a low profile, stay out of the way of the fae that I will be serving, and hide here until my birthday. Being a servant here is ideal, because this fae won't know me—unlike *all* of the other well-situated families in the city—and because I might be able to glean information that will help me run my raids more effectively.

There's no point in second-guessing myself. Mary already got me this job, and if I fail to show up now, I cannot get hired anywhere else.

I knock.

The door opens to reveal a sharp nosed, tall woman in a dark blue dress and starched white apron. She wears a cap over her tightly pulled-back hair. Every line of her face is severe. She studies me for several minutes, standing in the doorway, refusing to speak or open the door to me.

It feels like she is climbing into my brain and reading all my secrets.

This is the true test of my disguise, I think while my body goes stiff. There's no way this eagle-eyed woman is going to be fooled by my extra-large pants and chest binding. If she is, however, then I think I might be able to fool anyone.

I bow. "Ma'am. I'm here for my post."

"How old are you?"

I clear my throat. "Twelve."

"We don't hire children here."

"No, no, ma'am, I've already been given the job." I pull the notice out of my pocket. Mary thought of everything—brilliant girl—and leveraged her connections hard to get me this position. "I was to report here this morning."

The woman frowns at the note. "You're Mary's little brother?"

"Yes ma'am."

"You look nothing like her."

I wince. "I fear she got all the pretties, ma'am. She takes after our mother."

"And you got all the freckles, I see. Well, come in. You'll need a uniform if you're going to be working under my watch. I am Mrs. Banks, and you answer to me."

A potent mix of relief from my success and trepidation that the real trial is yet to come fills my blood. I follow Mrs. Banks inside. She gives me a new uniform: a pair of tighter fitting breeches that I almost am too afraid to wear for fear of them revealing my hips, a stiff, collared white shirt, and a pair of suspenders. I've never worn suspenders before. I do not like them.

She sits me down at a stool before a large bucket of potatoes and hands me a knife. "Peel these spuds."

And so begins my first day as a servant boy. I put my head down and peel those potatoes, trying to find a sweet spot between speed and minimal waste. As my pile of peeled vegetables grows, so does my confidence. I find myself growing distracted, however, by the people bustling around the kitchen. All unfamiliar faces. There is the woman who moves expertly about the kitchen, reminding me of Viola. A little girl sits in the corner, about eleven years old, with a pile of mending on her lap.

And Mrs. Banks said they didn't hire children!

There are several men. Two manservants in livery, and an older man in much dirtier clothes who must tend the grounds. When he walks through the kitchen, Mrs. Banks shouts from the other room, "I don't want your nasty boots on my floor, Clifford!"

Mrs. Banks returns twenty minutes later to inspect my work. I restrain my proud smirk.

"How are you only half done with those potatoes? Are you slower than a crippled horse?"

I bristle and stick my head back down, vowing not to let my focus waver one second.

When I'm finished with the potatoes, there is no word of praise. I quickly realize just how silly of an expectation that is. Mrs. Banks orders me out to the well to draw water for the kitchen. The buckets she gives me are alarmingly large. These will be *very* heavy when full. I'm an athletic person, but carrying heavy things is not my particular strong suit. That was always Mary. She has the strongest arms of anyone I've witnessed.

I'll just have to pretend I'm Mary to get these buckets of water back to the house.

Once they're full—or *mostly* full, as my courage faltered while I was filling them up—I wrap one hand around each handle and give a hefty lift. They barely budge.

"Saints have mercy on me," I mutter.

My limbs shake from hunger, even though I thought I'd eaten enough. Apparently not. No one has seen through my disguise yet, but with these breeches, I fear I might need to continue limiting my food. Whatever happens, I cannot risk being discovered.

An embarrassingly loud grunt slips between my teeth when I heft the water buckets up. *Saints have mercy,* I think again as I begin to worry about my elbows being pulled out of their sockets. The distance between the well and the kitchen door is far too long, and I perform an awkward shuffle-run in an effort to carry the water buckets for the least amount of time possible. I drag them inside, breathing hard, and pause as water sloshes over the edges. Where am I supposed to take these buckets?

"My five-year-old nephew is stronger than you!" exclaims Mrs. Banks from my left.

I whip my head to the side. She regards me from over the tip of her severe nose. I didn't realize she was in the kitchen. *Oops.* "Sorry, ma'am," I reply dutifully, instead of letting my instinctive snappy reply fly free.

I'm tasked with carrying wood to all the grates in the house. Mrs. Banks says that will be one of my everyday tasks, along with chopping the wood. When I dump the wood into the dining room hearth and soot shakes free and lands on the pristine red rug, Mrs. Banks threatens to box my ears. I scrub the soot out of the rug until my hand is shaking. When I am handed a dead chicken and told to pluck off its feathers, I swallow my instinctive need to vomit and pretend I'm Viola, unphased by a jiggly bird's neck with no head. I don't do that fast enough to please Mrs. Banks, who happens upon me mid task and announces: "Mary owes me one for asking me to hire you!"

"Yes, ma'am," I reply, just as Mary would have wanted me to.

I'm sent outside to collect eggs from the chickens. The slight reprieve from the hot and full kitchen is everything I needed—and yet my shoulders drop when I see the angle of the sun. It's only been a few hours. I count the rest of the hours in the day and nearly fall over.

"Mary must be a demigod," I conclude as I take a few pecks from the speckled chicken while fishing for her eggs. How she can handle this level of labor every single day is beyond me!

If I thought those first few hours of the day were difficult, the rest of the day only proves worse. Sweat pours down my face and I become endlessly thankful for the layer between my chest binding and my shirt, otherwise my sweat might have revealed my secret long before the day is over.

I work harder than I have ever worked in my life, enduring Mrs. Banks's endless displeasure, trembling from hunger, and there is no sign of this supposed fae master. I'm beginning to think I might not have a single opportunity to glean information that will be helpful on my raids.

This might just be the worst arrangement I could have possibly ended up in.

Marrying Lord Boreham grows oddly more appealing by the moment.

Then I think of Bartholomew. I clench my jaw and force myself to work harder. I will not let Agatha's schemes dictate my life. I will *not* let her win.

"Have you ever milked a cow before, lad?" Mrs. Banks asks mid-afternoon.

"No, ma'am."

She sends her gaze heavenward. Then she gestures sharply for me to follow her outside to the barn. The chickens scatter at her angry strides as she approaches the grazing cow with a soft brown coat and white rimming her black marble eyes. She takes a milk pail and a bucket of grain, opens the gate to the cow's pen and motions for me to shut it behind me.

"Missy is a good cow," Mrs. Banks says. I think that's the only praise I've heard her offer all day. "She doesn't need a milking stanchion. As long as she has some grain, she will usually hold still for you."

Mrs. Banks gives Missy the cow her pail of grain and then squats beside her. I steal a glance at the woman, somehow surprised that someone so perfectly starched and pressed would demonstrate for me how to milk a cow. I watch carefully, and when it's my turn, I mimic her movements. It proves to be a tricky task, but I pick it up quickly. My experience with Bartholomew seems to give me a slight edge. Mrs. Banks eventually stops giving me cues. It's as close to recognition as I think I'll ever get from her.

The milk is foamy and warm in the pail when I finish.

"Carry it back to the house. We must filter it. Finch will make butter from the cream for tonight's supper," Mrs. Bank says.

A grunt escapes me as I lift the heavy pail. It's several gallons—an awkward weight for one hand. I'm already sore from today's work and there was no midday meal provided for me. It'll be a steep challenge, but if I can get this all the way back to the kitchen, I will also consider myself a demigod like Mary. A much lower and far more pathetic breed of demigod, but still one nonetheless.

Mrs. Banks's eyes burn into me from ahead as I pretend this pail of milk isn't too heavy for me. I keep shifting it from one side to the other, which earns me a sharp bark of, "Don't you dare spill that!"

"Yes ma'am!"

Don't fall on your face, Kat. Don't fall on your face.

She disappears into the kitchen, too impatient for my slow pace. I hurry to stop lagging so much.

A new voice interrupts my focus.

"As you can see, Master, the grounds are well kept. There is a stream this way. I've found the water to be a refreshment after the way the human scent floods the city."

I follow the voice until I find a mop of curly hair, from which protrude nubby horns. Energy flashes through my body. *A fae.* A low fae, specifically. He isn't tall—a little shorter than the average human man. He wears a black uniform that is perfectly tailored to his form. If the horns were hidden, I might not have recognized him as a fae at all. Then he takes a few steps, and the movement is so unlike a human's, I take back my opinion. He's got hooves like a goat, complete with the strange backward-jointed knee . . . *thing* that goats have.

He walks toward the tree-shielded creek, talking to someone I cannot see because of a well-placed shrub. Whoever it is must be this very mysterious fae everyone is talking about. I keep walking, trying to get a clear look at him.

He comes into view between two shrubs. His back is to me, his hands resting lightly on his hips as he listens to the low fae speak.

It isn't his height or his warrior's build that makes my blood turn to ice. Nor is it the distinctly fae style of his clothes, with a long tunic, leather jerkin, and a belt designed to carry weapons.

It's the long, silvery-white hair that falls down his back.

The low fae points to something, and the warrior turns his head to follow, giving me a clear view of his profile: a sharp nose, prominent brow, severe jaw. It isn't necessary, however. I know who he is.

Prince Rahk.

I'm so shocked, so caught up in this sudden, horrible realization that my ankle rolls in a dip in the grass and, with my weakened strength, there's nothing that keeps me from flying face first into the dirt. And spilling all the fresh milk into the grass.

CHAPTER 8
RAHK

QUEEN VIVIENNE FINALLY agreed to see you, but only at a public event," says my new steward, Edvear, his large ears twitching in his mop of curly brown hair. He's a lowborn fae, so the air of the human world isn't as taxing on him. For me, on the other hand? The air has a quality to it that reminds me of a battlefield strewn with corpses.

The moment I arrived, I cursed Lord Nothril, Lady Nothril, and Ash for their errands.

As Edvear has already spent time in the human world, he's an ideal candidate to help me order my affairs here. "She specifically asked that you come unarmed, alone, and consent to being escorted by a unit of her guards everywhere you go."

I give a slow nod. "If that will make her feel less threatened, then I will comply."

Ash failed to mention in his original order that he was specifically sending me to the human kingdom with the most antagonistic view of the fae. So not only am I to aid the restoration of the stolen human lands, I am to work with a monarch who believes I will kill both her and her young heir if given the chance.

I'm beginning to think I might be here longer than a few weeks.

Edvear chuckles slightly. "These humans do greatly underestimate the capabilities of a fae warrior."

I shrug. "It is good that they do."

"Very true. There wouldn't be an opportunity for peace if they didn't."

A great crash and a groan of pain rips my attention up, away from the thinness of the air and my growing headache from the stench of grass, straw, earth, and manure. The *ollea* I applied earlier to take the edge off the flood on my senses is already wearing off.

There, a stone's throw from us, is a fallen servant boy and a spilled pail of milk.

"What did you just do? That was all the milk we had for today!" screams a tall woman, rushing out of what seems to be the kitchen, given that she's followed by a plume of smoke. "Curse Mary and her favors! I'm going to give you a solid thrashing and dismiss you without a recommendation, you imbecile!"

She drags the boy by the ear to his feet, ignoring his squealing protests, and I'm about to roll my eyes and move on, when she slaps the boy hard across the cheek.

Anger simmers to life inside me. That is not how my servants will be treated here. At Nothril, I didn't have a say. But here, I am master, and I will not allow such ill treatment. "Enough!" I shout, leaving Edvear by the creek and hurrying across the small length of pasture, the boy's cries of pain making me louder when I shout once more, "Enough, I said!"

My fist clamps around the woman's wrist just before she hits the boy again. She spins toward me, releasing the boy at once, and her eyes go wide as dinner plates. She swallows. "My lord—"

I lean over her, keeping my voice level and restraining my hand from tightening around her wrist. She smells of yeast and soap and that underlying current of decaying humanity. "Thank you for working hard to ensure the excellent care of me and my house. But you are not permitted to raise a hand against any of my staff. Understood? Miss . . .?"

"Mrs. Banks." She swallows and nods, but I don't miss the line of fury she shoots toward the boy. "He's no longer a member of this staff."

The boy scrambles to his feet, several paces away from the two of us. As though afraid he will be hit again if he comes too close.

"Are you very hurt?" I ask him.

"No, my lord," he replies quickly, ducking his head. His hair is dark and straight, falling into his eyes in shaggy clumps. His freckles stand stark against his pale skin. He looks like I could snap him in half with nothing but my hands.

"He showed up on my doorstep this morning. His sister—she's a good servant, that lass—told me she had a brother in need of work. She failed to mention he was weak, incompetent, and hasn't even had his voice deepen yet!"

Why am I dealing with this? I turn toward the boy, keeping my sigh under my breath, and ask, "You have need of work?"

"Yes, sir."

"Have you worked before?"

"No, sir. My sister has taken care of us, but it's getting harder for her to do it all by herself. I need this job, sir."

"Are you willing to learn?"

"Yes, sir. I might be clumsy at first, but I work hard."

I turn to the scowling Mrs. Banks. "Has he worked hard today?"

"Aye, my lord, but hard work doesn't mean much when you're using the day's milk to water the grass!"

There's something about the boy, about his earnest freckled face, and the unexpected flash of will in his gaze. He wobbles slightly on his feet, his shoulders stooping from strain, his chest heaving from exertion.

"Are you hungry?" I ask.

The boy hesitates, the rest of his face turning the color of the handprint across his cheek. "Yes, sir."

"Well, that's half your problem," I say to Mrs. Banks. "The lad's growing. Look, he's shaking with hunger."

The boy's eyes go wide—with horror—and he hides his revealing hands behind his back. "I can work. I don't—"

"What's your name, lad?" I ask.

The boy scratches the back of his neck. "Nat."

"Go to the kitchen and eat, Nat. Then report to my study. You will be my personal attendant. This should be a better arrangement for everyone."

The boy stares at me, dumbfounded. Then, at the snap of Mrs. Banks's fingers, he follows her inside. When he does, he comes closer to me than he has been this entire conversation, and I get a hint of his very human scent.

I am already turning to go, but that scent—mostly dirty clothes and sweat—shocks me so much I freeze and look back. Nat's scent is, unsurprisingly, distinctly human.

But it is also distinctly *female*.

I watch Nat's retreat with new eyes, following every inch of the supposed *boy's* frame. It's a good disguise. I wouldn't have caught it if I relied only on my eyes. But now I see the truth: the narrow shoulders, narrow waist, the way the shirt is slightly untucked to hide the definition of hips. The cut hair. Nat's face flashes before my mind's eye, and I watch as it transforms into a young woman's.

No wonder she's hungry. She's a grown woman, and she must have starved herself to aid her disguise.

I watch until she disappears inside the house, my mind spinning. Who is this woman? Not a skilled servant, that is for certain.

My mind turns over Queen Vivienne's requests for our meeting. Has she sent this woman to spy on me? If so, why would she send a woman disguised as a young boy? There are far more effective forms of subterfuge. Why would the queen set up an operation like this if it had so many points to fail? Surely, she has a capable spy who could masquerade as a stable hand or a maid.

What am I thinking? I shake my head and dismiss the idea. I'm thinking like a Nothril prince, looking for cutthroat politics at every turn. She is probably completely harmless, poor, and in need of work. Maybe she is unskilled and felt she had a better likelihood of landing a position if she were perceived as younger and more trainable.

Or perhaps she wears the disguise because she is afraid of being recognized. Has she accumulated debts or committed crimes? Does she fear being discovered and exposed?

Or . . . is she in danger?

It is odd, though, that of all places she would come to work, she would come *here*.

I'll keep an eye on her.

I will have plenty of time in her company, now that I've made her my personal attendant. It will not be difficult to unravel her secrets. A slight huff comes from my chest as I shake my head. I do not need yet another concern on my mind right now, but here we are.

Edvear's voice startles me from my thoughts. "How long will you stay in Harbright, do you think?"

I rub my jaw, still watching the door the young woman disappeared through. "I do not know."

"The human world will take some getting used to."

"Indeed, it will." I consider confiding my realization in Edvear, then decide to keep it to myself for the time being. "Help the boy out, will you? I'm afraid I've made him an enemy in that woman."

"You know, you could have dismissed him, my lord."

"I thought of it."

Edvear waits for me to elaborate, but I do not. I head back to the house. My mind lingers on the young woman, and perhaps it is my Nothril blood that makes me oddly excited about unraveling her secrets. No matter what angle I view this situation from, I cannot come up with a way she would be an effective threat against me. All that remains is an intriguing puzzle just *begging* to be solved.

A young woman masquerading as a boy?

I smile, and it is *definitely* my Nothril blood that makes me immediately think of dozens of ways to toy with her and her insistence upon this disguise.

Maybe my time in the human lands won't be so terrible after all.

CHAPTER 9

KAT

I BREATHE HARD as I shut the door to the outhouse. The stench is repugnant, but I don't care. I just need a quiet, dark corner for half a minute to let out a chorus of silent screams. My cheek still stings, but it's nowhere near as bad as the sting of my pride and frustration.

I need to give up my intention to continue undereating. I can't do basic things like fend off someone angry at me.

But more than that—bigger than all that—is the gut-filling horror of my new situation.

Prince Rahk. Prince Rahk. Prince Rahk.

Of the cursed Nothril Court.

"Oh dear saints," I gasp, clutching the sides of my head. "Oh dear saints. I'm going to get myself killed."

Memory assaults me of what it was like to be cornered by him in his room, fearing that he would take one of his great swords and slice me open. I think of the frightened woman I left behind. A woman who might be dead now, if my mask wasn't enough to throw the Nothril Court off the scent of the other servants.

Prince Rahk of the Nothril Court.

Of *all* the fae in Faerieland, he is the single worst person who could have come to Harbright. The single worst person for me to be living in the same house with—even one as grand as this one.

If he knew it was me who stole his *ollea,* he'd kill me.

If he knew I was freeing human slaves from Faerieland, he'd kill me.

If he knew I was lying to him about my gender, age, social status—*everything*—he'd kill me.

Brutally. Torturously.

Blast this all.

These servants here have *no idea* who their master is. They do not know that he is a notorious killer. They have not seen the coldness of his dead gaze—not like what I saw in Faerieland.

And now that I've begun this job, I cannot leave. There is no other place for me to work without getting a reference, which I cannot earn within the short time I intend to stay here. Beyond that, there is no other place for me to go. Not without leaving town and crippling my ability to run raids.

I have to do this.

The only way out is through.

"You've just got to be clever about this," I tell myself between panicked gasps for air. "You learned how to survive in the Long Lost Wood. You learned how to stalk fae courts and rescue humans. You can do this."

I have many things to my advantage, I tell myself, to make up for all the ways I'm egregiously disadvantaged. We're on human ground. He's not home. *I'm* in my homeland. I know the ways of the human world. He doesn't know who I am. He didn't pick up my scent at the Nothril Court. I'm good at staying beneath notice when I want to. I'll work hard. I'll *eat* and get back my strength. I won't give him a single reason to doubt me. I'll be the best attendant he's ever had.

"You robbed a fae prince blind and got away with it," I tell myself. *You've got this.*

Squaring my shoulders, I push open the outhouse door and face what comes next.

Over the quick but satisfying meal that the cook, Mrs. Finch, sets out for me, I learn that the low fae with the horns is named Edvear, and he is the steward. According to Mrs. Banks, I will now answer exclusively to him. She tells me to go report for duty to him. I wander the hallways of the manor looking for him, and I hide my wince when I find him speaking to Prince Rahk in a room that appears to be a study.

I'm *not* going in there while they are speaking. I will wait here. Awkwardly. In the hallway. And I shall pray that when Edvear leaves the study, the prince does not follow him.

My prayer is answered. Only a few minutes later, Edvear shuts the door to the study behind him and spies me with a pair of startlingly yellow eyes. His pupils are slitted like a cat's. They dilate upon seeing me.

"I am here to do your bidding," I say, ducking my head.

He sniffs—disapproval? He strides down the hallway past me, speaking as I launch myself forward to follow him.

"You will oversee setting out his clothes. I will check your work until I am satisfied with your skills in this area. You will serve his tea first thing in the morning. He is used to Faerie brews, so you must learn to prepare them properly. Any meals that he does not wish to take in the dining room, you will serve wherever he wishes. You will attend him on errands and outings. You will draw his baths for him and help him dress as he requires."

My eyes bug. I can only imagine how brutal my death will be once the prince learns it is not a young boy, but a full-grown woman who helps him bathe.

He will absolutely murder me.

"Your primary job is to ensure he is comfortable and happy in all circumstances," Edvear concludes.

A Nothril prince—happy? I almost snort at the ridiculousness of the notion.

It's just at that moment that I realize we've been walking these fine hallways, and I'm supposed to be an urchin who has never been inside such a building. I quickly arch my neck and feign gawking at the intricate, gold-painted designs on the ceiling panels. My gawking quickly turns real. These are *beautiful* ceilings. I cannot remember the last time I specifically looked up and admired a ceiling.

"Deliver any communications he wishes," Edvear continues. "Most will come through me, but he might send some directly through you. You will keep his chambers clean, his fire filled with wood and stoked as necessary. You must be available to serve him whenever he needs anything. More tasks will be added as needed, and as your competence grows."

"Where do I begin?" I ask.

"Unpack his clothes in his room and get everything ready for him."

He shows me to the prince's bedchamber. It is the largest, most opulent room I've encountered in this manor so far.

It's a dark room, with walls of plastered stone. Thick red curtains with corded gold tassels are drawn over the arched windows. They match the large stretch of woven red rug covering the cold stone floor. The bed, with its ornately carved headboard and footboard, is situated against a recessed arch. A great chandelier of wrought iron holds a host of unlit candles. It's going to be my job to light those things, isn't it?

Near the door is a large space occupied with a low table, surrounded by cushions for seating. The far side of the room is fitted with a luxurious vanity, a private bathing chamber with a clawfoot tub, and a mysterious door I don't explore in front of Edvear.

"There are his things." Edvear points to two trunks arranged against the wall near the table. "I expect you to be finished readying his room by the end of the day."

I survey the room. It is tidy, but having been unoccupied for some time, it is not clean enough for someone like Agatha, and this prince is well known for his sensitive nose. Considering that I can even smell the must, this room will be intolerable to him. My life and hope for the future depends on doing a good job—and not getting dismissed. As I note the dust balls in the corner, the dirt gathered in the grout of the stone floor, the stale angle of the curtains, I summon my will.

I'm going to work harder than any of these other servants.

I won't make the prince regret giving me a second chance.

I throw myself into my work. Returning to the kitchen, I collect a broom, duster, rags, and a bucket of soapy water. The first thing I do is pull back all the curtains, letting sunlight flood the dark room. I open all the windows and let fresh air circulate. The spring air is fragrant and cool. The chirp of birds outside becomes my companion as I endeavor to remove every single speck of dust in this room.

Edvear returns an hour later to find me on my hands and knees, scrubbing relentlessly at the floor.

"What are you doing?" he demands.

"Cleaning the grout," I say, tucking away the butterknife I was using for precision.

"That is not necessary. Unpacking his trunks is your first priority."

"I will stop."

When he's gone, I continue what I'm doing, sweat beading down my forehead. He might think I am being ridiculous, but Agatha was always fastidious about grout and I've heard dozens of lectures from her aimed at the unfortunate staff back home of the vast importance of clean grout.

I'm almost done, anyway.

Before I started on the grout, I cleaned out the wardrobe and opened all of its doors and drawers for the spring air to purify. Now that they are dry, I flip open the prince's trunks. The first thing that greets me is a bandolier of sharp, gleaming knives. I sweep away my momentary flinch and carefully set the bandolier on the ground. His clothes are beneath it. I set to work organizing them in the wardrobe. They are all distinctly fae make.

He will need proper human clothes if he wants to be accepted into society here.

I will not suggest such a thing. For one, it's not my place. For another, it is better if we all remember just how deadly and unlike us the fae are.

The sun angles low in the horizon, warm and bright, announcing late afternoon. I've still got so much work to do! One of those pressing tasks is chopping enough wood for the prince's fire. Considering that I've never chopped wood a single day in my life, I anticipate sacrificing a few fingers in the effort.

I consult Clifford, the groundskeeper, and he shows me where the wood pile, axe, and stump for chopping are. I heave a hunk of wood onto the stump, flex my fingers on the handle of the axe, and blow a short strand of hair out of my face.

I send the axe flying into the wood. I miss entirely, taking a chip out of the stump instead.

Perhaps I ought not to squeeze my eyes shut while I swing.

I lift the axe again and swing. It lands in the wood—and sticks. I yank hard, but the axe refuses to budge. *Don't panic,* I tell myself as pressure rises in my chest. *It'll come out. And if it doesn't, Clifford was a nice man and probably will only laugh a little if you go tell him you got the axe stuck.*

"You're doing it wrong."

The deep voice startles me so much I whirl, holding the axe in front of me like a weapon.

Only a few feet away stands the Nothril prince, his legs planted wide and his arms crossed over his chest.

He stands like he did when he found me in his room—like a warrior, and I decide that stance is far scarier than any of the armor and weaponry he lacks. His chin is tucked slightly as he frowns down at me.

I brace instinctively.

Then I realize I'm poised to fight. This is not what a servant boy would be doing.I force myself to relax and bow quickly. "Master."

"You've never chopped wood before," the prince states.

I wince. I've got to salvage this before he dismisses me. "I am a fast learner."

He only regards me coolly. Something about the way his gaze travels over my face and form makes me feel like he can see through my disguise straight to the girl beneath it all. I try not to squirm uncomfortably beneath his study.

He isn't going to recognize me. He isn't going to recognize me. It becomes a chant that I repeat in my mind to avoid being overtaken by the temptation to turn on my heel and run for cover.

Then he steps toward the chopping block. I scurry back several paces, too aware of how close I am to my own death. One of his broad hands lands lightly on the handle of the axe. The muscles of his forearm flex as he rocks it up and down until the head comes loose.

"That is how you get it out." He lifts the axe and faces me, deliberately placing his hands along the handle. His right hand lands just below the head, his left near the base of the handle. "This is how you hold it. And this is how you chop."

He turns, and in a swift, singular—and utterly terrifying—motion, he cleanly chops the wood. The two halves hit the ground with dull thumps.

That block of wood will be me if he discovers what I've done.

He's speaking to me. I drag my gaze up from the fallen wood to him. "It may take several strikes to split. If the head bounces, make sure that your face isn't in its way." He holds out the axe to me.

I have to take it from him.

Which means I have to come within a few feet of him. I try to pretend I'm not terrified of him as I inch just close enough to grasp the handle. One of his eyebrows twitches, but other than that, his face reveals nothing.

With one hand, he grabs a new log and affixes it atop the stump. He steps back to give me room, though not as much room as I want. My back prickles from his gaze.

I grind my teeth.

Gripping the handle of the axe, I brace my legs. My fingers flex. I've got to impress the prince. Or, at least, I've got to satisfy him with my progress.

I chop.

The sound that comes out of my mouth is not at all masculine. The head of the axe hits the wood and bounces back toward me. The prince reaches out and catches the handle just before it smashes me in the forehead. I stare stupidly at the thick veins of his hand and wrist.

"What did I say about keeping your face out of the way?" he says.

I bow my head. "I am foolish, Master."

He doesn't reply. I wait several long moments, and then cautiously peer up at him. Is the corner of his mouth *very* slightly lifted?

He returns the axe to me. "Try again."

I exhale through my nose and take the axe. Is it possible that he won't kill me? Or punish me some other way for my incompetence? This is the same prince who told me humans aren't allowed to serve him in the Nothril Court, and yet he deigns to instruct me on how to accomplish my chores. Is he on his best behavior while in the human lands so we will trust him and allow him to do whatever he came to do?

On my next swing, the axe gets stuck.

"Rock it as I previously demonstrated," says the prince.

I throw all my effort into it. Perhaps it would be easier if the log was rooted into the ground and not prone to moving. I use my foot to keep it still. Then I pause, the warmth of the day making sweat bead across my forehead. I give a hard upward jerk and the axe comes free.

"You might be doomed to chopping your own wood, sir." The words are out before I remember that I am not Kat, but a servant boy. My eyes fly wide with horror. "That is, my lord, I will master this. I promise. I—"

He blinks slowly. "Try again."

I manage to keep my girlish war cry behind the seal of my gritted teeth as I try again. The axe flies through the air. It bounces off again, but this time I succeed both in creating a small crack and dodging the sharpened iron coming for my face.

"Again," says Rahk.

I do as he says. Over and over again. Until, finally, a resounding crack splits the air. The log splits in two, and I stare bug-eyed at it. Then I blurt: "That was *awesome*!"

"I'm glad you think so." His flintlike jaw shifts, his mouth twisting, a lightness coming into his cold eyes. "Because there is a lot to do. If it's too much, one of the other servants can handle it."

"No, master! I will do this!"

He gives a single shrug and strides back to the manor. I stare after the retreat of his tall form, processing only now that I'm in full view of his study's window. I spin around and face the task before me.

"You don't stand a chance," I tell the pile of logs.

I throw every bit of my strength into my blows, honing my accuracy as I work. With each strike, I unleash my relief that he didn't recognize me.

I can finally relax.

If he hasn't figured out who I am by now, then he won't. My disguise—both then and now—has worked.

I chop the wood for his hearth and return to the project of his bedchamber. I take his unpacked trunks to Edvear and follow his instructions for where to put them. I draw fresh water from the well outside for the basin and pitcher of water in his bathing chamber. When I can see nothing else that needs to be cleaned, arranged, or sorted, I run outside to the garden and clip a few sprigs of flowering basil to put in a vase on each of his windowsills. I must do what I can to make this room a pleasant smelling, but not overpowering, room for him to be in.

The mysterious door in the bedchamber finally beckons me too much, and I crack it open. It's probably my responsibility to ready this room too, anyway.

What I find is a very small room with nothing but a rack to hang clothes, a bed for one person, and a small nightstand beside it. I'm not sure what to make of it, but I clean it like I did the main room.

Eventually, when the golden glow coming through the windows darkens, I look up. And I realize I've done everything I can possibly think of doing. I sag against the wall, my limbs threatening to give out completely.

I'm not sure I've ever worked so hard in my entire life. And I don't think I've ever been this exhausted—even after my raids.

There is something satisfying about surveying the room now. I give it one more study, and then I force my legs to carry me into the hallway. I shut the door behind me and hurry to find Edvear.

He is setting a single place in the dining room.

"What do I do now, sir?" I ask, barely hoping Edvear's activities indicate that I will not be required to serve the prince his dinner.

"Master Rahk will eat here. You are finished for the day. Go eat with the other servants and take your rest."

I nearly sag in relief. "Where do I sleep?"

He gives me a funny look, as if I should know these things—since I am the younger brother of a maid and all that. Still, he doesn't press, and only answers: "You sleep in the adjoining room attached to Master Rahk's."

That small room was . . . *my* room?

My entire body seizes up. I'm supposed to sleep only a few paces from the prince, with only a door between us? How am I going to run raids? How will I keep the proper distance I need between the prince and I?

"You are dismissed," Edvear says pointedly.

I slip out of the dining room, letting my feet carry me to the kitchen and the servants' hall, where the servants who do not have tasks keeping them busy have sat down for supper. Just as I shut the door to the servants' hall, I glimpse the prince striding down the hallway toward the dining room.

As though sensing me, he looks up. His black gaze pierces me, holding me in place until he strides out of my vision.

I release the breath I was holding.

There is an open length of bench at the table beside the young girl I saw in the kitchen earlier. Wordlessly, I take that seat and gratefully accept the bowl of stew and slice of buttered bread offered me.

The girl watches me while I eat. *Don't talk to me,* I think desperately. *Please don't talk to me.*

"Hello!" she chirps brightly. She's missing one of her front teeth. "My name is Rebecca, but you can call me Becky. What is your name?"

I sigh, then turn and offer her a smile. "My name is Nat."

"You are the attendant for the Master?" she asks. When I nod, she continues. "My mama is the one who cooks all the food. Say hi, Mama!"

The woman ladling stew into bowls smiles at me. "I'm Charity Finch. You can call me Charity. Except when Mrs. Banks is around. Then call me Mrs. Finch." She winks.

"I'm too young to be a servant," Becky says, ignoring her food in favor of talking. "But Mama has to work because Papa died several years ago, and I've got nowhere to be and it's not safe for me on the streets. So I get to mend all day. It's nice. I can go outside when the weather is beautiful, and I can stay inside when it's raining, and Mama will fix me a cup of hot chocolate. Here! Let me show you what I was working on before we stopped for dinner!"

She hops off the bench. I keep eating as she fetches her work. I didn't consider this dynamic of my disguise. This girl thinks I am a boy only a year or two older than herself.

She comes back a moment later with a flannel coat. My mind immediately leaps to Bartholomew, and I shove a bite of stew into my mouth, swallowing hard.

"There was a rip in the side seam. I'm almost finished mending it. Look!"

I look. I can barely tell where the original stitching ends and her mending begins. I'm genuinely impressed. "Those are very neat stitches."

Becky blushes furiously. I pretend I don't notice and return my focus on my food.

"Is the lad a connoisseur of stitching?" laughs Clifford, whose muddy boots have been left at the door.

"No, sir. My sister's stitching is very nice though, so I can tell a little bit."

The apples of Charity's cheeks are round and rosy when she smiles. "You should go rest, Nat. You look like you're going to fall asleep here at the table."

She takes my finished bowl and I could kiss her for giving me an excuse to not stay and meet the rest of the staff. I get to my feet, bid her thanks, and leave after grabbing my little bundle of things and my spare uniform that I left here this morning.

The dining room door is shut when I pass it, but the shadows beneath it remind me *just* how occupied it is. I pick up my pace and do not relax until I'm safely locked inside my new room.

I don't think I'll be able to sleep knowing that the prince can enter his room at any moment. Then I'll be trapped inside this small closet of a bedchamber. For that reason—and despite the way my ribs scream for me to remove my chest binding—I dare not undress.

I flop into the small bed as I am.

Then, remembering something, I sit upright and grab my bag. I rifle through it until I find what I'm looking for: the tailor's scrawled notes. My eyes land on one unfamiliar place in the column of familiar fae Courts.

The Star City.

Somehow, despite my long days and my employer ending up being the terrifying Nothril prince, I need to get information from him that will help me learn which Path leads to the Star City.

I return the paper to my bag and lay back down. My last thought is spent wondering how long it'll be until the prince comes to sleep. Then my exhaustion overtakes me.

CHAPTER 10
RAHK

A STRETCH OF farmland, empty at this dark hour, is what lies at the border of Caphryl Wood. I stalk along its edges, observing the sparks glowing along the ground. *The Wood is already beginning to recede.* I count the number of Paths that open from here and lead into the depths of Faerieland. There is the Path to Nothril, another to Valehaven, another to the recently sacked Ildreer Court, and more. I even come across a Path that leads to Caspar's precious Star City.

So many Paths.

I have no proof yet that the Ivy Mask uses this stretch of the Wood. He could be in Aursailles or another border kingdom. With Ash's errand, I didn't have a choice to come to Harbright instead of Aursailles, nor did I have the choice of which city within Harbright would be the capital. But if I *had* been able to choose, I would have chosen exactly here. I do not know of any other part of the Wood with this tight concentration of Paths. If I were the Ivy Mask, this would be exactly the place I would use.

I pause at the entrance to the Nothril Path, staring through the branches of the Wood down the winding length of its golden trail. I've yet to encounter a human who can see Paths, and yet I must assume the Ivy Mask can. How else can he navigate from Court to Court? Not even fae choose to navigate through the ever-shifting Wood without a Path.

Usually, I rely on my sense of smell to hunt quarry. That was how I found Pavi so quickly. But even the mask left behind from the Ivy Mask, which sits in a drawer in my desk, didn't have an easily traceable scent. That is an impressive feat for a human.

I ought to be frustrated. Instead, energy bubbles to life inside me. Will this hunt give me a challenge for once? It's been so, so long since I've experienced the true thrill of pursuit. The way my blood rushes when I'm closing in on a difficult quarry.

Still, my sense of smell isn't wholly useless. The Ivy Mask wasn't the only one to escape. Lord Nothril gave me a piece of his slave's clothes. I search for that scent now, following the miles of forest edge.

Suddenly, I catch it.

The rush returns. I follow that scent until I come across exactly the proof I need.

Hidden in the underbrush, halfway tucked into Caphryl, is a small, wooden cart. The slave's scent is strong here, along with several other human scents that come with a tinge of Nothril. A slow smile curves my mouth. The Ivy Mask *does* use this stretch of Wood.

It won't be long now until I catch him.

I investigate the driver's seat. There is no scent here except that of dusty wood. I scratch the back of my neck. How did he manage that? Does he have fae blood that allows him to glamour away his scent?

Or have we been wrong to assume that he is human?

I regard the towering Wood, the darkened stretch of farmland, and the sliver of sparking soil in between. Perhaps all this time, it has been a fae conducting these raids. Whether this fae lives in disguise in the human lands, or stays in his own part of the world, I do not know yet.

But I know how to find out.

I step onto the Nothril Path. The pressure of the human world's air immediately vanishes. I breathe deeply of the sweet Faerie air. With its power flowing in my veins, I weave my spell across the entrance to the glowing Path. Then I step back over the border and head to the next Path. I set my trap along every Path in the vicinity.

Now when someone steps inside Caphryl from the human lands, I'll know. If the Ivy Mask strikes a Court without triggering my spell, I'll know my quarry lives in Faerieland.

I finish as the sun crests over the horizon. It's time to return to the manor.

I think of the young woman sleeping in the adjoining room to mine. *Nat,* I must refer to her as, since I don't have her real name—yet. Briefly, I forget the intensity that hits me when I cross into the human world. I get to go from toying with one quarry to another. I can be mentally challenged and stimulated by one, and the other I can just play with for the enjoyment of it. She is completely harmless, after all, judging by her embarrassing performance chopping wood yesterday.

I have *many* questions for her to answer.

Am I actually excited for these next few days?

I shake my head, fighting the twist of my mouth as I spread my wings and launch into the sky.

Edvear is right. The wooded creek is the best part of this estate. Taking an early morning dip in its cold waters is exactly the rejuvenation I need after my long night. I grab my tunic off the bank and sling it over my wet shoulder as I climb out of the stream and enjoy the grass beneath my bare toes. The death cycle of the human world has stifled its magic and flow of energy, but with my feet flat against the earth, I can discern a tingling source—suppressed, but still moving.

As I step into the manor, Edvear's faint hiss from a few rooms down greets me. "Master Rahk is returning. Go to his chambers to serve him."

"Returning?" comes Nat's reply. "Where did he go?"

"Where he goes is not your concern. Only what he needs of you. Now hurry!"

I pause just inside the doorway as Nat's light footsteps hurry down the hallway to my right. I'll give her a few minutes of head start. Silently, I shake my head. If she truly is a spy of Queen Vivienne's, I think I will actually laugh at the sheer ridiculousness. They could not have sent a more incompetent spy.

The door to my bedchamber creaks when I push it open.

A hot breakfast is laid out on the table and the smell is unexpectedly appetizing. On the other side of the room, half of Nat's body is visible outside the wardrobe as she selects something to go with the black tunic already laid out on the bed.

"Black and more black!" she huffs, apparently not having heard me enter. "And there's the token dark blue tunic. Everyone is going to be afraid of him if he dresses like this!"

"Will they?" I drawl.

She lets out a squeak of surprise, bangs her head on the wardrobe door, and pulls herself upright. Her tied back hair is already mussed, her freckles standing out sharply as her eyes meet mine. Her gaze travels down to my torso and widens significantly. Color rises into her pale cheeks. I've already forgotten that I'm holding my shirt instead of wearing it.

I want to swipe a hand down my face. How can her subterfuge be *this* terrible?

"You're back!" she cries, and sweeps a hasty, awkward bow. "Would you like a towel?"

"Please." I sit cross-legged on a cushion beside the table and toss my wet shirt at the girl. She catches it—*at least she's somewhat coordinated*—and takes it to the bathing chamber. When she returns, she has a thick towel in her arms. She holds it out to me, hiding behind it like it's a wall between us.

There's no chance she is a spy.

I take the towel, hiding my smirk, and dry myself. When I hand it back to her, she blinks rapidly, averting her gaze from my chest. I sigh. Has she never seen a man's torso before? I turn that thought over. Actually, she probably hasn't.

Humans are far more modest than we are.

"I've got your clothes!" Nat cries desperately, pointing at them laid out on the bed. "What else can I do for you?"

She wants me to leave the breakfast I'm serving myself, which grows colder by the second, so I can dress? Am I not allowed to eat while shirtless, as my comfort dictates?

I study her. She wrings her hands anxiously, shifting her weight between her feet. Her face is bright red by now, hiding her freckles. The longer I study her, the more she squirms and avoids my gaze.

I might pity her and relent--if she wasn't actively trying to deceive me.

I know you're a woman, I say to her in my mind as I hold her gaze. She won't look at me. *And you're going to tell me the reason behind this disguise.*

She looks so miserable that I'm tempted once more to relent. Instead, I push harder. "Come sit beside me."

"No, Master!" she blurts back. When I raise my brow, her lips part as she realizes what she's done. If she were a slave in the Nothril Court, she would already be dead. She tries to recover herself. "That is, if you would like me to, I will. But I wish to serve you! How may I serve you?"

"You can serve me by sitting beside me while I eat," I reply coolly.

She looks like she is racking her mind for any excuse to keep from obeying. In the end, a muscle jerks in her neck, and she plops down on the ground three paces from me. She's so far away she's not even sitting at the table.

An inkling of impatience rises in my chest. My words come out firm. "Come closer. I won't bite you. If you're to serve me, you must overcome that hesitancy written on your face. Come. Closer."

She scoots forward. Not enough. I narrow my gaze at her. She scoots one more inch and then stares stubbornly back at me.

She wants to test me? Very well. I'll test her back. I take a swig of hot tea and return the teacup to its saucer. "If I threatened to punish you, would you obey me then?"

She has already planted herself at the table before I finish speaking, every visible inch of her skin a bright, flaming red.

My lip curls in amusement. "Good."

She sits still, a slight shiver working down her spine. She looks at the cushion she sits on—avoiding my gaze.

I eat slowly and watch her. She chews her bottom lip. *Trying to decide if she should break the silence.* I let the silence linger, curious to see what she might do or say to relieve her own discomfort. She's not difficult to read, and I watch as she waffles back and forth between keeping her mouth shut and saying something.

After several minutes, I decide to put her out of her misery. It's time to get her story out of her. "Tell me about yourself."

"Myself?" she blurts.

"You showed up dirty in ill-fitting clothes and said you'd been promised a job. And then we find you're not as skilled as your sister supposedly said."

"I will work on my skills!" she insists quickly. "I will master everything! Just please give me time. I will do it."

I take another sip of tea. It's not good, but it's not bad either. "Did I say I wasn't going to give you time?"

"Well—"

"You're talkative for a young boy," I interrupt, taking care not to let a single shred of my enjoyment show on my face. "If you work elsewhere after working for me, you might consider talking less."

She swallows hard and says determinedly, "I will talk less."

I am forced to wipe my mouth to cover the way a smile almost breaks free of my control. This is too easy. It is a good thing I have the Ivy Mask to challenge me. I clear my throat and put down the napkin. "I don't mind. But other masters might, so I tell you. Now, tell me about yourself."

She draws in a deep breath, bracing her shoulders. I lean back, more than ready to witness this phenomenon of a human lying without consequence.

CHAPTER 11
KAT

THE PRINCE WATCHES me. His body language is deceptively relaxed, the wrist resting on his knee loose, but there is a focus in his gaze that makes me think he is just waiting for the moment I slip so that hand can shoot forward and choke me.

I can hardly think under his study. My attention shifts away from his scandalously bare chest to the half-eaten biscuit on his plate. He didn't cut it open and butter it. Instead, he took a large bite right into the side of it. I might find it amusing in other circumstances. "My sister—her name is Mary—she has been taking care of me much of my life."

"What happened to your parents?"

I hesitate. Best to tell the truth whenever I can so I can keep my stories straight. "My mother was lost to the Long Lost Wood when I was a child—"

A glint comes into his black eyes. "You still are a child."

I'm so going to get myself killed. "When I was a *younger* child," I correct, hoping that's enough to cover my mistake. "My father waited over a year in hopes she would return." *Then he married Agatha.* "She finally did return." *And my father nearly went wild when he realized his love had finally returned to him—but he was already remarried.* "She wasn't the same person, and she died not even a week after her return. His heart gave out shortly after that. Mary and I have been on our own ever since."

There is no sign of pity in his hardened jaw. He eats the rest of his biscuit in one bite. "How old were you?"

"Nine."

"And how old are you now?"

"Twelve, my lord."

"So you've been an orphan these last three years."

Those words startle me more than I expect. *Three years.* Would that I had seen my mother and father only three years ago! Would that I hadn't been carrying their loss for eleven years instead.

He takes my silence as assent. "And tell me about Mary. She is how much older than you?"

Mary is several years older than me, and I run the calculations in my mind to see how implausible it would be that she would have a twelve-year-old brother. I decide it's safe to be honest—and I could hardly lie since her age is easily verifiable.

"She is twenty-five."

"She has been working as a maid for some time, then?"

I don't like these questions. Why is he prodding? Is he suspicious of me because I am not a skilled servant? Or does he simply wish to build rapport with his attendant? I don't like it at all. Especially while he's shirtless and only a foot away.

"Yes, Master," I answer. "She began working when she was fourteen."

That was when she began working in earnest as a servant—when my stepfamily entered the mix—but before that, when my parents were still alive, she'd been hired as a companion for me.

"Did any of your family ever go to the Long Lost Wood to look for your mother?" the prince asks, taking a deliberate bite after the question.

My world freezes. Memory flashes across my mind of that dark forest, and how terrifying it was when I first stepped foot into it as a child. Wailing my mother's name at the top of my lungs. I find my answer with difficulty. "My father looked into it. He was told that no one entered the Long Lost Wood and returned. Mama was gone and dead, they said."

"But she wasn't."

Curse it all! My throat thickens, my heartbeat turning to a painful pulse. I clamp down hard on the rising emotion with gritted teeth and look away.

"I've upset you," declares the prince.

If my job wasn't on the line, I would have scowled at him.

He pushes away his plate, empty of every last crumb. "This problem of the Long Lost Wood and the border between our peoples is why I am here. Your loss must have been hard on you. And your sister."

Did he just offer me consolation? A fae of the Nothril Court? I didn't think such a thing was even remotely possible. I steal a hesitant glance up at him.

He taps one finger on the table. "Did you or your sister ever go after your mother?"

This man is relentless! "Of course not," I lie, anger snapping back the emotion and making me pull myself under control. "It was too dangerous. You have to be a fool to walk into the Long Lost Wood." I almost let *Caphryl Wood*—the fae's term for the Wood—slip past my lips.

I'm not sure how many graves I can dig myself out of if I keep wagging my stupid tongue. I should take his advice and keep my mouth shut.

The prince regards me in silence for several minutes. Then, he says almost casually: "I'm sorry for what happened to your family."

Sorry, is he? The comment is more insulting than anything. I sniff. "It is what it is."

"You seem very accepting of your loss for a child."

"I'm not a child," I growl, because it seems like the sort of thing a twelve-year-old boy would say. And because I don't like it that he keeps referring to me as a child.

He nods, acquiescing. "I forgot. You are a grown man."

He says it with such a straight face that if I actually were twelve years old, I would have missed the gleam of amusement in his eye. He has the gall to press me about my family's losses and then mock me a moment later?

"I am a youth," I correct stubbornly, offended on behalf of the lad I'm pretending to be. If I let the silence linger, he will come up with more painful questions to ask. I've got to flip the dynamic. There is a reason I came to work for him. I need information. It's time to play the curious young boy. "What's it like living in Faerieland?"

His brow twitches. "It's never boring."

"Why? Because there's always war and such in Faerieland? I hear there are lots of wars." I do my best to sound ignorant and boyish.

"Faerieland is very vast," he says with a sigh. "I'm sure there are many parts of Faerieland that are always at war. My side of Faerieland, however, doesn't often have outright war. Instead, there is usually the looming threat of it."

I find it curious that he indulges my questions. It is not what I expected from someone who previously refused to have humans even attend him. "Is it exciting? The threat of war?"

He trails his finger on the edge of his teacup, and I tense as he regards me. "For some, I imagine."

"But not you?"

"I do not find it particularly enjoyable, no. I hear you humans love war so much you can hardly restrain yourselves."

"I do love war," I say, hoping that's the sort of thing a young boy would say. "I hope Harbright attacks someone soon so I can go to war."

To my shock, the prince snorts, his mouth twisting into a surprised smirk. "Do you, now?"

What's so funny? I cross my arms over my chest and scowl.

"What draws you to the idea of battle?" the prince asks, leaning forward slightly. He pulls his smirk away, but the shadow of it remains. Mocking me with his innocuous question.

"I want to fight."

"For what?" he presses.

For justice. For hope. For the chance the future can be brighter than the past.

I scratch the back of my neck. "I don't know. Anything."

"Not everything is worth fighting for."

"I would fight for my sister," I say, lest he think too little of Nat.

He nods slowly. "So would I." That glint returns to his irises. "We men have to protect our sisters."

"You have a sister?" I ask, even though I know of the Nothril princesses.

"Three."

"And you would go to battle for them?"

"I already have," he replies, getting to his feet and shrugging. "I'm sure I'll do it again."

I scramble up after him. Apparently, our conversation is over—which is both relieving and frustrating. I was just racking my brain over how to prod for information on the Star City, and now I've lost my chance. How am I to know when I'll get another?

"May I take your dishes, Master?" I ask as the prince strides past me toward the clothes laid out on the freshly made bed, taking his shirtless self mercifully out of my vision.

"Please."

I'm almost out of the door, his breakfast tray gripped tightly in my hands, when his voice arrests my movements.

"Tell Edvear to inquire after one of the city's tailors," he says with just enough wryness in his tone that I glance back at him. "Apparently I have need of one."

I flush. "Yes, my lord."

That night, my feet drag with exhaustion as I carry the prince's empty supper dishes from his study to the kitchen. I nearly drop the dishes at the sight of a familiar smile beaming at me.

"Look at you—so grown up in your uniform and working hard," Mary teases with a rare smile.

I'm so relieved to see her I could laugh. Catching myself, I glare at her instead while Charity Finch chuckles and the other servants look on in amusement.

"I had to come visit and see how you were getting along at your first job. I'm told you nearly got dismissed on your first day."

Mrs. Banks, who stands severely in one corner, arches a brow as the other servants laugh. My cheeks burn with embarrassment. "I didn't spill the milk on purpose."

She laughs and ruffles my hair.

"You should have come work for us instead of the boy," says Mrs. Banks. "We'd pay you more than what you make at Vandermore Manor."

"Tempting," says Mary with a wink.

She's so at ease here, among these people. The men in the room all seem to lean a little closer to her sparkle. I blink to clear my vision. I'm so used to Mary in the context of home. She is the bossy but loving sister-friend whose job is to worry about the things I neglect to. Here, however? Now I can see her infectious energy and the shine in her perfectly tidy red hair. Why has she never married? Why *has* she stayed at our estate, even after she was demoted from my companion to my servant?

Me.

I set the dishes down with a clatter.

"Mrs. Banks, could I steal him for a few moments?" asks Mary. "The evening sunshine is so lovely, and I hate to let it go to waste."

"Just so long as he's finished his duties."

All eyes turn to me. I nod quickly. "Master dismissed me after he ate, saying he had business to attend to in his study."

"Very well then."

Mary and I step out of the darkness of the kitchen into the glow of late evening. From this side of the estate, the manicured walking paths among the hedges are visible, but so is the forested edge of the creek and the lush field where Missy grazes in her corral and chickens scratch and peck.

"Look casual," Mary orders, her smile turning tense. "I bet they're going to watch us through the window."

I take up toeing a pebble in the grass, trying to look like the distracted schoolboy. She crosses her arms and eyes me—the perfect older sister.

"How's it going?"

"The fae is Prince Rahk of the Nothril Court."

Mary's face turns white. She may not know the prince by name, but she's heard my tales of the horrors of the Nothril Court. She hides her shock in a few blinks. "Do we need to get you out?"

"Is there some other place I can work?"

She shakes her head. "Not without a recommendation from this situation. Which, it sounds like, *you* haven't earned yet—even if you could on such short employment."

"I promise I'm trying! There's just a lot I didn't know!"

She lets out a long sigh. "I know. I was afraid of that, but I didn't have time to teach you everything. Is he very hard on you?"

I think of the intense power that follows his presence, the way he looks at me as if he knows all my secrets. And yet . . . "He has not been hard on me." In fact, he *should* be much harder on me.

"That's a relief."

"How have things been back at home? Is it too much to ask if they bought Bartholomew back?"

She gives me a sympathetic glance. "I'm afraid not. Things have not been well at the manor, actually. Your stepmother has been in quite a rage. Lord Boreham was furious too, and one of the girls overheard him yelling to your stepmother about how he's been putting up with you for this long and, '*this is what I get?*' She was pleading with him to not revoke his offer of marriage, but he stormed out in a fury."

"So . . . I might be free of him?"

"I wouldn't be quite so optimistic at this point."

"Did they give you trouble?" I wince.

"Oh, of course they did. I told them you'd been cooking up some scheme to keep your money and not get married, but that you refused to tell me any of it and I was surprised with the rest of them when your room turned up empty. In fact, I was the one who came running down saying you were gone. I think they believed most of it and moved their wrath on to other things."

The sun dips below the horizon, and the evening glow fades.

"I need to go," Mary says, glancing back toward the kitchen. "I hid your box of *ollea* and your raid essentials behind the outhouse. Send word if you need help. I'll drop everything and come at once."

I refrain from hugging her. I wish I could repay all that she has done for me. "You are too good to me. I promise to be careful. You must also promise me that you will get out of my stepmother's house if they are cruel to you."

"Don't you worry about me." She pats my head, even though we're the same height.

Then it's goodbye, and I'm left to head back inside by myself.

Right as I'm about to open the door, a tall silhouette in my periphery catches my attention. My head swivels just in time to see the prince stride casually toward the stream, staying in the shadows of the trees.

I stand there for a heartbeat, debating with myself, and then let go of the door handle and creep along the wall, trying to get a better glimpse of what on *earth* the prince is doing at this hour. An innocent evening walk? Somehow, I don't think so.

I angle my body until I find a good view of the prince. His back is to me, so he doesn't see me, and he's far enough away that he cannot catch my scent. Why has he stopped walking? Is he—

Suddenly, it's as though two great shadows emerge from behind him—massive and towering. They spread wide, and I'm still puzzling over what I see when the prince leaps into the air, and the shadows begin beating, carrying him into the night sky.

Wings.

My mouth falls open and I stand as though I've grown roots, watching until the darkness swallows him whole. Even when I was at the Nothril Court, he didn't have wings! Does he always glamour them away?

He's heading toward Caphryl Wood.

Why is he here, in the human world?

Did he come to hunt the slave girl I freed? She's long gone by now. He won't find her by searching along Caphryl Wood.

Or is he here for another reason?

I wish I dared follow him. But no, I need to stay alive. I have my raids to accomplish. How I will manage those without Bartholomew . . . I have no idea. But I'll figure something out.

Until then, I intend to figure out this prince.

CHAPTER 12

RAHK

I SPEND SEVERAL hours at the edge of Caphryl Wood, but when my spells remain untouched and the cart shows no sign of being moved, I return to Nothril briefly to meet with Pelarusa. She informs me that Pavi has kept herself out of trouble so far, and agrees when I ask her to have a servant leave notice for me on the Nothril Path when the Ivy Mask strikes. Not without vicious complaint however, and a promise to make my life miserable if I don't catch him soon.

After that, there's nothing more to do except trace the scents of the escaped slaves. I track them through the field into Ashbourne. Their scents—four of them—stay close together. They lead to a coach in the poorer part of the city and end there.

They've left the city. There's no tracking them from here. Not unless I wanted to spend a significant amount of time pursuing a few humans who might not even know much about the Ivy Mask themselves.

I mark the lead as dead and return home to catch a few hours of sleep. Humans need far more sleep than fae, but it still catches up to me every few days.

Quietly, I slip into my own room, not disturbing Edvear or the other staff. I toss away my jerkin and tunic, only to pause a second later. The memory of Nat's scandalized expression when she saw me shirtless resurfaces. I roll my eyes once more, but then I remember that she is supposed to be sleeping in the room adjoining this one.

Curiosity makes me approach Nat's door. I don't open it to respect her privacy, but I do place my ear close to the wood. I can make out her faint, even breaths from here.

She's asleep.

My brow puckers slightly.

Is the sob story she told me at breakfast true? The emotion in her body was clear: the haunted look in her eye, the slight inward curling of her shoulders, the shift in her breathing. I'm inclined to think it was, though the timeline she offered is inaccurate. Her parents have been dead for much longer.

If she did lose her mother to the expansion of Caphryl Wood, and her father not long after, then what turns did her life take to bring her here? Why would she have a skilled servant for an older sister, but she herself not be skilled? And the ever-present question: why the disguise?

I step away from the door.

Nat wasn't raised as a servant. Which means Mary likely isn't her sister.

I return to my spy theory as I navigate the darkness to my bed and lay down, staring up at the rafters. On one hand, it still seems the most plausible that Nat would be a spy sent from Queen Vivienne.

I just cannot believe an official spy would be *this bad*. Perhaps she *is* this bad, and I am letting my own bias cloud my vision. Still, it doesn't sit right. I could interrogate and threaten her until she broke and told me the truth. I could even use some . . . *forceful persuasion,* if she proved difficult to crack. If I was Pelarusa, or either of my parents, that is exactly what I would do.

But I have always been inclined to lean back and watch. To observe. To wait and see how things will play out. Perhaps part of me also enjoys the game of it.

Another theory has been stirring in my mind. One that grows more compelling by the day.

She's hiding.

From what, I do not know.

None of this is my business, and as long as she doesn't threaten my errands, I see no harm in letting her do whatever she came to do. The moment she does, though—and by consequence, Pavi's life—she'll be dismissed. Or worse.

For now, however?

I'll let her continue her charade as long as she likes.

KAT

"It was nice to see Mary yesterday evening. I thought the two of you looked nothing alike, but then she crinkled her nose like you do. I couldn't stop seeing the resemblance then," says Charity the next morning as she spoons oatmeal into dishes for the staff's breakfast.

"I wish I had a big sister," says Becky from her stool.

I give a little laugh as I take the prince's breakfast tray. I try to think of a proper response, and come up with nothing. So, I give an awkward shrug to Charity and carry my tray out.

I've already laid out the prince's clothes. He was measured for new, human-styled clothing yesterday. Soon, he'll look less like a warrior sent to destroy us all and, aside from his striking features and unusual hair color, he will *almost* look human. If he pulls his hair back in a way that covers his long, pointed ears, that is.

For the first time since I arrived, I woke to evidence that he slept in his bed last night. He was long gone by daybreak, however, if the coldness of the bedclothes I rearranged were any indication.

I lay out his breakfast on the low table in his bedroom. His approaching footsteps in the hallway make my spine stiffen, and I pray desperately that this morning, he will be fully dressed.

The door squeaks on its hinges. The prince's voice is low and monotone behind me. "Thank you."

I turn around. He wears the new set of black clothing I laid out for him. He hasn't donned his jerkin, but his tunic is embroidered with silver thread fine enough to make even a queen weep. I release the breath I'd been holding and bow.

He hardly even looks at me as he sits down to his breakfast.

I turn to leave.

"I'm attending a ball in three evenings." His voice arrests my progress. I turn around and fold my hands, waiting for his orders. "Some of my new wardrobe will be delivered by then. You will work with Edvear to select what I shall wear. I need a human's opinion on the matter, as it will be my first public appearance as ambassador in Harbright."

I cringe inwardly. I sent my intention to attend this ball weeks ago—before Agatha sold Bartholomew. The queen will be offended by my absence.

Well, there is no use worrying about it. I'll just have to deal with her displeasure when I return to court.

I bow. "I will do my best to pick out suitable clothes, Highness."

His head whips up, his eyes going sharp like a cat's. "Highness?"

My hand flies to my burning lips. "Master. I mean, *Master*."

The look he gives me is shrewd and calculating. His low voice takes on an edge that makes my teeth tingle. "How did you know I was royalty? I haven't told anyone here."

A rock drops into my stomach. I scramble for any excuse. "Oh, I just assumed—with being an ambassador, that you were someone important. Aren't ambassadors always royalty?" I try to thread my question with enough ignorance to cover my slip.

Stupid, stupid Kat. You're going to get yourself killed.

"I'd say they're usually *not* royalty," the prince replies.

"Oh. Forgive me." My voice pitches high, and I desperately drag it back down to my lower registers to exude curiosity instead of supreme discomfort. "But . . . you *are* royalty?"

He blinks once, slowly. "I am."

I lean slightly forward, feigning surprise. "Are you a king?"

To my relief, the question seems to genuinely amuse him. "No, I am a prince. Most kings don't do their own emissary work."

Slip of the tongue successfully recovered from.

Now time to make my escape.

I bow. "I will remember what you have taught me and will say foolish things less often."

"Don't." His mouth curves slightly. "Your foolishness is the only delight I have to look forward to."

He eats his breakfast, signaling the conversation's end. I leave the room as quickly as I can and head outside. I already have more wood to chop. When I walk into the sunshine, I let out the curse I was biting back. I think I'm offended—and not for Nat's sake, but my own.

I stomp over to the stump and woodpile. I grab the axe.

The violence of the task calms the simmer of my blood.

It's fine if he thinks you're an idiot, I tell myself, puffing hair out of my face. *Let him think less of you. It's only then that you can take advantage of him.*

Work keeps me busy until sundown. While my hands move, I occupy my mind with the problem of doing a raid without Bartholomew. I used to do them that way a long time ago, while I was still getting her used to Caphryl Wood. Until Bartholomew gets back, I'll have to go on foot. It'll slow us down, but I cannot use another horse—for so many reasons.

The prince summons me to his study after supper. I brace myself when I open the door. Almost immediately, a chest is dumped into my arms.

"Organize the contents of this chest in my room. It was misplaced during unloading," the prince orders.

"Yes, Master." I bow and turn to leave.

"I heard your sister stopped by to see you."

I go still. Then I force a smile, shoving away my growing premonition. "Indeed. I was glad to see her."

"Good. She is welcome here. You must introduce me when she comes next."

He speaks the words so casually, but I don't trust it for a minute. Is he suspicious after I called him by his royal title today? Does he wish to corroborate Mary's story with mine?

I make a mental note to *never* let him meet Mary if I can help it. "Thank you, my lord."

In the bedroom, I set the chest on the vanity and open the lid. Of course, right on top are several very sharp knives. I force myself not to be afraid of them and lay them out on the vanity, one after another. After that, I find a silver medallion on a long chain. The medallion is engraved with a crest: a jagged fang with a star in its center. I place it in a small drawer in the wardrobe.

The bottom of the chest contains two items of interest. A pouch containing two vials of *ollea*. They snag my attention at once, with their slender size and blue tint. It would be so simple to snatch one—and endlessly stupid. I go to place it on the bedside table where he will find it the moment he wakes up each morningonly to stop. That is where I would put it if I knew *ollea* was for him to dull the intensity of scents to his nose. But I'm Nat. A twelve-year-old boy who wouldn't have a clue what this is.

I set it on the vanity beside the knives instead.

The second item of interest is a flat, circular container of thin, carved wood. My heart leaps—not from fear this time, but pure excitement. *Fool's Circle.* A fae game that the tailor taught me when I was a child. A game I have not played in years.

I cannot resist sliding open the lid. There, on top of the board, is a carved piece with a red, painted cap and a comically long nose. A wave of comfort rolls over me, bringing a smile to my lips. This was how Tailor calmed my tears when he discovered me, frightened out of my mind, wandering the Long Lost Wood in search of my mother.

"Everything will be alright," he told me while we took turns moving our pieces. *"See how silly the Fool's nose is?"*

"That is a fae board game."

My throat slams shut in fright. I whirl, releasing the piece back into its container.

Prince Rahk stands just inside the doorway. I didn't even hear him approach—I must have been too caught up in my discovery.

"I was *not* trying to snoop," I say quickly, slamming the lid of the game shut. "I wasn't sure where I should put it, so I opened it to see what it was. That was when I saw it was a game. I love games and this one seemed interesting, but I promise I was just about to put it away."

His arms are crossed over his chest, his face utterly blank.

"I can put it beside your bed?" I rush over to his bedside table and set the game there. "I wasn't sure where you wanted your knives or your blue vials. I didn't want to put them somewhere where they'd break, as they seemed valuable."

In a few strides, he stands in front of me. I swallow, looking up at him, trying to read his thoughts in the impenetrable set of his hard, wide-set jaw and the black depths of his pupils. Have I pushed him too far this time? Have I proved myself untrustworthy and incompetent beyond redemption?

His hand slips behind me. I brace myself, forcing myself not to squeeze my eyes shut. He withdraws his hand—and I realize he's grabbed Fool's Circle.

He holds it up. "Would you like to learn to play?"

My jaw unhinges and falls to the floor. "Yes! I would love to. But I thought—I thought you were angry with me!"

His lower lashes twitch, the severity of his mouth shifting just slightly. "For having excellent taste in games? Certainly not."

He goes to the table and sits on the cushions as he opens the game. My relief sends my legs almost melting into water. I force them into motion and make them carry me to the opposite side of the table.

I fold my feet beneath me as he slides a thin disc of wood onto the table and dumps the painted pieces beside it. The board has a circular grid carved into it, with one center space reserved for—

"The Fool goes here," says the prince, setting the biggest piece in the middle. "The goal of the game is to surround the Fool with four of your minions—the smaller pieces—and claim your win. You arrange your minions like so, one in each of the edge spots on your half of the circle, and I will do the same. On your turn, you can move three spaces between any of your pieces. They can only move to the spaces adjacent to it. You can use all three of your spaces on one piece, or you can split it between two or three pieces. If you want to capture a spot I'm currently residing in, you must surround me on three sides—and thus force me to retreat."

I nod, already planning my moves out as I stare at the board.

"There are various strategies—"

"I prefer to learn as I play." I shouldn't have interrupted him. I kick myself.

He only looks up, settling his gaze on me. "Then let us begin. You may take the first move."

I take my leftmost piece and move it three spaces inward.

A slight smirk twists his lips. He mirrors my movement on the opposite side. I immediately veer into his territory, halfway to the one of the coveted slots.

"Aggressive," he mumbles.

"Am I doing it wrong?" I say, to cover my confidence in my moves.

"Not at all. I have a friend named Ash back in Faerieland who is good at this game, and this is his favorite strategy to use on those who are new to the game. It works well on those likely to get flustered and defensive."

"But not against someone like you?"

"It's not going to make me fall back on my defenses and give you the edge, no. That doesn't mean it can't work with someone more experienced, though."

"Hmm." I bite my lip, focusing on my moves. Adrenaline sharpens my attention. It isn't likely that I could successfully win against someone like Prince Rahk, but the force of my desire to do just that surprises me. I'm so completely focused on the game that I hardly even think about the prince until he speaks.

"You have a knack for this game."

I look up. He studies me intently, his head slightly cocked to one side. If I'd known he was watching me like that, I wouldn't have been able to think straight about my next move. I shift in my seat and look away. "I enjoy games."

"Even fae ones?"

"I haven't met a game I didn't enjoy," I reply.

He smiles. *Actually* smiles.

"Me neither."

I clear my throat to rid myself of the strange tickle that appeared. The pieces on the board shift in my vision. I blink to focus. I study the board, then sag against the table in realization.

Rahk's smirk widens. "I'm impressed."

"Impressed?" I blurt. "Impressed that I lost?"

He encircles my last piece and claims the fourth spot surrounding the Fool. "I'm impressed that you saw your loss that quickly. I thought it would have taken several more turns to notice."

I make a vague sound of displeasure.

"So, you like games," says the prince, sliding the board back into its container, "but you don't like losing."

"No one enjoys losing," I reply tartly. "Though I'm sure you're not very familiar with the concept."

He pauses just before he drops the Fool into the container. One eyebrow cocks slightly. "That is a bold assumption, considering you know nothing about me."

I shut my mouth, chastened.

"But you are correct. I do not lose often."

When I look up at him, surprised, his gaze holds an unexpected twinkle. I blink twice. Then, because he seems to be in a relatively good mood, I decide to test my luck. "My lord, may I speak plainly?"

"So long as you do not offend me," he replies, and I cannot tell if he is serious or if he is somehow teasing me with an unreadable deadpan.

"I know I am lacking in many ways," I begin cautiously, "but I wish to please you. I fear that I usually cannot tell from your face whether you are pleased or not."

There is no shift in his expression. He nods slowly. "That does put you at a disadvantage, considering that I can tell very easily when you are pleased and displeased."

I do not think he could have given a more frustrating reply.

"Nat: currently very displeased with his employer," the prince declares.

"My lord!" I cry, wishing I could hide the way my skin suddenly turns hot. "You must delight in tormenting me! I cannot tell if I am to get on my knees and beg your forgiveness or if you are merely teasing me."

He nods again. "I do delight in tormenting you."

My mouth falls open. I try to collect my composure. "Then . . . you do not require penance of me?"

"The penance I require of you is that you play Fool's Circle with me tomorrow evening." At this, he seems to allow himself a small smile. Enough to prove that he *is,* in fact, teasing me and that he is not angry.

At the mention of playing again, I forget my frustration and perk up. "Tomorrow?"

"Considering that your world smells like rotting animal corpses, I ought to indulge in anything that makes up for it. You've proven yourself an interesting opponent, and perhaps with enough practice, we'll turn you into something formidable."

That . . . is a compliment. Very backhanded, but a compliment nonetheless. I don't have a clue what to do with a compliment from a Nothril prince.

"Perhaps with enough practice, we can reacquaint you with the experience of losing," I reply, too cheeky for my own good.

"You are bold for one with years beyond your skill."

"Ouch." I rub my arm. "I will endeavor to bridge the gap formed by not growing up in Faerieland."

"Nothing would please me more," he replies.

CHAPTER 13
KAT

PRINCE RAHK RARELY requires anything of me beyond my usual service, but the next morning, he summons me to his study almost immediately after breakfast. I pass one of the parlors on the way, and think of Edith when a bust of Botsov glares at me from inside it.

"I do not like how these books are arranged," Rahk says when I enter his study, gesturing to the shelves lining his walls. "Rearrange them at once."

I shift my weight between my feet as I regard the six shelves. What doesn't he like about them? "Yes, my lord. Do you have a particular way you want them arranged?"

"By author."

I draw in a deep breath. This is going to take forever, and I have more than enough work already. I'll just have to be *very* fast. With another, "Yes, my lord," I set to work. I start at the shelf closest to me and carefully remove the books, piling them on the floor. The prince's quill scratches against his parchment as he works—on what, I have not a single clue. Whenever that quill goes quiet, I try not to let myself wonder if he watches me. It *feels* like he watches me. But I will not be spooked by him and his intensity.

I soon have sweat beading on my brow from carrying all the books in this small room and making myself move as quickly as possible.

"What are you doing?" the prince asks abruptly when I'm on the third shelf.

I look up. He sits at his desk, his knees and elbows wide, his black gaze moving between me and the piles of books I have lined up in a row. I open my mouth, close it, then frown. "I am reorganizing your shelves . . . my lord."

"Yes, yes, but what are the piles?" He gestures at my neat rows.

I blink. "The books sorted by author. The authors whose names start with A are in this pile, B in this one, and so forth . . .? I'll alphabetize within each group once I have all the books sorted."

He gives a single, solemn nod. "Efficient."

I take that as permission to get back to work. He doesn't speak to me for the next hour as I work as quickly as I can.

There are long stretches where his quill doesn't scratch, and I have to tell myself repeatedly that it is ridiculous to consider that he does nothing for over a quarter of an hour save watch me work. He probably is reading.

Or thinking important thoughts.

I slide the last book onto the shelf. Pride blossoms in my chest as I regard my work. I'd like to see anyone else try to do a better job more efficiently. I pull my face into a serious mask and turn around. "I am finished, Master."

He leans back in his chair, a single lock of his silver hair falling over his forehead. He regards me first, then my handiwork. Standing, he walks around his desk, one hand planted on his hip as he studies the shelves. Is he checking to see if I correctly alphabetized everything?

"This is not satisfactory," he says at last.

My neck cracks from how quickly I spin my head toward him. "My lord? How—how can it not be satisfactory? Everything is arranged exactly as you asked."

"I believe the appropriate response would be, *'How may I make it satisfactory, my lord?'*" the prince says.

I bite my burning tongue and suppress the mounting heat of anger in my chest. *You've just got to work here until you turn twenty-one. Then you don't have to deal with any of this.* Still, it takes me a minute before I trust my tone when I say, "How may I make it satisfactory, my lord?"

"I'd be much more satisfied if the shelves were arranged by topic. I could find what I look for easier."

He could have said that from the beginning. I am proud of the way I don't let a single fiery word pass my lips. If he is toying with me, that is his prerogative. I am his servant, and I am indebted to him for giving me so many second chances.

I bow. "As you wish, Master."

Then I face the shelves once more and begin dismantling all my careful work.

Sorting by topic proves to be much slower and more complicated. For one, I must decide the topics by which to sort the books. For another, some books could technically be placed under multiple topics. I take twice the time to arrange the shelves. When I finish, I want to flop on the floor and die. I tell Prince Rahk I am finished, and when his shrewd eyes narrow at the shelves, I can practically hear his low voice pronouncing, *"I am not satisfied. Do it all again."*

But he only sniffs and turns away. Evidently satisfied.

I sag, desperately relieved. "How else may I serve you?"

Please let me go. Please let me go.

"I require your aid in deciphering this passage." The prince holds up the book he is reading.

"My . . . aid?" I repeat, bewildered. "I'm sure there is nothing you cannot understand that I would."

"Excellent use of flattery. It will serve you well." The prince turns the book around and slides it across his desk toward me. "As it happens, you are a human, and I am not. Thus, your insight on this human text will prove enlightening to me. Read that passage aloud and tell me what it means."

I take the book and read the title of the passage. "The Clockmaker's Son? This is a fairytale."

The prince steeples his fingers. "I am aware. Proceed."

I hesitate, then clear my throat. "Once upon a time, there was a princess so beautiful that word of her radiance spread to the ends of the earth. Suitors traveled vast distances for a single glimpse of her face, offering wealth and admiration. Yet, she cared not for them or their gifts. The only gift she longed for was the ability to stop time, for her true love was her work—a grand tapestry, larger than any other in the world, portraying the history of her kingdom in intricate detail. Every morning, she rose early to work on her tapestry before she was forced to entertain her suitors. One morning, her clock broke. Unbeknownst to her, the day slipped away, and her suitors wept outside, grieving her absence."

I pause, looking at the prince to ensure he wants me to continue. When his gaze does not shift from my face, I swallow and keep reading. "The clockmaker's son, renowned for his intricately fashioned timepieces, came at once to repair her broken clock. 'Why do you care not for your suitors, who have come far and wide to give you the world?' the young man asked. 'They do not give me what I truly wish,' the princess replied. When the clockmaker's son asked what it was that she truly wished, she told him. 'You are a clockmaker's son,' the princess implored. 'You know the secrets of time. Teach me to master it, that I might bend it to my will.' The clockmaker's son answered her, 'Time is not a thing to be mastered, my lady. To kill time is to rob life of its sweetness.' Undeterred, the princess coaxed him into her service with her beauty and wit, and together they toiled on a wondrous clock. It was gilded and gleaming, each tick sang like a silver bell, each chime like a choir of stars. When at last it was complete, the clockmaker's son warned her: 'This clock will steal from you as much as it grants. For each moment you steal, another shall wither and fade. Use it wisely, if at all.'"

I stop reading, glaring at the book.

"Why have you stopped? Keep reading," says the prince.

"I do not like the rest of the story," I reply sourly.

He merely lifts one eyebrow.

I huff and keep reading. "But the princess, enamored with her newfound power, ignored his plea. She stopped the hours whenever she worked, skipping past the ones spent with her suitors. All the while, the clockmaker's son watched, his heart aching with unspoken love. One day, she bade him to stop the clock entirely so she might finally finish the grand tapestry. Reluctantly, he obeyed. When she tied off the last thread, triumphant and satisfied, she turned around, only to find the clockmaker's son collapsed to the ground—his life drained by the magic he'd given her. The princess wept over his body. For it was only now that she realized that the true treasure she possessed was not her work or the magical clock, but the clockmaker's son himself."

I slam the book shut and return it to Prince Rahk's desk. "Do you see why I don't like it? It has a horrible ending."

"I thought it a very fitting end for the selfish princess."

I restrain my impulse to defend the princess. Was it truly such a great fault for her to care about her work more than she cared about a bunch of men who wanted nothing but her beauty? Who cared nothing for her skill and diligence and passion? To me, it seems like the greater fault lay with the clockmaker's son—who could have just *told her* that using the clock would kill him. How was she to be blamed when he withheld that crucial information from her?

But twelve-year-old Nat would hardly identify with the princess in the tale, so I keep my mouth shut.

"There is a phrase in this story that I find curious," Prince Rahk says. "They mention *killing time*. Even with the magical clock, they couldn't kill time. Time kills you, not the other way around. Within the story itself, it even proves my point that in the end, time is the ultimate power. So why do they claim to have the power to kill time?"

"Oh, that." I shrug. "It's a euphemism. To kill time is to waste it. It doesn't mean they intended to destroy time altogether."

"Ah, I see." He takes the book back, flipping it open to where it was before.

I take a half step closer. "Why . . . why are you reading fairytales?"

"Do you require an explanation?"

"N-no, of course not. I was merely curious."

"If it will sate your curiosity, I read them because I find stories to be at the core of a culture. I wish to understand yours, so I read your stories. Satisfied?"

I nod, backing away toward the door. "Yes, my lord. If there is nothing else—"

"You read very well."

I halt my progress. I consider my disguise again, wondering if I have revealed myself. But no, twelve-year-olds can read. I cannot think of anything I've miscalculated. "Thank you."

"Do you have much education?" the prince asks.

Now *that* question is one I must be careful with. "Mary taught me to read. I've read the books she brought me."

There. Now I can be educated at any level.

"I've heard you humans have schools and universities. Have you ever thought of attending? You're a bright lad. You would be successful. Perhaps you could even find an occupation for yourself beyond being a manservant."

He thinks I'm smart?

He thinks Nat is smart. Nat, who is twelve. If he knew you were twenty, he would hardly find your mind impressive.

He's looking at me in a strange way. His mouth is slightly slanted, his eyes bright in a way that reminds me of last night. It's like he's testing me again. Why, or how, I cannot make sense of.

"I—I don't know," I say. "It would be a lot of pressure on Mary."

He nods in reply. "Of course. Off you go. I shall summon you if I need you again."

I let out an enormous sigh once I'm safely free of the prince's presence. I slip into the empty dining room for one moment of peace and silence. I survived this long and arduous morning.

My break is over. I straighten and slip back out of the dining room. With all the time I've lost, I've got to work extra hard to complete the rest of my tasks.

But if I thought Prince Rahk was finished with me for the day, I am soon proven dead wrong.

Edvear and I are busy sorting through a partial delivery of the prince's new wardrobe after the noon meal when he summons me once more to his study.

"Sit there," the prince orders, pointing to a new chair beside his desk that has materialized since I was last here. "And play this."

I've barely sat before he thrusts something into my lap. I look down at the object in bewilderment. It's a lute, with a rounded body and a long neck where its strings are fastened.

"I don't understand," I say bluntly.

The prince sits down at his desk, which now feels far too close. "I require atmosphere while I work. Play me a pleasant tune."

His tone offers no room for protest. So, with a silent huff, I position the instrument in my lap and begin plucking at the same string over and over again.

"Something pleasant, I said," he orders.

I grit my teeth. I pluck at a different string this time, bouncing in a discordant pattern entirely lacking in beauty, rhythm, and any consideration for those within hearing distance. I stop the moment he swivels his head toward me. "I don't know how to play the lute!

Or any musical instrument, for that matter! Where did this lute even come from?"

He wipes a hand over his mouth—to hide his smirk.

"My lord," I begin carefully, "is there a way I might become less delightful to torment?"

His lips quirk. He shoos me out of the chair with one hand. "Go back to whatever you were working on."

The moment I've shut his study door, I clench my hands into fists. This job is hard enough without him *purposefully* trying to make my life as difficult as possible.

Is he trying to make me quit? Why not just dismiss me outright?

I tighten my jaw. If he is trying to get me to quit, he is going to be sorely disappointed when I refuse to let his goading get to me.

Three blissful hours go by with no summons from the prince. Edvear and I select his clothes for the ball two nights from now. I head down to the creek with Charity and Becky to do the prince's laundry. As I finish pinning the laundry to the line to dry, fighting off a chicken that wants to roost in my basket of freshly cleaned clothes, Edvear pops his curly head out of the kitchen door.

"Master Rahk summons you. He is in his bedroom."

I let a very unladylike curse escape my lips. Then I remember my resolve to be unflappable. "Coming!"

I leave the gloriously sunny outside and tromp to the prince's bedroom. I knock on the door, praying desperately that this will be a short instance of torment like the lute, instead of the half-day project of reorganizing his bookshelves.

"Come in."

I push open the door. "I am here, Master. What can I—" The words die suddenly on my tongue.

Prince Rahk lays on his stomach on the bed, above the bedclothes. He is shirtless again.

I drag my gaze to the rafters and pin it there. "What can I do for you, my lord?"

"My back is sore from sitting all day. Massage away the aches. There is oil on my bedside table."

My mind goes completely blank at the thought of doing what he asks. I can think of little that would be more inappropriate than this—except that I'm Nat. It wouldn't be inappropriate for a servant boy to tend his master this way.

If he ever finds out I'm a woman, he will kill me.

"I am not skilled in massage," I say in one desperate attempt for a reassignment. "I could get Edvear—"

"He is busy, and this is your job. Attend to it at once."

You're going to have to do it, Kat, I tell myself. *And you're going to be unflappable about it.*

I leave the door open because it feels like I am doing something illicit if I close it. I march to his side, locate the oil, and slather it across my hands. *Unflappable. Unflappable. Unflappable.* I regard the broad expanse of his pale, muscular back. *Be unflappable, Kat!*

The first thing that surprises me is how warm his skin is beneath my touch. The second is that he immediately flinches.

I withdraw. "Are my hands too cold?"

"No," he says quickly. Gruffly.

Hesitantly, I lay my hands flat on his back. My heart threatens to beat straight out of my chest, but I make my hands move, spreading the oil across his back until his skin gleams.

Unflappable.

The tension has not left his muscles, and I get the distinct sense he does *not* enjoy this. Strange, considering this was his idea.

I move his hair to one side, only to pause when a dark lined tattoo is revealed.

It's a curling vine of ivy. I tilt my head to one side.

"What is your tattoo?" I ask.

The only visible side of his jaw tightens. His whole body feels like a coiled spring, tense and taut and ready to snap. I bite my lip and step backward. I shouldn't have asked, should I?

A minute passes, but the prince offers no answer. I decide eventually that he isn't about to leap up and strangle me for my insolence, so I creep back and continue my work.

I start at his shoulders, working the muscles at the base of his neck. His head lies on his folded arms, contracting his shoulders and making his arms seem even bigger than normal. My eyes dance around, trying to find anywhere safe to look where I can both see what I'm doing and still not see *him*. I settle on staring at the back of his head.

"Rub harder," he grunts. "Put your weight into it."

I drag my lip between my teeth. He wants more force? I'll give him *force*. I'll channel all my frustration and embarrassment into his back. I dig my knuckles into his flesh, driving my weight into his ribs.

"Yes, like that," he says approvingly, instead of crying out in pain like I'd hoped.

And yet, he still seems to brace against me.

I set it as my goal to make him flinch in pain while I work. That helps me set aside my discomfort. I roll up my sleeves and sink my elbow into his shoulder blades, which earns me another nod of approval. My frustration only drives me to work harder.

I work my way down his spine and then back up again, focusing on my efforts to make him flinch. When I use my elbow just beneath his shoulder blade, I am finally rewarded. It's almost more of a twitch, but to me, it counts. I smirk in satisfaction and then lean forward to similarly hurt his other shoulder blade.

My arms grow more tired by the moment. I'm going to pay for this dearly tomorrow in soreness. How long have I been doing this? Half an hour? Longer?

Abruptly, his eyes open. My hands go still.

"That is enough," he declares.

I pull my hands back as fast as I can and step backward, putting distance between us. "How else may I serve you?" I don't look at him for fear my discomfort will be plain on my features.

He swings his feet to the ground, sitting upright and gripping the edge of the mattress in either hand. I keep my gaze stubbornly downcast, so I do not know whether he studies me or if his own finds elsewhere to lodge. "For someone unskilled, you did fine work."

His praise catches me off-guard. Still, I refuse to look at him. I bow. "I am honored to please you."

He gives a dry snort, and now I can feel his attention settle on me. "Look at you. A rebel if ever I saw one, yet so tame and restrained. You were not exaggerating when you said you were a fast learner and would say fewer foolish things."

My blood simmers beneath my skin, but I won't open my mouth and ruin my progress.

"You must want this position very much. Pray, what is it, Nat, that makes you work so hard to overcome your deficiencies?"

Claiming my fortune and maintaining my independence. "I want to keep this position, my lord."

"But why?"

I shift my weight uneasily between my feet. "Because I need it."

"And why is that?"

"I . . . I cannot get another, Master. Since this is my first situation, no one will hire me until I've worked one place for several months without being dismissed."

He leans forward, his forearms resting on his knees. "Why would that be so bad?"

Is he seriously asking this question? I've already told him why. "Because Mary and I need money, and I've got to start pulling my own weight. I cannot ask her to keep giving everything for me."

"You wouldn't starve, though?"

"If something happened to Mary, then yes!" I cry. I just want to leave this room, eat my supper to quell the shaking in my exhausted limbs, and go to sleep. I don't know what games he's playing with me today or what is behind these questions, so I voice the fear I've carried all day. "Do you want to dismiss me, my lord?"

My question hangs in the air. He props his chin up on one fist. I stand where I am, waiting like my life depends on his next words.

"If I dismissed you, I wouldn't have anyone to play Fool's Circle with," he replies coolly.

Not an answer.

I exhale through my gritted teeth. "I have many more tasks to finish before sundown. Do you wish me to stay, or may I go finish them?"

"You may go."

I whirl on my heel and march out of the room, barely keeping myself from slamming the door behind me. He is playing with me, and I hate it. It's his cruel fae nature, his Nothril blood, that makes him torment me so mercilessly. He knows this position is hard for me, and he is trying to see how far he can push me before I break and release my own spitfire nature.

I won't give him that satisfaction. I won't let him see how close I am to snapping in half and railing at him for being the reason my mother died.

I throw myself into my work, disregarding my own exhaustion. The prince mercifully takes his supper in the dining room. Edvear serves him and I hide in the kitchen, eating and flinching every time the steward enters for fear he'll tell me the prince requires my service. Then, the moment I'm finished, I throw caution to the wind and go outside instead of remaining available. I stalk to the creek and let the cover of trees hide me from the windows of the estate.

Crouching beside the bubbling water, I stick my fingers into its frigid shallows. Then I flop onto the bank and stare up at the golden cast boughs.

Hiding here could cost me my position, but I decide to rely on the prince's parting words. If he dismisses me, who else can he torment? I pick up a twig, snap it in half, and hurl it into the water. What I would give to go back to working for Mrs. Banks!

"You're not going to let him beat you," I growl up at the treetops. I savor the flare of rebellion that keeps me planted where I am instead of returning inside. "You're *not* going to let him beat you. You're going to be the perfect servant. You're not going to react. You're not going to run your mouth. You're not going to vent your anger in front of him. The more controlled you are, the less interest he will have in tormenting you. You're going to keep this position until you can safely leave and claim your fortune."

The day after tomorrow will bring relief. The prince has his ball, and I have a raid. It'll take me out of this situation and remind me of all the reasons I put up with him.

I stay where I am, watching the sun go down.

Then, the sound I dread comes ringing across the distance. "Nat! Nat! Come at once! The master summons you!"

I groan, resist an extra minute, and then roll up to my knees. "Coming!"

CHAPTER 14

RAHK

I CANNOT FIND Nat," Edvear tells me, wringing his hands and eyeing the Fool's Circle laid out on the table before me. "I will keep looking."

I grunt. "Look outside. He didn't leave. He is here."

She might have been lying about why she needs this position, but she wouldn't have put up with me today if she hadn't truly needed it. She would have quit and left.

I would have quit and left. There is no chance I would have tolerated that nonsense. Yet she did. I thought for certain that if nothing else did, the back rub would push her too far—or give her an opportunity to harm me if that is what she had come to do. I was proven wrong.

"We found him!" Edvear shouts from down the hallway.

I set the pieces of the game in order until I hear Nat's familiar soft gait coming slower than usual toward my room. She appears on the threshold, her hair in disarray, a leaf stuck to the top of her head, wearing an uncharacteristically blank expression.

She's angry with me.

"Come." I beckon for her to take her spot opposite me. "You get the first move."

She obeys without a word. She makes her move and then waits for me to make mine. Not once has she met my gaze since she entered the room.

I move my pieces and watch her face carefully. We go six turns, and she claims the first spot surrounding the Fool. I nod approvingly. She doesn't acknowledge it. Five more turns, and I claim the second spot.

The eager energy and excitement of last night is gone. She is a silent storm cloud, threatening to release thunder and lightning, but refusing to be the one to break first. That restraint is more than I thought her capable of. Then again, she has grit, will, and determination in measures I did not expect from a human.

I'm the one who angered her, so I must be the one to solve the silence.

"You impressed me today," I say, moving my pieces.

She does not answer.

"You pleased me greatly."

Still, no reply.

I wipe a hand over my mouth to conceal my smile. She is a little fool to behave so much like a woman. A young boy would have accepted the praise quickly. "I am sorry for asking so much of you today. I do not anticipate having this many unusual needs again."

Her jaw works, and for a moment I think she might accept my apology, if not my praise.

But no, she won't accept that either.

"You want me to admit that I was testing you."

"Yes!" she cries suddenly, the storm finally breaking. "And I want to know why! Was it a cruel joke to see me struggling when I am exhausted and giving everything to please an impossible-to-please master?"

Her words make my hand, holding my piece, go still.

My mind flashes back to the cold hand of Lady Nothril wrapped around my young neck, smiling as she choked the life out of me, whispering in my ear: *"You will do as I say, or you will die, my dear heir."*

I move my piece forward and rest my palm on the tabletop. "I wanted to know if you were lying to me."

She freezes, her eyes going wide. Wide with *guilt*.

"I wanted to know if this position truly mattered to you, or if there was some other reason you asked your sister to get you this position."

"And what did you find?" she asks, making her move.

"That you needed this position enough to put up with a capricious master," I reply. "There. Are you glad you successfully passed the test?"

She clamps her mouth shut. She isn't going to forgive me so easily.

"You earned yourself a request." I drum my fingers on the tabletop, then move my piece to surround her spot near the Fool. "Ask what it is that you want, and I will endeavor to grant it."

"I do not want to be mocked or tested," she answers readily.

"Very well."

Her eyes dart up toward mine in surprise. They are a rather nondescript shade of brown, yet now I notice the way they shine golden in the sunset. She looks away just as quickly.

"Nat," I say, softening my voice. "Look at me."

Begrudgingly, she lifts her eyes to mine. Waning sunlight plays across her face, her wild hair. I lean across the table, too quickly for her to jerk away from, and pluck the leaf out of her hair. I drop it in front of her.

"I'm sorry."

Why am I doing this? I've only been in the human lands for a few days and I'm already apologizing to a servant who is actively lying to me about her identity, her history, and her motives. It must be the stink of this air combined with my constant dosing of *ollea* that influences me.

Yet I cannot find it in me to regret the apology. I mean it. I mean it more now after seeing just how much more frustrated and hurt she was by today than I realized.

She purses her lips, hesitates, then nods once.

Apology accepted.

Just for that, I let her claim another spot near the Fool. I'll win the game, of course, but she can have this little victory.

Neither of us speaks for the rest of the game. Unlike the beginning of the game, however, the silence is pleasant. I didn't lie yesterday—she is an interesting opponent, with unusual maneuvers, and it keeps my mind engaged in the game more often than when I play Pavi. Many of the maneuvers are careless and poorly thought out, but interesting all the same. I never would have thought she had learned the game only yesterday.

Night has fallen when we finish.

I slide the board into its container and we each dump our minions inside. The Fool goes last of all. "I regret that the queen's ball will keep us from playing every night this week."

She chews her lip, then admits, "Me too."

This time, neither of us are lying.

CHAPTER 15

KAT

THE NEXT MORNING, I am not as mad at the prince as I ought to be. True to his word, he leaves me alone. I work hard at my usual tasks, sore from yesterday, but I focus quietly instead of fuming. My body is already adjusting to my new routine of vigorous activity. There is something very satisfying and very *simple* about working hard all day, and then when I'm finished—I'm finished.

Prince Rahk leaves mid-morning and doesn't return until nearly evening. I'm not the only one who is relieved to have him gone. All the staff, even Mrs. Banks, are extra chipper, chatting more while they work. I find myself smiling when Becky waves from her stool. Edvear is in good spirits too, his characteristic furrowed brow smooth as he talks to Charity.

I'm not the only one frightened by the prospect of living with a fae prince, it seems.

The prince returns as I am setting out his supper. He strides into the room, a package tucked under one arm. He wears human garb for the first time—an embroidered vest over a collared shirt and a pair of dark brown trousers—and with his hair tied back, he . . . *still* doesn't look human.

I skitter to one side and bow.

The prince looks at me before noting his meal. He takes the package from under his arm and holds it out to me. I hesitate for a second before walking forward and taking it from him.

"Where do you want me to put it?" I ask.

"It's for you."

"For me?" I blurt, turning the package over in my arms. It's some large tome, wrapped in brown paper. "What do you mean?"

"Open it."

Curiosity overtakes me. I tear open the wrapping to reveal an embossed title. *The Complete Guide to Fool's Circle.* My lips part. I stare at the book in my hands, comprehending and yet more confused than ever. "I—what is . . . This is for me?"

His mouth is lifted in a smirk again, but this smirk is different than his others. There is no lurking danger behind it. "Yes, Nat, it is for you. I think you will like it. It's written by a human who lived in Faerieland most of his life as a slave. His story at the beginning is quite fascinating."

I run my fingertips over the title and stitching along the thick spine. Are my cheeks turning warm? "Oh," I say stupidly. Then I look up. "Do you want me to beat you, Master?"

He laughs. The sound is quiet, but deep and rich. It's far more pleasant than I ever anticipated a fae's laugh sounding. "I like to encourage potential when I see it. Now, sit down with me while I eat and play so I might trounce you once more before you become too good for me."

A smile spreads across my face despite my best efforts. The last thing I wanted to do last night was play Fool's Circle. Now, it is all I want to do. I sit down quickly and set aside my present.

We play until it grows dark. I take his dishes to the kitchen and then return to my own room for sleep. He seems to only rarely come to bed, and when he does, it is much later than when I do. Finally alone, sequestered safely inside my room, I hold the book to my chest and inhale the scent of ink deep into my lungs.

Then I dive into its pages, devouring the contents. The prince was right—the story at the beginning is *fascinating*. I'm immediately drawn in. This man, Abraham Felton, stumbled into the Long Lost Wood by accident and wound up a slave for "invading" the fae lands, like most of the people I rescue during my raids. He served a cruel master who decided to trick him by bargaining that, instead of fulfilling his sentence, he could remain a slave just until the day he beat the master in Fool's Circle.

The master was the best in all the Courts at the game, and opponents would come far and wide to play him. Abraham served his refreshments during the games, and while he stood silently and awaited his master's bidding, he observed. He quickly figured out the rules and began assembling different players' strategies. Soon, he could see the flaws in his master's opponents' games. He constructed his own board with a large leaf and smears of mud. Once every week, he would play his master, and every time, he lost. But soon he shifted from losing on accident to losing on purpose. He carefully wove different strategies into his attempts, testing how his master would counter each one. He finally acquired ink and paper and catalogued his findings until, at last, it was time to play the master in earnest.

He knew he had to be careful, however. If he wasn't, he could easily end up being killed the second he won the game. So he faked illness to be dismissed from service until he had recovered. Then, he disguised himself in tattered rags and smeared mud over every inch of himself. He fashioned a cane, made his voice crackly and thin, and made his appearance in front of all the Court of Valehaven, when his master was entertaining his challengers. Everyone thought this stranger, who gave no name, was curious. The master let him play.

Abraham played better than the master. So much better, that he made the master believe he was winning, until the very last second. When he claimed the Fool.

Silence fell in the court.

Abraham got up immediately and fled. Everyone was so shocked, and the Court was in such an uproar trying to find out who this mysterious stranger was, they lost themselves to confusion and no one could stop him. He'd smeared himself with fae mud, so they'd lost his scent and when he disappeared into the forest, no one could find him again.

He vanished, until the day his book was published in the human lands—

"Your candle is about to burn out. And you need sleep."

The voice startles me so hard I drop the book, knocking my candle, and snuffing it out. "Master!"

The prince's white hair stands out in the dimness, as does the flash of his pearlescent teeth when he smiles—a sight I am still adjusting to. "Do you have any clue how late it is?"

I blink.

"It's past midnight."

"Saints!" I cry, shoving the book away from me as the prince chuckles. "I'm so sorry! I hope I didn't keep you awake with the candle!"

"Get some sleep."

Then he shuts the door. I mentally kick myself. But when I lay down, my mind is so full I can barely let my exhausted body fall asleep.

The queen's ball falls on the night of my next raid. I couldn't have picked better timing. Prince Rahk will be gone all night and won't notice my conspicuous absence. I don't know how I will handle future raids when he is home, but I will deal with that problem later. For now, I count my blessings.

I am a bundle of nerves helping him get ready. He wears human fashion—a blousy linen shirt with ruffled sleeves, blue velvet doublet embroidered in silver thread, straight legged trousers, and leather shoes—and I watch Edvear struggle to fasten a bejeweled cravat to his throat.

Don't intervene, I instruct myself severely. I cannot reveal how familiar I am with upper class fashion.

Edvear steps back. It's a little lopsided. Prince Rahk looks at me. "Is it correct?"

I tilt my head, getting a better look at it. I shrug. "I think so?"

"It's not right," the prince interprets. He marches to the mirror and fiddles with it himself. Then he turns around. "Is it right now, Nat?"

It is, indeed. "That looks better, Master."

"Excellent." He turns as Edvear holds out a decorative knife for his belt. He shakes his head. "The queen doesn't want me wearing weapons."

"It's decorative," says Edvear. "It barely counts as a weapon. All the human men wear them at balls—as I'm told."

"I'm not wearing a weapon, no matter how impractical and silly the weapon may be." He then turns to me, spreading his arms wide. "Well, Nat, lend me your human eyes. Do I look presentable? Am I sufficiently humanlike?"

I look him over. In his new garb, tailored perfectly to his form, he looks human from the neck down. A very large human, yes, but still human. He followed my suggestion to wear his hair in a queue and cover his long ears. The color of his hair is very noticeable, but that cannot be helped.

The main problem, however, is his face.

It's like I realize for the first time just how overwhelmingly beautiful he is. Fae are always beautiful beyond imagination, and over the years I've learned to see past their glamours to their wicked core. I don't even notice their beauty anymore—only their power. Looking at the prince now, though, I do see it. It is a rugged sort of beauty, hard-edged and flintlike. One can scarcely look into his endless black eyes and think he was anything short of *other*.

I find my voice with difficulty. "I think we've done the best we can to make you look human."

Edvear shoots me a sharp glare, wordlessly chastising me to always praise. But the prince seems to appreciate my honesty and nods consideringly.

"You both have done well tonight. Are you ready, Edvear?" he asks, turning toward his steward.

Edvear wears his own finery, though it is significantly plainer than the prince's. A smart feathered cap hides his horns. "Yes, my lord."

The prince's gaze returns to me. His mouth tilts upward. "Don't stay up too late reading."

"You don't want me to wait up for you?" I ask. Mary always waited up for me.

He shakes his head. "Edvear and I will manage. Take your rest."

With that, the two of them head out to the waiting carriage. I run to the window, pushing aside the curtain to peer into the dusk as they climb inside the cabby and the footman clicks the horses into motion.

An enormous sigh whooshes out of me.

It's time for my raid.

I close the doors to the prince's bedroom and my own. Once it is fully dark, I push open my window and climb out.

I sneak to the outhouse and dig up the small box Mary left for me—my Ivy Mask costume and *ollea*. I dress quickly, keeping watch for signs of movement, and replace my uniform in the box. The *ollea*, I smear on the bottoms of my shoes and rub across my hands. I don't know how long it lasts or how much I need, but judging by the size of the bottle, a little goes a very long way.

Then I'm off. I rotate between jogging and walking the several miles across farmland to the Wood's edge, mourning the loss of Bartholomew once more, hoping she's doing well, panicking slightly but remind myself that I've just got to get through this month, claim my inheritance, and then I can buy her back.

If she's still alive. If I can even find her.

Stop thinking about the horse.

I make it to the edge of the Wood before midnight, panting and dripping in sweat. How dare this night be as hot as it is? I'm only hoping my *ollea* hasn't lost its effectiveness yet.

I stop before the Path I usually take, an image of the destination shining across my vision in fragments. It's so strange to be on foot again after all these years. It takes me back to that moment I stood here, on the edge of the Wood, as it came rushing toward me and Mama. I can still feel that cold sweep of wind that threatened to devour me, the gangly tree limbs that shot toward my throat.

I grit my teeth.

The cart is where I left it. I don't bother with it this time. Everyone will just have to try not to step off the Path.

I pull my mask over my face, yank my hood low, and plunge into the Wood.

CHAPTER 16

RAHK

IF I HAD thought the scent of the human lands was overwhelming, this ball is vastly worse.

I haven't even stepped inside the palace before the perfume, the soaps, the hair oils, the boot polish, and the melting candlewax is too much. I pull my vial of *ollea* out of my pocket and swipe one drop under my nose. My pulsing headache eases at once. I hold it out to Edvear.

He shakes his head, politely declining, but when his eyes linger on the vial, I pass it to him. Relief melts across his face as he applies it.

"It was too much even for you," I say with a smirk.

"Humans and their fragrances," he mutters.

When we reach the grand archway, several guards emerge from the nearby guardhouse and approach me. I step out of the line of humans in their finery heading inside and meet the guards. Edvear trails behind me.

"You are the fae?" one of them with forked facial hair asks. They all wear armor that immediately snags my interest. The recently shined plates of metal fit closely together, leaving hardly an inch of exposed skin anywhere—and yet if I had a blade longer than three inches, I could slip that blade right beneath the shoulder plates. Every step they take announces their movement and location.

I'd sooner go into battle in the ensemble I'm wearing now than one of those suits. How do they move fast enough to counter or avoid blows?

I drag my attention back to the guard. He is the oldest of the group, but I would guess he is barely thirty years old. "I am indeed. I come as the queen requested. My steward here will not enter with me."

The guard jerks his chin. "Dismiss him at once."

I nod at Edvear. He withdraws.

"I come without weapons. Do you wish to search me to verify?" I ask.

"I am afraid we must. Please, this way."

I follow them into the guardhouse, aware of the way they surround me and how two of them touch the hilts of their swords. I watch for threats, but there is no sign of a potential ambush—only fear.

I stand there, just inside the guardhouse, as three guards check me for weapons. They clearly intend to be thorough, and after several minutes, I grow impatient, but I let them do their work. This is about making the queen comfortable in my presence. I will tolerate what is necessary.

At last, they pronounce me clean. Then the fork-bearded one motions that I can follow him back to the entrance of the palace. Several other guards accompany me. I keep my movements casual and light—a contrast to their loud, hulking steps.

The hall they escort me into is grander than I expect. A vast ceiling soars above us, painted with a mural of . . . winged babies in clouds? Interesting. A red carpet unfurls across shining white tile. Guests walk ahead of us. Several of them peer back at me as though I am some strange spectacle.

Nat *did* make it clear that despite everything, I still look distinctly fae. Even without my wings.

The ballroom itself is smaller than I expect, but I watch as some partygoers drift through doorways into adjoining rooms. Even through my *ollea,* I can smell the thick stench of *human* as I step into the throng of colorful gowns. The men do wear decorative knives at their hip, and the concept amuses me more than anything else I've encountered tonight.

Everyone gives me a wide berth. One young woman whose back is turned when I approach openly flinches when she sees me, her mouth falling open as she drags her gaze up to mine. She immediately steps out of my way, her skin pale. Most stare openly and do not bother hiding their whispered comments to one another. A few try to be more dignified about it.

I exhale slowly and try to arrange my features in as least threatening of a mask as I can.

If Nat were here, she would likely say I have failed.

Why do humans fear so deeply anything that does not closely resemble them?

The queen sits on a throne at the far end of the ballroom. She seems tall for a woman, her back erect and her dark hair piled in a towering updo and dripping with jewels. On a smaller chair beside her is a young boy, about seven or eight, with soft curls a shade lighter than his mother's.

Queen Vivienne and her heir, Prince Lionel.

Her gaze meets mine across the ballroom, and her chin lifts. An invitation.

"Will you escort me to the queen?" I ask my guards.

"We will take you close enough to speak with her, but no further."

I end up parked twenty feet from the queen's dais, still surrounded by the guards. I shift my weight to one leg. "Queen Vivienne. Prince Lionel."

"You haven't aged a day since I last saw you," says the queen, speaking loudly to cross the distance over the hum of the orchestra. "You look exactly as you did when you escorted my sister away."

I nod once. Stella and her sisters all wore veils when Ash and I came to find a bride for him, so I cannot return the compliment. Still, I say, "You look well."

The queen is a handsome woman who makes the subtle lines of aging look regal. I search her face for resemblance to Stella, and find less than I expect. Her eyes, however, give her away. While darker than Stella's, they are the same rounded, overlarge shape.

She inclines her head in acknowledgement of my compliment. "What brings you to my kingdom, Prince Rahk?"

"It is as I wrote to you. Faerieland's border has begun receding, returning the land stolen by our last High King. I am here as emissary of the new High King and Queen to serve you during a challenging transition."

Prince Lionel watches me keenly from his place beside the queen. He has large ears that stick out from his head. Unlike everyone else in the room, he doesn't look at me with fear—only interest.

"It is kind of my sister to send an emissary," says Queen Vivienne, "but we do not need your aid."

"Of course, but there is the issue of a troll who might—"

She smiles coldly, cutting me off. "Whatever happens, I'm sure we can handle it."

I release a slow breath. She will not enjoy *handling* Ymer the Indefatigable. "Excellent. I shall stay out of your way, unless you change your mind."

"I do not see a reason for you to stay in Harbright, Prince Rahk. Not unless you intend to steal a bride as my sister was stolen."

Steal a bride?

I fight my snort. The very last thing I need on my hands is a wife—much less a human one. "I understand, Your Highness. I am afraid I am under orders from your sister and her husband to remain in Harbright, so remain I shall."

"In that case, I shall tolerate your presence." The queen rolls her eyes, sighing. The gesture instantly reminds me of Stella. "But if you cause any trouble, I will send my warriors to your estate and drive you away. Do we understand one another, Prince Rahk?"

Her warriors would not enjoy trying to do that.

I bow. "We understand each other."

I step away from the throne just as a middle-aged woman with a narrow jaw and chin takes my place.

"Lady Duxbury Vandermore," says the queen with the same ire she used with me. "Where is the young heiress? She said she would be here. If I cannot watch her fend off all the young men in pursuit of her fortune, then I shall have no entertainment for the evening."

The new woman curtsies. "Yes, Queen Vivienne, I've come straight away to give Lady Vandermore's regrets. She is very ill and cannot leave her bed."

"That is a shame indeed. Tell her that her queen requires her to heal quickly."

I move to the wall. I locate a chair without arms and take a seat. My guards prop themselves up on either side of me. If Ash saw me at this moment, he would laugh until he cried. I would give almost anything to be back at my estate, playing Fool's Circle with Nat.

"Hello. Are you the fae warrior?"

I turn toward the voice. A young man approaches to my right, a little cautiously, but the light in his eye reminds me more of the queen's son. Curious and eager.

"I am," I say, rising to greet him. "Lord Rahk. You are?"

"Lord Rahk, it is a pleasure to meet you. I am Lord Oliver, the son of Baron Cranswick. My father helped your steward choose your estate."

"Yes, my steward spoke highly of your father. It is a pleasure to meet you, Lord Oliver."

He glances at the guards, then back at me. I offer no explanation. He wears a small decorative knife at his hip like the rest of the gentlemen.

"What brings you to Harbright, then?" asks Lord Oliver, ignoring my guards and standing next to me along the wall. For a human, he does not seem half bad. "Everyone assumed you were coming to steal away Lady Vandermore."

That is the second time in the last few minutes I've heard that name. "Lady Vandermore?"

"That answers that question." Lord Oliver laughs, then takes a sip of the wine he swirls in one hand. "You have not heard of Lady Vandermore? She is a lovely young heiress. We all want to marry her."

"Why?"

"Well, not many would admit it is for her money, though I fear that is the honest truth. I like to consider myself one of the few who genuinely enjoys her company. If you are not here for our Lady Vandermore, then why?"

My attention flicks to the queen. She threads her fingers into her young son's hair, stroking gently. My view shifts suddenly, and it is Lady Nothril sitting in that throne, smiling coldly as she strokes Pavi's hair.

I clear my throat. "The border of the Long Lost Wood, as I believe you call it, has begun receding. I am here as an emissary to facilitate a peaceful transition."

"The queen doesn't trust you, though?" Lord Oliver says, gesturing with his wine goblet at my guards.

"We did not meet on the best terms previously."

His eyebrows rise. "Were you there when her sister was taken into Faerieland?"

"I was."

He nods vigorously, chuckling under his breath. "She probably thinks you will steal her heir and carry him off into the Long Lost Wood."

"I will do no such thing."

His chuckles die away slowly. He takes another sip of his wine. "So, Lord Rahk, how do you plan to win Queen Vivienne's favor?"

I've been considering that issue for the last several days. I have a few ideas, but none fully satisfy me. Even if one did, I wouldn't tell Lord Oliver. He has proved himself friendly and outgoing, but his first loyalty is to his queen and his kingdom. "Have you advice on the subject?"

"Well," Lord Oliver drops his voice to a whisper so even the guards cannot hear, "it is rumored that the queen is secretly a romantic. She always finds great interest in every blossoming romance between us young people. She is even known to use her influence to subtly matchmake. She will create opportunities for any unattached bachelor or lady to meet and socialize with potential suitors. *And* she has even been known to bring old flames back into the picture—just to stir up drama and see what happens. She loves watching stories unfold."

I do not approve. "And?"

"And I think you should create a story to catch her interest. Court a young lady. Make her fall in love with you. Show that you are trustworthy. You'll catch the queen's attention then."

What a horrible idea. "I am not in a position to marry."

"Who says you need to marry?" the young man grins. "Just court the girl. You might even find one who could benefit from the arrangement and then you wouldn't have to fear breaking her heart."

"I shall consider your advice," I say. Then I turn my attention to the way he lounges against the wall, one foot propped up on elegant white molding. "Why are you helping me?"

"I want the land returned from the Long Lost Wood," he answers without hesitating. "Most of my inheritance is currently swallowed up in Faerieland. I will be a pauper if I cannot get it back."

Now *that* interests me. "How much of the stolen land is yours?"

He shrugs. "Not much compared to Lady Vandermore's portion. Her family owns the majority of it."

"Do they?" This also intrigues me greatly. I turn the information over in my mind. This is *very* valuable information. I release a slow exhalation. I think I know exactly how to repair this situation with the queen. "Thank you, Lord Oliver, for your aid. It is generous of you."

"Hardly!" Lord Oliver laughs. "If you can get me my inheritance back, I will be much more successful in my efforts of procuring a wife."

"You are that desperate for one?"

"Desperate? I hardly think desiring a companion in the form of a friend and lover makes me desperate. I rather think it curious if you do not desire the same."

If only relationships were as simple in Faerieland as they are here. I know better than to even look at a fae woman, lest Lord and Lady Nothril decide to use her against me as they use Pavi.

I open my mouth to reply when something twinges in my chest. *My spells*. A second later, the invisible spell thread inside me snaps in half.

The Ivy Mask has entered the Wood.

"Lord Oliver, I must leave, but it has been a pleasure," I say abruptly, straightening. "I hope our paths cross again."

He gives a friendly wave. "Come to the sparring yard if you'd like to cross swords with me and some of the other men. None of us have sparred with a fae before."

I restrain my quiet snort. "I will see what I can do."

With that, I take my leave. The guards follow on my heel, trying to keep up with my quick strides. Edvear waits for me outside, cleaning his fingernails. His head pops up the moment he hears my stride.

"Already, my lord?" he asks, pushing up to his feet as my guards disband to their guardhouse.

Edvear follows me as I take the steps down to the courtyard two at a time toward our carriage. "Ivy Mask."

His yellow eyes, bright in the moonlight, widen. "You will catch him tonight?"

I will.

CHAPTER 17
KAT

THE ROAR OF the waterfall is so tremendous I don't hear Tailor until he grabs my elbow. "Kat!"

"We need to get over the bridge!" I mouth back at him.

His spectacles are sprayed with water, droplets running down the strained lines of his face. He does not protest further, however, and follows me as I swing onto the rope bridge. It sways wildly. I crouch where I am, holding the rope, balancing on the wood planks that keep me suspended in the towering green trees. Once it is steady enough, I start walking. Tailor is so clumsy on the bridge that my lungs nearly end up lodged in my throat.

We do not fall, thankfully.

We slip into the abandoned guardhouse, high in the trees, that we use for Revar Court raids. Tonight though, it isn't abandoned.

Four forms huddle in the darkness.

A man and his three sons.

I sigh in relief. They all got out. We don't have to hunt through the Court for them.

"This way," I whisper. "We've got to move fast."

Tailor grabs my elbow again. "Where is the cart?"

"Not here. Long story. I—" My words die as two of the sons, who look to be about sixteen and twelve, carefully lift their father to his feet. Or, rather, his *foot*. He is missing half of his left leg and balances between a crutch and a boy. Did a fae do that to him? Was it recent—could I have prevented it if I'd come sooner?

Of all the raids where I didn't have my cart!

"He won't be able to walk the entire stretch of Path," Tailor hisses.

His unspoken concern lingers in the silence: *We might have to leave him behind.*

I grind my teeth together. We are *not* leaving this man behind. We are *not* separating him from his sons. All of them have waited long enough for their freedom. I won't be responsible for their separation. I look at Tailor fiercely. "We will make it."

He meets my gaze, and there is resignation there. He always tries to make me more cautious. It will never work.

He would strangle me if he knew my current . . . *situation* with Prince Rahk.

"We've got to get him across the bridge," I say to the eldest of the boys. The youngest looks to be only four or five, and hides behind his brother. "And down a lot of stairs."

The oldest boy links his father's arm around his neck. "It will be slow, but we can do it."

"See?" I say to Tailor.

Then we're off.

It takes us nearly an hour to get across the bridge and climb down a series of stairs and ladders to get to flat ground again—without getting caught. We are soaking from the waterfall, but I will gladly accept it for the camouflage of its roar.

I make everyone stop and slather mud from the riverbank over their feet before I lead us onto the Path. Just in case someone tracks us. And just in case my *ollea* has worn off.

"I'll see you at the next raid." I give a casual wave as I take the little boy's hand.

Tailor waves back and then slips away.

Every time we say goodbye, I always fear it is our last.

"Follow me," I say, tugging the little boy after me into the Wood. He starts crying, snot dribbling from his nose.

"Be brave, sonny," says the father. He tries to hide his wince as he leans between his older sons. "We're almost free."

I crouch down before the boy and pull aside my mask to give him a smile. "Want to ride on my back?"

His little wet face turns to interest almost immediately.

"Climb on!" I say—and then freeze in cold-blooded horror.

There, in the mud, is a fresh pair of giant footprints. Coming from this Path.

Someone *followed* me. From the human world.

Grubby little hands wrap around my shoulders. I hike the boy onto my back and pull my mask into place. I keep my observation to myself, but my voice is overly bright when I say, "It's time to move fast now! Stay right behind me so you don't accidentally step off the Path!"

My heart thunders in my chest as I set a vigorous pace. The boy on my back grows heavier, and his brothers and father are all panting hard soon, but I don't dare slow.

I'm getting them out of here.

Even if it kills me, I'm getting them out of here.

"You're going to be the reason they die," the wind whispers.

I tighten my fists on the boy's ankles and grit my teeth.

No one is dying tonight. Not on my watch.

With every step, I miss Bartholomew. I curse Agatha and Lord Boreham. I curse my mother for being swallowed by this wretched forest, and my father for giving up on her. I curse them both for dying and leaving me behind.

At one point, I glance back to find one of the boy's feet dangerously near the edge of the Path. "I said to stay right behind me!" I snap, too harshly. He leaps back as though I've bitten him. I gentle my tone. "I'm sorry—it is just that you cannot see the Path, and if you step off of it, there is nothing I can do to help you. So please, try to walk exactly where I walk."

I always make sure to stay exactly in the middle of the Path.

After a few more silent moments, where the only sounds are the strange whispers of the Wood, I crane my neck to call behind me, "We're coming upon a troll. Just ignore him. He cannot hurt you."

The words are hardly out of my mouth before a gravelly voice booms, "Who goes there?"

"Ymer the Indefatigable! You are looking . . . indefatigable today," I call toward the troll. This Path doesn't take us as close to him as the last, but he still regards me with slitted yellow eyes.

"Small elf," he growls. "Ymer will flay your skin into fine layers and roast them on open flames!"

"You are adorable," I reply with a grin. "Maybe I can bring you some bones one of these days. To make your bread with."

"Elf lies, as elves always have since the ancient days," Ymer growls, smacking his club against his leathery hand.

"It's alright," I whisper to the little boy who buries his face in my shoulder. I increase our pace and leave Ymer's grumbling behind us.

Then, suddenly, we're free of the Wood.

We spill out into the stretch of farmland. Sweat pours from the older brothers and their father, their matching tawny hair wet. I set the child down. He runs at once to his father, who smiles down at him and praises him warmly for being so brave.

I press a hand to the stitch in my side, breathing hard, counting the seconds—knowing we cannot stop, but as desperate as them for just one moment.

"You've got to keep going," I finally gasp, bent and gripping my knees. "I'm so sorry, but you must keep going. That direction is the city. Don't stop until you get there." I give them directions to find Mary, who will be waiting for them outside the city's cathedral with their sacks of provision, since I can no longer make them. I gave her all my allowance before I left for this very purpose.

"Saints bless you," says the man.

They always thank me. I wish they wouldn't. Their thanks always settles uncomfortably in the pit of my stomach. I stay where I am, watching the four of them continue despite their exhaustion. Every time we part ways, I am acutely aware of all that I long to give them. And all that I cannot.

It never feels like enough.

But there is yet one more thing I can do for this family.

With a grim set of my mouth, I force my wooden legs into motion. I find my cart, hidden in the bushes, and pull a crossbow and a length of rope out from a hidden compartment. I don't know how much time I have, and I refuse to give voice to the fear humming in the back of my throat. I duck back into the Wood to set my trap.

I pick the first oak I come to on the Path—they are friendly to humans—and scurry up its boughs. My hands scrape against rough bark, my fingernails straining as I dig them into bark and hoist myself up. I unfasten the crossbow from my belt and set it carefully on one of the branches, aimed where I will direct my quarry.

I take my *ollea* smeared boots and stomp them deep into the ground right next to where I want this pursuer to walk. The length of rope I coat in dirt and half-bury across the path. I leave several different lengths to guarantee my pursuer won't miss it. Then I fasten them carefully to my crossbow with a few special knots I picked up for this exact sort of thing. I'm desperately careful not to trigger it as I climb down.

If anyone steps on these ropes, the trap I've rigged is sensitive enough that it'll shoot them.

Then I'm forcing my quaking limbs back into a run.

It is a long stretch of misery before I finally make it back to the prince's estate. I wash myself off in the creek quickly, the cold turning my pulsing limbs numb. Then I change clothes, shake out my hair, and climb back into my window.

I yank the blanket over my head and rub it into my hair, hoping to disguise any Faerieland scents before—

Voices from the hallway.

I stiffen.

"Nat!" comes Edvear's voice.

Dread pools in my gut.

"I've got it," growls Rahk in return. "Don't wake him."

"This is his *job*. This is what we hired him for."

My door is flung open and candlelight flickers into my dark space. I wince, pretending to wake up. "Sir?"

A short silhouette with curly hair and goat horns fills the space. "The master requires your service."

I get up, rubbing my eyes. "I thought the master was at a ball. Has he come home earl—"

The words halt on my tongue. There, sitting on the foot of his bed, is Prince Rahk. He still wears his ball finery, but his hair is in disarray, his boots coated in mud. There is a streak of dirt across his forehead, and a long cloak is clasped at his throat. Not the cloak he wore to the ball.

A stripe of crimson soaks through a torn sleeve.

Every drop of blood drains from my face.

Rahk looks up from his wound and sees me. He immediately glares at his steward. "Edvear, leave him alone. He looks as though he's never seen blood before. Go back to bed, Nat."

But Edvear presses a bowl with rags into my hands.

"Edvear—" growls Rahk.

"He needs to learn."

"I will learn," I say quickly, forcing the words out around the horror choking my throat. "What happened?"

"It's not your place to ask questions," snaps Edvear.

"Sorry." I set the bowl down on the vanity, going to the basin to pour water into the bowl. I wet a cloth and wring it out. When I approach the prince, he's still glaring at his steward.

"Take my boots and make sure they get cleaned," he orders Edvear.

"I can do that, master," I say quickly. "Once I'm done—"

"Edvear can do it."

Edvear bristles but picks up the filthy shoes that the prince kicks off. He's gone a second later, leaving me alone with Rahk.

My hands shake as I press the cloth to the wound.

"You can go back to bed," he says quietly. "I will handle this."

There is nothing I'd rather do! But I need to confirm what happened . . . even though I already know. Even though I knew the moment I saw those footprints in the Revar Court. "Please, master, I wish to learn."

He sighs. "Very well. The first step is to get better access to the wound."

A second later, he's stripped off his cloak, doublet, and linen tunic, until candlelight gleams off the chiseled edges of his bare torso. Blood runs down the toned muscles of his massive arm. I swallow and desperately hope he takes my discomfort as unease with the wound. I step closer and dab the wound with my cloth until it's stained red.

"Does it hurt much?" I ask.

"It is only a shallow wound."

"Will it need stitches?"

He shakes his head. "Even if it did, I wouldn't make you do it."

"I would do a rotten job of it, Master."

He chuckles, though his mind seems to drift elsewhere, his amusement fading into consternation. "It would be foolish of me to expect more from you."

Silence falls. I dab away the blood from the torn flesh. He's right—it's only a nick, really. Like an arrow came right for his heart, but he dodged it just in time, and it only grazed his biceps.

I am going to throw up.

"I will finish," the prince says, uncharacteristically gentle. He must have noticed my face changing colors.

But I still haven't gotten the information I need. I shake my head firmly and command my stomach to settle itself. I turn over different questions in my head, until I finally land on: "What sort of person stabs someone at a ball?"

His eyebrows shoot up, and I think he might be suppressing his amusement. He leans closer to me, his breath tickling my ear as he whispers conspiratorially: "Only the blackest of fiends."

"In Harbright?" I squeak, pulling back as fast as I can so his nose doesn't detect any traitorous scents lingering in my hair.

He's smirking again. Enjoying my naivete. But he doesn't offer an explanation.

It could just be a coincidence, I think desperately.

"I assumed humans at a ball would be no match for a fae prince," I say.

"Your curiosity won't be sated, will it?"

"No, master, but I can shut up if you like."

His smile is quick to vanish. "Did Edvear not bring the bandages? There are some in my study in one of the drawers."

"I will fetch them at once." I am all too glad to put some distance between us. My legs ache, but I refuse to let it show as I take a candle and hurry from the room.

The light from my candle trembles erratically as I open the study door and go to the desk. I curse my fumbling fingers as I struggle to get the first drawer open. No bandages. I open the second one.

I keep glancing up while I search, expecting the prince to suddenly be in the doorway, a catlike smile revealing long canines.

It might not be him, Kat. You have no proof.

I yank open the bottom drawer. Bandages roll toward the back of it from the motion. I grab my candle and bring it closer to locate my quarry at the back of the drawer.

A face stares back at me.

I swallow my scream and leap backward. The candle hits the ground. The room pitches into black.

I stand there, pressed against a bookshelf, my hand pressed to my heaving lungs.

That . . . that was my mask.

The one I left in the Nothril Court.

So it's true. His claim that he is here as an emissary—it's a lie. His true purpose is to hunt the Ivy Mask. *Me.*

I shot Prince Rahk of the Nothril Court.

He followed me. He's hunting me.

He's going to kill me.

"Oh saints," I whisper, staring at the splattered candlewax hardening on the floor. "I'm trapped."

I'm stuck in this position with no way out. Unless I marry Lord Boreham—which won't protect me from Prince Rahk anyway.

It is the thought of Bartholomew that brings my panicked heartbeat under control.

She is out there somewhere, and all I have to do is survive here until my birthday. Then I can get her back. I'm only three weeks away. I can do it. I've already outsmarted the prince thrice now. He clearly doesn't know I'm the Ivy Mask.

My mission tonight was successful.

"It'll be fine. It'll all be fine." I breathe the assurances under my breath as I collect the candle and fish out the bandages from the drawer, ignoring the mask.

All I have to do is keep going. This doesn't truly change anything. I already knew Prince Rahk would kill me if he knew who I was. So everything is . . . basically the same.

I gather my composure, pulling back my shoulders, and march to the bedroom.

The prince sits where I left him, his black eyes regarding me leisurely as I approach his side. "You took a long time."

"I burned out my candle by accident. It took me longer to find the bandages."

He lifts his arm, allowing me to wrap the bandages around the injury. I use an ungodly amount of it just to span the size of his arm once. He moves suddenly.

I leap back, dropping the bandage. The prince's gaze snaps to me. His other hand slows as he scratches his temple.

That was it—he was only scratching himself.

"Sorry—sorry!" I cry, mortified by my jumpiness.

Rahk leans down and picks up the fallen bandages. He returns them to my trembling hands. I quickly tie it off and step away. His attention seems to sharpen on me, his eyes scanning me to my toes and then back up. I hide my trembling hands behind my back.

"Not all of us are made for blood and guts," he says, glancing between me and the bowl of pink water and soiled rags. "There is no shame in being upset at the sight of an injury."

He thinks that is why I am unsettled?

"You've done well tonight, Nat," he adds quietly. "You can return to bed."

I give a half bow. "Thank you, my lord."

I don't wait a second longer, and barely keep myself from bolting straight to my room. Once I'm safely ensconced inside it, I listen to his footsteps as he strides out of the bedroom.

This changes nothing.

And changes *everything*.

CHAPTER 18

RAHK

SOMEHOW, I MISSED the Ivy Mask. I traced him into the Revar Court and back, only to discover a crude but clever trap left for me. I was too preoccupied by investigating the mud and scuff marks left in the bark of the oak to see the rope trigger until I'd already stepped on it.

I was certain I'd catch him tonight.

At least I have confirmation now that the Ivy Mask lives in the human world. In this very city. How he has managed to disguise his scent is beyond me.

But I will get to the bottom of it. I will find him.

While it is still dark, I return to the Wood. From the sky, its edge glitters brightly. The Wood is receding faster, already leaving several paces of restored land. I find the scent trail of Faerieland and follow it through the fields to a rise, and beyond toward the city. There are not many footprints, but the ones that I come across on the outskirts of town seem to indicate one of the slaves was only using one foot and supported by another. *Interesting.* Wounded? Maimed? Something else?

The trail goes to the coach like the last one, but it takes an unusual detour first—at the cathedral. There are so many scents here that I barely maintain my grip on the escaped slaves' scents. If they met with anyone here, it is impossible to discern who. Perhaps they came to honor their saints before they left the city.

I arrive on foot at the stop for the coach. A sheltered bench sits a few feet away from the road. A man wrapped in a patchwork coat sleeps there.

I draw on my glamours and shift away my long ears, soften my face, and take a few inches off my height. I haven't tried maintaining a glamour this demanding in a while, and never within the human world. It proves startlingly difficult, but I manage it.

I kneel next to the man and shake him awake.

"Eh? What's the matter?" he grunts between missing teeth. "I don't sell the coach tickets."

"Has anyone come here in the last few hours?" I ask.

"How would I know?" he grumbles, pulling his coat tighter around his throat.

"Answer my question." My glamours struggle against my hold, and I clench my fist to keep them in place.

"Ugh!" The man rolls over on the bench. "There were some boys and their papa it seemed. The papa looked like he got his leg bit off or somethin'. They must have left an hour or two ago. Now will you let me sleep?"

I step away, falling into the shadows between buildings as my glamour breaks. I exhale hard and press a hand to my chest. This human world is going to be the death of me.

But I am not done exercising my magic tonight.

The man returns to sleep, his back to the road. I use my foot to draw a rune in the dirt. It is the sister spell of the one I left at the edge of the Wood. I draw the last line of the rune, and it comes to life with a flare of blue that only I can see.

There.

I return to the darkened shadows of the city. They become my shroud as I take the way I came. When I am far enough away from the more populated parts of town, I release the glamour on my wings—sagging in the bliss of it—and fly the rest of the way to my estate.

The sun is still an hour or two from rising when I arrive. Smoke already billows from several of the chimneys, and the rooster lets out strangled crows.

I think of Nat and her pale face last night at the sight of my wound. The poor thing wouldn't last a day in Faerieland if she couldn't tolerate that small bit of blood. Even Pavi can stand much more than that, and Pavi is much younger—relatively speaking—than Nat.

I slip inside the open window to my study and let out a great sigh as I settle into my chair.

What a busy night! And it will be a busy day, for there is a certain heiress I've decided to pay a visit to.

My vision clouds slightly. I lean my head into my palm, finally admitting to myself that I am tired. Maybe I will let myself have an hour of rest or so . . .

KAT

I drag myself out of bed, blinking my blurry eyes and dressing in the dark. I never appreciated how early servants wake each morning! Had I realized, I never would have taken a single wink of sleep for—

A shadow passes across my window. The prince?

I go still.

It was so fast, like a cloak tossed over the setting crescent moon. I'm fully awake the instant I rush to the window and peer out of it.

I'm just in time to see five hooded figures pass out of view.

Not the prince.

Alertness rushes through my blood. I pull away from the window. Are they fae come to hunt down their stolen slaves? Did I leave a trail after all? My hand covers my mouth.

I rush from my room into the prince's. It is dark, swaths of curtains covering the windows, the thick blankets on the bed untouched save where the prince sat while I bound his injury. He is not here. My heart in my throat, I hurry to the window. My fingers shake slightly as I grab the curtain and pull it aside.

A pair of eyes stare back at me.

My blood screams.

I shove the curtain into place as if it will save me from the knife I saw glinting in that man's hand and throw myself in the opposite direction. I crash into the table where we play Fool's Circle, pain flaring in my leg.

Righting myself, I bolt out the door into the darkened hallways. My breath comes fast. That wasn't a fae—that was a man. They're all human men. Which means . . .

"Lord Rahk!" I yell, breathless, not thinking straight. "Lord Rahk!"

I careen down another hallway until I get to the door of his study.

It's locked.

"Lord Rahk!" I bellow, slamming the side of my fist into the door. It doesn't open. I curse and whirl around. The door to the parlor is open. Inside, faint moonlight gleams off the marble bust of Botsov. I say a prayer as I run to grab it. It's so heavy I nearly drop it. "Lord Rahk!" I scream again as I bash the heavy bust headfirst into the lock. The door buckles, but doesn't break. I give my next hit everything I have. The door flies open.

The prince lifts his head blearily from his desk, his eyes widening at the sight of me standing there, in the dimness, clutching a marble bust.

And behind him, in the window, are three silhouettes. One eases the pane open silently.

Assassins.

They've not come for me—they've come for the prince.

"Behind you!" I scream and hurl Botsov toward the window. Rahk dodges out of the way. It sails through the glass, shattering on impact. The assassins split to avoid getting hit.

Rahk curses, already on his feet as one assassin leaps through the broken window. He bounds over the desk and ducks behind it as he reaches beneath it to grab one of his long swords. The assassin corners him between the bookshelves I recently reordered as two more pour through the window. But Rahk is so fast I cannot even see what he does before the first assassin lies dead on the ground. The other two fly at him, their swords gleaming in the darkness. He counters and ducks beneath their strikes to dance away from the corner.

The fourth assassin creeps just outside the window. He lifts a crossbow, aiming at Rahk just as he cuts down the second assassin.

"Rahk! The window!" I cry, just as the assassin looses his arrow.

In a flash, Rahk seems to bend backward, almost folding in half. The arrow lodges in a book's spine. Rahk throws his palm upright and searing light fills the room. He growls in pain. Did one of them land a blow?

But no, the assassin with the crossbow has collapsed, the window blackened.

I need to get out of here or I will become collateral damage. I whirl. My nose rams into a hard, black-wreathed chest. I drag my gaze up to the black mask and hood, with only a slit for a pair of gleaming eyes.

The next second, he has me pinned, my back to his chest, holding me by the throat and pressing a knife to my temple.

"Rahk," I squeak as I grab the assassin's wrist, trying to pry his grip free.

"Drop your weapons," growls the assassin holding me. "Or this one dies."

Rahk's black eyes fall on me just as he yanks his sword out of the chest of the third assassin, leaving only one other standing—besides the one that holds me.

"You think he cares if I live or die?" I snap. "How about we go find better hostage material?"

His fingers tighten around my throat. I choke. His knife stings against my temple. Warmth dribbles down the side of my face.

Rahk's sword clatters to the ground.

My eyes bug. "What are you doing? Don't you know that they always kill the hostage anyway?"

"Why are you here?" Rahk demands, keeping his eye on both assassins, tensing as the other one circles behind him. "Did the queen send you?"

The second assassin lunges. Rahk sidesteps the knife coming for his back and holds up both hands.

"You know you cannot kill me," Rahk says as he dances around the assassin. "I don't need weapons to kill you both. So let the boy go, and I'll spare your lives."

The one holding me squeezes my throat so hard black spots erupt across my vision. I try to say, *"Rahk,"* but it only comes out in a wheeze.

The prince's tone changes. Darkens. "Let the boy go. Now. You hurt him, you die."

Hooves come clopping down the hallway. "My lord! What is happening? You, sir! It is too early for calling! Please come again at a—"

The assassin yanks me aside and pivots toward the approaching Edvear, still keeping Rahk in view. The hooves on flooring go silent and I manage a weak smile at Edvear's open-mouthed shock, illuminated by the single candle he holds. My vision swims.

"Much too early for calling," I croak.

Edvear's face turns a furious shade of purple. His voice drops. "That is one of my staff. You let him go at once."

Just then, a body goes flying past me and slams into plaster. Rahk is right in front of me, his hands closing around my assassin's wrists. I end up smashed between them as they both let out strained grunts. Rahk yanks the hand with the knife away, twisting his thumb at a hard angle until the assassin releases a cry and the blade clatters to the ground. Then he pries the other hand off my throat and anchors his weight, whirling the assassin off me and face first into a bookshelf.

Edvear catches me with an arm beneath my shoulder blades. With his other hand, he pulls a kitchen knife out of his belt and stabs it into the back of the assassin stuck in the plaster. It shocks me so much I stumble.

"Just making sure he's dead," Edvear says, yanking his knife free and wiping it clean. "He is. Come, let's get a bandage for that cut."

A strangled cry cuts off abruptly from the study as Edvear leads me away. My legs sway and buckle with every other step. How come I am fearless in the Fae Courts, but so unsteadied by a few humans? My throat is scratchy, and I suck in deep breaths to make up for the ones I lost.

"Nat."

Edvear pauses. I turn around to find Rahk standing in the doorway of his study, his tall frame flanked by corpses and busted walls. His expression, lit by the faint sunlight coming through his broken window, is strange. I cannot decipher it.

"How did you know about the mercenaries?" he asks.

My gaze travels to the body Edvear stabbed. Five men lie dead now who were alive only minutes ago. I swallow. It hurts. "I saw them out my window. They went to your bedroom first. I realized they had come for you. Did the queen send them?"

"Yes," he replies, planting his hands on his hips and shifting his weight. He studies the one dead assassin sticking out of the plastered wall. Blood smears down his back from Edvear's strike. He lifts his gaze back to me. Something flashes deep in his dark pupils. "Thank you. For warning me."

It only now occurs to me that if I'd let him die, my Ivy Mask problem would have been solved. *Great thinking, Kat.*

Still, in my heart of hearts, I know I could not have stood by and let it happen. "But . . . but I almost didn't even get there in time."

He smiles slightly, ruefully. "I am glad that you did." He scratches the back of his neck. "That marble bust—who was that of?"

"A composer named Botsov, my lord."

He nods, and his smile turns a little more genuine. "That was quick thinking."

He has offered praise before, but there is something about the way he says this that strikes me differently. *Deeper*. It's as if it is spoken by the real Rahk, the one beneath the hardened expressions. The one I have only caught tiny glimpses of.

"The lad is bleeding, my lord," Edvear says, firming his grip on my shoulder.

Something drips off my chin. I reach up, touch the side of my face—the side that is turned away from Rahk—and am surprised to see how much blood is on my hand. "Oh." I look back at the prince. He has taken a step toward me, but stops.

"Please, help him with whatever he needs," Rahk says to Edvear. He shifts his weight again, glancing at the damage around him, almost looking . . . *lost*. "I will deal with this. And Nat—I don't know if you meant what you said, but I was never going to let them kill you. You know that, right?"

My lips part slightly. I let myself be dragged away to avoid giving a reply.

Edvear takes me to the kitchen. Charity has her back to us, stoking the fire. She is the only one in the room; Becky still sleeps. My temple aches, my throat scratchy and sore. I sit down on one of the bar stools. My head turns heavy.

"Please do not be alarmed, Mrs. Finch," says Edvear. "Nat has had a little accident and needs some hot tea with honey while I bandage him."

Charity latches the oven and turns toward us. She inhales sharply, just as Edvear says again, "Everything is fine, Mrs. Finch. It is a little scratch."

"Well, the blood from that *little scratch* is falling on my counter! Nat, what happened? Here, sweetheart." She hands me a clean towel to hold to my temple.

I don't want to talk. My throat seems to close. I point to Edvear as he fishes through a cabinet for bandages.

"Edvear? What happened?" Charity briskly places a kettle on the stove and prepares a cup and saucer.

His ears twitch as he takes a wet cloth and wipes at the wound. I wince. He gentles his touch as he works. "It was nothing you need to worry about, Mrs. Finch. A few assassins came to kill Lord Rahk and for a minute or two used Nat as a hostage, but he quite easily—"

The kettle clangs against the grate. "Assassins?" cries Charity. "Kill Lord Rahk? Nat as a hostage? Nothing for me to worry about? Are you out of your mind?"

Edvear's skin turns bright red. His ears droop slightly as he turns away from her. "I forget this isn't normal for you humans. Please pardon me. Lord Rahk has taken care of these threats. Everything is safe now. You and Becky are safe. Lord Rahk and I both take the wellbeing of our staff very seriously. I do not want you to be afraid."

Charity pauses, peering at me strangely. "Nat? You don't look well."

She turns blurry on the edges. I swallow hard. Why does it feel so hard to breathe?

Hurried, heavy footsteps come from beyond the kitchen. The door bursts open.

"Lord Rahk!" says Edvear. "What is the matter?"

The next thing I know, the legs of my stool have been grabbed and rotated, and Rahk kneels before me. He swims in and out of focus as he takes my jaw in one hand and tilts my head so he can inspect the cut. He spits a vehement, unfamiliar curse.

"My lord—"

Rahk growls as he suddenly scoops me up into his arms. The ceiling blurs above me. "That blade was poisoned."

CHAPTER 19
RAHK

BLUE SPIDERLIKE VEINS spread out from the wound on Nat's temple. I carry her to the nearest bed, which happens to be mine. Her head lolls over my elbow, her eyes vacant and her mouth open. The cook comes, folding back the bedclothes so I can lay Nat down. Edvear has already left for a doctor.

"Is there anything I can give her?" Charity asks, fussing with the quilt. "I have herbs of many varieties, fresh and dried, but I only know their cooking uses, not medicinal."

I grind my teeth together. Fae poisons, I am familiar with, but I know nothing about human poisons. Its stench on each of the assassins' blades was unfamiliar.

How could I have overlooked something so significant?

"We will wait until the doctor comes," I say tightly.

"But what if that is too late? What if the poison moves too quickly?"

My gaze shifts from the concern wreathed across Charity's features to Nat's sweat-slicked face. The sun, only just rising, illuminates the spreading blue veins, reaching down to her cheek and up to her forehead. I look away quickly. "It won't."

Charity seems to take comfort in my baseless declaration. It is only then that I realize she referred to Nat as a *her*. I am not the only one to see through Nat's disguise, then. Or did Nat confide in the cook?

None of that matters. What matters is saving Nat's life.

Like she saved mine.

My guard shouldn't have been down. I should have suspected an attempt like this from the queen after I refused to leave. I should have set wards around the estate to alert me of trespassers.

I step away from the bed, raking a hand through my hair. I am a prince of Nothril. I know better than this—than *all* of this. Nat never should have been in a position to save me.

And why *did* she? What could she possibly gain from protecting me? She could have helped the assassins and earned the favor of the queen.

I cannot let her die. I owe her a life debt now.

And Prince Rahk of the Nothril Court never owed anyone a life debt, much less to a human woman.

I wipe a hand down my face. *Great Kings . . .*

The wait for Edvear and the doctor to arrive is agonizing. Charity stays by Nat's side while I pace at the far end of the room, thoroughly chastising myself in every way I can think of. The cook's daughter comes in at one point, and her little eyes grow wide at the sight of Nat's pale face and bloodied temple.

"We must ask the saints for help for Nat," whispers Charity to the girl.

Their murmured prayers hum in the air, turning it thick. Nat must have saved me because she didn't think things through properly. She must have reasoned that if I were killed, she wouldn't have been able to keep her position and would have been turned out on the streets. It is the only thing that makes sense.

The click of Edvear's heels makes all of us look up.

"We're coming!" he calls from down the hallway.

My relief is so sudden, I pull out a chair and drop into it. The white-haired, portly doctor follows Edvear straight to Nat's beside.

"Yes, poison," says the doctor in a strong accent immediately upon seeing her. He sets his case on the bedside table and pops it open.

"We can take it from here, Mrs. Finch," says Edvear to the cook, who looks at me.

"I don't want to leave the girl alone with three men," that look says.

I nod briefly, acknowledging her concern and bidding her to listen to Edvear. She purses her lips but leaves with her daughter. Edvear's eyes are glued to them, and when Becky glances back at him, he gives her a gentle pat and steps outside with them.

"I will be here if you need me," he tells me.

Only the doctor and I remain in the room with Nat. My fingers drum on the tabletop as the doctor places a tablet in Nat's mouth and holds it shut until she swallows, wincing. Then he withdraws a sharp scalpel and a small bowl. In his thick accent, he says, "Poison. Out."

He places the bowl beneath Nat's cheek and makes a small incision with the scalpel, just below one of the blue veins, until the dribbling violet blood turns red and thin. He works on each vein, moving clockwise around the wound. One of the incisions is dangerously near her eye. I briefly wonder if the doctor had come any later, would he have been forced to partially blind her?

She wouldn't have saved me if she'd known how much it could cost her.

I look away, clenching my jaw.

A moan drags my attention back to the bed. Just as the doctor is about to make the last incision, Nat thrashes her limbs.

"Sir, sir!" cries the doctor, just as Nat nearly rolls straight off the bed.

I am there the next moment, my knees digging into the mattress as I grip her arm in one hand and her jaw in the other.

"Still!" says the doctor, and I hold Nat's head still against the mattress, no matter how hard she tries to fight as the doctor slices into her forehead.

The last of that ugly, thick, purple blood clears to red.

KAT

The side of my face stings. My throat aches. I drag open my eyes to see a sharp instrument dripping with blood and an unfamiliar face. I let out an *"Uhh!"* of surprise as I try to throw myself backward away from him.

A large hand lands on my shoulder, restraining me. "It's alright, Nat. The doctor is helping you."

That is the prince's voice. I swivel my head toward it, only to find the great mass of Prince Rahk kneeling at my side, on the bed. Aside from when I massaged his back, I've never been this close to him before. What if he discovers . . .?

The assassins.

The poison.

I groan.

His thumb presses into the hollow above my collarbone. "Relax."

Absolutely not. What is happening? Why is he so close to me? What if he—

The doctor lifts the bottom of my shirt.

Nothing—not the assassins, not hearing Rahk declare I'd been poisoned, not even Rahk himself—terrifies me as much as that.

I grab his wrist. "What are you doing?"

"Stomach. Poison. Investigate," says the doctor with a thick Algravian accent.

"No, no investigate!" I try to get to my knees. They wobble and when I get one foot flat on the bed, I pitch to one side.

The prince catches me. Which is a horrible thing, it turns out, because he pulls me against his chest and captures my wrists in one vice-like fist, gripping them next to my face. "Hold still. The doctor is not going to hurt you."

My panic turns blinding white. They're going to remove my shirt and see my chest binding and there will be no recovery—for my job, my reputation, my fortune, my chance to avoid marriage, or my own dignity. "Please, please I don't want—"

The prince's low voice is a gentle murmur as he restrains me. "Nat, I'm not going to let anything bad happen to you. Trust me."

I'm panting, his long hair tickling my temple as I try to twist my wrists out of his grip. But I'm so weak, there is no chance of escape. I sag. A whimper sounds in the back of my throat.

"It is alright," the prince soothes again as his hand reaches down toward the hem of my shirt.

I breathe far too quickly, wriggling uselessly.

Swiftly, the prince lifts my shirt, revealing my middle. He stops, however, at the base of my ribcage just below my chest binding, my shirt fisted in his grip, only allowing the doctor access to my stomach.

Wait, does this mean I won't be disco—

Something cold presses against my stomach. My whole body seizes up. I yelp.

"Warm up the instrument first!" cries the prince. "The boy is in a delicate state!"

"Apology!" says the doctor, removing the cold metal *thing*. He holds it between his palms for a moment and then puts it back on my skin.

The doctor performs his investigation while the prince holds me. I grind my teeth and try to look anywhere but the doctor or the prince's hand that holds my shirt. My eyes land on striped wallpaper and stay there.

At last, the doctor pulls away. The prince immediately puts my shirt back down. I let out the breath I was clinging to. He releases my wrists. I squirm away from him at once.

"Stomach. Small poison, not big poison," announces the doctor, pointing at me. "Stomach sad. Eat cold foods."

The prince stares blankly at the doctor, then turns to me. "Does that mean anything to you?"

I tug on the bottom of my shirt. "I think he's saying only a little poison got to my stomach and that cold foods will help my body process it."

The doctor nods eagerly, apparently much better at understanding our language than speaking it.

"That is it for managing the rest of the poison?" asks the prince dubiously. When the doctor nods, he shrugs. "You humans have odd medical practices and odd poisons, but we shall serve you cold foods and see if it helps. You already look better."

I do feel better. I don't resist as the doctor bandages my temple. Rahk gets up, seemingly glad to put distance between us once again. When the doctor closes his case, all his things packed up, the prince calls for Edvear to pay the doctor.

Guilt stabs me at once. I clutch the quilts and try to sit up. "You must take the fee out of my payment. I'm so sorry to have created such a—"

Rahk shoots me such a look, one that is both incredulous and furious, that I immediately snap my mouth shut. Edvear leads the doctor away and closes the doorleaving the prince and I alone.

I lick my lips. I shouldn't fight him, but I cannot let him pay my doctor's fee. I'm his servant, not someone he is responsible for. I'm not *family*. "Master, it is more than generous of you to handle this, but I don't deserve it. Please let me pay for myself."

Rahk, who leans against the table, folds his arms across his chest and regards me. His mouth is drawn in a tight, thin line. "You don't deserve my generosity? How is this generosity, Nat? You saved my life. This doesn't even come close to repaying the life debt I owe you."

I draw back. "Life debt? Is that a fae thing? We don't have those here."

He shifts his weight, gripping the edge of the table in both hands. "I'm going to ask you a question, and you are going to answer it completely honestly."

The ache of my throat and temple vanishes immediately in the thrumming pulse of my blood. Does he suspect my secret? Did he discover it while I was unconscious?

"Why did you save me?"

I blink. "I'm sorry?"

"Tell me, Nat, why you saved me."

That's it? "Because you were in danger."

He shakes his head. "That is not why."

"What do you mean?" I cry, sitting up, indignant. "I saw them out the window. At first, I was scared they were going to kill me—they spooked me badly!—but they didn't, and then I realized they had come for you. So I had to warn you."

"I told you to be honest."

My mouth drops open. I try several responses, but none of them come out in my shock. Finally, I resort to, "What am I supposed to say? What response would satisfy you, Master?"

"I want the truth. I want to know *why* you came to warn me."

I give a wheezing laugh of disbelief. "I've already told you! Because you were in danger! Because I didn't want you to die!"

His finger shoots forward. "There! You didn't want me to die. Why not? Tell me why you didn't want me to die, Nat."

"Because you are a person?" I say, spreading my hands wide helplessly. "Because they wanted to commit murder, and that is wrong?"

"But me killing those five was not murder?" he challenges.

"It's different when you are defending yourself! What do you want me to say: that I didn't want to spend all day scrubbing your blood out of the rug?"

He shakes his head. "I want to know what you get out of it if I'm alive. That is what I'm asking. Did you save my life so you could keep your position? Were you afraid you wouldn't be able to get another if I died?"

"It was so early I thought my eyeballs were going to fall out of my head. I was not thinking of my position, except that it was because of this position I had to get up so early. Though now that you mention it, you dying *would* have probably put me in a tough situation."

A strange little smile, with a dangerous edge, creeps across his face. "Are you claiming that you saved me purely out of the goodness of your heart?"

I snort. "Hardly. It was just instinctual, though now this questioning is making me regret it."

His eyebrows rise at that. Strangely, my rude comment seems to be what convinces him. Of what, I'm not sure. His grip tightens on the table edge, and he looks away from me. He opens his mouth, pauses, shuts it again.

I wait, wriggling my toes beneath the quilt. *His* quilt.

He pushes off the table abruptly and heads toward the door. "Regardless of your reason, thank you for doing what you did. It . . . it was brave of you." Each sentence sounds disjointed, almost *awkward*. "I'm sorry you got hurt. And I will be paying the doctor's fee. You will rest."

With that, he marches out of the room, shuts the door just shy of a slam, and his footsteps echo into nothing. When quiet at last fills my space, I collapse against the pillow, my chest rising and falling fast. My limbs shake even more than before.

He still doesn't know I'm a woman.

I could almost laugh from relief. *He still doesn't know.*

A knock sounds on the door. I nearly leap out of my skin.

"It's just me, sweetheart," says Charity, coming in with a bowl of broth. "No need to look so frightened. I've come to see if you can take a little broth after your wild morning—cold, unfortunately, as the doctor ordered."

My hand shakes only a little as I take the bowl, but she places a hand beneath it, steadying it as I take small sips. The broth is good, spiced and salty, though I don't like it nearly so much cold. "Is the doctor gone? Will he come back?"

"He is just leaving. Do you want him back?"

"No!" I say, too vehemently.

She gives a gentle smile and winks conspiratorially. "Don't worry, he didn't expose your secret."

I nearly spit out my soup, setting into a violent round of hacking. "I beg your pardon?"

"Sweetheart," Charity says with a chuckle. "I've known the entire time. There's no need to hide it."

I stare at her, my mouth fallen open, and I don't know whether to be afraid or desperately relieved.

"I won't tell anyone, if that's what you're afraid of." She takes the empty bowl, sitting on the edge of the bed.

I groan, closing my eyes. "How did you know?"

"A woman knows another woman, sweet. Now, *Nat*, would you like a confidant in . . . *all this*?" She gestures around us. "Or shall I leave you to your secrets?"

The words come tumbling free without consulting me, anxious to be spoken. "My stepmother sold my horse, and I was afraid she would do worse if I didn't marry a man I *never* want to see again in my life. I had to get out before I would be forced to accept his proposal!"

The rest of the story pours out without restraint. I don't tell her my name, but I do mention that I have an inheritance that everyone keeps trying to steal. It's enough that she will know who I am.

I do not tell her about my identity as the Ivy Mask.

"It's all a mess!" I cry, throwing up my hands.

"That is *quite* the situation," Charity agrees. She sits beside me, her legs crossed and her black stockings poking out beneath the hem of her frock. "Have you considered confiding in the master?"

"*Confiding* in him?" I release a high-pitched chortle. "You cannot be serious."

"I am. Did you not see how worried he was about you?"

She should have seen him interrogating me only moments ago.

She continues. "I am not one to trust a fae, but his attentiveness is unusual—not even human masters care so much about their servants—and I find it to be a virtue. His steward is amiable, too, for that matter."

I shut my gaping mouth and wrap my arms around my knees.

"If you told the master, he might be able to help you," she adds.

I'm already shaking my head. "I'm not saying he has not a single virtue, but I just . . . I cannot confide in him. If he sent me away or exposed me to my stepfamily, I'd have nowhere else to go. What I stand to gain from his aid is nowhere near as much as I stand to lose."

Bartholomew, my fortune, my freedom, my ability to perform raids.

It feels like I am clinging to all the things I will inevitably lose because I didn't deserve to have them in the first place.

Charity gets to her feet. "I've got work to do, but I am glad you are doing better, and I will do what I can to protect your secret until you're ready."

"Thank you," I say earnestly as she takes the empty bowl and leaves.

CHAPTER 20

RAHK

I *DIDN'T WANT you to die . . . because you are a person.*

Those strange words rattle around in my brain. No matter how much I try to distract myself, they keep returning. Along with the image seared into my brain of her, eyes widened, face wreathed in panic, clutching the marble bust she'd used to break through my door.

She looked frightened. As if she genuinely cared whether I lived or died. And she took those injuries without hardly flinching—injuries that were supposed to be for *me*. She never should have been hurt. I never should have left myself so *vulnerable*.

I was wrong. Nat is not easy to understand. She must be telling the truth, that she saved me simply out of the goodness of her heart. There are precious few people I would willingly, without ulterior motive, put myself at risk for. Ash, his wife, their heir, and Pavi. That is it.

Does Nat just sacrifice her safety for anyone, then?

Why?

A question for another day. This day has more than enough trouble and work.

"Edvear," I call through the door of my study when his familiar stride reaches my ears. He pokes his head through my broken door. The bodies are all disposed of, the blood mostly cleaned except for a few stray droplets on the spines of unfortunate books. "Procure the address of the Vandermore estate. I must pay a visit at once."

Edvear tilts his head to one side. "The Vandermores? Isn't that the wealthiest family in the city, save the queen?"

"The same. I will call on Lady Vandermore."

"The mother? Or the heiress?"

"The heiress."

"Whatever for?"

I smirk at Edvear's bewilderment. "I think we can help each other, and in the process, give the queen a story."

"Oh no, oh no," groans Edvear. "I'm having flashbacks to working for Ash."

That surprises a chuckle out of me. "Have no fear, my good steward. This hardly compares to his machinations."

The Vandermore Manor has an enormous shrub trimmed into the shape of a rearing stallion at its entrance.

"The things I do because of Ash," I mutter under my breath.

Since Edvear was gone and Nat was sick, I had to ask Mrs. Banks for advice on which human clothes I ought to wear.

"What statement do you wish to make?" she had asked.

"I wish to appear unthreatening," I replied, thinking of how Nat had indicated that I often appear frightening.

She suggested a doublet of lavender, which I did not realize I even owned. I took her advice and wore what she selected, but now I do not feel like myself at all as I step out of the carriage. My shoulders are too wide, my stride too long, my feet too broad for a light shade of purple. The glamour on my wings shudders slightly, but I dare not let it slip. Least of all here.

I spare a singular, smug thought that the queen will be very put out at the failure of her covert attempt to be rid of me.

I am shown to a parlor, fixed with red upholstered chairs with armrests—*curse it*. These ones look particularly bad, with a very narrow seat and narrow arms. I might have to stand beside the mantel this entire meeting. Then, blessedly, I spot the singular bench, this one a striped, spring green.

The clock on the mantel chimes the hour as someone enters—the woman I observed speaking to the queen at the ball.

"Lord Rahk," says the woman with only a hint of trepidation in her voice. "We are honored by your presence. And surprised, as we have not had the pleasure of being introduced."

"Lady Duxbury Vandermore," I reply, bowing. "Forgive me if I have blundered. I am still learning Harbright culture."

"Consider it forgotten." She takes a seat by the fireplace, then gestures for me to sit as well. Behind her, two manservants step into the room and stay by the door like guards.

I take the bench and survey the woman. She must be well into her fifties, a touch of gray streaking away from her temples into her bound-up hair. She holds herself erect, her spine straight, her hands carefully folded on her knees.

The only tell of her fear is that she keeps glancing at her manservants.

Apparently, the purple doublet didn't do its full duty.

"I came to speak with Lady Vandermore," I say when the silence stretches. "Is she here?"

"Ah, yes. All the young men wish to speak with her."

That is a bitter tone. Is the lady angry I do not come for her hand? Or some other reason? I remember to return her smile lest I come across too *brooding*, as Ash always says. "Is she here?"

"I'm afraid not. She is out calling on one of her friends. But if it is marriage you are considering, I can tell you the process."

I'd rather speak to the girl. I do not need a wife, neither do I want one. I have no intention of marrying Lady Vandermore. But if we broker a deal between us to feign courtship, where she will help me create a compelling story for the queen and I will return her stolen land to her, then we might be able to help each other.

"There is no shame in desiring to wed the young lady," says Lady Duxbury Vandermore with a light chuckle that grates down my spine. "All the other young men do."

She keeps putting me with *all the young men,* as if I am one of them, and not a fae from another world. Still, I am here. I might as well collect the information. "Please, do tell me the courtship process."

"Are you familiar with it?"

"Is it similar to Aursailles?" I ask by way of answer.

"Oh dear me, no!" the lady laughs, and it reminds me of the way Pelarusa laughs when she is angling to get something she wants. "Here in Harbright, you sign a contract agreeing to pay the bride price and then she's yours. It's all arranged by the parents here."

Arranged by the parents? A bride price? What nonsense. Does she think me a complete fool? I shift on the bench. "I would like to meet the lady first, before we sign any contracts."

"Certainly! I can draw up the agreement and you can call again to meet her and sign it. As I said, she's out now, but we can certainly arrange a meeting. I know she would be *delighted* to meet you."

This plan of mine will not work. I'll have to come up with some other way to get the queen to trust me. I thank the woman anyway.

When I leave, passing between the manservants, they let out a huge exhale. They think I'm out of earshot. I shake my head and stride down the hallway. I scent another human servant, this one female, as I head toward the door. I glance toward it and am just in time to watch a red-haired maid carry a basket of clean laundry upstairs.

I saw her from a distance once, leaving my own estate.

Mary. Nat's sister.

I cannot remember if I knew she worked here. It should mean nothing. Yet my senses still tingle after that odd meeting with Lady Duxbury Vandermore, so this strikes me as a strange coincidence. I consider informing her of Nat's condition, but I cannot bring myself to call out to her. My pride is still very wounded that Nat would ever have been in danger at my estate.

I climb into my carriage and set off once more for home. No, no, I set off for my estate. Not for home.

The first place I go when I return is my room. Nat is no longer in the bed. Fresh sheets have been laid and the bed made to look untouched. Quietly, I make my way to Nat's door and ease it open. She sleeps soundly on her cot, a blanket pulled up to her chin, a cold cup of water beside her. Her short hair is mussed, her freckles standing out in the sunbeam that covers the upper half of her body. Her neck is mottled purple, and the bandage on the side of her face covers her healing wounds. She will have scars on her face. Because of me—because of my incompetence.

I will not be so foolish as to let my guard down again. Neither will I forget her bravery and devotion.

I leave, staying quiet to not disturb her sleep.

CHAPTER 21

KAT

I'M DESPERATELY WEAK as the remnants of poison finish working through my system the next day. So weak, I'm not sure I'll ever be able to do another raid again. Chopping wood, cleaning the prince's room, or hauling water—even setting out his clothes—feel like tasks so monumental I don't think I'll ever be capable of them now. When I peel away the bandage from my face, I discover eight small cuts scarring over. They're small enough I doubt they will be very noticeable, but I can already hear Mary having a fit.

The prince tells me to rest, to eat slowly, and to regain my strength. When I try to go back to work, he orders me to sit outside and soak up the sun, so I do just that. I find a sunny spot on the patio with my Fool's Circle book, and I read until my face is sunburned and hundreds of new freckles have appeared on my arms.

I do feel better though.

That night, when the prince suggests we play our game over dinner—dinner where he ordered I eat with him so he can make sure

I don't go too fast—I'm so eager to do something *normal* again I almost trip over myself getting the board.

Our first game we play mostly in silence. Until we near the end, and my gaze shoots up in outrage. "You're letting me win!"

The prince's gaze flicks up to mine. Is that a smile tugging on the corner of his lip? "You're improving quickly. I see the book is helping you."

"How dare you!" I cry, shoving the pieces off the board.

"You took a poisoned blade for me!" he protests. "It feels cruel to beat you."

"I want a fair game, or no game."

We lock eyes. I hold my ground, glaring at him, while he regards me mildly. He is the one who looks away first.

"Very well. Let us start again." He sets up the pieces. "If a merciless beating in Fool's Circle is what you need to feel better, then a merciless beating you shall have."

I take my minions and arrange them properly. "It's not that I want to be beaten. It's that I plan to beat you one of these days, and I want it to be for real. A false victory holds no satisfaction."

He places the Fool in the center and leans back, lacing his fingers together as his eyes run over my face, lingering on my new scars. "The number of strong opinions you hold as a twelve-year-old continues to amaze me."

You're acting too much like yourself, I think in self-chastisement.

I must have flinched or given some indication of my chagrin, because the prince adds: "I do not disparage you for your age. I compliment you. Few lads know their own minds. Few men do, for that matter. It's an admirable thing to be so young and yet so thoughtful."

He's teasing me. In what manner, I cannot fathom. But he's somehow goading me. He has done this before, but there used to be an edge to it that now seems to have . . . softened? It's as though he was previously trying to catch me in a mistake, but now it's like he wants to know me better. As if he conducts a curious study of my character.

None of it makes sense, so I shove it from my mind.

"I don't need to be grown to know I don't like to be patronized." The words are muttered, and I mean them in reference to him letting me win, not to what he said. But when he's silent, I realize just how bad those words sound. "I—I've misspoken, Master. I meant—I meant the game—"

"You haven't offended me."

I uncurl my tense fingers. Then, I blurt: "You are very kind to me, master. I don't mean to be ungrateful for your kindness and patience. I know I have much to learn, and I say things without thinking and act foolishly. You are merciful to not punish me. You have the patience of a saint."

He opens his mouth as though to say something else, but stops himself. "You don't need to flatter me to appease my moods."

I sag in further relief. "That is a relief."

He laughs outright at that. I hide my self-satisfied smile and quickly add: "But I mean what I said."

To my shock, he reaches across the table, his hand landing on the top of my head and ruffling my hair. "Your turn," he says.

I blink too quickly and steer my attention down to the game.

We're halfway through the next round—in which I'm getting thoroughly trounced—when the prince's face turns more contemplative, as if his mind is elsewhere. I take turns watching the board and his expression, and on one such occasion, he looks up and catches me.

"You look troubled," I say.

He lifts one shoulder in a casual shrug. "Much is on my mind."

Like how to quickly hunt me down. I curse myself for enjoying his laughter only a few minutes ago. "Like what?"

He moves his pieces. "Like marriage."

"Marriage?" I drop the minion I just picked up. It falls to the floor, and I scramble to retrieve it.

He gives a quiet snort of amusement. "Don't you think about marriage?"

My mind trips over itself for the right twelve-year-old boy reaction and I settle on screwing up my nose.

He chuckles. "Give it some time. You'll think differently sooner than you think." He winks at me—and it is a wink like we share some secret, just between the two of us.

"You think differently, then?" I probe, curious.

"It is complicated."

"Because you're fae?"

He moves his pieces. "That is part of it."

"Do fae marry?" I ask, knowing the answer.

"We do. We call it *bonding*. It's like a human marriage, but, because we are magical beings, our bonding is infused with magic. It is a powerful bond. Many fae choose never to bond, or if they do, they wait until later in their life. They may have many dalliances before and after a bonding, but once the bond is in place, it can rarely be broken by a force besides death."

"Is that why you haven't marr—bonded?"

"In part, yes. It is not something to do lightly."

I wait, and when he does not continue, I say, "But there are other reasons."

"There are." He inclines his head, then frowns down at the board. He considers it carefully for several long minutes before moving his pieces. "The Court I come from is especially notorious. It is not safe to get your heart tangled up with someone who can be used against you. In Faerieland, we cannot lie, but we are very good at deception. There has been no one I trust enough to bind my life to."

I bite back my initial pitying response, and instead say, "That's probably good."

He looks up, surprised. "How so?"

"Because if you wanted power in Harbright, you could woo the queen. She's the widowed regent for her son. You could be reigning King of Harbright until the crown prince is of age."

"Marry the queen?" His bark almost startles me. "She would sooner bite my head off."

"I think you can handle her."

"You do me credit."

I frown, and before I can stop myself, I gesture at his massive physique, his bulging arms and powerful shoulders. "You're a veritable mountain. You'd be fine."

He laughs again while I duck my head to hide my blush. I'm beginning to grow fearful of what foolish things I will say and do to elicit such laughter. The little *clinks* of our pieces moving on the board fill the silence for several long minutes, until the prince clears his throat.

"Nat."

The seriousness underlying that syllable lifts my attention to his. He shifts uncomfortably in his seat, refusing to look at me. I chew on the inside of my lip, hardly breathing as I wait for him to continue.

"I don't think I have properly thanked you for what you did," he says at last.

Now it's my turn to shift uneasily. "No, you have."

"No, I haven't, and I owe it to you," Rahk says, firmly, still not looking at me. "Frankly, I am deeply ashamed that those assassins ever made it onto my estate, much less inside this house—and it is an egregious offense that I ever let any of them close enough to hurt you. I would have lost my head if I'd proved such poor competence in the Nothril Court."

"How was it your fault?" I cry. "They are the ones who broke in. They are trained for this. It's not your—"

"*I* am trained for this, Nat!" It comes out in an angry snap. He rakes a hand through his hair. Is that a tremor in his fingers? My lips part.

He is serious. He truly is ashamed, which somehow succeeds in making *me* ashamed that I couldn't have gotten there faster.

Finally, his gaze latches onto mine. It is so strong, I immediately want to retreat.

"You were hurt because of me," he growls. The words falter slightly. "That is never going to happen again. I swear it. You may not trust me, and that is fine—I have not earned your trust. But I promise anyway that I will not let you down again."

"You haven't let me down," I insist. We haven't played any minions for several minutes now. I don't remember whose turn it is. "It is my fault that I didn't get there faster—"

His tone turns almost . . . *distraught*. "Why won't you accept my thanks? Why won't you accept my apology? You did nothing wrong—you were brave and courageous and sometimes I think it is impossible that you didn't have some ulterior motive for it because where I come from, aiding people is done for selfish reasons and protecting someone can cost you everything." His words are tumbling out, fast and breathless, and for this moment, he sounds nothing like the stern, quiet Prince Rahk I've come to know. "I've been forced to do things that I hate, been prevented from doing the things I want, and anyone I protect becomes a means of manipulation. I have this little sister and—" He cuts off with a growl, shaking his head. He runs a palm down over his face, as though trying to wrestle control back. When he speaks again, his voice is quiet. "What I'm trying to say is that I am envious of your ability to just *choose* to help someone. Simply because you want to. I admire that you did not just have the option, but you took it. I am thankful that you saved my life. If you hadn't . . . one of the only people I care about in the world would have likely died. So please, Nat, please accept my thanks and please accept my apology. It upsets me that you seem disinclined to do so."

I stare back at him, my mouth agape.

Little sister.

He must be talking about the youngest Nothril princess—Princess Pavi.

So the fae can *love,* I think, closing my mouth. But why would Pavi have died if Rahk had? Unless he was talking about someone else?

I run my tongue over my lips and try to find my voice. It feels impossible to get the words out. They go against every instinct inside me that screams I have no right accepting either thanks or apology. He is so distraught, though. I cannot bear to look at the expression on his face and refuse the one thing he asks.

"Yes," I say finally, quietly, ducking my head. "I accept them."

Rahk lets out a deep exhalation. He works his jaw, then abruptly leans forward and moves his minions. We play silently until he speaks again.

"I am told it would be wise to marry a human woman to secure my position in Harbright's court." The furrow between his brows returns.

"You don't want to?"

"I do not."

"Then don't."

He only smiles and then moves his piece to claim the last opening around the Fool. "I win."

CHAPTER 22

RAHK

WE'VE HARDLY PUT away the game before Edvear's hurried footsteps come down the hallway. By now, I know the variations of his stride well. This one has my spine stiffening.

"What's wrong?" Nat asks, just as she slides the game onto its usual place on the shelf.

I glance at her, startled that she should be able to read me so well, so quickly. A curt reply leaps to my lips, since I cannot lie, but I stop myself. I owe her better than that. "I hope nothing serious," I reply honestly.

Edvear's knock is insistent. I bid him enter. He doesn't even see Nat in the corner and rushes to hand me a crisp white missive. "I just received this from Nothril! I meant to go earlier in the day like usual but with the aftermath of the assassins—"

"Do not worry yourself," I say as I take the note. "You may leave."

The room is quiet a moment later. Nat stands like a ghost in the corner, clearly caught between retiring to her own chambers or awaiting my bidding. I break the seal on the note, my heart already quickening its rhythm. It is in Pelarusa's hand. Concerningly few words are written on the note. I skim it in half a second.

Pavi messed up.

Ice washes through my veins. I stuff the note in my pocket and cast around for my swords. They're not here—they're in my study.

"What's wrong?" Nat asks quietly. She has already gone into motion herself and a second later, she hands me a cloak and a pair of boots.

Gratefully, I swing on the cloak and yank each boot onto my feet. "I don't know. All I know is that it involves my sister."

"What can I do?" she asks, her tone serious, without a hint of her usual irreverence. She moves fast with me, following me toward the study. "Your knives are in the bedroom. Should I fetch them?"

I grab my two swords from under my desk, swing them onto my back, and fasten their buckles. "No, this is all I need. I will leave at—" My fingers slip on the buckles of the second sword. The weapon nearly drops to the ground.

But Nat is there, catching the buckle and tightening it for me.

I spare one second to look down at her as she fastens the buckle. She is focused, sharp, while I am caving for a second time. Part of me hates her for it, but it is only because I hate myself for these stupid weaknesses. For caring about my sister when I should let her survive on her own merits.

The greater part of me is relieved that for this one moment, there is someone who will compensate for my shaking fingers without requiring a hefty price in return.

She looks up at me with such concern in her brown eyes. That expression is dangerous. It will make me confide my fears in her when I shouldn't. It will make me want to trust her far more than I ought.

"I don't know when I will be back," I say as I stride past her, letting the glamours fall from my wings even before I shut the door behind me.

Pelarusa meets me at the iron gates of Nothril.

"What happened?" I demand as the guards let me through. Coolness washes over me as we step into the entrance of the deep cave that is the palace.

"Pavi and her young handmaiden decided to play a *prank* on one of her bodyguards. They stole his helmet and painted pink flowers across the whole thing." Pelarusa keeps pace with my fast strides, heading toward the throne room. "She is such an idiot sometimes. But that wasn't where things went wrong."

"Let me guess," I growl, frustration building up inside my gut, "Lord and Lady Nothril announced their intention to punish the servant instead of Pavi, and Pavi could not stomach that. She intervened—and then things escalated."

"Exactly." Pelarusa throws up her hands. "I should have just let them kill her. I don't know why I care at this point. She is asking to be put to death. Lady Nothril is simply too fond of her to have allowed it to happen so far."

"The punishment for the servant?"

"They took her hands. One for her fault, one for Pavi's fault. Pavi was supposed to be the one to do it."

I briefly let my eyes shutter closed. Pavi can never hurt another soul. That will cost her dearly if she stays at Nothril. Silently, I berate myself for not having caught the Ivy Mask already. Pavi could be out of here by now.

That little servant girl could still have her hands.

We reach the door to the throne room. Yelling penetrates the thick stone. Pelarusa and I share a look. Then I shove open the door.

"We didn't mean any harm!" Pavi cries. She stands before the two thrones, her hands extended in pleading. The tears are evident in her voice. "It was just paint! It washes off!"

"That warrior has sworn to give his life for you, and you humiliate him with tricks like this?" Lord Nothril shrieks back at her.

"I see that now, but it wasn't even Kava's idea! She just went along with me. How could you be so cruel? You should have taken my hands instead!"

"She is a *slave girl.* She doesn't matter. I find your care of her to be extremely disturbing, and I will gladly take your hands too if it will ingrain this lesson in your thick skull!"

"Lord and Lady Nothril," I call, my voice slicing through the storm cloud of fighting. I bow. "I pay my respects."

"What are you doing here?" Lord Nothril spits. "The High King's lapdog has finally returned home, but has he brought his quarry? It does not look like it."

I clasp my hands behind my back, bracing my legs wide. I can take Lord Nothril's redirected ire. Distraction is the name of this game—not trying to reason with either Lord Nothril or Pavi. I need only to revert attention to me long enough for Pelarusa to get Pavi out.

"I do not have the Ivy Mask yet, but there have been some interesting developments."

"Do I look like I care about updates on your errands?" Lord Nothril's vitriol is biting. If I was not used to it, I might have retreated a step from the force of it. "I want the Ivy Mask. I want him cut to pieces at my feet. I do not care about your *developments*."

Lady Nothril, who has been sitting silently on her throne in a gown of deep purple, taps one nail on her armrest. We all, as one, swivel our attention to her.

"I would like to hear," she says calmly.

I incline my chin slightly. "I have been able to effectively trace the Ivy Mask's movements to the Revar Court. I have also confirmed that he lives in the human world—and I have pinpointed the city. It will not be long before I collect him."

Lady Nothril's mouth twists upward. "The vigilante must be quite skilled to be giving *you* such a challenge."

I keep my voice devoid of emotion. "There is a reason he has gone so long without being caught. But I will catch him. I am close on his trail even now."

As we speak, Pelarusa drags Pavi out of the throne room. Pavi doesn't seem inclined to go at first. She does not know that there is nothing to be done for her friend. All there is, now, is the preservation of her own life.

But, being Pavi, she still has not realized that.

Lord Nothril does not seem to notice, but Lady Nothril's eyes flick from me as I speak to watch her youngest daughter leave. She returns her gaze to me. She strips me bare with that gaze, reading exactly what I am doing, and exactly why I am doing it.

This is why I bear the blood oath tattoo on the back of my neck. Because I cannot be trusted to act without consideration of the few I care about. Even though Lady Nothril herself is the softest on Pavi, the viperlike expression she shoots me is one of disappointment.

I can almost hear her voice slithering in my ear: *"You have never had what it takes to rise to the throne of Nothril."*

"Why are you not just sniffing the creature out?" Lord Nothril demands, missing entirely that Pavi is gone.

"The Ivy Mask does not leave a scent trail, but he is still trackable. I—"

"Then why have you not tracked him already?" It comes out in a violent shout. "You do realize your sister will die if you do not finish this—or are you too stupid to realize that is what a blood oath is? If you drag your feet, she may even be dead before you return."

My throat closes. I measure my breathing carefully. When I have regained my composure, I say only, "I will hunt him down. Have no fear."

"Have you at least finished the High King's errand?" Lord Nothril growls, flopping into his throne and running a hand down his face. "No, do not answer that. I already know."

"I will finish both of these things within the time specified," I say coolly.

Lord Nothril flicks his hand. "Then begone and finish your tasks."

I gladly turn on my heel and march from the throne room.

Pavi waits for me outside. She stands by the servants' door, ready to flee into it if it was not me who exited. Her shoulders are curled inward. She gnaws on her fingernails until her eyes fall on me. Tears bubble to the surface. She breaks into a run and throws her arms around my waist.

"I didn't mean for her to be hurt," she sobs against my chest.

I sigh as I wrap one arm around her. "I know."

I should berate her for her foolish behavior. I should give her a list of things she should never do again. But my stupidly soft heart cannot let those words pass my lips. Instead, I hold her close and let her cry.

CHAPTER 23
KAT

"WAKE UP AND get dressed."

The prince's voice startles me from my sleep. I bolt upright, my hand instinctively going to my chest to ensure I'm still wearing my binding. *I am*. This proves my insistence upon always wearing the binding, even while sleeping, is necessary. I exhale.

His words process in my mind.

"You're back. Is everything alright?" I ask. It's very early. I get up and gather my uniform but dare not change into it with him still in the doorway. It took me a long time to fall asleep last night after the way the prince rushed off after receiving that note. "Is your sister alright?"

"She is fine for now." He considers a moment, then adds in a quieter tone, "I'm glad I arrived when I did."

I lick my lips, something inside my chest easing. "Then I am glad too."

He steps outside of my room briskly. The honesty between us seems to make him almost uncomfortable. When he speaks again, it is in his usual tone. "The queen has summoned me. I want you to come along."

"The queen? Is she going to try to kill you again?"

He lifts one shoulder. "It wouldn't be wise. I'm prepared now."

I dress quickly once the door is closed, shake out my hair, and hurry to grab a quick breakfast from the kitchen before we leave.

The sun rises as we take the main road out of the city. It doesn't take me long to figure out where we're going when we veer onto a dirt road, and a cold shiver like ice descends, slowly covering my body.

We're going to Caphryl Wood.

Why are we going to Caphryl Wood?

Has he . . . discovered me? How could he have? It's been days since I even touched the Wood!

A hand lands on my knee. I jerk away from his touch even before I process that it is Rahk. I look up quickly. He withdraws his hand, his brow pinched, his scrutiny sharp as it roves over me.

"I'm sorry, Master," I manage.

"Are you—" He stops himself abruptly, his eyes widening. "Your mother. Nat, I—I am so sorry, I forgot you had such terrible memories of this place."

Is he . . . *sputtering*? I didn't think a fae could sputter. Much less the infamous Prince Rahk of the Nothril Court.

He yanks open the curtain and shouts out the window, "We must go back at once!"

"What?" I blurt.

He leans back in to say to me, "This is my blunder, so I shall fix it. You need not go near the Wood."

"The queen's caravan is already there!" Edvear shouts from where he stands on the footboard of the carriage.

Rahk releases a low growl of frustration. He looks back at me, and that appears to be genuine concern flashing in his black eyes. "Very well!" he calls to the driver. To me, he drops his voice and says gently, "You can stay in the carriage. We'll draw the curtains, and you won't have to look at the place."

So . . . he has brought me here for a different reason. He doesn't know I'm the Ivy Mask. I breathe a little easier, my body unwinding from its tight coil.

The carriage comes to a stop. Rahk looks at me again as he moves to exit the box.

"I'll go with you," I say, trying to hide the bubbling of my curiosity. I'm supposed to be a traumatized boy, so I keep my shoulders scrunched as I follow Rahk out of the carriage.

He smiles down at me. As though he's proud of my bravery.

We stand on the farmland waving with grass at the edge of the great, dark Wood. Knights in heavy armor stand at attention beside Queen Vivienne, who wears a shawl around her delicate shoulders. Rahk goes directly to her. I hang back, mussing my hair and slouching my shoulders even more. I don't want to go anywhere near her for fear she'll see through my disguise at once and recognize me.

So I stay with Edvear by the carriage.

"What's going on?" I ask, nervously.

"The border of the Wood has begun receding."

"It has?"

"It seems the queen is asking our lord to inspect it."

The prince leaves the group then. He strides through the tall grass, his white hair falling between his shoulder blades and sweeping around his face as the wind picks up. He doesn't slow until he reaches the edge of the Wood.

Queen Vivienne stays where she is, her chin lifted as she watches Rahk.

It hasn't even occurred to me that it might not be safe for humans while it is receding. I've just been going in and out as I please. The prince turns around, beckons Edvear to come. His eye catches mine and his eyebrow lifts—giving me the option to join if I want to.

It's probably a bad idea, but my curiosity gets the better of me. I follow Edvear out to meet the prince.

What I see takes my breath away.

The ground at the edge of the Wood isn't green like the rest, but sparking with a chorus of golden glows. As though millions of fireflies hover just above the soil. The wind, always strong near Caphryl, blows my hair in every direction.

I stop where I am. The prince beckons me closer. "It's safe."

"What's happening?" I ask.

"The forest is receding, but the land left behind is still saturated with magic."

I look up in alarm. "Will it always be this way? Will we get hurt if we get too close?"

Rahk shakes his head. "No, on both counts. The remnants of magic will fade as the human cycle of death overtakes it. It won't be long. It won't hurt anyone. Not the ground itself, that is." He says it with a dark furrow of his brow. "Though perhaps now the queen will be open to a dialogue about the Wood."

I stay where I am as he leaves to speak with the queen.

The land is being returned. After all these years.

But the Wood won't give back all it took.

I grit my teeth. Foolish as it may be, I cannot wait until my next raid. I walk back over, staying out of close range but within hearing distance just as the prince is saying to the queen, "I would be honored to attend your luncheon."

"Two days," says Queen Vivienne. "One discussion, and no more. We do not need fae here."

Rahk bows cordially. "I understand."

The next unexpected errand Rahk takes me on is to a sparring yard. I have no idea why he takes me, and not Edvear, but when he asks me to accompany him, I cannot think of an excuse fast enough.

The sparring yard is out of town again. I recognize the place as belonging to Baron Cranswick. My hackles rise as we step onto what seems to be a glorified courtyard, complete with barrels of weapons and an alarming number of shirtless young men.

Young men that *I know*.

There is Sir Alsbee and his crew, laughing and lounging on a few benches. There is Lord Oliver Cranswick, tossing aside his sword as he jogs to meet us. And beyond him, sitting fully clothed with no sign of exertion, is Lord Boreham.

Saints have mercy on me. What is Lord Boreham doing here?

I try to look anywhere at all, but nowhere is safe from the hairy bellies and pale chests. I happen to look up to find Rahk smirking down at me.

"This will be you someday," he teases.

My disgusted reaction is out before I can help it. He chuckles as Lord Oliver catches up to us.

"You came!" he cries happily, sweating profusely and planting two hands against his narrow hips. He has one of the nicer torsos of the group, and the fact that I notice only embarrasses me more.

I shuffle partially behind Rahk, keeping my head bowed, my heart pounding violently when Lord Oliver glances my way. *Please don't recognize me. Please don't recognize me.*

"I am grateful for the invitation," says Rahk with a warmth I'm not sure I've ever heard from him. "I hope it is no trouble that I brought my attendant. He is young, but he intends to go to war someday."

I could *murder* him. He all but grins down at me, his dark eyes twinkling.

"War, eh?" says Lord Oliver, turning his sunny smile down to me.

I squirm in my shoes. I pray like I have never prayed before.

"Well, you're in the right place, er . . .?"

"Nat. His name is Nat." Rahk ruffles my hair. "Would you like to join us?"

"I can watch," I squeak.

The two of them laugh. Rahk shucks off his boots, hands them to me, and then strips off his shirt. I frantically look elsewhere until the shirt drops into my waiting hands. When I brave a glance, he has mercifully left on his thin linen undershirt.

"Watch those for me," says the prince as he strides barefoot toward the barrel of weapons.

I scurry toward an empty bench and carefully prop up his boots, folding his shirt and draping it over the bench. Then I sit cross-legged and pray no one looks my way ever again.

There are several circular wooden fences scattered throughout the yard. As I watch, two men choose their weapons, climb into the enclosure, and begin sparring. Rahk is busy inspecting blunted swords with Lord Oliver. He tests the weight of each in his palm and does not seem fully satisfied with his selection. Once he has a weapon, he leaps lightly into a pit. Lord Oliver follows, far less gracefully, though not without his own dignity.

Is this the prince's way of connecting with the influential men of Harbright? I didn't know they all came here to fight together like dogs.

Lord Oliver faces Rahk, both with their swords lifted. Lord Oliver attacks first, darting forward and aiming at Rahk's forearm. Rahk blocks the blow and side-steps. Lord Oliver continues throwing quick attacks—faster and more precise than I would have expected from any young lord in Harbright's aristocracy. Rahk stays back, blocking and dodging, but not striking.

"Come now!" cries Lord Oliver. "I know you're better than me! You needn't protect my dignity!"

The next second, his sword goes flying upward. Rahk darts forward and snatches it out of the air, and an instant later, he has both blades against Oliver's throat. I press a hand over my mouth—and then rip it away when I realize how feminine of a gesture it is. I'm supposed to be excited about this. Nat wouldn't be worried about Oliver.

Oliver lets out a chortle. "How did you do that? You must show me at once!"

Rahk seems pleased with this response, tossing the sword back to his opponent. His neck cranes quickly, and I find myself trapped in his sparking gaze. He didn't search for me—he knew exactly where I sat.

Something about the look he gives me makes my cheeks flush.

He returns to his opponents. Many of the men have abandoned their respective matches in favor of surrounding the pit and watching Rahk. I cannot see a thing except the top of Rahk's white hair, which moves as he instructs the onlookers.

He and Lord Oliver do two more rounds—none of which I can see—and after that, it is Alsbee who saunters forward and demands his turn. He proclaims that he wishes to fight hand to hand, no weapons. I have no idea where he gets the boldness for that. Maybe the same place he found the boldness to try to seduce me when I was sixteen.

I lean forward on the bench, very eager to watch Alsbee get trounced. There is no viewing pocket available to me, so I leave the safety of my bench and venture closer to the pit.

Laughter erupts just as I find a spot, several paces away, but at an angle where I can see. Rahk's knees are bent, his hands gripping Alsbee's forearms. Forearms that are wrapped around his neck. My gasp is out of me before I can stop it. Why are they laughing? How dare Alsbee play so dirty?

And then one of the men shift, and I get the full view. Alsbee hangs on Rahk's back, his feet literally dangling off the ground. He is trying to pull Rahk down. Rahk, however, stays sturdy on his feet, and all he does is keep Alsbee from choking him. He isn't even fighting.

Everyone is laughing at how ridiculous the young lord looks.

I find myself smirking, delighted far beyond what I expected. Maybe this trip isn't the worst thing that ever happened.

Then Rahk pivots, prying Alsbee's arm loose of his neck and swiveling. I cannot even follow what happens, but one minute Alsbee is hanging from his back, and the next he is flat on the ground, Rahk's foot planted on his sternum.

I blush furiously.

"Now you *must* show us that one too!" cries Oliver.

One by one, all the young men want to challenge the prince. I don't know how their dignity allows them to be so competitive. The prince is half a head taller than the tallest of them all, otherworldly with his silvery-white hair, pointed ears, and exquisite beauty. Everything about him screams *warrior*, and I feel a flutter of something that should be fear, but isn't. The longer I watch, the more I see that he's actually holding himself back to make it seem like he is only winning by a margin.

After all the young men have been thoroughly trounced, they pepper Rahk with questions and beg him to demonstrate his unusual techniques to them. A few of them have bruised egos and slink off to pout elsewhere—Alsbee being one of them—but most of them seem like good sports, and eagerly accept instruction, asking questions and watching as the prince demonstrates.

"So, what is it like being a servant for a fae?"

I startle out of my shoes—not having noticed someone sidling up to me. *Lord Boreham.* I swear under my breath, tensing to run. Honestly, I don't even know why he's here, because his fine doublet and velvet pants suggest he isn't here to join the others.

I step to one side, putting distance between us and keeping my face downcast. *Please don't recognize me.* I pretend I didn't hear him.

"Will a little coin loosen your tongue?" Boreham presses, smiling like a cat in my periphery. "I understand. Money is hard to come by. Especially for one in your station."

I bristle, even while relief nearly makes my shoulders sag. *He doesn't recognize me.*

"Nat."

The prince's voice makes me flinch. He's standing right in front of me, and I didn't even notice his approach. *So observant, Kat. Quit losing your wits!*

"Master," I croak. It takes me a second to drag my gaze all the way up to his face. Several long strands of his hair have come free, and they blow lightly around his face in the spring breeze.

There is something almost electrifying about watching someone best over a dozen men in their prime . . . and then shift their focus to you.

I've outsmarted him twice now, I think with a plume of satisfaction unfurling in my belly. *Thrice, if counting the disguise.*

"Would you like a turn?" Rahk asks.

I stare blankly at him. A turn for what? A turn for—

Oh.

He means . . . he means . . .

"Definitely not," I blurt.

He smirks. "You said you wanted to go to war. You'll need a few skills to stay alive."

Lord Boreham has vanished, almost as if he was never here. I lick my dry lips, setting my brow in a stubborn line.

So Rahk insists, "You say you want to help take the burden off your sister. If you could defend yourself—and her, even—that would be a great peace of mind to her."

I scowl at him. I don't want to go to that pit and have all those eyes on me as I fumble around over some fighting techniques. I have nimble feet and I'm strong for my size, but my advantage as the Ivy Mask comes from avoiding confrontations that could get me killed. I'm not stupid enough to think I can go against a fae warrior several centuries older than me and escape with my life.

But Nat would want to learn.

So I force myself to follow him.

He offers me a hand into the pit, but I opt for a graceless scramble over the fence instead.

Rahk stands next to me, bracing his feet wide. "It all starts with the feet. Your strength and power come from properly engaging your feet."

I try to mimic him, my toes splayed on the dirt. He kneels in front of me. I almost take a step back, but his warm hand comes around my ankle, positioning my feet for me.

"Like this," he says. "See how solid you are now?"

I do not feel solid. Not with him so close. But I try to focus as he springs upright.

"You should know how to land a good blow," Rahk continues. He comes to my side and mimes a slow version of a blow into the empty air. "This is the motion. This is how your fist should be arranged."

I follow his example and give my own mimed punch.

"Just like that. Now faster and harder. Yes, exactly. You've got power in that blow!" Rahk grins, pleased.

I never thought a Nothril prince would be . . . *enthusiastic* about anything. Except meting out death, perhaps.

He shows me several different ways to dodge a blow. We go slowly, his fist coming toward me and giving me time to step left or right, duck, or retreat. This is starting to feel very useful for my raids.

"You're a natural," he declares.

I know his praise is only to encourage me—he's not impressed with my abilities at all—but I find myself wanting to please him even so. I throw more energy and passion into following his instructions.

"Excellent!" he cries as my blows land across the flattened palm he offers me. "Use that back leg to stabilize you. Yes, just like that!"

I pause, breathing hard, but I'm smiling. Then I get back into position.

"Don't tuck your hips so much," says the prince, coming round behind me. "You can engage the muscles running down the back of your legs better if you aren't tucked. It'll give your movements greater power."

"Tucked? What do you mean tucked?"

His hands land on my hips. I nearly leap away in shock but manage to do nothing but stiffen. "Easy," he says gently, his voice dropping. "Don't tense up so much. Relax. True power comes from being open and letting your strength flow out, rather than forcing it." He grips my hips and pulls them back and up. I try to force away the heat in my cheeks. "Now, fill your ribs and try to expand them to every side. Your feet, hips, and ribs are all key areas to supporting your body and allowing your strength to flow."

His hands start to go to my ribs, and my mind turns white-hot at the thought of him discovering my binding. Quickly, before he can touch me, I place my own hands at my ribs and do as he instructs, filling them wide.

"Excellent job," the prince praises again, stepping away from me. His eyes somehow seem a shade darker than before. "Now we can start practicing in earnest."

He takes his place opposite me. I gulp. His mouth quirks. "We'll go slowly."

I nod, face him, and take up my stance.

"Kat!" someone cries.

My attention breaks. I instinctively turn toward my name—

And the next thing I know, I'm hitting the edge of the fence, my head snapping back. Pain roars to life in my face a second later, followed by a terrible pressure and something hot and sticky sliding down my cheek.

"Nat!" Rahk is there a second later, crouching over me, horror stitched into every line of his expression. "You were supposed to dodge that!"

"I thought someone called for me," I say stupidly, my face throbbing and my back pulsing from hitting the fence. I turn to the side, only to see a stray cat dart across the yard and disappear.

The prince's shirt is off a second later, and he presses it to my face. It comes away red.

I stare at the blood in shock.

He mutters something under his breath, flicks his wrist, and returns the shirt to my face. The shirt is shockingly cold. He—he used magic to make it cold!

He's talking to me, I realize belatedly.

"I'm so sorry. I never meant to hit you. Great Kings, I hit you *very* hard. Are you alright? Can you hear me? Nat!" He gives my arm a little shake. My attention snaps to him.

"What?" I taste copper.

Running footsteps come up behind me. Rahk looks up and shakes his head. "I've got him. Come on, let's get you home. To think you've only just recovered from poison! I never should have pushed you this hard."

He reaches for me, hands going to my armpits to lift me up. I can't let him carry me. I can't let him feel that much of my body—there is no way he wouldn't realize at once how I've lied to him. My brain might be rattled, but I can deal with it later.

I knock his hand away and grab hold of the fence to pull myself up.

"Nat—"

The world spins once I'm on my feet. I hold on to the fence to keep from falling. With my other hand, I press his cold shirt to my swollen face. At least now no one will recognize me as Lady Vandermore! I choke back a hysterical laugh.

Then I face the prince. "Again."

He's on one knee still, as though he means to propose marriage. I fight back another delirious giggle and repeat firmly, "Again. Let's keep practicing. I assume we ought to go over dodging once more?"

Laughter surrounds us. I startle and glance around, only to realize most of the men in the place hurried over in concern the moment I was hit.

"The lad's fine!" one guffaws.

"He's got the skull of an anvil!"

"Brings a new meaning to the mind being a steel trap, eh?"

I want to laugh along with them, even though the barest chuckle makes my head feel like it is splitting in two. But the prince is staring at me with such an iron focus, it's almost as if he's angry I would suggest such a thing.

"We're leaving," he growls, his voice low and cold. When I start to protest, he comes very close to my face and says, "At once."

I clamber over the fence, mopping up the blood still seeping out of my nose, and try to move quickly despite my dizziness so the prince won't decide I need to be carried. A few men clap me on the back and give me wishes for my speedy recovery or proclaim I'm as tough as nails. I'm reminded once again why I've tried so hard to avoid them and their marriage proposals. Most of them seem to be genuinely good-hearted people and I simply cannot risk being tempted to give up my fortune.

I sway. The prince's hand latches onto my upper arm. He doesn't move too fast for me, but we quickly exit the sparring yard.

He doesn't speak a word to me the entire way home.

CHAPTER 24

KAT

"MINOR CONCUSSION. REST day and day. No better—me," pronounces the doctor.

Rahk looks to where I sit on the settee in his foyer, his magicked shirt still pressed to my face.

"I think he's saying to rest two days and if I'm not better, to summon him again," I say dully.

The doctor nods. Rahk flicks his attention to Edvear, who produces the coin to pay for the doctor as he leaves. Mary is at my side the next minute. She kneels on the rug, tsking her tongue and trying to get a look at the swelling on my face. "How can you be such a boy? Every time I turn around, you've gotten yourself injured again!"

The prince sent for Mary the moment we got home, and I could not be gladder to see her. It takes the edge off the radiating pain through my skull.

Rahk stands by the door, watching us, arms crossed over his chest and I'd almost think the emotion that flashes across his near-inscrutable face is guilt. "I'll be in my study. If the boy needs anything, send for me or Edvear."

"Thank you, my lord," says Mary.

We wait until there is no chance of his hearing, and then Mary hisses: "What were you doing? You're supposed to be staying out of trouble! And Charity Finch tells me you were bedridden with *poison* only a few days ago!"

"I thought someone called my name—my real name. I thought Lord Boreham had recognized me!"

"He was there?" she demands.

"And Lord Cranswick and Sir Alsbee and—"

Mary covers her face with her hand. "I cannot decide if you're the most or *least* lucky person I've ever encountered."

She helps me to my own room, where she shuts the door and helps me change. She gives me a new chest binding so she can clean the old, browning one. The moment we peel it off my skin, I take in a deep lungful of air. I've gotten so used to the garment I forgot what it feels like to be free. But we cannot dally, no matter how glorious those few seconds of freedom are, and I'm once again tightly bound up in the new garment.

"How are things at home?" I ask in a hushed tone, after updating her on all of my recent misadventures.

"Lord Boreham has stopped by several times," Mary replies grimly. "He and Agatha were yelling at each other in the parlor only last night. It was horrible. Bridget and Edith come up with every excuse to stay out of the house as much as they can, and then Agatha noticed and demanded to know if they were *sullying* their reputation with men. Bridget cried for an entire day after that accusation, saying she *wished* there were men trying to sully her reputation. Edith took it better, but she spent the day drilling her harpsichord again—a punishment for the entire household."

I wince. "Poor girls."

That night, after Mary leaves, the prince returns from an errand and knocks on my door. I shoot up in my bed—only to regret the movement when my head starts pulsing like a drum—and make sure my shirt is pulled all the way down as he enters.

He has a wrapped package under one arm. Without a word, he hands it to me.

Curiously, I take the package and unwrap it. It crinkles loudly in the quiet. When the wrapping falls away, a small round tin sits in my palm. "Is this—" I tear off the lid. Then I stop.

There are the pieces. The tall and goofy looking Fool. The green-painted minions and the opposing, red-painted ones. Rahk's version has silver and gold minions, but I like the bright colors better.

"Fool's Circle!" I cry happily, grinning as I pull the pieces out so I can inspect the board.

"It's a miniature version. It is easier to carry in your pocket. It was hard to find, but I hope you'll enjoy it."

It's an apology.

His distraught voice from only a few days ago echoes in my mind: *"Please, Nat, please accept my thanks and please accept my apology. It upsets me that you seem disinclined to do so."*

A strong part of me wants to argue against him giving me this gift, no matter how much I love the gift, but that voice makes me swallow my words. I'll only make him feel worse if I refuse to accept this.

"I'd gladly get punched ten times over for one of these!" I cry, instead of protesting, and dump all the pieces on my bed and arrange them.

The prince gives a rueful twist of his lips. "Next time, you can just ask for what you want. No need to be punched to get it."

A new piece catches my eye. It isn't as large as the Fool, but neither is it as small as the minions. It has a painted brown cape and a hood. "What is this?"

"It's a variant. That piece is called the Thief. You can play it the original way, or if you want something new, you can add this piece."

"Is that in my book?" I slide the book from under my cot and start flipping through it. "I haven't—*oh,* here it is! At the end of the book. I haven't gotten this far. We should try—"

The door shuts before I can finish my sentence. A muffled, "Sleep. You need extra rest. Your master commands it," comes through the door.

At first, I shoot a glare at the shadows of feet beneath the door. Then, when they've disappeared, I inspect my present again. My smile cannot be suppressed. I set both of my treasures by my bedside, my throbbing head forgotten, and I stare at them until it's so dark I can see nothing but the whites of the Fool's eyes.

RAHK

I will never forget the sound of Nat hitting the fence.

She might have forgiven me, especially after the gift, but I will never forgive myself. Though it wasn't my full strength, I hit hard.

I slump into the chair at my desk and lean my face on one palm.

What am I going to do with her?

She isn't a spy of the queen's—I'm sure of that by now. She's far too harmless and good to have been sent to hurt me. I'd bet my blade that she isn't here for any reason to do with me. She is hiding from something, and the estate of an unknown fae was an easy place to do it.

But *who* is she hiding from?

The temptation grows stronger every day to pull her aside and tell her I know she's a woman and make her tell me why she is here. I want to know if she is in danger, if she needs my protection. I've tried to indicate in every way that I can without words that I know her secret. Either she doesn't want to acknowledge it, or she truly believes she has fooled me.

In the end, however, the reason I don't ask is because—for some inexplicable reason—I want her to *choose* to confide in me. She's made me trust her. I want her to trust me. Maybe it is because I want to show her that, even though she is an orphan because of Faerieland, not all of us hate humans. Not all of us enjoy seeing them degraded. And that, no matter what Court I hail from, I am truly sorry for what she has lost.

But she won't trust me now. Now that I've struck her.

My attention falls to the chest of fae medicines Edvear brought back from Faerieland. Is there something here that will help a human's concussion? I press my thumb to the lock mechanism. It clicks. I flip open the lid.

There, on top of the various jars and bottles, is a sealed missive. The stamp on the seal is of a star and fang. The Nothril crest.

Dear brother,

Lady Nothril is making me write to you even though you were just here. I don't know why she doesn't just do it herself—selfish miscreant. She wants me to remind you about Mirror Tide coming soon. You are expected to be there, of course. Ideally with the Ivy Mask, because I. Do. Not. Want. To. Go. To. The. Human. World. So bring the creature, and we'll make a spectacle of him at the ball. You know, the whole "deter others from rebellion" and "there is no such thing as hope" spiel our lovely parents adore so much.

I don't tell you this because I like you, but yes, despite her best efforts, Pavi is still alive and well. There, now will you be a good big brother and catch the vigilante, so I don't have to come?

Now Lady Nothril should leave me alone. Finally.

Pelarusa

I release a low exhalation, my eyelids shuttering. What am I doing, spending my mental energy worrying about my servant girl? Catching the Ivy Mask is my highest priority—far above even Ash's task. Pavi's life is at stake, and the Ivy Mask is proving more formidable than I anticipated.

But I do check my medicines for something for Nat. I grunt when I find nothing, and then shut the lid of the chest with a click.

CHAPTER 25

KAT

THE QUEEN'S LUNCHEON is not in Ashbourne, but in Bellmast, a city on the coast a day's journey away by carriage.

Mama and Father took me to the coast a few times when I was a child, and while I wait to hear if I will accompany the prince on his journey, I am a bundle of desperation to go and desperation *not* to go. What if it's nothing like I remembered, and that piece of my parents is gone? What if it's everything I remembered, and I will be flooded with how much I miss them? What if the prince sees through my attempts to hide my emotions? Is it feasible that Nat's parents would have taken him? Or will I have to make something else up?

My complex tangle of emotions isn't unraveled when I overhear the prince telling Edvear: "I plan to leave the boy here. I wouldn't want to take him away from his sister." That night, I am tempted to silently cry my disappointment into my pillow, but I roll around the Fool from my Fool's Circle set in my fingers instead, letting the sharpened parts of it—its cap, its long nose, its pointy shoes—bring pain to my palm when I squeeze it.

The next morning, when I serve the prince's breakfast, he asks, "Would you like to come to Bellmast with us?"

I nearly drop the tray I'm holding. "Come with you? But—but I thought . . . Well, I overheard you speaking to Edvear, and you said you were going to leave me here!"

He lifts his brows. "An honest eavesdropper you are, Nat. Yes, I was planning on it. Upon further consideration, I realized it would be better if I had a human servant with me. Someone who knows more of the culture than Edvear or I do. I will let you decide what you'd like."

All this time, I thought I didn't know which I preferred. The second he gives me a choice, however, the words are pouring out of me. "I want to go with you, Master!"

He smiles, pleased. "Then you shall. Pack your things and help Edvear pack mine. I'll be out the rest of the day. We will leave at dawn tomorrow."

The question—of where he is going—is on the tip of my tongue. But I've learned to be a good servant, so I swallow it back.

The other servants and I work until well after dark to prepare for the journey. It is almost midnight when I finally fall into bed, utterly spent. Hours later, I'm woken by the shuffle of boots in the prince's room.

He was hunting for me again.

Despite my shiver, my mouth twists upward. He will catch me one day, but that day is not today. A dangerous sort of thrill shoots through my blood—thrill that, if left unchained, will get me killed, and yet I cannot fully suppress it. He lives with me, and yet he still doesn't know it's me. I roll over and pull my blankets over my head and let my warm breath fill the cavernous space until it's almost impossible to breathe.

The next morning, I come out in my normal clothes, packed and ready, only for Edvear to order me back to change.

"I have the nicer clothes in my bag!" I say, holding it up. "I don't want to get them messed up while traveling!"

Edvear holds up a firm finger pointed back at my room. "You are representing the staff of your master. This is why you have two sets of your nicer uniform. Change."

I swallow my grumbles and obey. When I reemerge, dressed in starched black breeches, a crisp white tunic, a black overcoat that scratches, and silly shoes with buckles, I feel more uncomfortable and self-conscious than ever. The pants are tighter, and I'm constantly afraid someone will look at my legs and hips and decide they're a little too feminine. My chest binding feels especially oppressive. I want to readjust and wiggle it around, so it doesn't dig into my ribs so much.

I march into the kitchen, hating Edvear's insistence of my wardrobe, and grab a freshly baked cranberry scone, two patties of sausage, and a glass of milk for my breakfast.

"You look quite dashing today," teases Clifford while scraping mud off his boots at the door under the watchful eye of Mrs. Banks.

I scowl at him, and everyone—save Mrs. Banks—laughs. I intend to eat quickly and then run out to ensure everything is properly loaded into the carriage. If only I could ride Bartholomew instead of sitting in a stuffy carriage all day!

A hand gently tracing my arm makes me nearly drop and break my glass of milk.

It's Becky, come to sit on the bar stool next to me. She almost never leaves her seat against the wall with her basket of mending. "This stitching is very fine," she says, running her fingers up to inspect my shoulder. Her cheeks are pink, and she is decidedly *not looking* at me.

If I were actually a boy, I would think nothing of it except irritation. But I am very much not a boy, and I know flirting when I see it. I cast a helpless glance at Charity, who rolls her eyes and bangs her wooden spoon on the edge of the pot.

Becky yanks her hand back but persists. "When you are finished wearing them, may I borrow your clothes? To study the stitching better?"

That's enough. I down my glass of milk and stuff my mouth with the rest of my scone and sausage and shove to my feet.

"Becky, help me carry this to the sink," says Charity.

I turn to leave and nearly spit all my food back out.

The prince stands in the doorway of the kitchen, smirking at me and Becky. "Master," I garble around scone. I clamp a hand over my mouth so no food escapes, bow, and run outside before anyone can stop me.

The prince only follows me and once I've swallowed the rest of my breakfast, says blandly, "I was coming to see if you were ready, only to find you dashing in your uniform." When I make no reply, furiously red-cheeked, he adds, "I hope I didn't interrupt anything. Or are girls still unappealing at your age?"

In lieu of an answer, I whack him with my bag. Immediately, I yank it back, horrified as I blurt, "I shouldn't have done that! I am thoughtless and foolish, Master!"

But the prince is laughing as he climbs into the carriage, his dark eyes sparkling and his white hair catching the earliest glints of sunrise.

The road is long and boring. The carriage rattles so much we cannot play Fool's Circle, and any attempts at conversation soon fizzle out. I'm sore and bored out of my wits by the time we finally arrive at an inn in Bellmast for the night.

The sun hangs low in the sky when we arrive. As the prince's only attendant, I spring into action with the footman, wrestling his trunk off the back of the carriage. It lands harder on the ground than I intended. I cringe, feeling Rahk's eyes on me, and hoist it up.

But he is at my side the next minute, grabbing the trunk in one hand.

"My lord!" I cry, attempting to wrestle the trunk out of his grip. "I must take this for you! You must let me serve you!"

"I do not like things being grabbed from me," Rahk says.

I let go at once and step back. "Forgive me, Master, I—" I trail off when I find him smirking down at me. I slam my mouth shut.

Rahk's smirk isn't like Sir Alsbee's: devious and with a hint of cruelty. Neither is it like Lord Oliver's, which is just shy of a grin. Rahk's is subtle, and it is easy to miss. One half of his mouth remains in that unreadable flat line, but the very corner of the other side lifts slightly. There is a dry-humored amusement in that lift.

I turn my back on that amusement and gather the rest of the load before following him inside the inn. I give one forlorn glance toward the shoreline I can see between buildings—it's so close!—with the sun sinking into the horizon, and force myself to be satisfied with the salty air playing with my hair. It smells like happiness. I miss running on the beach and throwing myself into the waves despite Mama's anxiety that I'd be dragged away in a riptide.

The inn is lovely, with a pristine emerald carpet leading to a wide, grand staircase. The rooms are on the second floor, gold-inlaid doors visible behind the balcony rails. It occurs to me as I walk in that I should be the one getting the key from the innkeeper—but Rahk has already obtained it, and strides toward the staircase.

I'm such a terrible servant, I think shamelessly, as I consider how glad I am to not have to carry Rahk's trunk up an entire flight of stairs.

"The innkeeper said there is a door on the other side of the room that leads to the servants' staircase and kitchens," Rahk tells me as we reach the line of doors. He pulls the brass key from his pocket. "You can fetch us supper that way."

"Yes, my lord."

He unlocks the door and pushes it open.

It suddenly occurs to me that this room might not have a small adjoining room for me. It's a large space, with its color scheme of sea green and sky blue, canopied bed, separate bathing chamber, and living area with chairs around a table. There is one door at the far side of the room. I bolt toward it in desperate hope, only to open it and find an outside staircase that leads to another door on the ground floor.

It is confirmed: there is no separate room for me.

How on *earth* am I supposed to keep my gender hidden when I have not a shred of privacy?

The prince shows no sign of thinking anything of the arrangement. He deposits his trunk beside the wardrobe, pulls a small book out of his breast pocket and settles himself at the table to read. A moment later, he pulls a small blue vial out of a different pocket. *Ollea.* He swipes a drop under his nose and the line between his brows eases away.

I dump my own bag in the bathing chamber to keep it out of Rahk's way.

There isn't even a servant's cot. Am I expected to sleep in the copper tub in the bathing chamber?

Well, I am *not* going to bring attention to the problem and ask about it.

There is one window, facing east, so none of the dying sunlight makes its way into the room. I light the candles above the fireplace and beside the bed. Maybe if I keep myself busy, I won't have time to work myself into a tizzy about this arrangement.

"Shall I fetch your supper, Master?" I ask.

He looks up from his book. Swiftly, his eyes drop from my face to the hands I didn't know I was wringing, before moving upward again. "Is something the matter?"

I shove my hands behind my back. "Not at all! I simply wanted to know if you were hungry, or if you'd rather I waited. . .?"

He glances around the room, as though in search of what is causing my anxiety. His face clears suddenly. "They did not leave a cot in here for you, did they?"

"I am *very* comfortable sleeping on the floor," I lie quickly.

He frowns, then waves his hand. "Sleep in the bed. I did not plan to rest tonight."

"Me? Sleep in the bed? But Master, I'm your servant! I dare not—"

"You dare not do what I say?" Rahk replies, that subtle smirk of his returning.

I bow quickly. "I will do whatever you say, Master."

"Then I order you to sleep in the bed and to get good rest. I won't have you being useless tomorrow because you weren't able to sleep."

"But won't you be useless tomorrow, my lord?" I say, and then realizing how it sounds, quickly add: "If you don't sleep."

"Hopefully not entirely useless," Rahk replies dryly, shutting his book with a snap and leaning forward. "Why don't you go fetch supper instead of arguing with me?"

"Because you didn't tell me whether you wanted it or not," I answer. "I will gladly go get it now."

His warm chuckle echoes in my ears as I scamper out the door in search of his meal.

The kitchen is livelier than expected, with inn staff preparing exquisite trays of food with gleaming silverware and embroidered napkins. I let out a grunt when I pick it up. That is one *heavy* tray. I pray to all the saints as I heft it up that I will not drop it on the way back to the room.

Just outside the kitchen are three servant boys, sitting on an empty staircase. I wouldn't think anything of them, except they stare at me as I walk past them. One of them is a freckled redhead, while the other two could be brothers with how similar they look. The three of them wear uniforms similar to mine, except their suspenders hang loose to their knees and the redhead has his shirt tails untucked.

They have a mischievous, no-good twinkle in their eyes as I pass them. They seem to all be around thirteen years of age and despite their youth, are taller than me. I keep my eyes fixed ahead and find the staircase to Rahk's room. Surely these boys cannot tell that I am a woman, right? Young boys are not supposed to be perceptive, yet they stare at me like I am their prey.

I make it safely to Rahk's room and serve him his meal. He regards the tray, a brief frown flickering over his features. "Where is your food?"

They didn't have trays for servant suppers, and I highly doubted I was supposed to take one of the fancy ones for myself.

I open my mouth to respond, but before the words leave, he takes one of the side dishes of two pillowy-soft rolls and sets one aside. Then he fills the plate from his own, giving me the chicken leg quarter, one of the rolls, a generous serving of steaming, spiced yams, and the entire plate of cherry tart.

"My lord!" I cry when he sets the plate before me. "This is more than half of your meal!"

Rahk only lifts one brow. "Sit and eat."

If I protest, he will ask me why I do not obey him. Restraining my frustrated whimper that he is treating me far better than he ought, I plop into the chair across from him and begin eating. The food is delicious, and I didn't even realize how hungry I'd grown. My consternation sweeps away as though with a wind. I devour the meal with zeal.

"Excellent job," Rahk says with a smirk when I clean my plate. "You have pleased your master greatly."

I glare at him—a mistake—but I earn a chuckle, not a reprimand. I get up to take the empty dishes back to the kitchen. The air is colder now with how dark it has grown, and I shiver in my uncomfortable shirt and breeches. Will the prince sense that anything is amiss if I use the bathing chamber to change? And why does he keep being so sacrificially *kind* to me in a way that feels out of place and disconcerting? In some ways, his kindness is more confusing than his capriciousness. What sort of a fae prince offers his food and his bed to his servant without expecting anything else in return?

And a *Nothril* prince, for that matter?

"Hey! Psst!"

I startle out of my thoughts as I leave the kitchen empty-handed. It's the three boys from earlier. They aren't on the staircase anymore, but hang around the corner of the kitchen, away from the servants' entrance.

"Come on!" one of the brunette boys calls, waving his hand for me to follow them.

"I have to return to my master," I say, immediately on-guard.

"Is he going to beat you?"

"No."

"Then come on! We've got a game, and we need a fourth player!"

The mention of a game perks my interest. I quickly shove it away and keep walking. A second later, all three boys block my path. I try to step around them, and they move to block me again.

"Let me past," I growl.

The redhead—the tallest of the group—folds his arms across his chest. "We need a fourth player."

"It'll be fast," one of the others says. "Your master will not realize you've been gone."

"I shouldn't—" I start to say.

"Aw, come on." One throws his arm around my neck, making me flinch, and forcibly pulls me toward the corner of the building. He's surprisingly strong. "We just need a fourth player. We've been waiting for hours to find one."

"Where are your masters?" I ask, changing my tactics. "Don't they miss you?"

"Nah, they're old and they go to bed before the sun goes down. We've got hours to kill tonight."

"Fine," I say, when they clearly won't take no for an answer. "But just one game. Then I must leave."

The boys holler in triumph and all but drag me to the base of a tree where they sit in a circle and beckon me to follow suit. I sit in the dirt and spare a thought for how Edvear will rebuke me for getting my nice breeches dusty.

"That is Jack," says one of the boys, gesturing to the redhead who shuffles a deck of cards. "I'm Finn, and that's my brother Arthur. What's your name?"

"Nat."

Arthur pulls something from behind a raised tree root as Jack deals the cards between us. My eyes bug when I see what it is. "Is that—"

"Whiskey?" Arthur says. "Yes. Don't you dare tell anyone. We worked *very* hard to get this, and you're not going to ruin it."

"If you do," says Jack, finishing his dealing and sitting back on his haunches. "We'll steal your clothes, and your master will be furious."

Steal my clothes? They don't even know how dire of a threat that is. I shut my lips tight, suddenly afraid that if I try to leave, they'll dogpile me and do exactly what they've threatened. My voice comes out a little shrill as I ask, "What are we playing?"

"Crowns," Finn replies.

"I'm terrible at this game!" I cry.

"That should work in your favor," laughs Arthur. "Whenever you win a trick, you have to take a swig of the whiskey."

I get up. "I did not agree to a—"

Arthur and Finn lean forward and grab the edges of my trousers and yank. I barely grab the waistband and hold on tight before disaster ensues.

"Fine! Fine!" I growl, sitting back down. "I'll play your stupid drinking game! And I won't tell our masters and I will lose every trick on purpose!"

"I told you we should have gotten Count Buchard's servant boy instead," says Finn under his breath. "Even he would be better than this stick in the mud!"

"He is a tattle," says Jack. "But Nat here isn't a tattle. Right?"

I huff irritably and pick up my cards. One game—that was the deal. I'll play this game, lose it on purpose, and then get out of here.

As we begin, it quickly becomes apparent that I'm not good enough at Crowns to lose every trick. I waste all my low cards at the beginning, and before I know it, I have nothing but high cards for several rounds.

"Your trick," says Jack with a toothy grin, sliding the pile of cards my way.

"Drink up!" says Finn, shoving the bottle of whiskey into my hands.

"I really shouldn't drink," I whine. "And I don't like whiskey."

"Stop being a blubbering *girl* and drink!"

I'm acting like a girl, am I? *Fine*. I grab the bottle, uncork the top, brace myself, and take a swig. It is like drinking liquid fire, which burns all the way down. I cough and sputter as Finn pulls it away, laughing hysterically.

"He drinks like a girl!"

"What is that supposed to mean?" I demand furiously, blinking against the fire that has somehow made its way up to my eyes.

"You act like it's going to bite you!" laughs Finn.

"You've got to be the whiskey's master, not let it be master over you," says Jack.

"Don't worry," I reply. "I'm just letting it *think* it has mastered me before I destroy it. You've got to let the whiskey put its guard down. Don't you know anything about drinking?"

The three of them stare at me in surprise, then seem to silently contemplate if this might be a valid approach to alcohol. I would smack them upside the head if I thought I could get away with it.

Then it's my turn. I look at my hand and curse violently. The boys laugh and shove the bottle of whiskey back to me.

"Drink it! Drink it!" they chant, and then nearly roll around on the ground in their laughter at the way I cough and sputter the drink down. "Make it put its guard down!"

We lay out our cards for the next round. I win the trick yet again.

CHAPTER 26

RAHK

NAT IS TAKING a *very* long time to deliver the dishes to the kitchen. I tell myself to stay focused on this book I'm trying to read on Harbright's history—it is mind-numbingly dry—but as the night darkens and the shadows of my flickering candles lengthen, I grow more worried. I don't want to be overprotective when everything is almost certainly fine. She is probably tending to one of her various feminine needs that she avoids me knowing about. I want her to have her privacy.

Still, the sharpness of my concern makes reading impossible. I give her half of an hour. When she still isn't returned, I regret applying *ollea* when I entered this room—it deadens my ability to scent her. I push up on the table, rising to my feet, slamming the book shut.

Privacy or no, I need to make sure she's safe. And if I invade her privacy at the wrong moment, perhaps it'll make her finally confide in me. Maybe then I can finally find out what is wrong, and how I can help her.

Maybe, at last, I can learn her real name.

I'm not even halfway to the door before the scuffle of shoes up wooden stairs reaches my ears. My awareness prickles, my relief almost frightening in its intensity—until I realize her gait is not what it usually is. In fact, it might not be her at all.

I swing open the door just as a loud thump and grunt burst from beyond. And there is Nat—collapsed in the stairwell, her arms and head on the floor while the rest of her body is arranged awkwardly across lower stairs.

"Nat!" In two strides, I'm at her side. My blood turns into a dark, lethal rhythm I know so well. I grab her upper arm and pull her upright. "Nat! Are you hurt?" If she has gotten hurt again because of me, I will never forgive myself. I scan her body for signs of injury and find none.

Then she belches. I stare at her, shocked, but only for a second. My lids shutter. "Great Kings help me, you're drunk! You little fool!"

I pull her head to my shoulder, getting one arm under her ribs and another beneath her legs before I hoist her up. I carry her inside our room, kick the door shut, and drop her onto the seashell-colored bedspread. "You were alone for thirty minutes. How in the Mountains of Ildrid did you come to be drunk?"

She giggles, rolling to her side. "I cannot hold my alcohol. Not at all!"

"Clearly!" I reply with a huff, marching to the door and throwing the bolt. "Where did you get alcohol?"

She mimes sealing her lips and tossing away the key. "I'm not a tattletale."

I stand there beside the bed, one hand on my hip, the other one dragging down my face. "I'm not asking so I can go punish someone. It's just . . . This isn't like you!"

I forget she's supposed to be a twelve-year-old boy. It's impossible to think of it when she's giggling in that very distinctively girlish way. And when she grins up at me, I find it impossible to believe that I bought her disguise for the first few minutes of our acquaintance.

"Am I drunk?" she asks, her arms flung wide on the bed, her body at a crooked angle.

"Very."

"Oops." She covers her mouth with her hand. "I didn't want to get drunk."

"What were you trying to do?"

"Lose a game."

I cross my arms over my chest. "Did you succeed?"

"I lost the game. But I won a lot of tricks. It wasn't good."

A drinking game with other servants. That is . . . a choice, I suppose. Not one I thought she'd make, though she is not the type to walk away from a challenge. She will have a killer of a migraine tomorrow morning while we get ready for the queen's luncheon.

I wave my hand and march back to the table. "Go to sleep. The alcohol will wear off during the night."

I drag back my chair and drop into it with a sigh, refusing to look over to where Nat is lying on the bed. I open my book and stare unseeing at the page. What an unexpected turn for this evening! Did she forget she was playing the part of a young boy? Who should *not* be drinking? She has a tendency toward chaos, but this is *not* the sort of chaos I thought she'd—

There's a tap on my elbow. I look up.

Nat stands right next to me, her face flushed, her hair standing out in every direction.

"Go to bed," I say sternly.

She holds up her hands, pressed together like in prayer, her eyes rounded and pleading. "Please, Master, there is something I must tell you."

My heart skips a beat. I hope my voice doesn't sound as gruff to her as it does to me when I reply, "What is it?"

She wraps both her arms around one of mine. I startle sharply and only barely restrain my instinct to toss her across the room. "Nat—"

She brings her face toward mine. My eyes widen. I find myself going very still. I search for her pleasant scent in the air, but I can only detect a muted thread of it. Why did I have to apply that *ollea*?

The turn of my thoughts shocks me. How could I think like this? I'm glad she cannot read my mind and see what a fool I am.

"It's a secret, my lord," she whispers into my ear.

I fight to keep my composure with her so near, my hands fisting on the armrests of my chair. "A secret?" It comes out in a rasp.

What *is* this? What is with me?

She wobbles slightly, her grip on my arm tightening as her lips brush the shell of my ear. "Oops. Sorry. I am a little dizzy."

You need to lie down and sleep, I almost say as she leans into me, but withhold it for fear she'll forget to tell me her *secret*.

"I have a secret," she says again, clutching tighter to me. I resist the urge to catch her by the waist to steady her—and then immediately give in when she pitches forward. Her hands brace on my elbows as I hold her, her face coming close to mine.

Our eyes lock. Her mouth is open, her pretty eyes catching the flickers of the candle above the fireplace. "Prince Rahk."

I flinch slightly at the title. I'm the one who told her I was a prince. Her use of it still strikes me as very strange. "Nat," I say gently, "you need to go lie down on the bed. I don't want you to fall and hurt yourself."

"I'm a woman," she blurts suddenly.

My shoulders sag in relief. *Finally,* the truth is out. Finally, she confides in me. Now I can get to the bottom of this ridiculousness. I smile slightly. "I know."

Her mouth drops open even more. "You *know*? How long have you known?"

She seems to be drifting closer and closer to me. I swallow and find my voice with difficulty. "From the beginning."

Her punch to the shoulder is not what I expect, and if she was sober enough to aim properly, it might have had enough gusto behind it to hurt a little. "Fae," she spits. "You all are so annoying."

I lift one eyebrow. "Last I checked, Edvear and I were the only fae you know."

She blinks. That is, unmistakably, a bolt of fear that just sliced into her gaze.

I silently kick myself. "Forgive me. After what happened to your mother, you must have a very negative view of us. As you should."

I don't realize how close she has drifted until her knee presses into my leg. I hold very still, caught in a debate over whether I should pick her up and deposit her back in bed where she should be in hopes that she'll get the rest she needs—or if I should stay here and wait to see what she does.

"I do hate fae," she whispers. "But I don't hate you."

"High praise," I murmur.

"I want to hate you," she clarifies. "I want to very badly. It's just that the longer I'm with you, the less I hate you. Except when you made me do all those pointless tasks. It was *so* inappropriate for me to rub your back!"

The resurgence of that memory brings with it a new emotion. It is not *quite* embarrassment, and yet heat crawls up the back of my neck—something I've never experienced before.

"Aside from that, you've been kind to me," she continues. "I don't really know what to think of it. I don't know why you do it."

"Because I care about you." Why would I not care about her? She is a diligent servant who makes me feel less alone in this world away from my world, and she entertains me. I also owe her a life debt. Of course I want her to be healthy, well-fed, and rested.

I can almost taste iron from the lie I tell myself right now.

"Do you?" Her lips quirk slightly. Then suddenly, she darts forward and presses a quick kiss to my cheek.

I freeze, too stunned to react. Too surprised by pleasure blossoming in my chest.

"You terrify me," she breathes. "I'm always afraid you're going to kill me."

Those words yank me out of my stupor. "Kill you?" The idea is revolting to my very core. I've killed often, violently, and without apology. But the thought of hurting Nat makes me want to crawl out of my own skin. "Why would I kill you?"

"Because I'm a human. And because I'm a woman."

I lift one eyebrow. "Those are hardly crimes worthy of death."

"Some fae might disagree."

I acquiesce to the point with a nod. "But I am not like those who disagree. I will not hurt you. As long as you are under my roof, you are under my protection."

"Promise?"

"I promise."

She wrinkles her nose. "I'm still afraid of you."

"Then I will endeavor to ease your fears whenever I can."

Her weight has shifted and settled, my awareness of her ripping away my ability to breathe. I've barely moved a single muscle, but now she's sitting on my knees. Leaning over me with such a focused intensity I wonder how *anyone* is fooled by her disguise. She doesn't look at all like a boy. Her sharp nose and chin are softened by her freckles and full lips, and the eyes I once thought rather plain now devour my attention. I keep my hand firmly on her waist to keep her from falling.

Her face drifts above mine. Her eyes wander over my features, lingering on my mouth. As though she is trying to decide if she's going to kiss me again.

If she did . . . I would let her. Great Kings curse me.

"Please," I rasp, lifting my chin toward hers. "Tell me your name. Your real name."

"My name is Kat," she replies.

Kat. I smile. "You're not very creative with your pseudonyms, are you?"

She blushes, and it pleases me very much.

"Kat," I whisper, dropping my tone. "Are you in danger? Why this disguise?"

She swallows hard. "Yes."

My stomach pitches. My brow hardens. I tighten my grip on her, pulling her closer to my chest. "Tell me how I can protect you."

"Let me remain as your servant—and don't kill me."

I roll my eyes to the ceiling. "We've already established I'm not going to kill you. But yes, of course you can remain with me. As long as you need."

My very bones demand the answer to another question: *who*. Who has frightened her so much that she resorts to these measures?

"Are you hiding from someone?" I ask. A foreign impulse to cradle her close to my heart, to physically surround her so she cannot be hurt, almost obliterates my defenses.

She looks away from me, toward the window that views the night-darkened city. Her profile is a mix of sharp and soft. She nods once.

I press harder. "Who are you hiding from?"

She doesn't answer. She's turned into a very solemn drunk.

"You don't have to tell me anything you don't want to. But I want to help you."

Her eyes flutter closed, and her weight shifts on my lap. "I'm so tired."

This conversation is over, then. I temper my disappointment at not learning more with the celebration that I've learned as much as I have.

Kat. Her name is Kat.

She slides to the floor. I watch each of her movements. She doesn't move like anyone else I've seen before: nimble, with quick but slightly unsteady feet—exacerbated by the alcohol. It is an unusual combination that I do not know what to make of, yet one I find fascinating.

Suddenly, she whirls, nearly toppling over. I sit up and instinctively reach to stop her fall, but she catches herself. The next instant, she catches my face in both her hands.

I go still.

She stares at me, intently, her lips parted. I do not breathe. My command to go to sleep dies in my throat. Her fingers are warm on my rough cheeks. She pulls me slightly toward herself, and brings her mouth to—

"Kat," I croak just before she kisses my chin. It is featherlight and soft and yet no less shocking than the first. My voice comes out in a rasp. "Please go to sleep. You are drunk and you don't want this."

"I just want to say thank you," she whispers. "You are good. I didn't think so at first, but I see it now."

Her words are even more shocking than her kiss. I don't want to think about them, what they mean to me, what they make me feel. No—I must get this Great Kings cursed woman to sleep before she makes fools out of both of us.

"To bed," I order, gently but firmly pushing her away from me. "Now."

To my relief, she obeys. I stay where I am as she slides to the bed and flops beneath the covers, fully clothed. She's asleep in seconds, her chest rising in even breaths.

A huge exhalation gusts out of me, and I sag in my chair. I cover my face with one hand. Then I release a groan. Somehow, I must get back to work after . . . *that*.

Stubbornly, I pull the boring book I was reading into my lap and stare unseeing at the page.

"Kat," I whisper, tasting the name on my tongue. My eyes flit up from my book every few minutes to linger on her. I find the longer I look at her, the more my mouth tilts down.

I'm going to find out who she's hiding from, and it'll take a great deal of self-control to not let the Nothril prince in me rip him limb from limb.

It is after midnight when I rise from the table. I snuffed out the candles hours ago, and Kat is lost to a deep sleep. She does not stir as I slip across the room and take the servants' door out.

I stay close to the shadows as I traverse the streets, heading toward a very specific destination. It does not take me long to find the city's stop for the coach. My *ollea* dose has worn off, leaving my senses sharp as I cover the area, scenting for anything familiar. The freshest scents are not familiar at all. I investigate past those, hunting for the broken trails, the ones that have been almost completely buried.

And there, I find one tiny sliver remaining. One that immediately registers in my mind.

I take off, following that scent. Several times, I almost lose it, but every time I slow down, retrace my steps, and I pick it up once more.

The trail ends in an alleyway. I pick my way around debris, broken slats of wood, and jagged bottle caps until I reach the alley's dead end.

Four bodies lie huddled together, all male. I survey them from the youngest to the oldest. A father and his three sons. The father is missing half of a leg. He is the source of the strange arrangement of footprints I noticed.

Soundlessly, I approach. I crouch before the oldest boy, who sleeps on his side, half in front of his father as though to defend him. Quickly, I lay my hand over his mouth.

He jerks awake. His eyes immediately go white-ringed.

I lean close and whisper, "Come with me and don't make a sound, or I will kill your father."

The youth trembles as I release him, but he does what I say. I prod him to walk in front of me to the mouth of the alley. I expect him to start blathering the moment I motion for him to speak. Instead, he remains silent, fingers flexing at his sides.

His time in Faerieland has increased his courage.

"Tell me about the Ivy Mask." I keep my voice low.

"Or else you will kill my father?" asks the boy.

I don't intend to kill his father, so I let my silence be taken as affirmation.

He draws a deep breath. His exhalation is shaky. "What do you want to know?"

"What is his name?"

". . . the Ivy Mask?" the boy replies.

"You do not know his name?"

He shakes his head.

"Then what does he look like?"

He shrugs. "He wore a mask the entire time."

"His height then." I sit on an empty crate, drumming my fingers on its splintery side. "His build."

"He was almost as tall as you," the boy replies. "Though somewhat slenderer."

What a little liar. I saw the footprints from the Ivy Mask's last raid. None of them could have belonged to someone of my height. I withdraw a three-inch blade from my sleeve and twirl it casually on my fingers. The boy visibly swallows. I lean forward. "I think he is a little shorter than what you are describing."

"He probably is," he replies. "I was not paying close attention."

So he remains loyal to the Ivy Mask. I can change that. I can also drag one of his other brothers out here and get him to talk. If they had information that would be crucial in identifying the Ivy Mask and sparing Pavi's life, I'd do it.

But they don't have what I need.

I sheathe my knife and jerk my head toward the alleyway. "You're free to go."

CHAPTER 27

KAT

I WAKE WITH a headache strong enough to shake the foundations of the world.

"It's no fun, is it?" rumbles a low voice that comes very close. "Here. Drink this."

A hand slides under my back and shifts me upright while the world spins. The lip of a warm bowl presses against my lips. I open, and he pours a savory broth into my mouth. When I'm steady enough, I take the bowl in both hands and drink it all greedily. I still can't bear to open my eyes all the way, but the fog has cleared enough to recognize the prince.

"I doubt I can take all of the headache away, but I can take the edge off of it, if you'd like," he says.

"Yes please," I groan.

His hand, pleasantly cool, lands on my forehead. I flinch instinctively at the contact but force myself to relax. Then I flinch again when I realize belatedly that he's about to work *magic* on me.

"Easy, there," he murmurs, and then he mutters a string of unfamiliar words under his breath.

Like a wave washing away a castle in the sand, the pounding of my head dissipates. All that remains is a faint twinge. My whole body goes liquid from the relief, and Rahk catches the bowl before I drop it. I turn my head toward him, to find he's kneeling beside the bed. His silver hair is loose and falls in waves to his chest.

He smiles at me, his eyes twinkling in the morning light.

My shoulders stiffen. Why does he look at me so . . . so . . . *softly*?

And what in the *saints* is going on? What happened last night? Why is he tending to me instead of me tending to him? I glance at the window, at the angle of sunlight. The sun has been up for some time already.

Am I decent beneath these covers? I can feel my chest binding with every breath, so I know I'm still wearing that. But last night is a complete blank in my mind.

I'm not sure I've ever felt so vulnerable in my entire life.

The prince seems to catch my rising panic. His expression shifts at once, and he gets to his feet. He somehow seems taller when he turns his back to me. "Does a drinking game with servants ring any bells in your mind?"

I see Jack, Finn, and Arthur with their game of Crowns and their bottle of whiskey. Horror fills my gut. "I got drunk!"

"Very, very drunk." His tone changes slightly. "Do you . . . remember anything?"

My mouth goes dry. "Remember . . . what? Oh, I said things, didn't I?"

I blathered all my secrets to him last night, didn't I? I want to throw myself from the bed and just try to run away as fast as I can. Maybe I can put some distance between us before he catches up and slaughters me.

The prince turns, regarding me impassively. Gone is the warmth of his smile. He's the stoic prince I cannot read at all. He moves to the table, drops into his chair, and flips open the book he was reading. He's almost finished with it. "You went to bed shortly after you returned drunk."

A tiny glimmer of hope sparks in my chest. He doesn't *look* like he's about to murder me.

"Did I say foolish things? You know how terribly foolish I can be when sober! It must have been even worse when drunk! I never wanted to get drunk! I tried to leave, but they said they'd steal my clothes if I did!"

His attention flicks up from his book at that, a frown etched into his face. "Who? Did they hurt you?"

I shake my head.

"Who were these people?"

The boys' names are on the tip of my tongue, but I swallow them back. "They didn't mean harm. I'd rather not get them in trouble. But please, my lord—I must know what I said last night."

Rahk does not seem pleased with my silence, but he doesn't press. "Ease your worries. You said almost nothing."

"Nothing?" I blink twice, expecting to wake up again and realize I'm dreaming up this good fortune. "Nothing at all?"

"Almost nothing. There was one thing you said."

I gulp.

"You said you were in danger. You were afraid I was going to kill you."

Oh no. "Well—you're a fae. You're a warrior, and you have those great big swords back home, and you're practically the size of a mountain. And I saw you kill all those assassins in just a few minutes. You're scary!"

He just looks at me without a stitch of emotion on his face.

"And then you do that!" I cry, gesturing at him and completely forgetting to not behave so much like myself. "You make it impossible to guess what you're thinking!"

He sighs, and if I didn't know better, I'd think he was frustrated. "Well, I will tell you what I told you last night. I'm not going to kill you. I'm not going to hurt you. You're safe with me. As long as you are under my roof, you are under my protection. I won't let anyone hurt you. If you are ever afraid—of anything—you need only to tell me. Understand, Nat?"

I shuffle back one step. I nod, trying to ignore the sinking dread inside me. I wish my fears were so easily soothed by taking them to the prince. I almost wish I didn't know he was here for the purpose of hunting me down and, likely, bringing me to justice in the Nothril Court.

My stomach turns queasy. I grab my spare change of clothes, cup my hand over my mouth, and bolt out of the room.

I manage to make it all the way outside before I vomit.

RAHK

I stare at the door Kat disappeared through. I drop my book, lean back in my chair, and let out a low groan. All the progress we made last night—gone. It shouldn't surprise me. She was drunk. She said things she wouldn't have otherwise said. But I wanted her to remember. I wanted her to remember that she kissed me.

I could have just told her everything instead of lying and letting the sting of iron fill my mouth. The picture of her face and its utter horror flashes across my mind's eye. I had my chance, and I couldn't do it.

I want her to confide in me when she is in her right mind. I want her to choose to trust me. I want her to feel safe around me. Like she did last night.

It feels like we are back at the beginning again.

When Kat returns, she's dressed in fresh clothes, her old ones draped neatly over her shoulder as she carries a tray of breakfast for me. She doesn't meet my gaze, but sets the tray down on my desk and asks, "How else may I serve you, Master?"

I don't like giving her orders. I don't like her serving me. Last night, however, that was the one thing she asked for—that she would be allowed to continue serving me.

So I say, "Please ready my clothes for the luncheon."

She bows and hurries to do it, leaving me to my breakfast.

The luncheon itself is hosted on the shoreline. The salty air is pleasant enough that I test my ability to go without *ollea*. A large white canopy is set up on the green lawn beside the sandy beach. Musicians with stringed instruments sit in one corner, playing a cheerful song that threads through the well-dressed guests and the tables of refreshments.

The queen herself sits on a small white throne, wearing a gown of pastel yellow and a high updo. Her son has his own chair beside her. He wears his own soft-colored finery and an expression of boredom that shifts to curiosity when he spies me.

Kat is dressed in her starched livery and shifts uncomfortably every few minutes to tug on her scratchy collar. I suppress a smile. When she sees the gentle waves of the ocean, however, she brightens. With dilated pupils, she seems to gobble up the sight of the shore. I wish I could ask questions of the woman at my side, and not the boy she's pretending to be.

Her lips part, and I remember how soft they were on my cheek and chin last night.

I turn away from her, clearing my throat, and focus on the people milling around. Now would be a good time to meet Lady Vandermore, if she is present, though the idea of doing so in front of Kat sits in my gut uncomfortably.

I spot Oliver the moment he sees me. He has just taken a sip of punch when he offers a broad, tight-lipped smile and waves.

"So you got yourself an invitation to the exclusive Queen's Luncheon," says Oliver, sidling up to me. Kat slinks to my opposite side and remains quiet. “Impressive, though it doesn’t mean as much as you might think it does. She sometimes invites her enemies just so she can keep an eye on them.”

As though summoned, Queen Vivienne levels a sharp-eyed glare upon the two of us speaking, lingering on me. I incline my head.

“Come, before you address the queen, let me introduce you to my nemesis,” says Lord Oliver.

My eyebrows rise. “Your nemesis?”

“What? Did you think humans didn’t have them?” he asks with a wink. “This particular gentleman is my nemesis—and many others’—because he somehow managed to convince Lady Vandermore’s guardian that he was the most suitable suitor and now she aids his efforts at winning the young lady’s heart. It is a shame that Lady Vandermore is not here.”

She is not here, yet again?

“I will get you refreshments, my lord!” says Kat before running off, even though I gave her no such command.

“Guardian?” I repeat, returning my focus to the conversation. “Lady Duxbury Vandermore is not her mother?”

“Oh, no, not at all. She is Lady Vandermore’s stepmother. I don’t think they get along well.”

“Then your nemesis’s alliance might not aid him well,” I say dryly. “Who is he?”

“That gentleman over there.” Oliver points to a short man with ruffled sleeves and unsteady balance. I recognize him as having been the one to approach Kat in the sparring yard and presumably try to bribe her with coin for information about me. Oliver marches over, expecting me to follow, and offers a slightly dimmed version of his cheery grin. “Lord Boreham, you must meet Lord Rahk.”

Lord Boreham, startled, fumbles his drink. My hand darts out and catches it, preventing it from spilling across his ruffled sleeves. I return it and offer a nod. “Lord Boreham.”

“Lord Rahk,” he replies stiffly, taking his goblet and retreating one step. His posture is atrocious, back curved and hips collapsed forward. I find it hard to respect a man who cannot even hold his own body upright. There is a thread of tobacco and hard liquor that wraps around him, making me regret my decision to not apply *ollea*.

I glance over the tops of the heads of those around me until I find Kat. She stands awkwardly at the edge of the tent, a plate of dainties in one hand. She flushes when I catch her gaze. I lift one eyebrow in return. What nonsense is she up to now?

"Do you spar often?" I ask Lord Boreham. "I did not have the pleasure of crossing blades with you this last week. We must remedy that."

"I'm not much of a swordsman," Lord Boreham says with a nervous laugh.

You don't say.

"He does not spend much time at the sparring yard because he does not live in Ashbourne," Oliver explains.

"Where do you live?" I ask.

"Commington. It is not far from here."

I could ask more questions, but Boreham clearly has no interest in the conversation. Judging by the way he shifts his weight between his feet, he is very uncomfortable in my presence. That is not surprising. Oliver seems to be the only person who does not mind my company.

"I bid you a safe journey home," I say before putting the man out of his misery and striding away. Oliver continues the conversation while I make my way to the queen.

"That is close enough," Queen Vivienne snaps when I come within five paces of her throne. Her hand falls protectively to her son's head.

I sketch a bow. "As you wish. I have come to pay my respects."

"Have you?" she replies. "What respects might you have for a human ruler? Not much, I'd wager."

"More than you would wager," I answer, refusing to respond in kind yet also refusing to grovel before her. "The human rulers I hold in contempt earn that privilege."

The king of Aursailles, who I have had the unfortunate privilege of meeting, is one of them.

Queen Vivienne's gaze moves past me to the ocean beyond the canopy. "What must I do to get you to leave our land?"

It is the closest she will come to admitting she sent those assassins to kill me. "Cooperate with me over the border issue when it becomes relevant."

She waves a hand. "Besides that?"

I soothe my irritation with a deep breath. "That is the only way. You will soon have a troll squatting on the land that belongs to your people, and he won't take orders from me. As the ruler of the land, you will need to order him to leave yourself."

"A troll?" she laughs. "If you want to help us so much, just kill it."

"I am under orders not to kill him."

"And if I ordered you to kill him?"

"I would not listen."

"I am finished speaking to you," Queen Vivienne announces abruptly.

Is she, now? No wonder Ash was concerned about this transition. The troll isn't even a problem yet, and the queen refuses to cooperate. I bow and leave, as glad to be rid of her company as she is of mine.

Kat slips back to my side, offering up the plate of refreshments she filled for me. Of all the things I feel upon her return, *comfort* was not what I expected. I take the plate, only to notice that there is the outline of something missing on the plate.

"Have you taxed my refreshments?" I ask.

She shoves her hands behind her back and bites down on her lip—a guilty expression if I've ever seen one.

"What have you robbed me of? Confess at once." I almost call her *Kat,* and barely bite back the name in time.

"A chocolate strawberry!" she blurts. "It was delicious. I went to get you another one, but they were all gone. I'm afraid I am not sorry. I really loved eating that strawberry."

I cannot help my laugh. Several people startle, turning to stare at me, as though they never thought a fae capable of laughter. I hold the plate out to Kat, offering her choice of the dainties.

"You may select another tax," I say.

She eagerly inspects the plate. I watch her gaze swivel between a morsel of sweet meat and a tiny cranberry biscuit. She chooses the meat and closes her eyes to enjoy its flavor. My mouth tilts in a smile. When she opens her eyes, I hold out the cranberry biscuit to her lips.

"Another tax?" she asks.

"Only because I feel generous."

She glances a little uneasily around to make sure no one is watching us when she opens her mouth and lets me feed her the biscuit. Her enjoyment is deeply satisfying to me.

I pull the plate back to myself and eat without tasting. Every piece of food is so small it barely counts as a real bite. I will need a substantive meal after this—unless they want me to eat entire trays of tiny sandwiches and biscuits.

Kat stands at my side, bouncing on the balls of her feet, her hands clasped behind her back. No one gives her a second glance and it baffles me. What do they see when they look at her? Not what I see—they could never look past her if they saw what I saw.

My ribs suddenly feel squeezed tight in this doublet. I do not know what to make of these thoughts that keep invading my mind. Or, rather, I know what they mean, but their meaning is so preposterous I decide they must have some other meaning. Something that has nothing to do with how quickly my eyes are drawn back to my attendant.

I cannot court Lady Vandermore.

The realization is so sudden, so stark, I can do nothing but surrender to it. I will find some other way to win the queen's favor.

I need to meet with Lady Duxbury Vandermore and withdraw my suit.

We leave for Ashbourne after the luncheon and travel well into the night before we arrive home. Kat is stretched across the opposite bench inside the carriage, fast asleep. For the thousandth time, I wonder what I'm going to do with her. Her pleasant scent fills the carriage to the point it is impossible to ignore it. Not that I *want* to ignore it.

The carriage pulls to a stop, but Kat doesn't stir. I lean close and lay a hand on her shoulder. Still, she does not wake.

I sigh and lift her gently into my arms.

"My lord!" cries Edvear, rushing out to greet us. "What can I—oh! What has happened?"

"Hush!" I mouth at him with a glare. *"Nat is asleep."*

Edvear's jaw sags. "Why . . .?"

"Because it's in the middle of the night," I reply through my gritted teeth.

"No, why are you—" He wisely cuts himself off and goes to take care of our luggage instead.

Kat's arm hangs limply from her shoulder as I move carefully. Now that I've chosen this route instead of waking her up in the carriage, I'd rather she didn't wake at all.

Quietly, I lay her on her own cot and tug the covers over her. She lets out a soft moan and rolls to her side, toward me. I withdraw my hands and mutter, "Don't fall off your bed."

Then I leave, breathing harder than I should.

Edvear brings the luggage inside. I had originally planned to visit the border tonight, but I'm tired as well—and I have this prickling sense that I will want to be rested tomorrow night. Since I've placed wards around the estate to alert me of people I don't know stepping onto the grounds, I am comfortable letting my guard down for a few hours. So I stretch out on my own bed and let my exhaustion claim me.

The next evening, my intuition proves true.

I am at my desk, staring into space instead of tending to my work, when an invisible thread, pulling taut against me, snaps in half.

I'm on my feet in an instant. The Ivy Mask is back on the prowl.

My swords are strapped to my back within minutes. I don't bother to check in on Kat or inform Edvear that I'll be gone. Instead, I open the window and leap into the night.

Tonight, I'll get him. Tonight, I'll make him my ally and find some way to make him rescue Pavi from Nothril. And then the rest of my plan will fall into motion.

CHAPTER 28

KAT

I DON'T HAVE the luxury of the prince being gone for my raid this time. I wait until after dark, after he has dismissed me for the day. I left him in his study, and now I ease the window open and slip outside.

The night is unusually chilly, with a biting wind and a smell like rain. Clouds cover the stars and the moon.

I grab my Ivy Mask bundle from behind the outhouse. I must keep Prince Rahk off my trail, and judging by how things went last time, using *ollea* isn't enough. So I've hatched a new plan. A very different, risky plan, but one that I believe will pay off well. I put all the things I need in a sack—including a little present for Ymer—don my usual Ivy Mask garb, swipe the *ollea* on the bottoms of my shoes, and start my run toward the forest. I keep my eyes sharp, and several times a tree's moving shadow in the wind spooks me and I duck into hiding.

When I get to the forest, drenched in sweat and hot despite my cold ears, I pant for a moment, and then I hurry toward my cart. My task is made difficult by the forest's recession, which has left faint shimmers like fireflies along the ground. The ground itself almost seems to vibrate beneath my feet. *Strange*.

"Who goes over yonder?" booms a loud voice.

I startle straight out of my boots and whirl.

There, sitting with his thick legs stretched out in front of him, his back bowed forward, is the enormous form of Ymer the Indefatigable.

On *this* side of the border.

His moon-wide yellow eyes latch onto me.

For a moment, we just stare at each other. I'm not sure which of us is more shocked.

Then his rocklike fingers clench around his club and he lurches to his feet. "You nasty elf! Ymer will skewer you and roast you over a spit!"

Well, this is going to complicate things.

I throw myself into a somersault as Ymer smashes his cudgel into the ground where I was just standing. I roll back up to my feet only to nearly fall on my face as I try to dodge his next blow. "Ymer the Indefatigable!" I cry, and yelp as he tries to grab me with his other hand. "I come in peace!"

"You have stepped foot into Ymer's territory, and now Ymer will eat you!" he roars.

I spew a string of curses as I dart behind him, taking advantage of his slow maneuvers. If I'm not careful, he really will eat me, and I would never get over the shame of that. "You're not supposed to be here! You need to go back to Faerieland—*saints*!"

The cudgel lands mere inches from my foot.

"Ymer will not leave unless the ruler of this land bids Ymer go!" he roars. "Which *you* are not. So now Ymer will eat you!"

I trip. I catch myself on my hands and knees. My heart slams into my throat as stoney fingers clamp around my waist and lift me straight off the ground.

"Ymer!" I shriek as he brings me toward his craggy lips. "You can't eat me because I brought you a present!"

His mouth is open, a rotting stench assaulting me mid-air, so I get a clear view of all the lumps on his blackened tongue. But he pauses, my legs dangling a solid four or five feet above the ground, his grip digging painfully into my waist.

"A present?" he echoes.

"Yes!" I cry, wiggling to loosen his grip. "I brought it for you because I felt bad that I kept passing you and not letting you eat me!"

He narrows one of those massive eyeballs at me. Something is growing on his eyelid. "How does Ymer know you are not trying to trick Ymer?"

I lift both my hands. "If you put me down and let me open my bag, I will show you the gift."

"Ymer does not know if he should trust the nasty elf." With that, he turns me upside-down like I am a doll to abuse. I cling to one massive, rusted fingernail and brace myself as blood rushes to my brain.

"If I am lying," I say between gritted teeth, "I will leap into your mouth myself. You have that on my word as a nasty elf."

He drops me unceremoniously on the ground. I roll in an effort to not snap my neck clean in half. Then I cast about desperately on the ground for my dropped sack. My fingers close around the cloth and I nearly sigh aloud in relief.

"Here!" I say, digging around in my sack until I find the smaller sack inside. I yank it out and hold it up.

He studies the knotted kerchief and sniffs. He tilts his head to one side—*curious*.

"It smells good, right?" I fumble with the knot until I get it open, revealing the present. It is a picked over chicken carcass. Charity served several for dinner last night, saying she would make chicken stock today with the leftovers. I swiped one of them when she wasn't looking. "It is all for Ymer."

Ymer's hand, the one with the cudgel, slackens as he leans forward, his nostrils flaring with interest. I toss the carcass toward him and grab my pack, skittering back a step.

He picks up the chicken's ribcage and inspects it. I'm not sure if he enjoys herbal seasonings, but surely he cannot hate them, right? He snaps a rib and brings it to his jagged teeth, taking a tentative bite that crunches down my spine.

"Enjoy!" I call, a little shrill, as I turn on my heel and race toward my cart as fast as I can while he is distracted. To my vast relief, he seems content with the chicken and does not chase me. I reach the cart with no incident.

I duck behind it and change as swiftly as I can, tossing my *ollea* coated shoes into the cart inside a bag with the rest of my Ivy Mask garb. Now my clothes are all fresh, never worn before, and carry their own scent.

I tuck the bottle of *ollea* into my pocket. Then I allow myself one moment to feel the splitting in my heart for Bartholomew's loss. "I'm going to get you back," I vow into the night. "And I will give you so many carrots you'll be sick of them."

After that, I have no room for anything but the task before me. I glance back at Ymer's great, hulking shadow as he digs into his meal. Maybe he will be satisfied enough that he won't chase me when I return. I've got other things to worry about now.

I don't know how Rahk tracked me before, but this time, I've got to outsmart him. The saints know I haven't a hope for success otherwise!

I don't take the Path to Nothril.

I search along the edges of the forest, watching for those faint sparkles. It takes about a half a mile of walking before I find the right Path. The end of the Path shimmers in the ether—barren trees and green mud slung between their dead branches.

"If you let this kill you," I mutter under my breath, "Mary will skin your hide."

Pulling the hood of my new cloak low and affixing my mask, I slip onto the Path and let the forest swallow me whole.

This Path is darker than many of the others. I've never walked it before, but Tailor always warned me not to step foot on it. My awareness is tight and tense, listening for any sign that something is already following me.

The trees begin shrinking slightly. Lush greenery gives way to broken, sad stalks of wood. The ground shifts from well packed earth and pine needles to something wetter and slicker.

A pungent rot makes me press my sleeve against my nose. I dare not cough and draw attention to myself, but my eyes water from the stench.

My foot slips.

I catch myself with both hands in the muck. It is sludgy, green, and already deep enough to bury my wrists in. I restrain the sound of disgust in my throat and push myself upright again. This time, I move slower, more carefully, dodging around the muddier parts as I enter the swamp.

A low hum reaches my ears just as the Path ends.

I stand on the edge of a swampy pit. The remnants of blackened trees stand like blades as far as I can see. The horrible green mud is everywhere, sliding down the sides of large, sunken boulders, covering the rest of the way into the pit.

I reach one of those boulders, gripping it tightly with the pads of my fingers and leaning to get a better look inside the pit.

My heart stops beating.

A great . . . *thing* rests in the center of the pit, mostly buried in the mud. It has a smooth, bulbous body that protrudes from the mud like a dome. And that is all I can see of it—though I know there is much beneath the surface. The hum comes from the creature, the mud around it shivering from that noise.

I refuse to breathe, scooting behind the large rock, putting it between me and the Path—exposing myself to the monster and its reach.

As silently as I can, I change clothes. It's so vulnerable to be half naked in Caphryl Wood, at the mercy of this monster that can wake at any moment, knowing Rahk can be here at any second. But I do it anyway. When I'm finished changing, I pull the bottle of *ollea* out of my pocket, unstopper it, and smear it on the bottoms of my usual boots. I glance at the vial. Less than a third is left. I chew my lip and determine to worry about that problem later.

I sneak out of my spot and hide my first change of clothes as close to the monster as I dare.

Now it's time to make my escape.

But just then, a long shadow falls over the pit.

I slip back into my hiding place, barely willing to breathe, my heartbeat thrashing in my ears, and squeeze my eyes shut. I had hoped it wouldn't come to this, but it looks like I have no choice.

Kneeling silently, I search along the ground until I find a mud-coated stone. I wait as Rahk's silhouette, with the shadows of the hilts of his two great swords rising above his shoulders, comes down the Path I just trod. He silently approaches the monster—following the scent of the new clothes I wore.

His tracking ability is frighteningly good. How did he get here so fast?

I crush my teeth against one another, not daring to move, watching his shadow as it falls over the form of the sleeping monster.

He will catch me some day.

The realization strikes with the force of a whip. The question isn't *if*—it's *when*. It is only a matter of time until I make a mistake. How long can I stay a step ahead of him?

All it takes is one stumble, and then he'll be upon me.

I squeeze my fist.

Not tonight. He is not getting me tonight.

Rahk stops a few paces away from the sleeping monster. I watch his shadow as his nose lifts into the air. When he turns his head, so his profile is clearly set against the smooth surface of the monster, his mouth is downturned. Confident in his own stealth, he silently marches toward the monster, and if not for his shadow, I never would have known he'd come. His right hand goes to the hilt of one of his swords, but he does not draw it as he approaches.

He kneels right in front of it. Where my discarded clothes are.

Then his head jerks upright. He scans the area. Looking for me. I keep my shriek firmly locked behind my teeth. I shift the rock in my grasp, but hesitate.

What if something happens to Rahk? What if this monster kills him—or both of us? The idea of him suffering harm is more upsetting than I want to consider.

But he's the prince of the Nothril Court. He's a fae warrior. He took down those assassins without hardly a thought.

He's got to be able to handle this monster.

I have no other option to shake him off my trail. There are humans in the fae world right now, being ruined by their fae masters. As much as I may want to believe Prince Rahk isn't like the rest of the fae, I have no choice in the matter. I will always choose my fellow humans over one of their kind.

So I throw the rock with every bit of power I can muster. Straight at the lidded eye of the monster.

The monster surges with a roar that sends shockwaves through the mud. Its tentacles—lined with long, sharp blades—unwind from around its body at a dizzying speed, sweeping the area around it with the force of a tornado. Rahk flips backward out of the way, catches the low hanging branch of a nearby swamp tree and hoists himself upright.

The monster's tentacles come for him even there, slashing into the tree branch. Rahk swings to the opposite branch as he withdraws his sword and slices through monster flesh. The air splits with a rumbling roar. Then he drops to the ground, dodging another attack. The tentacle misses him, but slams hard into the rock I'm hiding behind. The force knocks me to my knees.

Rahk's attention whips to me, no longer concealed. I stare at him through the slits of my mask. His gaze widens slightly.

Another slicing tentacle shoots for me at once, the large, gray monster eye fixing on me. The heel of my boot snags on the uneven terrain, and I fall backwards. I catch myself with my palms, unable to do anything but watch in the split second before the tentacle slices open my chest.

Rahk's body suddenly blocks me, both of his swords swinging. The sliced bit of tentacle goes flying. I gasp. Mud sticks to my clammy skin. *Why is he defending me?* My senses return with that thought, and I scramble to my feet and try to run.

It's Rahk's own foot that I trip over next. I barely keep from swearing aloud in fury.

"I'm not here to hurt you! I need your help!" he shouts to me, his swords slashing as one of his feet presses into my ankle, keeping me from running.

I dare not speak to him for fear my voice will give me away. Instead, I grab my one not-very-good knife and, out of desperation, slice it lightly across the skin of his ankle. Barely enough to draw blood. Surprised, he shifts his weight, and I take the meager advantage to yank free.

He curses, then shouts as he dives and rolls back to his feet, dodging another flying tentacle: "Ivy Mask! Please! I need you to save my sister!"

His sister. The one he loves.

My heart fissures. He's lying to me. He's lying to trick me. To trap me. I hate myself for the way it almost works—the way I nearly stop running, pausing, to hear his case. I desperately want to believe that he hunts me for the purpose of gaining my alliance instead of hunting me down for his wicked parents. I want so badly for him to be on my side, and not working toward my death.

But I am not a fool. I saw what these fae did to my mother and many others. I know what they're capable of. I've seen Rahk in the

Nothril Court. He isn't to be trusted—no matter how much I long to do exactly that.

I cannot risk my raids and the future of the people I rescue.

The monster shoots tentacles out of the pit. They latch onto trees, the few boulders, wrapping around them and then *pulling*—dragging itself out of the pit. Rahk hacks at each tentacle, but he's not fast enough. New ones shoot past him with every second. He leaps backward to keep from being skewered. I take the window of opportunity and run as fast as I can away from the scene. I glance back once to see Rahk trying to follow me, but tentacles keep coming for him.

I run and run and run, leaping onto the Path, but just as I think I'm safe, a snap resounds behind me. Fire erupts across my leg, followed by wet warmth. I manage to withhold my scream, but I fall hard to the ground.

The back of my calf has been sliced open. Blood soaks through the torn fabric of my trousers. I curse viciously under my breath. That is a deep cut. But I don't have time to tend it. I push myself to my feet, ignoring the screaming pain, and keep running—limping violently. Blood streams down my leg.

I make it to the end of the Path before I stop, breathing too hard, and use my knife to cut a strip of cloth from my cloak. It's not clean, but that doesn't matter right now. I wrap it around my calf and knot it so tightly I nearly cry out from the pain.

A thousand questions flood my mind, panic about how I'm going to manage this raid, how I'm going to keep this wound hidden from Rahk when I return to his house. I shove them all away. There is nothing except the task before me.

I keep running. I take the right Path this time, one that goes to my next target: the Pyrenar Court.

I don't know how much time until Rahk frees himself from the monster, but I have to act fast. Pushing past the pain, I sprint through the Path, careful not to accidentally fall off it and into the unforgiving depths of Caphryl Wood.

Waiting at the end of the Path, before a white, ornate gate is Tailor. His spectacles sit askew on the bridge of his nose, his face wreathed in fear. "Kat!"

"No time!" I gasp. "We need to get them out—"

"I've already gotten them out," he says. "But you—you're bleeding!"

"Bless you. Prince Rahk is on my trail," I say by way of explanation. "I've got the lead on him, but I cannot go back the way I came."

"I have an alternate Path for you. This way! How bad is the injury?"

"I can barely feel it, to be honest." I duck after him around the gate. In tall rushes, a young couple hides. They look only barely older than I am. He has his arm around her shoulders, and she grips his hand in hers. I spare a relieved thought that they both look like they can move quickly.

"Thank you, Ivy Mask," says the young woman. "We owe you everything."

"You've given us a chance to live—and to marry." The man gives me such a look of earnest gratitude as he pulls the woman I assumed was his wife—but apparently is his intended—to her feet.

Their praise turns my stomach. "Don't thank me yet," I mutter, reapplying *ollea*. The three of us follow Tailor through thick foliage until we reach a new Path that shimmers before us.

"He won't be able to track you here," the tailor says. "It'll take you to Valehaven, and from there you can take the usual Path to your part of the world."

I cannot help myself and I grab him by the collar and kiss his cheek soundly—a slapping of my mask against his face. "You are a miracle, Tailor. I couldn't do this without you."

"Yes, yes, now go!"

It's a longer distance than usual, and I could weep from missing Bartholomew, but we make great time for being on foot. When I stumble, the fabric tying my wound soaked through, the young man scoops an arm beneath my shoulder blades and under my armpit, dragging me back to my feet and helping to bear my weight.

"Thank you," I gasp.

We make it to the edge of Caphryl Wood an hour later. My leg shakes from the ill use. But I don't stop as I yank out my precious little supply of *ollea*. I cannot take chances tonight. "Put a drop on the bottom of your shoes!" I tell them. Now that I know Rahk is here in the human world, along with Ymer, I'm painfully aware of how unsafe this place is. It's like the shimmering ground of the receding border is only a reminder of how dangerous Ashbourne is while Rahk is on the hunt.

I search the darkness for sign of Ymer. In the distance, a great lump is sprawled on the ground, and if I strain, I can hear something resembling snoring. I exhale in relief. As long as we stay quiet, we should be fine.

The couple does as I say, and I give them the usual instructions. Sweat streams down their faces as they pant. The young man's eyes flick between my face and my wounded leg. "We're not leaving you like this."

"Absolutely not!" insists the girl.

"I will be completely fine," I lie. "You're the ones in danger. I have only a little way before I am safe. Please—you must make it to the city. For me. You'll leave me in worse danger if you stay."

They look dubious, but accept my explanation and break into a run.

I watch them disappear into the darkness and spare a prayer that they will rebuild their life together and have a long, happy marriage. Then I take stock of where I stand, a good half of a mile from my cart and the Nothril Path. My limbs shake from the exertion and pain, yet I have no choice but to work as fast as I can. I need to be back in bed at Rahk's house before he returns—and I must be free of all signs of Faerieland when I do. I rip off my mask and stuff it into my pocket.

It seems impossible.

But I must make it happen. There is no other option.

Thunder rumbles overhead, low and menacing. I take another strip of my cloak and wrap it around my leg. I cannot leave a trail of blood behind me. I find a stick I can lean on and hobble my way as fast as I can back to Rahk's estate. It's agonizing work, sweat streaming down my face and salt stinging my eyes. Each step is more painful than the one before it. I grit my teeth and push onward.

I'm beginning to believe I'll never make it when the light woods near Rahk's house and the burbling of the creek nearly make me gasp in relief. I pick up my pace, ignoring the throbbing that now shoots up my entire leg.

With a whimper, I collapse against the side of the stream. I breathe hard, leaning against the trunk of a tree, my head tilted back toward the night sky. The reprieve from the sheer agony of walking is almost pleasurable. But I cannot sit still for long.

I groan as I unwrap my makeshift bandages. The cut is nasty, still bleeding, and deep enough to require stitches—though not deep enough to leave permanent injury. *I hope.*

I sift through my sack until I find Mary's makeshift bag of injury treatment tools. She always keeps me prepared. I'd be dead without her so many times.

I open the bag. A flash of lightning overhead illuminates the long needle I had hoped to never need. The thread is a high-quality silk. I thread the needle and bring it to my torn flesh.

"There's nothing to it," I mumble with a quiet laugh.

The first puncture of the needle through flesh nearly makes me pass out. I clench my jaw, refusing to slow down—lest I be here all night until Rahk returns and finds me like this. By the second stitch, tears stream down my cheeks. The third stitch hurts worse than the injury itself.

"Keep going. Don't stop," I growl at myself, forcing my shaking hand to keep going. "The faster you go, the faster it'll be over."

I curse every inch of this wound that requires another stitch. Despite my intention to not stop or slow, I take a break halfway through. My hands are a bloodied mess.

I sag against the tree trunk, tilting my head up. Tears stream down my cheeks. "This is all my fault. And it's *your* fault, Mama. You never should have come after me. Why did you have to go into the Wood? I *needed* you. I—I need you now. But you're not here."

It's hatred that rises from deep inside me, fueling my needle as I begin stitching again. The worst part is the tug of the thread through the skin. I cannot yank too fast or risk tearing the skin, so I'm forced to pull long and slow. It's agony.

I hate my mother for getting lost in the Wood. Even though she was a captive, enduring horrors I can only begin to guess at. I still hate her for it. I hate her for not abandoning me when she should have. I hate her for the empty shell of the person she was when she returned.

And I hate Father too—who remarried for *me*. Father—who died of a broken heart when Mama returned from the forest only to find he'd moved on.

But most of all, I hate myself. My family was torn to shreds, leaving me among ashes. Leaving me with a stepfamily that I never belonged to. All because of my *idiocy*. If it wasn't for me, I would be with my family now, instead of pretending I was part of Agatha's.

"Better I was left destitute," I snarl through the tears.

I miss Bartholomew so terribly much. I must believe I will get her back. If I don't—

"You're going to get her back." I wipe my nose on my bloodied sleeve, swearing into the darkness. "That is the end of the story. You're going to get her back, and all of this will be worth it."

I pull the last stitch through. I knot it quickly, then fall against the tree, my mouth open as sweat drips from my cupid's bow onto my tongue. My leg pulses, and every heartbeat brings a fresh wave of agony.

It's a mercy, a blessed mercy when the rain begins. Each drop stings against my stitches, but it is cooling on my fiery skin. A soothing balm. I let the rain soak me through, washing away my blood into the creek, washing away the scent of Faerieland.

It gives me just the scrap of determination and energy I need to push to my feet, still leaning on my makeshift cane, and hobble to the outhouse, which is empty—yet another blessed mercy. There I switch my clothes and hide my bloodied Ivy Mask garments to be cleaned later when I have a chance.

My luck cannot hold forever, however. When I get to my window, I nearly crumble in anticipation of the pain of climbing inside. I'm so exhausted the thought of just sleeping on the ground in the rain sounds far more appealing.

"This isn't just about you," I growl to myself. "You cannot let yourself get caught. For the sake of all the other raids that still need to happen. For the sake of those you haven't rescued yet."

So I toss away my walking stick, hoist myself into the open window, and endure the brand of fire that sears all the way to the bone when I swing my legs inside. I land on the floor of my small room, soaked and shaking. The jump slightly ripped a couple of the stitches, and fresh blood leaks into my wet trousers.

I change as fast as I can without dislodging more of my work. I rub my wet hair with the quilt on my bed, drying it as best as I can. Then, because Rahk still isn't home, I sneak out of my room and go to the roll of bandages in his wardrobe. I fumble with the clean white bandage before cutting a good length. I scurry back to my room, leaving everything exactly as before, and the moment I shut my door, Rahk's heavy boots thud down the hallway.

He survived the tentacled monster.

I didn't realize how afraid I was for him until this moment. It strikes me like a wave on the seashore. *He is alright.*

Then, the relief passes, and panic nearly overtakes me. I hide the bandage, fling into bed, and pull the quilt over myself. I hide my still-wet head beneath my pillow and try to calm my breathing.

I listen as the door to his bedroom opens and closes. His boots thud a few steps, and then they land in a pile. His steps are quieter then, but the slight shuffle is enough to give away that he has also gone to the bandages. I listen to the sound of scissors clipping the bandages, the splash of water in the basin on the dresser, a singular grunt.

Not once does he come near my room.

Finally, I release my tightly held breath. I keep my eyes on the light under my door, watching for any sign of his approaching shadow. As quickly as I dare, I pull out the bandage and wrap my calf before I bleed on the mattress. It still throbs, but my fear has deadened the pain slightly.

When the wound is sufficiently bound and hidden beneath the legs of my night clothes, I lay back on my bed and stare at the ceiling. Waiting for the racing thud of my blood to calm enough for sleep. Tremors move through my body.

I keep waiting for Rahk to come, for his shadow to appear beneath my door, for him to rip me out of bed and hold up proof in front of my face. Some mistake I made, something I overlooked, something I forgot. Something that betrays my identity.

Then he will drag me to my knees, take one of those great swords, and break his promise of protection.

But he never comes. It's not until dawn do I realize that I have successfully lived another day.

As I swing my wounded, aching leg to the floor, I do not feel comforted at all.

CHAPTER 29

RAHK

MY WOUNDS FROM killing the kravok are minor. My frustration stings much sharper. I had the Ivy Mask right there. He was in my grasp—I had touched him.

And yet, he got away.

When I first realized the Path he'd taken, I assumed it was by mistake after the likely fright of running into Ymer the Indefatigable, who is now officially a problem.

I was afraid I would lose my chance to catch him because he walked right into a monster's lair. But that was hardly the case. The Ivy Mask knew exactly what he was doing. It was a ploy to outsmart me—and it worked. I grudgingly admire his tenacity and quick thinking. It does reveal that he knows I hunt him. How he figured that out, I do not know.

My spells alerted me exactly when the rescued slaves got onto the coach and fled the city. I could not have made it in time due to the time lost fighting the kravok. Still, I would not have stopped their flight.

This wasn't supposed to be a difficult assignment. But I'm already nearly three weeks in Harbright, and I'm no closer to catching him than I was at the beginning.

The tattoo at the back of my neck burns. Pavi's full-lipped pout returns to mind.

I'm going to get the Ivy Mask. No matter what.

Kat brings me breakfast first thing. The skin under her eyes is darkened and saggy, as though she slept little. She says nothing as she places the tray before me and moves to leave.

"How did you sleep?" I ask, watching her instead of the cup of tea I bring to my lips.

She shrugs, her eyes skittering to mine and away. "Not very well, I confess."

The tea is too hot. I blow on it and set it down. "Then you must rest this afternoon."

She winces, and at first it strikes me as though from a physical pain, but then I realize I must have activated her fear of dismissal. "I wouldn't want to leave my work undone."

"You will work better if you are properly rested. You will rest."

She nods once. "Yes, my lord."

No more arguments? I breathe through my discomfort at her address, and stare at the door she disappears through long after she's gone.

There is far too much on my mind, too many matters of greater weight, and yet the thing I find myself thinking about is Lady Vandermore. I haven't yet gone to Vandermore Manor to withdraw my addresses. I can always change my mind—perhaps the heiress's alliance will be exactly what I need to earn the queen's favor and shorten my stay in the human lands. What if courtship isn't enough, though? What if the only way to gain the queen's favor is to actually *marry* the girl?

If Ymer the Indefatigable leads me to such drastic measures, I might defy Ash's orders not to kill him.

The thought of bringing a human wife into this house, into this very room, all while Kat serves me in charade, is far too repulsive to be considered. My relationship with Kat would become different. I couldn't sit with her each evening and play Fool's Circle. I couldn't even keep her so close in the room adjacent to mine. I couldn't tease her, watch over her, or enjoy her presence while I was married to another woman.

I couldn't think about what she said to me in her drunken haze.

"You are good. I didn't think so at first, but I see it now."

"Edvear!" I call.

My steward comes at once. His cheeks are reddened, his ears bent backward, and his crisp shirt is untucked slightly.

"You look upset," I say, instead of issuing my order.

"Well, of course I'm upset!" he declares, wringing his hands. "The cow isn't producing much milk anymore, so we don't have enough cream to make butter for tonight's rolls. Mrs. Finch is at her wit's end. She is doing her best, but I've hardly given her enough to work with. Apparently with these cows, if they stop producing milk, they are useless until they have another spawn—which will take months!"

"That is unfortunate," I reply. "I am sorry you must deal with such trouble."

Edvear pulls himself together. "It is no matter, my lord. I suppose we can buy butter in the market. I won't let such a fine cook as Mrs. Finch go without what she needs. What can I do for you?"

There is a note in his tone that gives me pause. Has my steward taken an interest in the widowed cook? He will be sorely disappointed when it is time to return to Nothril.

I pretend I noticed nothing. "Please arrange a meeting with Lady Duxbury Vandermore."

"At once, my lord."

An ear-splitting crash echoes from the opposite side of the house. Both Edvear and I turn toward it.

Edvear tsks. "It's that boy again. He's as clumsy today as he was on his first day. He's driving Mrs. Banks insane. It's barely past breakfast and she already looks ready to box his ears."

I shoot to my feet and shove past him. If that woman lays a hand on Kat—

The yelling in the kitchen is enough to guide me through the hallways. I throw open the door to find Kat on the floor, grimacing in pain next to my fallen breakfast tray. The china has broken to pieces, tea spilled everywhere, and chipped dishes scattered across the floor.

"—useless, clumsiest—"

"Enough!" I demand, grabbing Kat under the armpits and pulling her to her feet, away from the broken china immediately. I cannot keep my voice from betraying my temper this time. "Mrs. Banks, I have been clear that you are not to raise your voice or your hand against Nat. It is nothing but a few broken dishes. I will clean it up myself if that would please you!"

Mrs. Banks stares at me in shock. She looks like she wants to shift her tirade to me and yell that I shouldn't have so obvious a favorite among my staff. Which she might be right about—but I couldn't care less.

I put Kat gently on her feet, shielding her from Mrs. Banks with my body. She stumbles slightly, grabbing my wrist with a tight grip as though she might fall.

She's injured.

My blood turns hot in my veins. Was I too late? Did Mrs. Banks already lay a hand on her? I barely restrain the burst of violence inside me. I am not in Nothril, and I will not be hasty in meting out judgment.

But if Mrs. Banks did this, she will be immediately dismissed.

I don't release my grip on Kat. "Edvear, please see that this is handled. If it's too much trouble for the staff"—these words come out with far more bite than they ought—"then wait for me and I'll deal with it myself."

"I will clean it up—" Kat starts to protest.

"No, you will not," I reply firmly as Edvear shuts the kitchen door, giving us the privacy I need to bend and scoop her up into my arms.

"Master!" she cries, at once wriggling to free herself. A flash of pain crosses her face at the movement. She tries to hide it, but she's not fast enough.

"Where are you hurt?" I demand, taking her to my quarters for privacy. I kick open the bedroom door, then shut it with my heel.

She colors brightly. "I'm not hurt. I only—"

I stop before the bed, holding her firmly so she cannot squirm free. "You are going to tell me exactly where you are hurt and how it happened, or else I will search you for your injury."

Her head draws back sharply. I knew that threat would loosen her tongue. I set her down on the bed gently and place my palm on the footboard, waiting for her explanation.

"I sprained my ankle," she blurts. "It's really nothing. It wasn't Mrs. Bank's fault. That was mine. I just took a misstep and sprained my ankle and spilled your tray everywhere. I am the worst servant! Please forgive me, Master. I promise to do better."

"Let me see your ankle."

She draws in a hiss. "Please, my lord, do not trouble yourself."

"Too late. Show me. Or else I will summon the doctor."

Her skin goes pale. "No—no, my lord! Such a thing is not necessary. You can see for yourself that it is a minor injury."

I withhold my sigh. It is so ridiculous that she still does not believe I know she is a woman. If only she would confide in me—when she is *sober*—all of this would be tremendously simple. We wouldn't need to maintain this ridiculous charade.

She pulls her right leg onto the bed and rolls up her breeches enough to expose her ankle, and nothing more. "See? It's not even swollen. It's a silly injury that will be healed in no time."

Her slender, delicate ankle shows no sign of injury. I bend to get a closer look and find not a single thing wrong with it.

It is possible I overreacted.

I straighten my spine, clasping my hands behind my back, trying to forget the violence toward Mrs. Banks that had stirred in my gut only moments ago. "I am glad it is nothing serious. This is even more reason, however, for you to rest this afternoon."

She rolls down her breeches and nods. She doesn't seem herself at all today. I want to press her, to find out what it is that turns her bright gaze cloudy. As long as she thinks I know nothing of her secret, however, the most I can do is offer her rest this afternoon.

"Thank you, my lord," she says, using both her hands to push herself to her feet. "I will work hard this morning and then rest as you have ordered. I promise I shall not be clumsy anymore or break any more valuables."

I study her for a moment. Sunlight plays across her freckled cheekbones, illuminating her lashes. Then, because I cannot help myself, I reach out and ruffle her hair. It's the only show of affection I can give. She wrinkles her nose, and it's a reminder that the lively Kat is still there beneath the lack of sleep and her injury.

Then an idea occurs to me. A slight smile twitches at my lips. "Come with me."

She eyes me suspiciously before following me out to the back patio. The weather is already notably hotter than it was when I first arrived and is on the outer edge of pleasant unless I step into the shade, or a breeze picks up.

I make sure to glance back at Kat every few minutes to ensure she isn't having trouble walking. Once, when she seems to be slowing down, I say, "If your ankle is bothering you too much, I can carry you the rest of the way over my shoulder."

Her gaze shoots up to mine, her face coloring deep red. I laugh and slow my pace for her, pleased by her reaction.

"Are we going to the creek?" she asks.

"Cool water is good for reducing swelling. Especially on a hot day like today."

When I glance back at her, her step has slowed. I chuckle again, reaching back to take her arm so she doesn't slip when we reach the smooth, wet stones of the creek. "There is nothing more revitalizing than a dip in the cold creek. Your ankle will thank you."

"You don't need to tend to me like I'm a wilting flower," she whines, sounding almost petulant. "That water is *cold*!"

I roll my eyes. Yes, it's cold. And yes, I do need to watch over her carefully, since she doesn't seem inclined to do it herself. I strip off my shirt without a thought and it's only when I glance back and find her very pointedly averting her eyes that I remember yet again the human sense of modesty. It's only my back. I spare an amused thought for how utterly shocked she would be if she spent any time at all in Faerieland. It is a wild place.

I jump into the creek and dunk my head under, taking the shock of cold in all at once. It's a moment of frigid, and then a second later, a pleasant contrast to the heat of the day. I turn around, grinning, looking to see how Kat is coming along.

She stands on the bank, still fully clothed. Staring at me with an expression like that of a trapped animal. I sigh, wiping a hand down my face. The words, *"Listen, I know you're a woman. No need for scruples,"* nearly pass my lips. But I cannot shock her if I want her to join me.

So I march to the bank, shaking the water out of my wet hair and crossing my arms over my chest, as I tell her: "Don't act like a little girl. Be a man!"

The words have their intended effect. She moves into action, kicking off her shoes, determination flashing across her features. But when she dips her toe in like a delicate maiden, my patience has worn thin.

I grab her around the thighs and pull her off the bank. She shrieks—a very girlish sound—and instinctively wraps her arms around my neck. Laughing, I wrap both arms around her, holding her to my chest, and dunk both of us under the water.

She spews water out of her mouth the second I let her go, shoving away from me and growling, "I was *coming*!"

"You were being a *delicate*," I reply, happy to forget everything in the pleasure of teasing her. "I couldn't wait all morning."

Her mouth drops open in outrage, her wet hair sticking to her face and neck. She sweeps her hands across the surface of the water, sending a large splash at me. I take it, squeezing my eyes shut as the water pelts them. Then I open them, and she's looking at me with such dread, I laugh again.

"That's right. You *should* be scared. Because I'm not letting you get out of here until I splash you in revenge."

She squeaks, turning to run, but the creek is full of unsteady rocks, and I cannot let her run without risking her ankle being sprained again. I grab her arm, which she protests with a loud squeal. My splash drenches her all over again. She shrieks, gripping my elbow to keep from falling.

"You are evil!" she cries.

I grin down at her. "And you are about as tough as a pillow."

My comment lands exactly as I hoped, and she tries to shove me backwards into the creek.

It's right then that my attention drops slightly, noting the way her clothes stick to her skin. The outlines of a close-fitted undergarment beneath her tunic are completely exposed. It catches me off-balance, and Kat's shove succeeds. I hit the water. Cold rushes over me, but I barely notice it. It feels like I've glimpsed her in a vulnerable state, not meant for me.

"Ha!" she cries, triumphantly, pointing at me as I pull myself back to my feet.

I make myself smirk back at her. "Two can play at this game."

She turns and tries to run, though the waist-high water slows her progress significantly. My amusement fades when my gaze drops to her back. Should anyone glimpse her when she heads to her room to change and dry off, her secret will be exposed.

I pull myself out of the creek and settle on the warm grass. She seems to have realized what I did, for she has already ducked below the stream, keeping herself covered from my gaze. Something about her wet hair and that look of determination to bear something she hates shifts some of my discomfort back into amusement.

"Have you decided you like the cold now?" I tease, marveling yet again that she seems to believe me fooled by her scheme. Perhaps she has not been among men enough to know how they behave amongst themselves. Does she long to believe so much that I am fooled, that no matter how I tease her, she refuses to see the truth?

She lifts her pert little chin, which does not disguise the chatter of her teeth. "It's . . . revitalizing. As you said. Since it's so c-cold, all the pain is gone from my ankle. It's just numb instead."

I give a small snort. "How much longer do you think you'll swim?"

Her series of blinks are a smidge too fast. "I d-don't know y-yet. I'm loving the c-cold."

Part of me wants to stay here, testing her, knowing she won't leave the creek until I do, wanting to see how long she'll keep up the charade. The gentlemanly part of me, however, makes me stand and pull my shirt over my wet torso. "I'll leave you to your soaking. Just be sure to finish within the hour, lest I be forced to fish you out with a hook and line."

She shoots me a face and I laugh before I turn around and make my way up the hill.

CHAPTER 30

KAT

I *HATE* HOW cold this creek is! It is true that my wound hurts *far* less, and he was right to drag me here. Still, it's infuriating that the water is cold enough to freeze my blood and I can do nothing but endure it until Rahk's tall form vanishes inside the house.

Then, as quickly as I can without hurting myself, I scramble out of the water and shake out my shirt, peeling it from my wet skin. My heart still pounds from how close he came to realizing my lie. If he had found out by my shirt sticking to my chest binding, I would have never forgiven myself for allowing such a stupid discovery.

It wasn't as though he gave me much choice though, I think bitterly as I wring out my shirt. He threatened to carry me out here, and then he dragged me into the water despite all my protests!

I cannot be completely angry, though. The relief from the constant biting ache of my wound is so tremendous I could sigh.

It's a quarter of an hour before I feel safe enough to risk going inside. In the beeline I make to my room, I only encounter Edvear, who speaks to Rahk in the dining room about the kitchen incident.

I cringe and move past them. In a few minutes, I'm safely dry and dressed in fresh clothes that do not betray my femininity.

"Between the raids and being thrown into the creek, you're going through clothes far too quickly," I mutter under my breath to myself.

The day goes by fast, and I find the afternoon rest Rahk insisted upon to be just what I need. I sleep as the dead for several hours. When I come out rubbing my sleepy eyes and recoiling from the sunlight coming through the windows, Rahk smirks at me but withholds any comment.

My leg still hurts tremendously, but the edge of the pain has gone down since the cold plunge. My movements are more inclined to stiffness rather than heavy limping.

It's one small mercy.

That evening, before I am to serve Rahk his meal, I pass his study on the way to the kitchen. I glance inside and find him standing in the middle of the room, an open book in one hand, a furrow in his brow, and his other arm lifted in midair. Curiosity makes me pause.

As I watch, he keeps glancing between the book and his feet, moving his feet in a pattern well known to me.

I almost laugh. He's trying to teach himself how to dance! In that second, I forget the deadly arc of his swords last night, my injury, and the certainty that he will be the one to sever my head from the rest of my body. Instead, I think of how adorable he looks—one so mighty and otherwise graceful struggling with the basic steps of the waltz.

My quiet snicker betrays me. Rahk whirls. I duck away from the slim opening in the door, but he crosses the distance and swings it open fully. Revealing me staring up at him and trying to swallow my giggle.

He isn't angry. If anything, he looks pleased that I caught him. "You're not a very good spy."

"I shall improve, master."

The corner of his mouth lifts. "I know a sufficient punishment for you."

"Punishment?" I bow quickly. "I believe Mrs. Finch is ready with supper! I must be going!"

He laughs, blocking my escape by planting his arm on the opposite wall of the hallway and leaning down toward me. I flush despite myself.

"You'll not evade me so easily. I need to practice with a partner, and since I've caught you snooping, I'll make you do the woman's part."

Oh no. Now I'll have to pretend I don't know how to dance—or try to pull off the illusion that I'm better at the man's part. The way I screw up my face isn't at all an act. "I will do anything you wish, my lord, but my ankle still bothers me."

He cocks his head slightly and lifts one eyebrow. "You're going soft on me, Nat. There's no swelling, you took a dip in the creek, and you rested all afternoon. Surely it does not pain you so terribly?"

I don't know what to reply to that. If I say it does, indeed, pain me greatly, he'll summon the doctor, who will discover my true injury. If I say it doesn't, then if I ever show pain again, Rahk will immediately be concerned. I do my best to shrug nonchalantly. "It definitely feels better than this morning."

"Good. Now, step inside my study. We'll go slowly—for your sake and mine."

I do as he bids. The thought of dancing only makes my leg ache more than before, but I shove it away as best as I can. *Remember to pretend you don't know the woman's part,* I tell myself. *Be clumsy and ignorant!*

I'm afraid that Rahk will shut the door and enclose us in this small, intimate space by ourselves. To my relief, he leaves it cracked.

"Have you ever danced before?" he asks, and the way he fixes his attention on his book when he asks the question makes me feel as if he is pointedly *not* looking at me.

"My sister has taught me a little."

His eyes glitter. "Did she teach you the woman's part?"

I swallow hard and shake my head. He studies me a second longer and then turns the book my way. The page has diagrams of the foot patterns of the waltz. "Here's your part," he points, and runs his finger along the illustration I need to pay attention to. "You'll have to endure any censure you feel at playing the woman."

I am, instead, looking at the man's part, telling myself I need to do the exact opposite of everything I know in dancing. I nod. "She's taught me a little of the waltz."

"Good. Now, let us get in position. Don't look at me with such fear—I told you, we'll go slowly."

Chastised, I shift my gaze to the floor so he cannot read anything on my face. I pretend I'm focused very intently on my feet as I scoot close enough for us to touch, the tips of his boots filling my vision. Then, in an effort to make my act convincing, I hold up the opposite hand for him to grab.

There's a smile in his voice when he says—his breath stirring hair on the top of my head—"The other one, Nat."

"Oops."

I give him my other hand and try desperately not to instantly savor the feeling of his fingers interlacing with mine. They are far rougher than any of the gentlemen that I've danced with before. I find I don't mind it at all. I give a spare thought to hoping that, upon the contact, he doesn't notice how very feminine mine are.

His other palm slides to sit just below my shoulder blade. I freeze, suddenly terrified he will feel my chest binding. But he gives no indication of the discovery.

He applies gentle pressure on my back and tugs on my hand—drawing me closer to him. I determinedly keep my gaze on the floor, lest my blush give me away.

"The waltz moves on a count of three," he says, and his voice has gotten very quiet for some reason.

"I do remember that much," I reply, laughing slightly to distract from my discomfort.

"I shall count to three and then we shall begin. One, two, three—"

I stop him. "It's more of a lilting rhythm, not so stiff." I demonstrate for him. "*One two three, one two three, one two three.*" Then, when he arches an eyebrow at me in surprise, I add, "At least, that was how Mary said it was to be done."

"Well, then I am glad for Mary's correction. Let us begin again. *One two three—*"

As the woman, I'm supposed to move backward while he moves forward. But, because I've got a ruse to keep, I go forward—except that I overcompensate with my opposites, and begin with my right foot instead of my left.

We collide. My nose smashes into his throat, his chin hitting my forehead, our chests nearly crashing together.

"Forgive me! I am foolish!" I cry at once, pulling back. "I've gotten the parts confused again. You really should get someone else to help you. Someone who is familiar with the women's part."

"I will not allow you to sabotage us to get out of your punishment. No, we shall be here until we've got it down—even if we must be here until dawn."

"Ugh!" I whine in frustration.

He chuckles, and I might have thought his grip on me tightened just slightly. "You shall not escape your punishment so easily."

"Mrs. Finch will be infuriated that I'm late to get your tray of food. She'll complain that it was all perfectly hot and now it'll be cold."

"Your attempts to avoid this won't work. Now, remember: you go backwards."

This time, I go backwards, but with the wrong foot. Rahk only resets us, pulling me close to him, and counts us in again. I can think of only so many ways I can mess this up, so on the third try, I do as I'm supposed to. I allow myself seven perfect steps before I take another misstep.

My attempts to frustrate Rahk prove in vain. He only smiles at my mistakes, pulls me closer, and begins anew. By our sixth try, he holds me noticeably closer than at the beginning, and his head is tilted down toward mine, enough that I can feel every one of his exhalations in my hair. This strikes me as very strange. I frown. If he tries to dance with courtly ladies at this proximity, they'll all call scandal.

"I don't think you're supposed to be this close," I say, wrinkling my brow. I dare a single glance up at him, at his handsome face, and immediately regret it. "Mary said I was always to keep the ladies at a further distance or else they'll think I have ill intentions."

"Mary to the rescue yet again," Rahk replies, and adjusts our stance.

I can breathe again with more distance between us. We do several perfect turns around the room before I forget I'm supposed to be making mistakes. "You've picked this dance up very quickly," I say to cover my blunder. "I've not seen you make a single misstep."

"High praise indeed, coming from the servant boy."

I take my arm that is resting on his elbow and, without thinking, smack his shoulder. He smirks.

"I mean no insult to you, Nat, as you well know."

"You enjoy insulting me for sport."

"I'm afraid you might be correct in that assessment. There is an easy solution, however."

"Oh?"

His smirk widens, his voice dropping to a low, conspiratorial tone. "Don't be so fun to tease."

I scowl, which only makes him laugh harder.

"How is your ankle faring?"

His reminder of my injury brings the pain roaring back. He was so distracting I'd almost completely forgotten about it. "It is fine."

He releases me, stepping back. "There, you are sufficiently punished. If either Mrs. Banks or Mrs. Finch give you trouble for being late, tell me at once."

I'm dismissed, then. *Finally*. I turn toward the door, ready to flee the premises, when I nearly stumble back for the shock of Edvear standing there. He wears a strange expression, his ears turned back like Bartholomew's when she is upset. He regards me silently. I bow, not sure what else to do to hide my hot cheeks.

He steps aside and lets me scurry past. Once I'm halfway down the hallway, the door to Rahk's study shuts with a firm click.

RAHK

"Nat is a woman," Edvear says flatly.

I look up from the book I've been studying on human dances. I shut it firmly and set it down on my desk. Then I make my way to my chair and sit. I arrange my hands behind my head and lean back. So the dancing was what tipped my steward off. "Yes."

"Great Kings," Edvear curses. "How long have you known?"

"From the beginning."

"And you never told anyone?"

"I intended to find out the reason behind the deception before I so flippantly revealed her. You are displeased with me?"

Edvear opens his mouth and shuts it again. "I am worried."

"About?"

"How do we know she has not been sent to orchestrate our downfall?"

I take a deep breath through my nostrils and sigh. "She is not a threat to us. I have spent a great deal of time trying to understand the situation, and she has admitted to me that she is in danger and in need of protection. That is why I have let her stay."

"So she has told you that she is a woman?"

I keep my face motionless. "She has not."

A small noise of concern emits from his throat.

"Do not expose her to the servants," I say. "I'm doing what I can to protect her."

Edvear nods, unhappy, but obedient. "Lady Duxbury Vandermore is free to call on first thing tomorrow, if that suits you."

"That suits me well. Tell Nat to be ready for an outing. I'll take her with me."

CHAPTER 31

KAT

RAHK TAKES HIS meal in his room and asks me to stay and play Fool's Circle with him. I gladly oblige and bring both his game and mine to the table. We've been playing with the variation he gave me every now and then, to the point that I cannot decide which I enjoy more.

It's Rahk's move when he says casually, "Since you have grown older since our last discussion on the topic, do you ever think about marriage now?"

Just like in our prior conversation, I drop the piece I'm holding. I look up to find him studying me intently. Swallowing, I make my move and try to feign nonchalance. "No."

"Ah."

"But I take it that you do?"

"Indeed, I have been."

"None of these human women will marry you," I say.

He snorts, but I didn't mean to tell a joke. I was merely stating a fact. He doesn't know how terrified they all are of him.

Surely, he noticed the wide berth they gave him at the queen's luncheon!

"There is one who, rumor has it, will marry me if I ask."

"Is there?" I ask, trying to withhold my dubious chortle. I cannot think of a single young lady—except maybe Bridget, if she felt like the only alternative was spinsterhood—who would willingly marry a fae.

"I haven't met her yet," says Rahk thoughtfully. "I've tried on multiple occasions, but she has always been out. Her family was willing to accept my proposal on her behalf, however."

I scoff. It reminds me at once of Agatha and how hard she has worked to make me marry Lord Boreham, which still strikes me as vastly strange.

"Why do you find that amusing?" he asks.

I pull my face back under my control. "Nothing. I just wouldn't want to marry someone I'd never seen before."

He smiles, looking slightly conspiratorial as he leans closer to the board. "Would you think me incredibly shallow to hope I like how she looks?"

I scowl. "I would, my lord."

He laughs outright at that, a warm twinkle in his eyes that I cannot make sense of.

"Shouldn't you think more of the girl?" I ask, chewing on my lips and frowning. "What if she is scared to marry someone she hasn't met? Or someone she doesn't know if she can even tolerate? Or someone she finds *disgusting*? What if she doesn't want the marriage, but her family is only forcing her into it? After all, as the man, you have most of the power in the situation."

"Do I?"

"Of course you do." I place my move, then look up. He's still studying me. Why does he look at me with that focused expression like he's testing me? "I don't know what it's like where you're from, but here . . . marriage can be a vulnerable thing for a woman."

"You are very sensitive to this subject for a twelve-year-old lad."

I try to keep my wince internal. "I listen to Mary complain, is all."

He thoughtfully considers the board, then places his piece. He seems to take more time with each placement, as though I give him more challenge than I did at first. "You are right, Nat. I shouldn't think of myself in this potential marriage. My concern ought to be for her, whether she is comfortable, respected, cared for, and amenable to the marriage itself."

It's better I keep my mouth shut and not betray myself any more than I already have.

"Your sister . . . She is not married, correct?" Rahk asks.

I shoot a playful glare up at him. "Don't get any ideas."

He laughs. I bask in the satisfaction of that moment, but a very unpleasant emotion niggles at the back of my mind as I make my move. If he marries, he won't play Fool's Circle with me. He'll take his supper privately with his wife, probably.

His wife.

I want to shake out of my skin at the discomfort of that thought. It feels so ironic that Lord Oliver warned me so thoroughly against the infamous fae coming to town and how he might want me as a bride. Now here I am, the most suitable of wives for him, and yet wholly unable to claim that privilege.

Did I just think of it as a . . . *privilege?*

Saints, I've let myself forget my own head. I don't have to survive as Rahk's servant for much longer. I only have two and a half weeks before I turn twenty-one. Soon I'll be able to go back to my life, with my fortune, and I'll be free of Agatha's influence.

It doesn't matter if Rahk marries. I will probably be gone before he does anyway. I will miss him—a thought that feels like a betrayal of all the human slaves still imprisoned in Faerieland—but it will be good to put distance between us. He shows me so much overt favoritism, and aside from Mary and the staff back at Vandermore Manor, it's been so long since someone cared for me without regard for my money. I've let it matter more than it should.

"Mary hasn't enough influence or money to tempt someone like you," I say, trying to fill the silence between us. "Though she has better character than anyone you'll meet at those fancy balls."

He sighs. "I'm afraid I cannot marry for character, and certainly not for love. Influence is what I need, if I am to be accepted by the queen."

"You'll not get influence if you cannot properly count the rhythm of a waltz."

"I have mended the error of my ways. I shall never count it so *stilted* again."

I snicker, searching the board for any alternative to losing yet again. "You should find a proper teacher. You've got lots of money."

The crinkle of the skin near his temples turns his gaze sly. "Why should I? You make an excellent womanly partner."

The comment strikes me so hard I blush furiously, more from fear of discovery than anything else. He sounds like he's goading me, and if I didn't know better . . .

No, he cannot know I am a woman. He would say something. He would probably yell at me, enraged at being deceived. No, he cannot know. He's only trying to goad me by poking my *boyish* pride.

I scowl and hope he doesn't notice the color of my skin. I decide to change the subject back on him. "So if you are thinking of marrying, does that mean you plan to stay in the human lands indefinitely?"

Rahk moves his pieces. "I do not know. That is, I will go back to Nothril. I *must* go back."

There is something about the way he says it that makes me pause. "You are not sure if you want to."

He freezes. It is only for one moment, but that moment tells me a wealth of information. His black eyes flick up to mine—as if to check if I caught his slip. "I must go back," he repeats. "This time, here in Harbright, has been a reprieve. Perhaps to you that seems strange, considering the assassins' recent attack, but truly, I . . . I have enjoyed these three weeks."

"What takes you back?" I ask.

He chews on his lip. "My youngest sister needs my protection."

"Is someone trying to hurt her?" I do not expect him to answer my question. It is none of my business. But I get the sense he wishes to have a confidant. I wonder if he has ever had one before.

"My parents will probably kill her, eventually," Rahk replies.

His honesty shocks me. "What? Why?"

"She does not conform to Nothril's standards. She is not vicious or cold. She is sweet, adventurous, and a little stupid. If she does not learn to behave, they will cut her down. I do what I can to protect her, but I often fear it will not be enough."

I often fear it will not be enough. The sentiment rings in my ears, reminding me of the inevitable end of my work as the Ivy Mask. The work Rahk will end himself. I don't know how I can leave it behind, knowing so many others haven't been saved.

"I'm sorry," I whisper. It strikes me then, just how much I assume about the fae—that they are cruel to their core—when here is a brother giving up a chance at freedom for the sake of a sister who is too good for the world she was born into. I have seen many, many wicked fae. But maybe some of them aren't. Maybe some of them are just trapped in a life they cannot hope to escape.

"It is the reality of Faerieland, I'm afraid." Rahk places his pieces. I didn't even pay attention to where I moved mine. "You get used to it. Pavi is not the only thing that calls me back. I have a friend who is like a brother to me. I would miss him greatly if I didn't return. Then there is my throne to consider."

I snort.

"What?" he demands, his gaze finding mine in genuine confusion.

I shrug. "You said it so casually. *Oh yes—the throne, too!*"

His mouth tips very slightly. "I do not think of it often. It will be centuries before I ascend. I have plenty of time until then to lose all sense of morality and become a jaded tyrant."

He says it as though he jests, but the Rahk before me has, for whatever reason, decided not to mask his expressions for me. It makes me want to comfort him somehow, with words or touch. As Nat, however, I have little I can offer—a fact that burns me with frustration.

"I don't think you should worry about that," I say.

He lifts one brow, a slight brightness coming into his expression. He expects me to say something ridiculous, doesn't he? Something that will amuse him.

"I think you should only be concerned if several millennia go by before you get your throne. A few centuries won't do much."

His smile spreads. I've succeeded in cheering him up. "Do you speak this from experience?"

"Have I not told you I am twenty thousand years old?" I reply. "I have seen many kingdoms rise and fall. I also saw the invention of the pocket watch. No one was on time before that."

He doesn't laugh, which is good, since my comments didn't deserve one. Instead, he smiles at me. That smile pins me to the spot and makes me forget every thought in my mind. It is soft and liquid, warm and sweet, and what I want in that moment is the chance to be closer to him.

"I am glad you came to work for me," Rahk rumbles quietly. "You do my soul good."

His words bring a flush climbing up my neck to my cheeks. I cannot handle the intensity of his attention, so I shift away again to a question I've been needing an answer to. Clearing my throat, I drag my Fool's Circle book closer and flip it open after I take my turn. "Master? May I ask you a question?"

"Of course." He peers around the board to watch me page through the book.

I find the page, turn the book around, and push it toward Rahk. I point at the page. "What is the Star City?"

He reads the section I pointed at. "I didn't know this book was recent enough to have a mention of the Star City. It is a city separate from the Courts, which is very unusual in Faerie. I do not know how long it will remain independent."

"Have you seen it?" I press. "What does it look like? Is it full of stars like the name suggests?"

"I have seen it. Recently, in fact. It is not named for an abundance of stars unique to the place, but for the tall spires that reach toward them. It is a beautiful city."

Tall spires.

That is what I need for my raid. I smile and drag my book back. "It sounds beautiful."

Rahk nods as he places his piece in the final spot surrounding the Fool, claiming his win.

"One of these days, I will beat you within an inch of your life." I vow.

He grins at me.

The next morning, Rahk is gone early and does not return until after sunup. It's not a *guarantee* that he was trying to track me down, but I cannot imagine what else he could have been doing. If my life was not on the line, I might be smug about his unsuccessful trip.

He strides inside, his hair wild, a twig sticking out above his pointed ear. I serve him his breakfast in his room as usual. His breakfast tray grows heavier each day as Charity tries to calibrate her serving proportions to his appetite. Every time, I return the tray empty, and every time she throws up her hands and vows that the next time, she will finally serve him too much food.

"You've been trying not to smirk at me this entire meal," Rahk says mildly as I clear his empty tray. "To what do I owe this honor?"

That twig sticks out of his hair, one remaining leaf stuck to it like a flag. "I am not smirking at you, my lord," I lie outright for the fun of it.

He tilts his head to one side. Then he gets up and marches to the mirror. "Ah, you mock my organic decorations."

My laugh spills out of me. His gaze snaps to me at once, surprised. Have I . . . have I never laughed in front of him before? He is looking at me like I'm a different person. At first, I fear his disapproval, but he pulls out the chair from the vanity he's never sat in, and when he sits, his mouth curls upward.

"If you disapprove, then come fix the mess yourself," he orders, gesturing to his hair. "This should be part of your job, anyway."

"Fix the mess?" I repeat, not taking a single step toward the vanity. "You want me to tend to your hair?"

"I do."

I retreat slightly. "I am *not* skilled in hair." It is a very honest truth. Mary has always done my hair.

He waves one hand impatiently, gesturing to his head. "Then practice. I've got an errand to run today and you're coming with me, so you need to get started."

My reply is a grumbling, "As you wish, my lord."

I find a brush in the vanity and position myself behind Rahk. Is there a way to do this without touching him? He watches me in the mirror, his black eyes following the way I hesitate to bring the brush to his scalp.

"You could start by removing the debris," he says.

My cheeks heat. That would, in fact, be the first step. I pluck the twig and its leaf out of his hair. Then, before I can doubt myself, I stick the bristles into his hair and pull. A muscle in Rahk's face twitches.

"That was too rough, wasn't it?"

He doesn't reply, but I force myself to lay a hand against the back of his head and start brushing from the ends of his hair like Mary always said to. His hair is soft and silky, which is entirely unfair. Why is it that someone like Rahk, who probably cares little for beauty, must have all of it, while the rest of us who actually want it are left with nothing?

I work my way up closer to his scalp. When one lock is shiny and free of tangles, I move on to the next, until his whole head of hair is almost luminescent in its perfection.

Now, what to do with it? He usually wears it tied back in some fashion. He probably hates having it get in his face. I use my fingernails to pull back the hair above his ears and gather it at the back. He blinks fast every time I comb back more.

"Give me your hand," I order. He does, and I take it to the gather of hair at the back of his head. "Hold this. I need to find a cord."

He obeys. I shuffle through the drawers until I find a few thin leather cords. I scoop one up and bring it to his hair. I'm about to start tying when I suddenly can take it no longer, and the question bursts from my mouth: "Why are you staring at me like that?"

His black gaze, which has remained unmoved from my reflection in the mirror this entire time, flees mine for all of one second before it returns. "You are making a lot of different faces while you work. I am playing a game with myself to decipher their meanings."

My eyes widen.

"For example, the face you made just now says you are afraid I will have noticed something incriminating in your previous expressions, which begs the question: What are you afraid I will discover on your features?"

"That I have no idea what I'm doing," I growl as I tie off his hair and step back. "It's a little crooked, but it should stay out of your face."

He regards his hair in the mirror. "Excellent. Prepare to leave for our errand."

CHAPTER 32

KAT

EDVEAR ORDERS THE carriage, which comes round to the front of the mansion. I stand at attention, waiting for instructions as Rahk—wearing a dashing long coat—strides into the sunshine. His eyes find me immediately.

"Into the carriage with you," he orders.

Clifford, who drives, shoots me a sidelong glance as I hurry to obey.

"Is your ankle troubling you much?" Rahk asks as he settles across from me. "You still favor your leg."

I've been sneaking out to soak it in the freezing cold creek early each morning, which has helped with the pain management. But last night, I removed the stitches, so the pain is reinvigorated.

"Only a little," I lie.

He doesn't say anything else as we drive. He has his chin propped up on his fist, his elbow on his thigh as he stares out the window.

"Where are we going?" I venture after several minutes of silence.

"To sort out the matter of whether I shall be wed soon," he says, and I'd almost think there was a note of dry sarcasm in the statement.

"Oh," I say stupidly, focusing my attention on my hands in my lap. Horse hooves clip-clop on the cobblestone streets. I watch out the window, noting the familiar streets and houses. That's the Fairfax manor. Two streets over, the Ludlum family has their beautiful estate with enough grounds to make one forget they were in the city.

It occurs to me that I likely know which family he intends to marry into. I'm probably acquaintances with the girl. I want to ask, but force myself not to, in fear I might give away knowledge a boy of my supposed station shouldn't have.

"Mary's situation is nearby," I say absently.

"Perhaps we can visit after our business is settled."

I shake my head. "She'll be far too busy, but she's promised to visit me soon."

"As you wish."

We sit in silence, and when I look up, I find him watching me intently yet again. His scrutiny makes me shift awkwardly in my seat.

The carriage comes to a halt. I peer out the window.

What I see nearly makes me go blind in panic.

That is the trimmed shrub of a rearing stallion. A stallion I know better than my own name.

"It looks like we're here," says Rahk, stretching his legs as the footman opens the carriage door for him.

Is this some terrible joke? Is this a horrible nightmare I'm about to wake up from? Has he found out every one of my secrets and intends to force my hand in the cruelest of ways?

But when I look at Rahk, there is not a shred of understanding or significance on his face. No gloating *"Aha! I've got you now!"*—not a single smidge of it. If anything, his expression shifts very slightly to concern when he looks back into the carriage and sees I haven't followed him.

"Come along then," he says.

I could plead ill. I could claim my leg is thunderously painful. I could—

All of my options create more problems. I *am* in disguise. Perhaps my disguise is enough to fool my stepfamily? I could slip in, stay at the back, and slip back out again. No one will be the wiser.

I draw in a deep breath and climb out of the carriage, hiding the flash of pain that shoots up my leg at the effort.

I hang back among the footmen, but Rahk waves me to his side as he strides up to the front of the manor I've lived in all my life. My mind races faster than a galloping horse. Mary is here. She'll recognize me for sure. Perhaps she can pull me aside, away from the prying eyes of my stepfamily.

"Lord Rahk," says Charles at the door, bowing. "Lady Duxbury Vandermore has been expecting you. This way."

I finally process the reason for this visit.

"I haven't met her yet. I've tried on multiple occasions, but she has always been out. Her family was willing to accept my proposal on her behalf."

I stagger slightly, but I'm situated behind Rahk so he doesn't notice. Charles's gaze snaps to mine, however, and at once his eyes go wide with recognition. I hold up one finger to my lips, silently pleading with him not to reveal me. He swallows and quickly looks away.

I'm the bride Rahk is considering. *I'm* the woman he's been trying to see.

I stare in shock at the broad expanse of his back, the way his coat swishes with each purposeful step. Am I . . . engaged?

The parlor is as I remember it, though it suddenly feels *very* cramped with Rahk taking up so much space.

"I know you've been eager to meet Lady Vandermore," says Agatha, all smiles and ease as she receives Rahk into the parlor. She wears one of her nicest dresses—a raspberry colored silk. "I am happy to inform you that she is here."

My head whips up in shock. But Agatha isn't looking at me. She gestures to Bridget, whose curls are groomed to lush perfection, wearing the same spring-green gown I wore to the ball where Lord

Boreham told me his intent to propose. It is far too fine for a morning reception—as is Agatha's dress. Are they trying to flaunt their wealth to Rahk?

Bridget rises, smiling beautifully as Rahk bows over her hand and kisses it.

I could vomit.

"Lord Rahk, may I present Lady Vandermore," says Agatha.

"It is a pleasure to make your acquaintance." Rahk straightens and releases Bridget's hand.

"Likewise," says Bridget.

"Please, be seated and make yourself comfortable." Agatha gestures to the bench drawn up near the empty fireplace. "I've rung for tea, so you must stay as we discuss the terms of the marriage."

Rahk clears his throat. "I do not intend to stay long. I came to—"

"But you must stay! Sit at once. We have much to discuss that cannot be delayed."

Rahk subtly glances my way in irritation, and either his glance is so short or my playacting at not being utterly panicked is excellent, because he doesn't give a second glance of concern at my expression. He sits, hiding his annoyance under a silent, blank mask.

I hang against the back of the room where I desperately pray neither Bridget nor Agatha notices me. My hands and feet have turned ice cold.

"I've drawn up the papers for the bride price," says Agatha as Mary enters with a tea tray. She must have heard the news that I am here, for she does not look at me a single time but focuses on pouring each cup of tea with grace and efficiency.

Meanwhile, it takes everything inside me not to gape in shock. *Bride price?* We don't do bride prices—we have dowries. The husbands get paid to marry us, not the other way around. There hasn't been a custom of bride price in this kingdom for hundreds of years.

I stare, utterly dumbfounded. They're trying to hoodwink Rahk because he does not know our customs. They're trying to benefit from my fortune, which gave me influence, and thus made me a prize for Rahk—and then they won't give him any. They will steal his money in return.

I cannot even listen to the conversation as it plays out before me. Do they intend to have Bridget marry him under the guise of my name?

Suddenly, something hits me with such clarity, my knees almost buckle.

Somehow—in a way I cannot know or understand—my marrying Lord Boreham came as a benefit to my stepfamily. There's no other reason Agatha would work so hard to make that marriage come about. Perhaps there is an agreement that Lord Boreham would pay some of my fortune to them if they persuaded me to marry him before my twenty-first birthday. And if that is the case . . .

Agatha is trying to kill two birds with one stone. She is trying to farm my fortune from me by Lord Boreham's payment, and by fooling Rahk into paying a bride price.

I cannot let her do this.

I *will not* let her do this.

"As you can see, this is a very reasonable bride price for a woman of such standing as my stepdaughter." Agatha passes the papers to Rahk, who shows not a shred of emotion on his placid face.

He takes the papers and reads them. "Twelve thousand crowns?"

My jaw falls open. I shove off the wall and slip out of the room. I hear the shift in Rahk's seat as he glances at me, but he does not stop me as I leave. Heart pounding, I rush out to the carriage, where I pace for the count of thirty, trying to bide enough time to fool my stepfamily.

"Kat!" Mary hisses, her voice cracking as she rushes to meet me. "What are you *doing* here?"

"They're trying to trick Rahk—Lord Rahk! They're charging him a bride price! I'm going to go back in one moment and tell Lord Rahk that a missive came with urgent business. Once we are gone, I will explain the situation to him."

"Explain *what* situation?" Mary demands, a single strand of red hair standing out of place. "The situation about your identity? The situation that you are a woman? The situation that you are—"

The Ivy Mask.

"No, just that they're trying to fool him because he doesn't know any better."

Mary clicks her tongue, a sound of disapproval at the back of her throat. "You've got to be careful. This is *your life* on the line. So what if Agatha tricks the fae out of a significant portion of his wealth?"

I grind my teeth. I cannot explain this to her. So I only grab her hand and squeeze. "I'll be careful."

Then I run back into the house, my leg throbbing, and I don't even have to pretend to be breathless when I barge into the parlor. I drop to my knee beside Rahk's bench. His attention swivels to me at once.

"What is it?" he asks.

"Your steward sent a courier to bring urgent news from home. My lord, we must go at once."

He stands, reading my signal. "Lady Duxbury Vandermore, I'm afraid our meeting must be cut short. I shall send you word tomorrow of my answer to the proposal. Lady Vandermore, it was a pleasure to meet you."

But Bridget is staring at me, her hand pressed against her mouth. "Katherine?"

It is like the entire room swivels its attention to me.

Agatha shoots to her feet and catches herself on the mantel. Bridget takes in my clothes, my haircut. "What . . . are you doing?"

Rahk glances between the three of us, puzzled. "You know Kat?"

Kat. How does he know my nickname? And why does he not seem shocked that I have been called by a woman's name?

He knows. He knows I'm a woman. He *has* known.

I stand frozen. A dozen terrible scenarios play out before me. Rahk will hand me over to Agatha, and she will make me marry Lord Boreham. I'll be forced to wed a man I cannot respect and give him my fortune. Or Rahk won't hand me over—he'll chop me to pieces for deceiving him.

Rahk's hand comes toward me—most likely to take my elbow—and I panic. My panic mobilizes my feet, and I turn on my heel and bolt down the hallway as fast as I can.

There is no room for rational thought in my head. All I know is that I am the prey, and everyone in that room is a predator.

I careen down the hallway, shoving past Matthew and Viola in the kitchen, and fly out the backdoor. Escaping through the front lawn and into the city isn't likely to work, so I throw myself toward the hedge in the back. Every step, my wound pounds with agony.

Heavy footsteps pursue me. It's Rahk.

I shove myself faster.

"Kat!" he shouts. "Kat!"

His use of my nickname only makes me run harder. I approach the hedge, hoping that at least will slow Rahk down. There's the hole I use to crawl through for my raids. I dive for it now.

My wound jars with impact when I slam my knee into the ground and haul myself through the hedge. My shirt gets caught, held fast. I yank as hard as I can and hear a rip. I pull harder, determined to make it through the hedge and on to freedom.

A large hand catches the ankle of my good leg. The shriek that leaves my mouth isn't at all dignified. I kick hard, but Rahk is stronger. Vastly stronger. He drags me back through the hedge, no matter how hard I struggle.

And then, suddenly, I'm lying on my back in the lawn, staring up at Rahk as he pins me.

"What are you doing?" he demands. His gaze falls to my chest and quickly looks away, the muscles of his throat jerking.

Several of the buttons of my shirt ripped, and I look down to find that much of my chest binding is visible through the gaps in my shirt. Mortification overcomes me. I sag, looking anywhere but Rahk's penetrating gaze as he studies my face. To my horror, tears gather behind my eyelids, pressure building in my throat. He's got my arms pinned above my head with one hand, the other planted firmly on my hip to keep me from rolling to my feet and running.

More running footsteps pound behind us. Agatha's voice, turned unusually shrill, calls out, "Oh I'm so glad you found my daughter! I've been so worried about her! Katherine Vandermore, what has gotten into you?"

Rahk twists toward my stepfamily who hurries across the lawn. Then his gaze returns to me. I watch, helplessly, as full realization sinks into his face. Grimness overtakes everything else. His face shutters, and I watch the exact moment he closes me out—just like he did with my stepfamily. I can almost feel the fury rolling off his shoulders, though who it is directed at, I cannot know.

My leg throbs from the exertion, and out of a desperate need for relief from his gaze, I twist my face into his arm and swallow obsessively to keep from weeping.

It's Agatha's voice calling my name that brings sense back into my muddled brain. Rahk is about to turn me over to them, isn't he? He cannot just keep me as his servant now that he knows who I am.

I cannot marry Lord Boreham. I cannot have endured everything of these past several weeks for nothing. If Agatha punished me for refusing his initial advances by selling Bartholomew, what will she do to me now?

"Please," I gasp, pleading, clenching my fingers in his grip. "Please don't give me back to them."

His black eyes devour me, like a pit I have fallen into where only death awaits me. I want to remind him of Fool's Circle, of our dip in the creek, all the long conversations. But there is nothing I can do but wait.

Rahk releases my wrists abruptly, getting to his feet. His movements are brisk but careful when he pulls me to mine. He doesn't look at me now. Not as he removes his coat and sweeps it around me. Covering what my shirt doesn't.

Then, he takes me very firmly by the shoulders and, despite how much I try to resist, pushes me toward my approaching stepfamily. When he speaks, his voice reminds me at once of that cold, icy tone he used in the Nothril Court. "This is Lady Vandermore."

It's not a question.

Sweat glistens on Agatha's brow, her perfect hair falling out of its careful arrangement. I've never seen her so disheveled. "Yes, Lord Rahk, I'm afraid she is. Please forgive the deception. We could not find her, and we knew she would have wanted to accept your proposal of marriage, so we concocted the deception to keep both of you happy."

I want to snarl at her. How *dare* she? How *dare* she try to—

"I will marry her."

Rahk's voice brings all my thoughts to a sudden and shocking halt. My attention whips to him, but he still refuses to look at me. His fingers dig into my shoulders.

"I will accept the terms of the proposal," continues Rahk, "on two conditions."

Agatha's neck cranes, a note of surprised optimism entering her voice. "Yes?"

"First, that one of my servants inspects her today and the day of the wedding, to ensure she is an unblemished virgin."

Unblemished virgin?

My whole body goes hot with anger at the humiliation of those words. Is *this* Rahk's most important quality in a wife? What happened to our conversation last night, when he said he would be thinking of the bride's comfort in the arrangement? Instead, he bargains for me like chattel!

"And second," Rahk says, "the wedding will be moved to tomorrow."

CHAPTER 33

RAHK

KAT GOES RIGID for a second time beneath my grip. Meanwhile, Lady Duxbury Vandermore says immediately, "Deal."

She's afraid I'll rescind my word. She's afraid I'll realize how she has supposedly *fooled* me.

My world has narrowed to what is right before me. The Ivy Mask, the blood oath sealed with Pavi's life, Ash's task, the Faerieland border—all of it is gone. Even Kat's own feelings don't matter, much less the reasons for her deception.

I just have to get her out of here.

I will deal with the repercussions later. I will deal with my own simmering fury later. I will get answers later. And I will endlessly regret my choice not to force Kat's hand about her disguise—*later.*

Right now, there is room for one truth: I vowed to protect Kat, and for whatever unknown reason, she is not safe with her stepfamily.

"Let us go sign the papers at once," I say.

"Yes, of course," says Lady Duxbury Vandermore.

The daughter who is most definitely *not* Lady Vandermore says nothing. She hangs back, glancing with something akin to guilt between Kat and her mother. Every now and then, she braves a glance at me when she thinks I'm not looking. As we step into the house, she promptly disappears, and I am glad for it. I know a coward when I see one.

As we sign the marriage contract, Kat is a silent witness to the purchasing of her future. I keep one hand on her. I do not know which I fear more: her running away again or handing her over to her stepfamily.

When at last I can delay no longer, I pry my fingers off her, sketch a bow, and force myself to leave without her.

Sunlight streams across my face as I storm to the carriage. I dare not look back. The footman hurries to open the carriage door for me, but I beat him to it and barely keep myself from slamming it behind me.

Once I'm safely ensconced in the privacy of drawn curtains and rattling horse hooves, I bury my face in my hands and groan.

"Why didn't she tell me?" I growl under my breath. "If she had just *told* me, I could have kept her safe, away from her stepmother. I wouldn't have had to resort . . . to *this*!"

What am I going to do now? I can't be married! What am I supposed to do with a wife? It's not as if I can bring her back with me to Nothril! Do I leave her here when I return to Faerieland? If I do, will I have to visit her?

One thing is clear: I cannot marry her my people's way.

Carriage wheels on cobblestone fill the silence as my thoughts storm through my mind.

No matter what way I view this from, it is a disaster of colossal proportions. I should have handed Kat over, rescinded my intention to marry as I'd planned, and *left*. That is what I should have done.

So why didn't I?

Her wide, frightened eyes return to my memory. I will never forget the way she turned her face into my arm and begged me not to give her back to them.

I clench my jaw hard.

The carriage finally comes to a stop. My foot is on the ground the next second. Edvear rushes out to greet me. He reads my expression and falls back a step.

"My lord! What has happened?" He looks behind me. "Where is Nat?"

"Go get Mrs. Finch," I order.

He obeys at once. When the cook meets me in my study, I tell her, "Go immediately to Vandermore Manor." Then I lay forward all that I require of her.

CHAPTER 34
KAT

KATHERINE ELEANOR VANDERMORE, I should have you beaten!" Agatha, earrings shaking, skin reddened to the hue of a cherry, looks nothing like her normal self. "I should have you horsewhipped! Anthony—"

"She mustn't be touched, my lady," Mary interrupts, bobbing a curtsy. "Lord Rahk made it clear he won't have her if she is damaged."

I sit in the parlor, huddled in Rahk's cloak, shaking with wrath I can barely contain.

Bridget hangs beyond the door, a hand over her mouth. She watches the spectacle, but ducks out of view whenever Agatha turns around. Edith came when she heard the shouting, muttered, "No, thank you," and left again. I wish I could have fled with her.

Agatha rounds on Mary. "You were part of this, weren't you?"

"I had no role in the matter," she replies, clearing out the tea dishes.

"If you are lying, Mary, you will share Katherine's punishment with her."

Mary curtsies. "Yes, ma'am."

"She didn't do anything!" I cry, finally finding my voice. "It was all me. You must not punish her for my wrongdoing!"

"So, you admit it was wrong of you to run away, disguised like a common servant boy, to avoid your duty of marrying Lord Boreham?" Agatha sticks a shaking finger in my face.

I try not to look at Mary as she makes her escape. I breathe easier once she is gone. Swallowing my pride and stubbornness, I take the route of placation and nod.

"Then you will submit to whatever punishment I deem appropriate?"

The blood drains from my face. I do not reply.

"Since I cannot have *you* beaten, you will watch as Mary takes your punishment. Do twenty lashes sound appropriate?"

I've never seen Agatha like this. I never liked her, but part of me always believed if the circumstances of our sharing a family had been different, we might have loved each other. Now I cannot believe I ever thought such a thing. I jump to my feet. "You will *not* lay a hand on *any* members of this staff! Not to punish them, and certainly not to punish me. If you do, I will take every cent of my fortune and apply it to your ruin!"

Agatha raises her hand to strike me across the face. I flinch, bracing myself, but the blow doesn't come. Instead, she barks to her favored servant: "Sylva! The slippers."

Sylva comes silently, bearing the once-pink velvet box. Cold fingers close around my heart. I watch as she hands the box to my stepmother. Agatha takes the lid off and moves aside the fabric to take one of the slippers.

"Agatha—" I plead.

She smashes the slipper to the floor.

"No!" I scream, diving for it. I'm not fast enough. The slipper shatters.

Except—it *doesn't.*

The slipper lies there on the hard floor, not even slightly cracked.

In a rage, Agatha grabs both slippers and flings them into the burning fireplace. “Your mother is dead, and she isn’t coming back. Is the crushing of your little fairytale enough punishment?”

Matthew knocks quietly on the doorframe and announces, “Lord Rahk’s servant is here to inspect Lady Katherine.”

He doesn’t meet my eyes when he says the words, and the moment he finishes, he shuffles away. My whole body burns as Mary sweeps in and ushers me upstairs to my room.

I think I might prefer Agatha’s rage to what I’m about to experience.

Charity is the one waiting in my room. I blink when I see her, and then a cord of tension inside me dissolves.

“Everything is going to be alright,” she says by way of greeting.

My shoulders drop. Before I can start arguing with Charity that everything will not, in fact, be alright, Mary shuts the door and brings me a robe. Always focused and efficient.

“Turn around, Mrs. Finch. I will help her undress,” Mary orders.

Charity does as requested, and I change into the robe. Once I’m ready, she silently and quickly conducts her inspection of every inch of my body, moving aside the robe as necessary. There is nothing I can do to hide my poorly stitched wound from either her or Mary, and Mary shoots me a look.

“Look what you’ve done to yourself!” that look says.

I dread the moment Charity bids me to lie down—but it never comes. Instead, she finishes quickly and gives me a pitying smile. It is the sort of smile that I would normally despise, but today I want to be pitied.

“Please,” I plead, keeping my voice no louder than a whisper, “you must ask Lord Rahk to hire Mary. My stepmother has threatened to punish her on my behalf, and I—”

Charity nods once. “I understand. I will tell him. Tomorrow morning, at dawn, I shall be back.”

She leaves me alone with Mary.

"Oh, my little sister," Mary whispers, and then wraps me up in her tight embrace.

I sob into her shoulder.

"This is so much worse than I could have imagined. I've failed at staying single until my twenty-first birthday. Lord Rahk will have all my fortune."

She gives a choked laugh. "That is your first concern? Not marrying a fae? A fae with a death wish for you?"

My nose is sniffly, my cheeks wet. "Oh Mary, what am I to do?"

"I don't know." She combs her fingers through my short hair. "I don't know."

My wedding day dawns with heavy rainclouds that threaten a thunderstorm. I did not sleep a single wink—and that wasn't even due to my tumultuous mind. Agatha ordered me to a different room without a window and locked the door so I wouldn't escape during the night. I spend hours staring at the dark outline of that lock, wishing I'd learned how to pick it. Faerieland locks doors with spells, and human blood is an easy bypass. I haven't had to learn to properly lock pick. It sure would have come in handy tonight though.

Charity returns. I bristle slightly, drawing my robe tighter around myself when she enters. But the cook only lifts one hand. "I don't need to check you again. If no one has touched you since yesterday."

I shake my head numbly.

Instead, she aids Mary's effort to dress me in one of my nicest gowns. I am to commit the heinous social crime of re-wearing a gown, made even more odious by the fact that the event is my wedding.

"Word of your sudden nuptials have reached the queen," Agatha says briskly, sweeping into the room as thunder rattles the walls. She holds up a piece of paper. "She has ordered that the wedding take place at the palace."

"At the palace?" I blurt, just as Mary cinches my stays. "Wh—*why*?"

"Who understands the whim of a queen?" Agatha asks, throwing up her hands. "She favors you, certainly, but she does not trust or like that fae."

Maybe the queen doesn't believe the rumor that I would marry a fae unless she sees it unfold before her. I don't believe it myself.

So now the small, intimate ceremony Agatha had arranged at the cathedral will no longer happen. It'll be an *event* at the palace. I would normally care. I'd probably throw a fit about it.

At this point, however, what is the use of fighting it all? I have fought hard to stop this from happening, and yet here we are. Maybe my wedding is a prophecy that I've fulfilled in my attempts to avoid it.

I'm just not marrying Lord Boreham.

I'm marrying Prince Rahk of the Nothril Court—the prince and fae warrior sent to kill me.

Why did he agree to marry me? He certainly doesn't *want* to. Our unusual friendship will be gone, replaced by something neither of us desired.

The thought of marrying someone who does not want me makes me sick.

The gown is heavy and very, very *wide*. Are gowns always this heavy and wide? It's been so long since I've had to remember the size of my skirts before I go through a door. While I prefer the familiarity of stays over the rib-digging discomfort of the chest binding, the rest of the ensemble is vastly less preferred to trousers and collared tunic.

"This is my nightmare," Mary grumbles, fussing with my hair. "Having to arrange someone's hair for their wedding when it's been recently chopped against the scalp!"

I wave my hand. "Just leave it. No one cares."

She shoots me a look of such venom, it actually makes me crack a smile. "And what are these scars on your forehead? You know what—I don't want to know!"

I shake my head. "No, you don't."

Once I'm ready and we are unexpectedly alone, Mary says, "By the way, I have a wedding present for you. It's from the staff."

That perks my interest at once.

Mary holds up her palm to stay my hope. "It's not Bartholomew."

I shrug, trying not to give away the pang in my chest. Mary produces a parcel wrapped in unassuming brown paper. She places it in my lap. Curious, I open it quickly.

My mouth drops open.

Inside the box, carefully protected by cloth and paper, are a pair of soot-darkened glass slippers. My mother's slippers!

"We managed to rescue them when her ladyship was occupied," Mary says, smiling. "It was *quite* the feat to convince her they'd melted in the fire. Charles went all the way to the glassblower with a pair of glass vases to have melted versions made that we returned to the fire."

A laugh bubbles free of my lips. "You were betting a lot on my stepfamily knowing nothing about glass!"

"They are wise in other ways," says Mary with a wink. "They don't look pretty as they are now, but between your fortune and that fae's, they shouldn't take much to restore."

"You are so good to me!" I cry, flinging my arms around her neck.

She pats my back affectionately. "Aren't I? I'll give them to Charity to take to Lord Rahk's estate."

When I'm finally ready, my dress feels even heavier and more claustrophobic when the footmen hand me into the carriage. I considered making a mad bolt for freedom when I stepped outside, but I cannot get far in this dress. Agatha sits across from me in the carriage, silent and statuesque.

I curse the queen the entire ride to the palace gates. *Why* must this be at the palace? If I must marry in disgrace, why must I do it in front of my sovereign and probably the entire gentry of Harbright?

There is a chapel inside the palace. A unit of guards meet us at the palace entrance and escort us there. Bridget is already seated inside, and apparently Edith is to play the organ as I walk down the aisle. Agatha shows not a stitch of emotion on her face as we come to the arched doors.

It's happening so fast. I have no means of processing it all. It's like I'm a ghost trapped in someone else's body, watching through her eyes as the doors swing open into a thunder of sustained organ chords. Agatha steps backward, leaving my side. I never thought I would miss her absence, but I miss it now as my feet root to the spot before the full pews lining the chapel on either side. I cast a helpless glance at her. Her mouth is drawn in a thin line as she jerks her head, motioning for me to move.

I am supposed to walk down the aisle by myself?

The organ drones loudly, filling my entire skull, as I face the chapel.

The first thing I see is Rahk. He stands at the end of the aisle, beside the priest. His back is straight, his form tall. His hands are clasped behind him, his jaw set forward. He wears a formal doublet with creamy lace at the throat, dark breeches, and tall boots. His long hair is half pulled back the way I did it just yesterday, revealing his long, pointed ears. Despite the human fashion of his clothes, he has an otherworldly beauty that I usually try to ignore. I cannot ignore it now. He takes my breath away.

I barely remember to move my feet forward.

I'm marrying Rahk.

The sentence doesn't even make proper sense in my mind. There is no space for fear or gladness. Only a dull sense of disbelief dictates my feelings.

It is heightened by the fact that he isn't looking at me. His gaze, which sweeps over me in a split second as the doors open, fixes just above the fake bun and pearls Mary worked into my hair.

I feel like a mouse in a roomful of predators. The silent onlookers who ask a hundred questions with their disapproving gazes. The queen, who sits to the right in an elevated throne, is a vision of regal beauty. The sting of Agatha's attention burning at my back. Rahk suddenly becomes the only comfort in the entire room. I silently beg him to look at me, to communicate even the tiniest shade of emotion or thought. Instead, he stands like a veritable pillar of night lit by the moon-white of his hair.

I used to be able to read him. I used to make him laugh. We used to be . . . *friends.*

Now he won't even acknowledge my presence.

When I reach the front, Rahk steps down to me and without looking, offers his hand. I take it, and he draws me up the steps to the priest.

I don't hear a word of the ceremony. It passes in agonizing slowness, and yet I wish it would slow down even more. Maybe if the priest talks for forever, he will never get to the part where he says—

"You are now man—er, fae—and wife," stumbles the priest. "Lord Rahk, you may kiss your bride."

I forgot about the kiss. *How* did I forget about the kiss?

He isn't going to kiss me. I look up at him, at the attention he fixes squarely on my forehead, and I do not believe for one moment that he will kiss me. What are we to do, then? Stand here awkwardly until the priest says we can leave without kissing?

Nothing will announce more clearly to everyone present that Rahk has no regard for me.

I usually do not care about creating spectacles. I've been rude at balls often—though always in retribution—but this humiliation burns sharper than anything I've ever felt before. Rahk doesn't want me, and he will reveal that fact to everyone.

He startles me when he steps close to me. I swallow a gasp. His eyes finally, unexpectedly, meet mine. I drown in those black depths. He catches the bottom of my jaw with his right hand and prompts me to tilt my chin.

Wait—surely, he isn't—he won't—

He ducks his head toward mine.

"Rahk," I whisper.

He holds my gaze, and then his eyes close. Mine flutter shut in reply. My heart flies away from my chest. I wait for his lips to land on mine.

They never do.

His breath touches my mouth, his hand on the side of my face, but he does not kiss me. I open my eyes to find his still closed, a slight gather between his brows.

He's using his glamour to create the illusion of a kiss.

He senses my movement and pulls back. I stare up at him, blinking. Our eyes lock for just one moment. Then his return to my forehead and I am left to think bitterly: *I knew he wasn't going to kiss me.*

But at least he didn't publicly disgrace me.

The chapel is quieter than a graveyard. My feet lock in place. I cast around, searching for some indication of what comes next. The many seated people give none, and neither does Rahk or the priest.

It is the queen, finally, who relieves my misery.

She rises from her throne and claps her hands once. "The celebration will continue in the feasting hall with drink and dance."

There is a celebration after? *Why?* We were supposed to leave and immediately return to Rahk's estate. I could groan, my misery renewed. The last thing I want to do is paste a smile on my face for the next many hours and dance on my bad leg.

Rahk bows to the queen. "You are far too generous."

She lifts her chin in reply, but there is something sparking in her expression as she glances between the two of us. *Curiosity.*

I'm supposed to act like I'm in love with Rahk, aren't I?

Maybe I will take one of his moves and, instead of looking at his face, fix my gaze just between his eyebrows. Somehow, that makes it easier to force my own smile.

I slip my arm in Rahk's, and the pipe organ resumes as we retrace our steps down the aisle.

We make it out of the chapel. Several armed guards take up places surrounding us. There are more now than when they escorted me through the palace. Rahk watches them with an unreadable expression. They, in turn, watch him back.

And I'm caught in the middle of it all.

I want to say something. I want Rahk to look down at me, wink, and whisper, *"Isn't all of this ridiculous?"* I want this to be a shared joke between us. Maybe then I could make sense of it. Maybe then I would be comforted that, if nothing else, I married a friend and ally.

Instead, it feels as though I have wed a stranger.

Somehow, when we arrive in the banquet hall, cleared of tables to leave room for dancing, the queen is already there. She sits on another throne, on a dais. There is no sign of her son.

"Lord Rahk," she says, her clear voice carrying across the space, mingling with the sounds of the stringed quartet tuning their instruments. "You have won the favor of the illustrious Lady Vandermore, it seems."

Rahk releases me and bows low while I curtsy deeply. "Lady Vandermore is gracious to offer it."

This is the part where I do not behave like a trapped bride. I swallow, trying to find my tongue, willing it to work properly. I struggle to find something to say and then decide on the most honest thing I can offer. "He has been kind to me, Your Majesty."

Queen Vivienne regards me shrewdly. "What is the reason behind the sudden marriage?"

Rahk, being a fae, cannot lie. That leaves the job up to me.

"We have been secretly engaged, Majesty," I say, "but there have been . . . *complications* with the matter of my fortune. You know that I have been the object of unwanted advances because of it. It reached a point where I needed to be wed for my own protection. Lord Rahk was generous enough to move the wedding sooner."

"Your protection?" repeats the queen, lifting one elegant eyebrow. "Which suitors drove you to the point of needing *protection*?"

I give a nervous chuckle. "There has not been a singular person, but rather the many."

That one eyebrow does not relax. People stream through the open doors, however, and the quartet begins a lilting rhythm. Rahk takes my arm lightly and leads me to the dance floor, away from the queen's interrogation. She watches us as our hands clasp, as though to read the things we aren't saying in the press of our palms and the way he slides his fingers beneath my shoulder blade. She must think ours a marriage of convenience rather than a love match, and I suppose that is the case.

The dance begins. It is a waltz. This is a ridiculous parody of our dance practice in his study only two days ago. I do not purposefully mess things up this time, but dance proficiently. Rahk himself, to my surprise, has notable improvement. Did he fake his own uncertainty?

Well, he knew I was a woman. His little comments return to me in a new light.

"You make such an excellent womanly partner."

"The number of strong opinions you hold as a twelve-year-old continues to amaze me."

He has known this *entire time*.

We sweep across the polished floor, moving in time to the music. To anyone watching, it appears as though we stare into each other's eyes. I try to read the inch of space between his eyebrows to even a sliver of emotion, but I could be staring at a sculpted stone for all the life in his expression.

We are surrounded by curious members of the court. The atmosphere has shifted from silent to musing, pleasantries and quiet talk being exchanged around us. I wish everyone was gone. I wish we didn't have to be here at all.

I cannot bear the silence any longer. "Lord Rahk—"

"Please be silent, Lady Vandermore. We will speak later."

I'm Lady Vandermore now? I clamp my jaw shut and grind my teeth, but don't reply. He spins me. Our eyes meet briefly, but his flee as he pulls me close again. He physically holds me further away than he ever did when we danced in his study.

After several dances, Rahk abruptly comes to a stop. "This is enough. We are leaving."

And leave, at last, we do.

CHAPTER 35

KAT

AT RAHK'S ESTATE, he immediately hands me off to Edvear. "Have Mrs. Finch tend Lady Vandermore. I shall be in my study."

Then he strides off without another word.

Edvear's yellow eyes seem brighter in the darkness. He ushers me into Rahk's room. Charity comes and helps me undress, making me miss Mary. It also makes me confused about what this night will hold for me.

For . . . *us*.

I haven't thought this far ahead. There are hundreds of more important things to consider. For instance, how I shall keep my head intact while married to the Prince of Nothril. For another, how I shall continue my raids.

The wedding night just didn't make the top of the list. But now that I'm here, I suddenly wish I'd spent a great deal more time considering the possibilities and preparing for each one.

"Wait here," says Charity, when I'm in a soft-spun nightgown and robe with my short hair combed. "I'll go get the master."

"You don't have to," I say with a nervous laugh. "I'm just fine here by myself."

She looks at me pityingly, and then leaves.

After several long minutes, I pace back and forth down the length of the room. When I grow weary of that, I sit on the bed, only to leap away from it and start pacing again. Then I sneak into my old room where my things are. My shoulders ease. The box with Mama's slippers is set beside the bed. The sight of that box comforts me further, though I have no desire to open it and find the blackened remnants of Agatha's fury. I find my Fool's Circle board, sit on the foot of my bed cross-legged, and begin playing a game against myself.

I'm finished with the second game before I regard the window and consider whether I ought to climb out and make a run for it.

Footsteps thump down the hallway. The door creaks when it opens.

I stiffen. My first inclination is to hide my Fool's Circle, but I force myself not to. Maybe if he sees this reminder of our friendship, he will be less inclined to murder me.

The footsteps pause briefly in the bedroom. They come toward my room.

Rahk pushes the door open.

I stare up at him. With the light at his back, he's nothing but a featureless silhouette. A featureless silhouette that I know far too well.

"Come," he orders.

I've gotten so used to taking orders as his servant, it is not until I'm halfway out of my room that I wonder if I should have given a petulant rejection instead of obeying.

It's warm enough that there is no fire in the grate, so the only light comes from several flickering candles on the mantel. Without a word, Rahk grabs two chairs from against the window and drags them toward the center of the room. He plants one down, and drops the second two feet away, facing the first. Then he finally looks up at me. Candlelight catches in his dark eyes and plays across the sharp contours of his face, the broad line of his jaw. "Sit."

I sit.

He takes the chair across from me and leans forward, resting his elbows on his knees, his chin propped up on one fist. His countenance is deceptively mild. I do not buy it for an instant.

We sit there in silence for several long minutes. His chair is too close to mine, and I struggle to not fidget nervously from the awkwardness of it. I spent our entire wedding ceremony wishing he'd look at me. Now he studies me intently, and I wish he would look anywhere else.

"This is how things will go," he begins at last. "I will sit here. I will ask you questions. You will answer them. We will talk. And you will not lie to me."

I swallow hard. A pang goes through my heart.

"Is that amenable to you?" he asks.

I nod.

"Good. Now, my first question. Why did you disguise yourself as a boy and come under false pretenses to be my servant?"

This is vastly worse than the interrogations he's subjected me to in other situations. I don't want to continue lying to him, but he cannot know I am the Ivy Mask. I rack my brain for answers that are truthful but omit that part of my reasoning.

"My stepfamily wished me to marry someone I did not want to."

His lips twist humorlessly. "You certainly avoided that well, didn't you?"

His sarcasm stings.

"So, your stepmother picked you a husband, and you decided that your only recourse was to run away from home, cut your hair, and pretend to be someone you weren't?" He gestures at my hair and the rest of me.

That is hardly a fair characterization. I grind my teeth to keep from snapping. "She was going to force me into the marriage."

"Yes—I understand that. But why this route? Why this scheme? You're a clever girl. You wouldn't do something this extreme without good reason. So tell me, Lady Vandermore, what this good reason is."

He says it all so calmly, but there is just the slightest edge to his tone that betrays his anger.

For a second, I consider telling him that my motive was to kill him to avenge my mother's death. But I am no killer, and he knows that. "I had to hide in a place where they would never find me. Some place here in Harbright where I could stay hidden until my twenty-first birthday."

"Why?"

I itch the back of my neck. "Because the terms of my inheritance are that if I remain unmarried until the age of twenty-one, the money reverts to me, and not to my husband. If I married before I was twenty-one, my husband gets the money."

He massages his chin, a furrow appearing between his brow. "So, this elaborate scheme was for the sole purpose of claiming your inheritance."

"There were several purposes!" I snap.

"Then enlighten me."

"It's hard to do so when you're staring at me like you'll bite my head off if I give the wrong answer!"

Rahk leans back in his chair, one hand resting on his thigh. "Better?"

"Hardly!"

"Would you find it easier to talk if we snuggled up in bed together?" He nods his head toward the bed a few feet away.

The cruel remark makes me shove to my feet so quickly I knock my chair over. It hits the ground with a thud. I put as much distance between us as I can manage. When that isn't enough, I take up pacing. All while Rahk remains seated, watching me with that dreadfully unfazed expression.

"I didn't know how to avoid the marriage. I needed to be able to stay in town so I could claim my inheritance the day I was due it. I have friends and acquaintances, but I did not feel like I could ask any of them to hide me away from my stepfamily. Perhaps there were plenty of alternatives I could have chosen, but I didn't have much time to develop an elaborate plan. This was what occurred to me, and seemed to best accomplish what I needed."

Rahk nods, offering his satisfaction on the subject. I nearly let out a sigh of relief that he accepted my explanation. But we're far from being finished with this conversation.

"Did you lie about your mother being lost to the Long Lost Wood?"

I shake my head adamantly. "No—well, that is, I lied about the timeline of it. But everything else I said was true. Even the age I was when she was lost."

"So it is true that Mary is your sister?"

I grimace. "No. That is, she was hired to be my companion when I was younger. When my stepmother and her daughters came into the picture, Mary was reassigned as a house maid instead of my companion. She's like a sister to me, but we do not share blood."

He shakes his head, tinges of frustration coming through. "Why did you not confide in me? I would have protected you."

That elicits a burst of laughter from me. "Yes! Yes, let me run away from my stepfamily and find refuge among the fae who imprisoned and tortured my mother! Yes, let me confide all my secrets to one of their lethal warriors!"

He actually looks taken aback. "After all I have done for you, after all the time we have spent together, do you still believe I intend you harm?"

I throw up my hands, aggravated that he doesn't seem to understand my situation at all. "Don't you see? Your intentions never mattered! Yes, it's true that you've been kind—more than kind—to me, but *you are a fae*! Why would I show up on your doorstep and beg you to keep me safe? Do you hear how ridiculous that sounds? How far out of my mind I would have to be to do that?"

"I'm not suggesting you should have told me *then*," he replies, at last struggling to keep his composure. "You could have told me at any point after that. Or did you really think I would turn you out on the street?"

"What does it matter?" I cry. "You've clearly known for ages that I am a woman! I am a fool for not realizing it sooner."

His fingers flex, then curl into a fist. "I was trying to give you the opportunity to tell me of your own will. I worked very hard to avoid forcing your hand."

I stop pacing, my gaze shooting to his.

His expression has cracked slightly, revealing an underlying sadness that shocks me. "I wish you would have confided in me."

My gratitude at his unexpected gentleness is swept away yet again by frustration. He still doesn't *understand*. And he won't entirely, because I cannot tell him that I know he hunts me. I growl and rip at my short hair. "But you are a *fae*! You are *scary*! I knew you were kind to Nat, but I didn't know if that kindness would extend to someone who had lied to you. You've only validated my concern by the way you've behaved since discovering my identity! You've been nothing but terrifying, refusing to look at me, then looking at me too much—"

"Because I've been *worried* about you!" Rahk exclaims. He seems to regret the outburst a second later, groaning and covering his face with his hand. "Please, sit down. You're giving me a headache with the constant pacing!"

My feet go still. Then, in a huff, I right the chair, sit, and cross my arms over my chest. Waiting for him to speak.

He pulls his hand away from his face. "Nat—Katherine—whatever I'm supposed to call you. I've been worried about you from the day you showed up here. I knew from that moment that you were a woman. At first, I feared that you were a spy sent to be my undoing."

"What convinced you that I wasn't?"

A muscle twitches near his nose. "Watching you handle that axe."

I give a humorless snort.

"As long as you were here," he continued, "you gave me some cause for worry. First your poisoning, then when I accidentally hit you, then when you got drunk. And another thing you lied about . . ."

I'm not expecting him to lean forward suddenly, to grab my left ankle and bring it to his lap. I startle, trying to pull away, but he swishes aside the fabric of my nightgown to reveal the long, jagged cut down my shin.

His jaw works as he looks at the crooked stitching, the way my skin bunches and folds around the edges of the wound like misaligned fabric. Then he lifts his gaze to me, and it is the Nothril prince who looks at me.

"Tell me what happened."

I curse inwardly. I have no choice but to lie. I lick my lips. "It's not much of a story. I had a mishap while chopping the wood and I was so embarrassed . . ."

"You stitched it yourself," he says flatly.

"How can you tell?"

"Aside from the fact that you never summoned a doctor? Anyone who stitched an injury like this would be accused of malpractice. Look at these stitches! You'll be scarred for life—and an ugly, jagged scar at that. I could have stitched you myself, had you asked!"

I yank my foot free of his hold, and he lets me. I cover my leg with my dress once more. "I can suffer an ugly scar. How did you even hear of it?"

"Charity told me."

"Ah yes!" I cry. "When she inspected me like chattel! *Unblemished virgin!*"

His gaze flashes. "I did that to protect you."

"Oh really? And I suppose if she hadn't found me sufficiently *virginal*, you would have canceled the marriage?" I fling the words at him, too humiliated to acknowledge their unfairness.

"I did *not* stipulate those requirements because I cared about them." Rahk pinches the bridge of his nose, massaging his furrowed brow. "I stipulated them because *you* begged me not to return you to your stepfamily. Do you remember that?"

The sheer desperation of that moment, the way I turned my face into his wrist and begged him not to send me back . . . I am forced to look away to compose myself.

Rahk's tone gentles slightly. "They have not treated you well—that is easy enough to gather. I did not know the . . . *manner* of their ill treatment, and I had to make sure no one would lay hands on you while you were out of my protection. I couldn't take you back into my house, knowing who you were, without ruining both of our reputations here in your human circles. All that I could do was create barriers that your stepfamily or whoever else was mistreating you would be unlikely to cross."

"It worked," I say dryly, laughing humorlessly. "My stepmother nearly ordered me horsewhipped."

His black eyes shoot to me, a violent flash in their pupils that startles me. But he does not move.

"I wish we could have spoken before you signed that marriage agreement," I mutter. "She hoodwinked you out of your twelve thousand crowns."

"I was not hoodwinked."

"You were!" I cry. "We don't have bride prices! I'm not sure we've *ever* had bride prices, no matter how far back in history you—"

"I know you do not have bride prices. I did my research. I knew they intended to take advantage of my ignorance of your culture. At first, I visited them to cancel our arrangement and discussions. Then your identity was exposed, and suddenly I had no choice. I let them take advantage of me. Because, once again, you were going to be under their roof. If they were giving up you and your fortune, they wouldn't be incentivized to deliver on their promise. If I promised to pay a handsome sum in exchange for you, however, they wouldn't dare renege on their promise."

He sits in that chair, coolly regarding me, and I see reflected in his expression the same frustration I feel: the anger over having our hands tied, and that this sudden, horrible arrangement between us was the only option to rectify the situation.

"Well, I suppose that means you bought me!" I mean it as a joke, but it falls flat—likely because it's true. I try to recover myself and fail miserably. "You've bought yourself a bride you didn't want. Just think—if only you'd cut off Agatha instead of tolerating her politeness when we visited, things never would have changed."

He clasps both his hands together, leaning his forearms on his legs. "The discovery would have been made. Sooner or later."

"But it might have been made in such a way that didn't make us get married."

"Indeed."

The sound of my own short breaths fill the room. I rub my arm, and my gaze finds refuge in the dancing flame of the candles.

Rahk opens his mouth and shifts on his chair. "Listen, Kat, I—"

His use of my nickname stuns me yet again like a lightning bolt. I pull away, wishing this chair didn't have a back so I could retreat further. "How do you know I go by that?"

"Because you told me."

"When?"

Something in his expression twinges. He looks very subtly uncomfortable. "The night you were drunk."

The blood drains from my face. What did I tell him? He said I didn't say anything! I try to return to that memory, but I find nothing except that cursed drinking game.

"Yes, I lied to you," Rahk says coolly. "You said *lots* of things. For one, you confessed to being a woman."

My jaw unhinges. Then blood pounds in my ears. "How dare you take advantage of me like that!"

A muscle jerks in his throat. "I did not!"

I laugh. "That's right. You're a fae. You must have different definitions of what it means to take advantage of—"

"You threw yourself in my lap, kissed me, and declared that you were a woman!" Rahk snaps. "I was sitting at my desk. Minding my *own* business. Telling you to go to bed. *You* threw yourself at me. *You* told me your secrets. All I did was ask if you were in danger and what your real name was. Great Kings!"

I . . . *what*? I stare at him, mortification coming in such a flood I can hardly bear to be in the same room as him. All at once, my apologies bubble to my lips. "I'm so sorry. Please forgive me, my lord. I never should have—"

He gets to his feet. One of his broad hands rakes through his long white hair. "I am not your lord anymore. I am your husband. Please address me as such."

I clamp my lips shut. Those words, that declaration, my mind cannot process.

I am your husband.

"Call me Rahk," he says, and his voice is quiet once more. He doesn't look at me. He turns his back, his head bowed as though in thought. Then he gestures to the room. "Please, make yourself comfortable. This room is yours now. You know the servants, so do not hesitate to request anything that you need."

I watch, not understanding the way my stomach drops at his words.

His hand lands on the door handle. He pauses. Then, without looking at me, he says, "Goodnight."

The door shuts behind him. I collapse onto the bed, my shoulders vibrating from the belated shock of the day. Just as soon as I do, I bounce upright again. This is *his* bed. It's not mine, no matter what he says.

I take myself to my old room, with its familiar comforts and privacy, and slam the door shut.

I drag my hands through my short hair, grabbing it at the roots and pulling as hard as I can. A growl of frustration rips from my throat. The confusion is too overwhelming, too infuriating.

"What now?" I demand into the silence of my room. "What now? What now—*what now*?" My voice breaks, my knees buckling as I fall onto my bed and bury my head between my knees. I squeeze as hard as I can, wanting crushing pressure, wanting pain, wanting something to drive all of this away from me.

In one fell swoop, it's as though I've lost everything. My old home. My freedom. My fortune. My easy friendship with Rahk. There is no soothing presence of Mary, no good-natured teasing from my new *husband*. No ridiculous antics from Bartholomew. Even the servants I've gotten to know here feel like strangers now that I am myself and not young Nat.

I do not know how things can proceed. What do I do, now that I'm married to a fae? The very prince of Nothril I despised so vehemently only a few weeks ago? He's going to kill me. It doesn't matter how kind he is to me. It doesn't matter all the sacrifices he endured to save me from my stepfamily. I am a criminal to him, his people, his court.

"Oh dearie."

The voice startles me so much I shoot backward in the bed, get tangled up in the sheets, and nearly go flying out the window.

It's only Charity.

She clucks her tongue at my fright and sets a small tray on my short dresser.

I move a few of the blunt strands of hair out of my face. "Forgive me. I didn't hear you enter."

"Nothing to apologize for." She sits down on the edge of the bed and passes me a hot cup of tea on a warm saucer. "Drink this."

The tea is spiced and rich, and warmth blooms in my gut with each sip. I drink it slowly. She has taken some small jar, unscrewed the lid, and mixed the contents with a small spoon.

"Your left leg, please."

I oblige her, sticking out my wounded leg and lifting my skirt enough for her to see the extent of the gash.

"I've never used this before," says Charity, peering into the jar and eyeing the consistency. "It's some special fae medicine. The master bid me bring it to you."

"He did?" The words are out before I can stop them. Emotion clogs my throat. "Oh, Charity, what am I to do? I came here to *avoid* getting married!"

She sets down the jar and gives my foot a gentle squeeze before applying the salve. It's cold on my skin. But even as she starts applying the second dab, the first part of the wound is already tingling pleasantly. "Marriage is full of trials and travails, even when you enter into it voluntarily."

I snort dryly. "I suppose that doesn't leave much hope for those of us who don't have the privilege to enter it voluntarily."

"That is the funny thing about marriage," she says, smiling in the dimness. "I've seen those madly in love with each other end up unhappy only a few years in, while others who married for practical reasons have the sweetest relationship that lasts long beyond the grave."

"So marriage is a gamble. You take it, thinking it'll increase your chance of happiness when it is just as likely to only increase your misery."

She pauses her application of my ointment. "My dear, you are too young for such cynicism."

She says it with such kindness, my welling tears nearly make it past my guard. The lid goes back on the jar with a satisfying roll. She gets off the bed to retrieve a fresh roll of linen bandages.

"What makes marriage challenging," she says, gently wrapping my wound, "is that both parties must be equally committed. If only one party is committed, you will have such a recipe for heartache and unhappiness. Equally destructive are two apathetic parties. But where there are two people who are committed to working through every little thing, to being strong where the other is weak, to receiving the goodness the other has to offer—there will always be, if nothing else, deep and mutual respect. I was married to my husband ten years before he died. We did not know each other well before the wedding, but we grew to love each other deeply. I have never known a better man."

"I'm sorry you lost him," I say quietly. I rub my arms, and the teacup in my hand clatters on its saucer. This is a nice sentiment and all, and I know Charity means every word, but the last priority on my mind is making this *marriage* with Rahk work. My biggest priority is finding a way to survive and keep rescuing humans from Faerieland.

It just feels like there is only one inevitable outcome for this marriage: that it will end with my death, at Rahk's hand. I don't see how there can be an alternative. Now that I no longer have a claim on my own fortune, I cannot even run away and settle elsewhere.

Charity takes my empty cup and saucer, freeing my hands to wind up in my bedspread. "Get some sleep, my lady. I probably shouldn't let you stay in this servant's chamber, but I think it'll be fine for tonight."

I flop under the covers with a groan. "If he doesn't want me here, he'll have to drag me out himself."

She gives a light laugh, blows out her candle, and shuts the door.

I wait several minutes after her footsteps fade away. Then I fling off my covers, hurry to my dresser, and change swiftly into trousers, a dark tunic, and my coat. All parts of Nat's uniform, but that cannot be helped as it seems my clothes have not been delivered yet from Vandermore Manor.

Finally, I push open the window and climb out into the night.

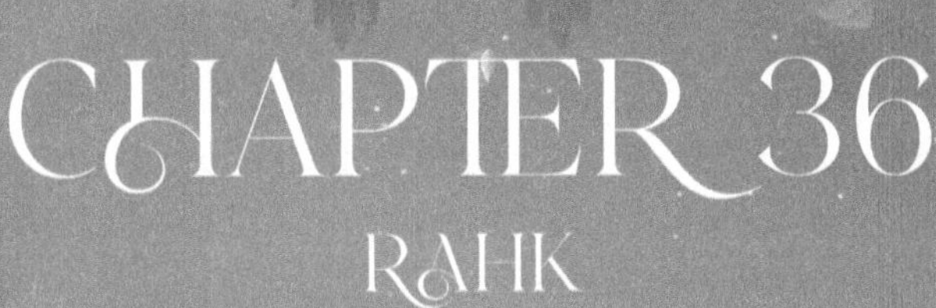

CHAPTER 36

RAHK

ONCE, I TOLD my old friend Ash, right before his wedding night with his new human bride, that he didn't need to be nervous—he just had to be sweet to the poor girl. I'm not taking my own advice very well, now am I?

I rub my sore temples.

I'm trying to wean off my *ollea* and adjust to the scents of the human world, if that is even possible. The result is a constant headache.

A knock at the door. "Master Rahk?"

"Come in, Edvear."

He comes in, wringing his hands. I go back to scribbling away at the letter I'm writing to Queen Vivienne.

"You think me foolish," I say when he shuts the door.

"It seems . . . sudden," he replies, somewhat diplomatically.

"I didn't have another alternative."

"None at all?"

I sigh, put down my quill. "If I did, they didn't present themselves to my consciousness at the time of necessity. I had to protect the girl, and I couldn't kidnap her."

"Why did you have to protect her? She's not your responsibility."

I give a dry chuckle. "That is the question, isn't it? I suppose I could have handed her over to her stepmother and washed my hands of the mess."

"No one would have blamed you."

I would have.

I clench my jaw. I couldn't have lived with myself if I had knowingly placed Kat in danger and walked away. It's like Pavi all over again. I'm doing things I don't want to do because I cannot let someone I care about be hurt.

"What are you going to do with her now? Surely you won't take her back to—"

"I will not take her to Faerieland. Whatever happens, she will stay here."

I cannot take her with me into Faerie without creating such a scene as would rival the overthrow of the last High King. There is nothing to gain from bringing Kat to Nothril. Only many, many things to lose.

"So you will leave her here when you go—"

"I need to spend more time hunting the Ivy Mask," I interrupt sharply, twirling my pen. "It's been three weeks since we came, which means I only have little more than a month until Pelarusa comes to join me."

Once she's here, there is no way I'll be able to get the Ivy Mask to free Pavi.

Edvear shudders at the mention of my sister. The thought of her here, in Ashbourne of Harbright, is laughable. And frightening.

"You should have more credibility with Queen Vivienne, now with Lady Vandermore as your wife," Edvear says. "It might help solve the problem of the troll."

I tilt the feather of my pen toward him. "Indeed. I suppose it wasn't such a terrible idea to marry the girl after all."

Edvear hesitates, and I brace for the question I won't want to answer. "Do you have a better idea now for how long you plan to stay in the human lands?"

I cannot leave until I have the Ivy Mask, but even then, I might have to stay longer to finish Ash's errand. Now that I have a wife . . .

I shake my head grimly. "I'm sorry. I do not know yet."

He nods quietly, trying to hide his anxiety over not being able to plan.

I hand Edvear the sealed letter I've written. "See that this is delivered to the queen immediately."

When he's gone, I wipe my hand down my face. At least I haven't married her my people's way. That will spare me a more . . . *permanent* bond. A permanent bond would be the worst possible curse I could give either of us.

I get to my feet. My swords rest beneath the heavy desk, tucked away so no human will find them and fear. I pull them out and strap each one on, pulling the leather buckles tight across my chest. Their weight is familiar—a reminder of what I am. And what Kat *isn't*.

Still, my mind flashes back to when she tightened these buckles for me when my fingers slipped, her face upturned and concerned.

I leave my study, keeping my steps quiet, and make my way outside.

I cannot keep dallying. I need to catch the Ivy Mask. Thus far, I've been more passive in my search, believing that he will quickly fall into my hands with the traps I've set.

I've underestimated him. He is skilled at evasion, which has enabled him to rescue so many of our slaves. My respect for this nameless vigilante grows. Perhaps if Pavi's life wasn't at risk, I would enjoy savoring the hunt longer. Who knows when I'll get such a good chase again?

Well, I'm not underestimating him anymore. I will tighten my net. One of these nights, he's going to make a mistake. A mistake that will cost him everything.

ANASTASIS BLYTHE

I spread my wings. The night smells of wood and wind, strong enough that I can almost forget the constant thread of decay beneath it all. I leap into the air, flying as swiftly as I can through the night sky to the forest's edge. There has been something niggling at the back of my mind since the Ivy Mask's last raid. I knew the exact moment he entered the forest, and the exact moment he left—thanks to the spells I set up. The time was shockingly brief, especially since a large portion of it was spent at the kravok's lair.

My memory of him resurfaces: a sweeping cloak meant to conceal the form of the wearer, but he wasn't large. He was slender, neither particularly tall or short, and the ankle that I caught beneath my foot was thin boned. His mask made a sad face, stitched ivy leaves covering every inch of it save for the eye slits—slits that were so thin I couldn't even glimpse the color of his irises.

He can move quickly. Since the cart has not been moved, I must assume all his progress was made on foot, speaking to his physical fitness—and he has excellent knowledge of the Paths in Caphryl Wood. The Paths that transcend time and space and make travel through the Wood possible instead of a death sentence.

But no matter how quickly he moved, there is *no* possible way he was able to successfully sneak the slaves out of their posts in that short timeframe. He has allies in Faerieland. People—or a single person—who gets the slaves ready, and then the Ivy Mask is the one who escorts them out of Caphryl. I need to find this person.

To do that, I need to find out what Paths the Ivy Mask took on the last raid.

I pull out my human pocket watch. One hour and fifty-three minutes—the entire time the Ivy Mask was inside Caphryl Wood. Twenty-nine spent traveling to the kravok's lair, hiding, fighting the monster, before he escaped. That leaves eighty-four minutes between the moment he left the kravok and the moment he left Caphryl.

"Who goes over yonder?" cries a loud voice. "Ymer will grind your bones to make Ymer's bread!"

I sigh, turning toward the great lump of troll not far away. "You know you're going to have to leave, Ymer," I call. "You don't want to stay in the human lands. Why don't you make it easier on both of us and just leave now?"

"This is Ymer's land!" he roars, swinging his club into the ground. He reeks of rot even at this distance. "Ymer will not leave it!"

"The ruler of this land will bid you go. You know it will happen. You might as well go squat somewhere else instead of waiting."

"You are not the ruler of the land! Ymer does not listen to your poisonous lies!"

"You couldn't have sent *anyone else* to deal with this, Ash?" I growl under my breath as I steer clear of the troll's club and march through the sparking, tall grass to get to the Wood.

Now comes the fun part: spending the night walking Paths to see which ones fit the timeframe. It's not as daunting of a prospect as it would be if I didn't know the targeted court based on news I received this morning.

The Pyrenar Court.

I mark the minute on my watch and begin.

The Ivy Mask went to *Valehaven*. I shake my head in disbelief, staring down at my watch as I stand on the rocky shore of the Maltun Sea. A bridge spans the rushing river emptying into the sea, and beyond it, a white stone palace rises above the cliffside. A thin crescent moon hangs above the towers.

He used the Path from the Pyrenar Court to go to Valehaven, and then from there back to the human lands. Since he left no scent trail, I couldn't have tracked him.

That is how he managed to lose me and make it back to Harbright before I caught up.

It's brilliant.

It is a great shame that this fellow must die.

CHAPTER 37

KAT

THE TREK TO Vandermore Manor takes forever on foot. I would *kill* to have Bartholomew back. Or even just some random horse from the market who wouldn't buck me off the moment I sat in its saddle. It's also a feat to avoid the notice of the patrolling city guards, but I am getting better at it.

Between these two matters, it's been well over an hour since I left—judging by the height of the quarter moon.

When I finally arrive, I slip around to the back, climb through the hedge, and reach the trellis I always used to sneak in and out for my raids.

This time, I stop at Agatha's window. The room is dark and empty, as expected. I pry open the window with some effort, then slip inside. I expect the impact of my feet hitting the floorboards to jar my injury and send a bolt of pain shooting up through my body, but Rahk's salve is working miracles, and I only feel a deadened ache.

"Maybe I should be stealing their medicines along with their slaves," I mutter to myself in the darkness. I could make a fortune selling them to humans. Since I no longer have my own.

The only light comes from the stars outside. I'll need a candle. I grab Agatha's shawl from the back of her chair and stuff it under the door. Then I return to her desk, my hands gliding over the surface of the wood until I find a stubby candle and a match.

The quiet glow of the candle doesn't illuminate much, just the span of her desk. It fights against the oppressive darkness of the room and fails miserably.

But all I need is the desk.

"There's got to be something here," I whisper under my breath. Everything is neatly arranged on the desk. There is a vase of trimmed roses from the front landscaping and a little picture frame with the busts of her two daughters. Of course there wouldn't be one of me.

Not what I'm looking for.

I ease open the first drawer. Stacks of fresh parchment and unopened bottles of ink. I close it and open the next.

There are two rows of letters, organized upright so one can flip through them quickly. My pulse quickens. I begin sorting through them at once, reading the return addresses.

Baroness Cranswick
Mr. and Mrs. Hudson
Lady Hornbuckle
Miss Ingham
Lord Boreham
Lord Boreham
Lord Boreham

My fingers move faster than the blood pounding in my ears. I flip through the letters, counting the number of exchanges. *Over two dozen.*

I place a hand over my mouth. "This must be it. The proof has got to be here."

I take one of the most recent letters and open it.

Dearest Mother,

Neither of us have time for pleasantries, so I shall skip them altogether. If that offends you, just insert the usual pleasantries here in your mind.

I do not like Lady Vandermore and I do not want to marry her. You and I have been over this many times, but perhaps with recent events it'll finally stick in your head. Forty percent of her fortune, however significant it may be, is not enough to put up with all this will cost me. I have an established living. Josephine will never forgive me if I go through with this.

Unless, of course, you were to give me a more substantial cut of Lady Vandermore's fortune. Seventy percent, at least. My sisters have their charms and shouldn't have trouble finding men to marry them with ten percent of the fortune for each of their dowries. I do not see why, if we are to go to the vast trouble and great social embarrassment that comes with convincing Lady Vandermore to marry me, that so much of her fortune should be immediately given away to other men who marry into the family. As the heir of my late father's estate, the bulk of the money should go to me to be passed down our line.

That is all I have to say on the matter. If you disagree, perhaps you should find a fourth husband and birth another son who might be more easily commanded to act outside his own interests.

Yours,
Malcolm

I stare in shock at the letter. Lord Boreham is Agatha's *son*? But—how is that possible? She had no other children besides Bridget and Edith. My father couldn't have known of this son. He wouldn't have married Agatha if she'd had a son. He wanted his fortune to go to me. He wouldn't have risked it by marrying a woman with a son who could take precedence over me.

Lord Boreham and Agatha both hail from Commington.

Fourth husband.

My father wasn't Agatha's second husband. He was her third.

It all makes sense now: the obvious disinterest Lord Boreham had in me and yet the way he still made me an offer of marriage, Agatha's obsession with me marrying him, Bridget calling him by his first name, my entire stepfamily being shocked and appalled at the idea of one of them marrying Boreham.

I press a hand to my roiling middle. So Agatha, for all her pretending as though she cared about me like a daughter—for all that she made me out to be the unreasonable one between us—really does despise me. And the girls, who at times I thought of as friends, also kept this secret from me. Even Edith, who acts like she cares about nothing but her lonely instruments.

Josephine must be Boreham's mistress. Someone who stood to lose if he married.

Floorboards creak outside the door. I leap almost a foot in the air. I tuck the letter into my tunic, ease the drawer shut, race to pull away the shawl from the door, and then scramble out the window as quickly as I can.

Just as I close the window, the study door swings open. A candle enters, followed by the illuminated features of Agatha, drawn and pinched, her hair tucked in her nightcap.

As I cling to the lattice outside the window, I realize I've left out the matchbox. I hold still, not daring to even breathe, as she sits down at her desk. She freezes, then whirls around. Everything inside me jumps like a frightened cat, but I hold still.

Slowly, Agatha turns back to her desk.

I puff out a silent sigh of relief.

Inch by inch, I ease myself down from the lattice to the ground. It's long after midnight before I return to Rahk's estate, but the bedroom is as empty as I left it. I shut myself in the servant's chamber and find sleep as elusive as ever.

I curl up in a ball and growl angrily at myself, "You're not allowed to cry over this. You knew Agatha didn't love you, and you knew Bridget and Edith didn't either. This only proves what you've long suspected. So it's good. This is good. *No. Crying.*"

I smash away the one disobedient tear like it is a mosquito come for my blood.

CHAPTER 38

KAT

THOUGH I SEARCH Rahk's chambers high and low, I find nothing to wear except my usual servant's uniform. I pull on those clothes, complete with the chest binding because I have no other suitable undergarments besides what I wore beneath my wedding gown—which is nowhere to be found.

With a sigh, I rake a hand through my short hair, grown out to an awkward length, and emerge from the bedroom. I feel like a prison inmate rebelling against orders, despite knowing I am—theoretically—the lady of this house now.

Edvear is the first person to see me. He is in the storeroom with a ledger and a quill in his mouth as I return from visiting the outhouse. His ears turn sharply backward. "My lady—"

Rahk steps around the corner just then, the purpose of his stride indicating he is heading somewhere, but at the sight of me, he stops and does a double take.

"Why are you wearing those clothes?"

He sounds angry, like I've defied him in the worst of ways.

Instinctively, I fall back a step. "Because there was nothing else . . .?"

Rahk's ire whirls at once on his steward. "Edvear! Did no one think to get Lady Katherine's clothes? Bring them at once."

Edvear turns tail and disappears, his hooves clopping all the way down the hallway.

"Please pardon the oversight," says Rahk, drawing my attention back up to him. His hair is tied back at the nape of his neck, and though he wears human styled trousers, his tunic is one of the long ones he brought from Faerieland. It's probably more comfortable.

I shrug. "I don't mind."

I intend to walk past him, but he steps into the hallway, blocking my path so my only alternative is retreat. He frowns down at me. I cross my arms over my chest, and after delaying, I find I have no choice but to drag my gaze to his.

"If you're so bothered by my clothes, give me one of those long tunics. It'll look more like a dress on me. Albeit one at a very scandalous length, but if I kept my trousers on—"

He waves a hand. "You're troubled by something."

I chortle. "An astute observation, my lord."

"Katherine—"

A flash of red hair at the end of the hallway immediately drags my attention away. Is that . . .? "Mary!"

She balances a basket of laundry on one hip, but when she sees me, a bright grin bursts across her face. She sets down the laundry just as I barrel into her arms.

"What are you doing here?" I cry. "Oh, I am *so* glad to see you!"

"Lord Rahk sent an offer of employment to me yesterday and paid off my contract with Lady Duxbury Vandermore. I am to be your handmaiden. Now what are you wearing?"

I turn around to find Rahk watching us. He stands there so severely, arms crossed over his chest, face utterly unreadable, and yet there almost seems to be a question in his gaze. I don't know what to say to him. I want to thank him, though that itself feels too insufficient, but I also don't want to bother him after all the trouble I've put him through.

I cannot bear the shift between blankness and slight emotion in his black eyes, so I whirl back to Mary. "Edvear is getting my other clothes, but I hope he's slow about it. Trousers are very comfortable." Though the chest binding isn't so much.

Mary clears her throat and bobs a curtsy to Rahk. "I will return to my work, Master."

He waves a hand again as if he doesn't care and strides to his study. He shuts the door.

"That means you can worry about the laundry later," I say, grabbing Mary's forearm and dragging her back toward the bedroom. "There is something I *must* tell you."

She yanks her arm out of my hold. "I will get your breakfast and bring some mending, lest Mrs. Banks think I am slothful at my work. Then we will talk."

"Fine," I say. "But hurry!"

We take breakfast outside on the patio, sitting on the steps that lead into the manicured lawn, me with a plate in my lap and Mary with her mending work.

"You're going to have to pretend *you* discovered this and that you're telling me it because I can't have anyone knowing that I snuck into Agatha's study last night."

"Kat!" Mary hisses. "You did *what*?"

"Never mind that. The important thing is—"

"Katherine Vandermore, you are going to get yourself in such trouble one of these days! And if it's with the fae—"

"Just *listen*, alright? You can flog me later. But right now, let me tell you what I found."

I go on to explain the letters, and I pull the one I stole from my pocket and slide it to her. She arranges her mending mostly on top of the note so she can read it. Her jaw clenches as she reads, her cheeks turning the color of a ripened summer tomato.

"If I get my hands on any of those women, or this worthless Boreham fellow, I will make them wish they'd never been born," Mary seethes. She turns to me and her expression softens at once. "Oh Kat, I'm so sorry."

I set down my plate and draw my knees up to my chest. "It's fine."

"It's not fine! This is a serious deception! If you could prove it, they could be ostracized from society."

"That isn't even the worst part!" I fling my legs back down the steps, stretching them out as I gesture with my hands. "You see it, don't you? She wanted to claim my fortune *twice over*! Once, by deceiving me and forcing me into a marriage with her secret son—and then again by deceiving Rahk into marrying Bridget and paying that ungodly sum in a bride price! And she succeeded on one of those counts!"

"Kat," Mary hisses suddenly.

I turn around to see Rahk standing next to the door, his arms crossed over his chest, and at first I think he's too far away to have heard us, despite the two furrows between his eyes and his intense study of me. Then I remember fae hearing and bite the inside of my cheek.

"Mary," says Rahk, pushing off the wall and striding toward us. "Kindly clear Lady Katherine's dishes to the kitchen."

"At once, Master." She gathers up the mending but manages to slip the letter back to me as she collects my dishes on their tray and leaves me alone in the sunshine.

With Rahk.

I cast one last forlorn glance after her disappearing form.

Rahk lets out a sigh as he sits on the step next to me, where Mary was a moment ago. His long legs stretch out in front of him, his hands clasped together before he turns his black-eyed scrutiny upon me once more. "Explain to me what you were just discussing with Mary."

My mouth goes dry. I sit there awkwardly, not knowing what to say. "How much did you hear?" I finally ask, so I can know how many lies I am obligated to tell.

"I came out as you were exclaiming about someone wanting your fortune. I assume you speak of your stepmother. Lady Duxbury Vandermore."

I hand him the condemning letter. "Mary found this last night and brought it to me. Lord Malcolm Boreham was the man Agatha was determined to force me to wed."

He reads the letter quietly and gives no indication of his thoughts as Mary did. Once he's finished, he returns it to me. "What was the manner of her attempt at forcing you into this marriage?"

I rip at the grass growing between the crevices of bricked stairs. "She sold my horse."

"A horse that meant something to you?"

"My father gave me that horse when he was still alive." Already, a lump grows in my throat. *Curse it all.* I'm not going to let myself cry in front of Rahk. Especially not now that we're *married*. I pull myself together, only to find that my voice still trembles. "She and I grew up together. She's an old thing now, and the morning after a ball, while I was still asleep, she ordered our manservant to sell her. I found out several hours later after it was too late. Agatha promised that an effort would be made to recover the horse . . . but only *if* I married Lord Boreham. I'm not even sure she's still alive at this point. She's old enough that most people wouldn't want to buy such a horse."

The typical panic when I think of Bartholomew clenches my lungs tight, making it hard to breathe. I shove it away and shift my thoughts.

"Agatha also found my mother's wedding slippers. They're very unusual, made of glass, and the most exquisite glasswork you've ever seen. When she saw that I wanted them back, she threatened to sell them if I didn't accept the proposal."

"These slippers meant a great deal to you."

I fidget with the lowest button on my shirt. "Yes. Mary managed to get them back to me, but not before . . ." I trail off, my mind returning to that moment when Rahk left, and Agatha tried to destroy the slippers. He looks at me expectantly, so I swallow and continue. "She was furious that I'd run away. She tried to destroy them."

"She didn't succeed?"

At that, I give a small laugh. "She tried to break them, but they didn't even so much as crack. So she threw them in the fireplace. They're all stained black now."

"Where are they?"

I get up and beckon him to follow. We return to the bedroom—I cannot and *will not* think of it as *ours*—and I pull the box from my room.

I hand it to him. He takes it, shifting his weight to one leg as he opens the lid of worn, gray velvet. Inside, the tip of the slipper's blackened toe is visible. My ribcage tightens.

He hands the box back to me and watches me replace the lid and set it beside the bed. Then he bids us return to where we were sitting outside on the steps. Birdsong and the distant gurgle of the creek surround us. He props his foot up on one of the higher steps and leans his forearm on it.

"Tell me about your stepfamily," he says.

I shrug, scratching uncomfortably at my elbow through my starched shirt. "What do you wish to know? When they became part of our family?"

"Let's start there." His penetrating gaze shifts away from me, mercifully, and focuses on the rolling lawn that disappears into forest. I can finally breathe a little easier. "You told me that your mother was lost to the Long Lost Wood when you were nine. Your father died a year later. When did your stepfamily come into the mix?"

"Well . . . after Mother vanished, Father kept hoping she would come back." I feel the compulsion to explain that, instead of just answering the question. It is the most important part of the story, after all. That Father didn't want to marry again. "After a year, he'd given up hope. He kept telling me that I needed a mother. At first, I thought he meant Mama would come back, but then it became clear . . ." My throat clogs and the words don't come out.

"That he had no hope of her return, but he didn't want you to be without a mother."

I nod. "He met Agatha in Commington. I think he thought it was fate that she was a widow with two daughters in need of a father, and he was a widower with a daughter in need of a mother."

He nods once. "It is rational."

"Rational," I huff, "until you realize that he never would have married her otherwise. He was blinded to her faults because of the *fortuitous* nature of their meeting—and apparently caught up in her deception. I don't know how she hid her son from him, but she rightly knew he wouldn't have married her if she'd had a son to inherit."

"Your mother returned after the wedding."

I gnaw on my lip and shove away the trembling that tries to overtake my hands. "She did. Shortly after the wedding. She looked like a ghost when she came out of that forest."

"You were there? When she came out of Caph—the Long Lost Wood?"

Yes, I was.

"I saw her when Father brought her back home," I say truthfully, side-stepping around the condemning truths. A shudder manages to work its way through my body. "She was a shell of the person she once was."

I remember sitting beside her rocking chair, holding her cold hands as she stared vacantly at the wall. Not speaking a word to me. Not acknowledging me—even when I wept and buried my face in her lap. The Wood had taken too much of her soul.

"And she didn't survive long?"

I swallow back the emotion. "Eleven days."

"Your father?"

"Followed her to the grave but a month later."

"You've lived with Lady Duxbury Vandermore and her daughters since?"

"I have. It would have been vastly easier if Father had left me an orphan," I spit bitterly.

"Was your stepmother often cruel to you?"

"She was rarely *cruel*. But she did have a way of forcing my hand to do things I didn't want to do. She always made me seem the unruly, unreasonable child any time I didn't immediately obey her."

Rahk shrugs. "To be fair, you *are* unruly."

"You're not supposed to agree with her!" I cry, whacking him on the arm before my brain catches up to my actions, and I yank my hand back. I stuff both hands in my lap. "I know I am a difficult person to manage."

"I wouldn't say that," Rahk replies, shifting his gaze back out to the lawn. "From the letter, it seems your stepmother deserved every bit of your rebellion. This is a dark betrayal indeed."

"She might have done it *because* I was rebellious. Maybe if I hadn't tried so hard to make her life difficult—"

"You were a child mourning the shocking and unexpected loss of your parents, and placed in the care of a woman who did not love you," Rahk cuts in, shaking his head. "I've seen a lot of black deeds in my time, but taking advantage of someone under your protection to swindle them out of what is rightfully theirs might be one of the worst I've encountered."

I don't like Agatha, but I can think of plenty of things much worse than what she's done. Murdering me in my sleep, for one. That would be worse. "I hardly doubt she could stand up to the faults of the fae," I argue.

Rahk doesn't reply at first. He runs his thumb along his jaw, considering. "If you don't mind me asking . . . what were the circumstances of your mother's disappearance?"

"Circumstances?"

"Yes. Why was she down at the Wood's edge? Was anyone with her at the time?"

I rub my shoulder. I don't like thinking about that day, but if I don't answer him, he will think I'm hiding the truth from him. "Father took Mama and I to see the harvest. It was something we did every year. He would bring us to see the full fields and we would eat a picnic in the grass."

Rahk nods slowly.

I force my voice to be steady. Careless. This happened ages ago—none of it matters anymore. "We were playing hide-and-seek among the stalks of wheat. Then . . . the border moved. It just came like a wave, swallowing up the wheat—and Mama."

That haunting image of trees surging forward, of Mama's smile suddenly turning to terror right before she vanished from my view, brings a need to retch. I keep myself controlled, however.

"What happened then?" asks Rahk.

I look away. I hate looking at him when I lie. "The Wood stopped. I screamed and tried to run in after Mama, but Father grabbed me and wouldn't let me go. He shouted her name for a long time. I don't know what happened to her. I've heard there are many Fae Courts, but I don't know which one she was imprisoned in."

"I'm sorry that happened to you," says Rahk.

He says it so simply, so gently. Suddenly, we're not basically strangers in a sudden marriage, but friends on either side of a Fool's Circle board. My barriers, so carefully erected to keep him out, are swept away before I can prevent it.

The next thing I know, I'm crying. I swivel my body away from Rahk's, covering my face. Why did he have to say that? Why does he have to care? He doesn't want to be married to me—he made that clear last night. So why does he show me kindness today and make me cry when I *don't want to cry*?

His large, warm hand lands between my shoulder blades. That touch breaks me even more, bringing the tears harder. He doesn't say anything.

"I'm sorry," I gasp between ugly sobs. "I will stop. I promise."

His thumb moves slightly at my shoulder. "I hate crying in front of others too."

That shocks me enough to stop the flow of tears and whip my attention toward him. "You cry?"

"It has been a few decades, but I never enjoyed it."

A delirious chortle bursts from me. It seems to break the spell, and I draw a shaky breath of composure. "Crying is horrible."

"A wretched experience, indeed."

I truly laugh this time. A slight smile cracks his impenetrable facade.

He gathers his long legs and gets to his feet. "I will leave you to your day. Please be kind enough to join me for supper this evening."

"I . . . well . . . of course," I say, not able to come up with anything else as I watch him walk away.

CHAPTER 39

RAHK

MY MIND TURNS over this new information as I march into the house. The image of Kat's trembling shoulders refuses to leave me. I think of all the times she didn't buckle—like when she took a knife from an assassin. I don't want to care about her past. She lied to me so many times, refused to trust me, and got us into this mess of a marriage.

Truly, though, I care. I care a frightening amount about the wrongs done to this woman. I successfully kept my composure in front of her.

But I am furious.

I want to march to Lady Duxbury Vandermore's home and demand restitution. I want that woman crawling through the mud in the filthiest part of Ashbourne. The dark fae part of me, the Nothril part of me, wants her blood.

"Master Rahk! The queen has replied!"

I pause in the hallway as Edvear rushes toward me, carrying a sealed letter. The door across from my study is open, and I can just see the chipped shoulder and curly hair of the Botsov bust from where I stand.

"This is good news that she has replied so quickly, right?" asks Edvear, who knows nothing of what I wrote to her. "Maybe she will cooperate now that you married Lady Vandermore."

I don't reply as I accept the note, step inside my study, and break the seal.

Lord Rahk Varadirth,

My sources have confirmed reports of the troll. Give this troll the enclosed note and bid him leave.

It is signed with a stamped crest instead of a name. The enclosed note slides into my palm. It is not even sealed. I open it and read.

Troll,

As the ruler of this land, I bid you return to the Long Lost Wood forever.

The queen of Harbright

I sigh and slide the note into my pocket. Ymer will not take kindly to this. Still, I will give the note to him, if for no other purpose than to show the queen that she must come speak to him herself if he is going to leave.

This is good, I tell myself as I make my way out of the house and try not to search for a glimpse of where Kat might be. This is an excellent distraction from the last two days.

I find Ymer exactly where I left him last night. He does not call out to me as usual, but glares between slitted rocky eyelids as I approach. His knobby fist closes around his cudgel, threatening me silently.

"Ymer the Indefatigable. I come bearing word from the ruler of this land," I call, holding up the letter.

Several thick, corkscrew hairs protrude above his lip. He scrunches them in a snarl. "Ymer sees no ruler of the land."

A sudden thought occurs to me. I almost groan. "Does Ymer the Indefatigable discern the mystery of these human symbols?"

It is the reverent way of asking if he can read.

His curiosity allows me close enough to slide the note with my foot up to him. I retreat quickly as he bends forward, squinting at the page. "Ymer knows many symbols."

I wait, arms crossed over my chest, my wings folded close to my back.

Ymer grunts. He plants both giant hands on either side of the page, which looks comically small compared to him, and bends his face down to it. Slowly, he lifts his snarl to me. "You play tricks on Ymer. There are no symbols on this page."

I dart upward into the sky, my wings carrying me out of reach of Ymer's grabbing fist. Sometimes I forget how bad troll eyesight is—regardless of whether Ymer could have read the writing anyway.

"Ymer will rip your limbs apart for trying to trick Ymer with paper!" He stabs a long nail through the paper and lifts it to his teeth, where he shreds it to pieces. "You are no ruler of this land!"

That went well, I think as I fly back the way I came. Maybe now that I've exhausted the easiest option, the queen will leave her comfortable palace and come to the border. One word from her—*one word*—and this whole thing is over.

But that would just be too easy now, wouldn't it?

When I fly back to my estate, I find myself watching the grounds, looking for a sign that Kat is still outside. I find none.

CHAPTER 40

KAT

MY CLOTHES ARRIVE shortly before noon, and Mary immediately sets to unpacking the trunks. I join her, having nothing else to occupy my time, and she only gives a few words of resistance before she lets me help her.

"This works in our favor," she declares, sorting through my collection of petticoats. "I am well overdue in sorting through your things. You've had some of these clothes since you were twelve years old."

We spend the afternoon dividing the clothes into separate piles. Clothes that need adjustments made, clothes that are too small, clothes that both of us hate and should never have been purchased in the first place. Rahk comes once to retrieve his *ollea*. His eyes go wide at the sight of his room covered in gowns, lace, and enough trimmings to rig a ship.

"You might have to sleep in your study tonight," I say absently as I toss aside well-worn undergarments that are due for retirement.

Mary shoots me a look.

"That is," I add quickly, "we will be sure to have everything cleaned up before supper."

One of his eyebrows twitches slightly. "Then do not let me distract you."

He leaves and I've sorted through half of the pile on my lap before I look up and find Mary staring at me. "What?"

"Do you always talk to him that way?"

I hesitantly place the next undergarment in the proper pile. "What way?"

"So . . . *casually* and flippantly?"

"I have *tried* to be respectful and demure!" I shoot back. "My tongue just blurts things out and I have no control over it!"

"Don't give me those excuses. You know as well as I that impulses can be restrained, but they won't be if you won't *practice* restraining them! You ought to be glad he seems to like it. No other master—and not many *husbands*, either, for that matter—would enjoy being talked to so."

"He has been very good to me," I admit. "Better than I deserve."

Mary huffs as she closely inspects a petticoat. "For that, I am glad. I do not doubt you gave him more than ample opportunity to dismiss you."

"I did often deserve dismissal," I agree.

She gives me a look—a funny sort of look that I cannot interpret. It embarrasses me enough that I bend my head and focus on the task at hand.

By mid-afternoon, we realize we need to increase the pace of our work if we are to have any hope of finishing before supper. My back is sore by the time we finish, and I have no desire to switch into one of my own gowns, but Mary will not be put off.

"You *cannot* have supper with the master in your servant's clothes. I will not allow it. And, tolerant of you as he is, he won't be pleased. You know he won't be pleased."

I sigh. "*Fine.*"

Mary helps me put on a proper dress—one that is cream trimmed in blue lace. She pulls out the false bun and secures it to my scalp with an ungodly amount of pins.

"He knows my hair is cut," I protest.

"This isn't about deception. This is about presentation. You will wear this bun until your hair has grown out, understood?"

I send a stream of air out through my nose, blowing the loose strands near my face that are too short to be pinned back. Mary curls these as a final touch, which will not last more than an hour at best. She fusses again over the tiny scars surrounding my temple and applies a little powder to conceal them.

"I've done what I can," she says at last, stepping back.

I look at myself in the mirror, and it's like looking at my old self before I ran away from home. "What if he doesn't like me this way?" I mouth under my breath at my reflection.

Rahk is waiting for me in the dining room, standing behind his chair. He gives a bow of acknowledgement when I enter. The gesture strikes me as uncomfortably formal, especially with me in this gown. When he rises, his eyes quickly flick over me before returning to my face and giving not a single indication in his features of whether he is pleased or not by my appearance. He pulls my chair out for me and pushes it into the table after I'm seated. Then he nods at Mrs. Banks, who begins serving the meal. It is an exquisite spread of a roasted turkey, buttered rolls, deviled quail eggs, savory meat pies, and a medley of honey-glazed root vegetables. Charity must have worked so hard to make this meal special.

We eat in silence for several minutes before Rahk asks, "Have you and Mary successfully accomplished your redecoration of my room?"

"Indeed. We have repapered the walls with my petticoats," I say.

A high-pitched sound comes from the back of Mrs. Banks's throat as she brings out a leek and herb soup.

"What I meant to say," I correct, sitting up straighter, "is yes, we finished, and your room is as it was before. Except your wardrobe door is harder to close now."

Rahk's spoon has paused halfway to his mouth, though his expression remains mild. He tips one eyebrow and replies, "You are in luck that I am very good at closing wardrobe doors. As for decorations, I have nothing but my tasteless male eye, so I shall leave any changes up to your discretion."

"In that case, I shall make many changes and endeavor to horrify you with each one."

He chokes on his spoonful of soup and coughs into his napkin. He collects himself, sipping from his wine. "And why, pray, should you endeavor to horrify me instead of please me?"

Bolstered by the subtle twinkle in his eye, I lean forward. "To prove your eye is not tasteless."

"What a price I shall pay," he replies dryly, "for a careless choice of words."

I hide my smile by taking a bite. I want to think of something to say, something that will make him laugh outright. My mind turns blank. Several minutes pass, until the silence has stretched so long it would be strange to reply now.

The rest of the meal passes that way. I find that the warm pleasure inside my chest at his attention has turned to abject misery at his silence. I cannot think of a mildly clever remark or even a single question.

Nothing worthy of his acknowledgement.

So I sit. I eat, and I taste nothing.

When dessert is brought out—a beautiful custard tart—I finally realize that his initial question was a way of asking about my day, and that I never asked about his.

"How was your day?" I ask, and the question comes out more painfully awkward than I could have even imagined.

"It was full," he replies.

"A good sort of full? Or the bad sort?"

"Somewhere in between."

"Ah."

And that is the rest of our conversation over supper, save for a few, "Shall I pass the berry sauce?" or "Is this not delicious?"

It's a relief when he leans back in his chair and sighs. "The first time I came to the human lands, I couldn't decide if I liked your food or not. Now, I find it very interesting and enjoyable."

"Oh?" I ask, hoping he'll offer more information about his life before he came to Harbright.

"I especially like how you humans do dessert." He pulls my chair out for me and offers me a hand. I don't see it until it's too late and kick myself for not looking his way faster. His stoic expression does not even flicker.

"Supper was delicious," I say, as if he is the cook or the host of a party.

"I'm glad you enjoyed it."

He doesn't move from where he stands. I realize he is waiting for me to leave first, though I do not know where he intends for me to go. I step into the hallway and then freeze, trying to decide if I ought to go read in the parlor—now that I'm not a servant—or if I should just go lock myself in my servant's closet like last night.

I decide to get my Fool's Circle book from my room and then return to the parlor. But once I'm halfway there, it becomes clear that Rahk isn't going to his study as I expected, but following me to the bedroom.

It is confusion that first turns my mind blank, and then sudden panic. Is tonight to be our *actual* wedding night—since last night was so . . . *last night*?

I do not know what that would be like. Would he kiss me then? The whole scenario feels impossible to imagine. He is by far the handsomest man I've ever known, and he has always treated me with kindness. I do not expect that would change. Even last night, in the heat of his anger, he sent that medicine for my wound. For those reasons, I do not think it would be a terrible experience.

It just feels like too large of a step when we cannot even sit comfortably together at supper. In many ways, it is like we are getting to know each other now for the first time.

I suppose that would be one way to get to know each other . . .

I rub my arm in discomfort. Also, he will kill me someday. That's another complication.

I'll just . . . follow his lead, I decide. If I become uncomfortable, I'll tell him so. He will not touch me against my will. Of that, I am certain.

I enter the bedroom. It suddenly feels vastly confined when he steps inside behind me and shuts the door. I intended to get my book, but if I do so now, it'll send the signal that I don't want his attentions. Which . . . I think I do want. Maybe not *all* of his attentions at this very second, but some?

Not knowing what else to do, I turn around. Rahk's back is partially to me as he pulls something off the bookshelf. The rustle of my skirts catches his attention, and he looks my way.

I don't know what my face looks like, but Rahk's eyes visibly widen—first surprise, then confusion. It's a relief to be able to read his emotions.

"Katherine?" he asks, his hands slowing.

My gaze trails to the object in his hand. *His Fool's Circle boardgame.* I pause, my mouth slightly open, as I try to quickly recalibrate my brain from the sudden whiplash.

"Are we going to play?" My voice comes out slightly shrill.

His gaze flicks from my face to my hands, then beyond me to the bed. Understanding seems to dawn in his expression, which seems to soften infinitesimally. "If you would like to."

I nod vigorously. My cheeks flame hot.

He sets the game on the low table. Then he comes to where I stand. He stops too close—the kind of close one stands when kissing happens. My instinctive reaction is to step back, but I don't want him to think I'm afraid of him. I manage not to move, but my eyes shift away from his gaze, latching onto the evening sun pouring through the window and melting across the rug. When he doesn't speak, I drag my eyes up to meet his.

He seems to be measuring my reaction to his closeness.

I swallow. His hand lifts and the pad of his thumb lightly brushes my shoulder. His voice is low and rumbly when he speaks softly. "Why don't you get your Thief?"

He speaks of the variation piece from my game. I drag in a deep breath, nod, and then escape his presence. The moment I'm safely ensconced in my room, I find my game and fumble around for the special piece—all while I mouth a silent stream of curses.

Then I return, forcing a sunny smile and dropping the piece onto the half-set board. He sits on his cushions while I take my usual spot opposite him.

He might chop off my head in the future, but I'm determined to keep it screwed on properly in the meantime. He can try to unnerve me with his proximity all he wants. I am not undone by intense black eyes or muscular chests. Or, at least, I can make strides in that direction.

I cluck my tongue. "You can go first. I'm feeling especially lucky today and I think you need all the help you can get to beat me."

Those black eyes of his flick up to mine for a brief second before he moves three of his pieces a single spot each. I spend all my moves on one piece.

We go back and forth in quiet, until he makes a specific move that has my finger flying out to point and the words bursting from my mouth: "I know that trick! I just read about it since the last time we played!"

His lips curve. "Do you remember the proper defense?"

"I'm sure I do not," I confess.

A full, true smile bursts upon his face, followed by a low chuckle. "Shall I show you? Or will your luck carry you through?"

I shoot to my feet and all but run to my room to retrieve my strategy book. "I don't trust anything you say once the game is going! You've got a conflict of interest. Now let me find the page . . ."

When I sit down, he lightly snatches the book from my grip. I immediately begin protesting and reaching for it, but almost as fast, he returns it to me, opened to the proper page.

"Unnecessary, but thank you anyway," I reply, sticking out my tongue as I read. "See! This is why I didn't remember it. It's a five-step defense. It'll take me two turns to properly recover."

He watches me huff impatiently as I move my pieces. "The best defense to this move is to not create an opportunity for it. And to recognize when your opponent might be setting up for it."

I glare at him. "Your turn."

He makes his move. I make mine, finally recovering from his snotty little maneuver. He moves again.

"Nope!" I call at once, picking up the piece and returning it to its spot.

"What?" he replies, his eyes twinkling, though the rest of his face doesn't betray anything. "Too clever of a move for you?"

"I know when you're purposefully making stupid moves to throw the game. I've told you before—I'm going to beat you one of these days and it isn't going to be from charity!"

Now he definitely fights a smile. "How is this a stupid move?"

I lean over the table so I can show him the moves for the next three turns. "See? You just gave up one of the spots surrounding the Fool. It is a stupid move, indeed, and you know it is."

I glare up at him, only to find that he isn't looking at the board. "It's rude to call your husband stupid."

My flush is hot enough to light a fire in the grate. "I didn't call you stupid! I said your *move* was stupid. And I said you were doing it on purpose—that means I'm calling you the opposite of stupid. I'm saying that you're being clever in a way that annoys me."

He's leaning over the gameboard now, bringing his face close to mine. "Why do you assume I did it to throw the game? Do you not think me capable of making mistakes in my Fool's Circle strategy?"

I narrow my eyes at him. "I've been playing this game with you for weeks now. I've not observed a single mistake in that entire time."

"You weren't a strong player when we started. You could have missed plenty of mistakes."

I give up trying to rationalize with him and only declare firmly: "You were throwing the game. Deny it."

He gives me a very Nothril prince smirk. "I don't take orders from you."

"Fine! Then I'll make your move for you." I put the pieces back the way they were before he made his stupid move, study the board carefully, and choose a move.

He shakes his head.

"What?" I demand.

"So it's not fine if I throw the game, but it is if you do?"

My jaw drops open. "It's a good move!"

He tilts his head back, loosing a full-bodied laugh. His silvery hair turns golden in the light of the setting sun.

I cross my arms across my chest and glare at him while he laughs. Then he reaches across the table and ruffles my hair, as he used to do. My hair isn't very ruffle-able, carefully pinned as it is, and he seems to catch himself when he feels the difference. He pulls back at once.

It's like the reality of our current situation becomes a shroud over our once-easy interactions. I bite my lip and try to pretend I didn't enjoy him touching me.

He wins the game, as usual, but it involves a long siege against my successful capture of two of the spots surrounding the Fool. We pack up the game and I take my Thief in my palm to return it to my own game.

The sun has disappeared below the horizon, though I don't notice how dark it has become until the game is over. My eyes strain against the dimness as Rahk returns the game to the shelf. The piece is sharp in my palm. He goes to the mantel. I don't see a matchbox there, but a second later, the three candles there are lit. They cast a dancing array of light and shadow across the quilted bedspread.

"I will call Mary to help you ready for bed, if you like," he says as he turns to leave. The way he says it, the tone coloring his voice, indicates he doesn't intend to stay with me tonight either.

I rub my sleeve with my knuckles. "Yes, thank you."

He opens the door, then pauses when he's halfway through it. He does not look at me, his mouth a thin, firm line. It's only a moment before he speaks, but it feels much longer. "I think I ought to state clearly, Katherine, that I had no objection to marrying you."

My mouth goes as dry as paper.

"It was the means that troubled me and . . . frustrated me. I did not like feeling like my hands were tied and the only option to pull us out of that disaster was sudden, rushed matrimony with no consideration for the prudence of it."

I mean to nod, but the muscles of my neck lock up.

He still doesn't look at me. "There were many objections I had to the marriage, but I think you should know that *you* were not one of them."

My heart stutters to a halt. I blink several times.

He moves to shut the door, but I must offer something in return, despite the way his confession has upended my world. "Please call me Kat."

He pauses in the doorway once more. His gaze flicks to mine and holds it.

"Agatha is the only person who calls me Katherine," I blather, as if my request is anywhere as near as vulnerable as his confession was.

There's that subtle shift in his features—a shift I cannot describe because it is so subtle. It's like his expression remains exactly as it was a moment ago, but it now has a different feeling to it. A softer aura that eludes my efforts to place it in the lines of his mouth or an alteration of the jaw, a refraction of candlelight in his irises.

His voice is low. "Goodnight, Kat."

I stare at the door long after it shuts. I stare until I hear Mary's footsteps and remember to move before she catches me like this.

She helps me ready for bed, frowning when she takes down my hair. "Were you messing with your hair? It's frizzy."

"Yes," I reply, not wanting to admit the truth.

She makes me sit down and show her the healing wound on my leg. She applies the special salve from Rahk. I watch her work, marveling at how quickly the wound is scarring over. The pain is very manageable now—enough that I can ignore it most of the day.

When I'm ready for bed, she watches me slip inside my own room and frowns. "You shouldn't sleep there," she says gently, almost apologetically.

I cast her a look of desperate pleading.

She doesn't relent, even though she seems sorry for it. "You're the lady of this house and the master's wife. You have to act like it."

With a heaving sigh, I plop down on the bed. Rahk's bed.

Mary lowers her voice. "Edvear caught the master sleeping at his desk early this morning and he's already shut himself in there again. I think you're safe for tonight."

She blows out the candles before she leaves. I slide under the quilt. Rahk's scent rises from the cool bedclothes to wrap around me—a scent of clear creeks, wind and sky, and that tickle of magic like autumn spices.

I feel small in this dark room by myself, alone with the magnitude of a future I cannot untangle. Up until now, I haven't been willing to admit it to myself, but now I see that I cannot keep running raids into Faerieland. When I had the privacy of my own room, it was possible. But now? Rahk can come into this room whenever he pleases. Because it's his room and his saints-cursed bed.

The thought of not continuing my work brings such an overwhelming panic it nearly cuts off my ability to breathe. My heart demands with every beat that I must continue, even if it costs me my life.

Despite having known for some time that Rahk will one day kill me, it occurs to me for the first time that he may not want to do such a thing. That killing me might cost him dearly.

A storm of such conflict brews in my breast. Half of me demands that this isn't my fault—it's Agatha's, for forcing my hand and making me resort to the drastic measures that led me to Rahk's doorstep. The other half, however, berates myself mercilessly for what this will inevitably do to him.

There is no more hiding from the truth: Rahk, despite being a fae from the Nothril Court, is the best man I know. He is good and kind, strong and protective, earnest and straightforward, gentle and considerate. And he will suffer because of me.

"What have I done?" I whisper to myself in the darkness.

CHAPTER 41

RAHK

THE ROARING WATERFALLS of the Revar Court coat my wings with a fine mist. I go straight to the palace, flying past the rickety bridges and navigating the maze of tree dwellings.

This palace is not situated in the biggest tree, but the oldest. Its winding trunk is wider than my entire Ashbourne estate, with stairs and rope ladders that drape between elegant, moss-covered platforms. Everything smells of earth, vanilla sap, and wood.

I go to the nighttime cleric. He is a short man of sticklike arms and legs, a greenish tint to his skin, and ears twice as long as mine.

His eyes go wide when he sees me. "Prince Rahk! To what do we owe this . . . ahem . . . pleasure?"

I lean one elbow on the wooden counter he stands behind. "I need a list of everyone who visited this Court in the last sixteen days."

"Sixteen days?" the cleric squeaks. "You do not have clearance for this. And such a task is impossible! I'd need to get access to the ward spells—"

I lean a little closer, dropping my voice. "You will do it. At once. And you will have it ready for me by tomorrow night."

"But Prince Rahk, I cannot—"

"We would not want to see the alliance between our Courts come undone, would we?"

The cleric balks. "The Nothril Court wouldn't."

"We would. So please get me this information."

He gulps. "Yes, yes, Prince Rahk. Of course."

One Court down, several more to go before dawn. One step closer to finding the Ivy Mask's accomplice—and thus one step closer to finding the Ivy Mask himself.

Normally, this is one of my favorite parts of the hunt; when I am almost there, but there is still enough unknown to keep the thrill alive. Instead, my mind keeps drifting away from the task at hand, counting down the minutes until I can return to my estate in Ashbourne.

KAT

Around midmorning, while I am reading my Fool's Circle strategy book with a warm cup of tea, Edvear comes in and bows. "Lady Katherine. The master wishes to see you."

I will never get used to him calling me *Lady Katherine*. I leave what I am doing and follow him to Rahk's study.

Rahk is standing with his back to the door, reading a letter he holds. A letter with something else—a remittance of money? My curiosity has me leaning closer to his tall frame. He folds the note, turns upon my entry, and places it in my hands.

Then he walks around his desk, takes a seat, and leans back with his hands linked behind his head while I peruse what I hold. "Is this your fortune that everyone speaks of?"

It is indeed a promissory note. I inspect the amount, and I cannot help my small smile. "This is the monthly allowance from my fortune."

Rahk lifts one eyebrow. My fortune has impressed even a fae prince, apparently. "How did your father come to be so wealthy?"

"Management of land, from my understanding, though he was only continuing the family legacy. The Vandermores have owned much of the agricultural land in Harbright for generations. It is a distant cousin of mine who manages the estate itself."

A furrow appears between his brows. He leans forward in his chair, steepling his fingers beneath his chin as he stares at the bookshelf across the room. Then his black eyes return to mine. "Do you have a copy of your father's will?"

I wish I knew the thoughts that turn through his head. He is so beautiful, and he doesn't even seem to be aware of it. I cannot believe that when I first met him, I didn't see it myself. It is almost overwhelming to have his attention on me like this.

But I've got to answer his question so he doesn't know I've been admiring the way his hair falls over the square plane of his forehead, and the perfection of his wide cheekbones. I clear my throat. "I do not have a copy of the will. Agatha has one, and I would say a servant could get it for you—none of them like Agatha—but she keeps her own personal maid and doesn't let anyone else near her things. Not even her own daughters. But my cousin, the one who manages the estate, would also have a copy." The more I talk, the more I forget his beauty and instead grow cautious, trying to keep my stomach from dropping. He wants to know what is his, now that the money is *his* and not mine. Perhaps he won't want my cousin to continue managing the estate. He might want to do that himself.

Rahk holds out a hand to me, and I reluctantly hand over the promissory note and the letter. To my surprise, he only takes the letter. He points to the address on the seal. "Is this your cousin's address? I would like to write to him for a copy of the will."

I stand there, still awkwardly holding out the note. "Yes, it is."

He looks between my face and the note, then back at my face. He does not take it. I purse my lips and set it on his desk.

"Why are you giving that to me?" he asks.

I blink. "Because . . . it's yours."

He places two fingers on the slip of paper and slides it to the edge of his desk toward me. "Actually, it's yours."

I stare at him stupidly. Did he forget the terms I told him of the will? "No, no, you misunderstand. It was only going to be mine if I remained unmarried until I turned twenty-one. As I am still two weeks away from that deadline and since you have married me, the money is yours."

A muscle twitches in his throat. He does not reach for the money. "No, it is you who misunderstand me. This is your money. Your inheritance. You are only days away from your birthday—that counts as fulfillment of the requirement. I will not touch it. It is yours and yours alone."

Then he picks up the promissory note and holds it out to me. His jaw is firm and unyielding.

My mouth falls open. "Master—I—"

His eyes flash at the title. I didn't mean to use it—it slipped out by habit.

I try again, suddenly unsure if I ought to call him *my lord* or Rahk, and end up blurting, "My Rahk—!" My face goes hot with mortification. I swallow hard, straining the tendons in my throat, and repeat clearly, "My lord, Rahk. I couldn't—that is, I don't think the will works the way you're speaking. It is very set to the date, not just near the date. I couldn't accept this."

He peers at me over the tent of his fingers. A slight smile tilts his severe mouth at my slip. He quickly hides it and clears his throat. "Kat, what use do you think I have of your money?"

I shake my head, frowning. "Well, just the same as anyone would have . . .?"

He gets up from his desk, walks past me, and shuts the door, wrapping us up in privacy and the soft sound of his steps as he returns to me. He stops very, very close, peering down into my face as I forget to breathe.

One of his fingers touches a strand of my hair that has come loose from Mary's meticulously arranged fake bun. My eyes feel very, very wide as he traces the lock down my temple to my ear, only to continue and gently trail to my jaw. His touch is a flame, soft but unbearably hot.

My thoughts scatter.

"Kat," he murmurs.

My mouth is open. I shut it abruptly.

"Do you have any clue how rich princes of Faerieland are?" he asks, his lips pulling to one side in a smirk. His finger curls to a knuckle under my jaw, and he brings it slowly across my skin to just below my chin. "I mean no insult on your fortune, but truly I couldn't possibly come up with a use for it."

A flush scorches my cheeks. I wasn't trying to disparage his means or imply he needed anything from me. I only meant—

His voice is a soft caress against my forehead. It is warm, with a smile in the timbres. "Take your money, wife. Nothing you do will convince me to touch it."

Then he kisses me. It is just a whisper of his lips against my hairline, but I could fall over from the shock of it.

Not knowing what else to do, I swipe the promissory note from the desk. "Alright. Thank you. Goodbye."

I scramble out of that study as quickly as I can, pretending I don't hear his warm chuckles following me.

I run straight to Mary, who hangs the laundry outside. She looks up as I skitter to a stop and wave the money in front of her face. I hope she assumes the tomato red of my face comes from the running, and *not* because I am replaying how it felt to have Rahk caressing my face.

"I can give them more than a single stagecoach ticket and a loaf of bread!" I burst. "And I can get Bartholomew back! We must go at once! I need to talk to Charles and find out who bought her!"

CHAPTER 42

RAHK

KAT'S COUSIN LIVES in the city, so he sends a manservant with a copy of the will at once. I spend several hours poring over it. Then, when I inquire after Kat's whereabouts and find out she's trying to track down her horse, I take one of my own horses from my stables and ride out to Vandermore Manor.

"Is Lady Duxbury Vandermore home?" I ask the maid who answers the door.

The maid curtsies at once. "She is. Please come in, sir."

The citrus scent of wood oil is the first thing I notice as the maid leads me to the parlor. Perfume floats on the air, not strong enough to induce a headache, but unpleasant still. A fresh wave of perfume—definitely strong enough to induce a headache—announces Lady Duxbury Vandermore's arrival, as does the swish of her red gown. A curious second face, framed in curls, pokes around the corner before Lady Bridget steps fully into the room and curtsies with her mother.

I rise and offer a bow.

"Lord Rahk," says Agatha, smiling as though we are friends. "What brings you here?"

"Have you decided to return Katherine?" Bridget asks, suppressing a giggle. "I'm afraid you're stuck with her now."

I don't bother giving her or her comment the honor of acknowledgement. Instead, I slap the will on the table and take a seat, fixing my full attention on Agatha. "I'm here on matters of the late Lord Vandermore's estate."

"Oh, I don't manage that," says Agatha. A different maid brings tea, serving the three of us. I don't touch my tea, though Agatha stirs a sugar cube into hers. While her spoon clinks against the china, a new scent makes me look up. The second daughter—whatever her name is—peers into the room until she catches me watching her. Her eyes widen, and she ducks back out. Her light footsteps scurry away. "The late Lord Vandermore's cousin manages everything. Speaking of which, I must say that I am quite put out by your hiring of Mary. We relied on that girl—"

I cut in. "I understand you sold my wife's horse without her permission."

Agatha looks at Bridget, who is in the middle of sipping her tea. The daughter hesitates, glancing at me. Then she takes her cup and saucer and removes her odious presence from the room, much to my satisfaction. The delicate wrinkles on Agatha's throat constrict as she swallows. "Oh, Lord Rahk, you must understand. It was an old horse—"

"You did sell it then."

She places her teacup down with a rattle. "I had to! There was nothing else to be done. It was by Katherine's own testimony that the horse kept throwing its shoes and having all sorts of issues."

"Did you sell it without her permission?"

"Lord Rahk, as I stated, Katherine often complained of the horse's many issues—"

I narrow my gaze at her and lean forward, dropping my voice. "Answer the question, Agatha. Did you sell it without her permission?"

The blood drains from her face, enough that I almost wonder if I've let the glamour on my wings slip. But apparently, I don't need to reveal my wings to reveal that I am a prince of Nothril. When she does not answer, I ask in quiet calm, "Do you need me to repeat the question?"

"I did sell it without her permission," Agatha finally admits, turning her pale face away from me. "I sold the horse to make Katherine cooperate. She is a foolish and headstrong girl. She has declined every offer of marriage that has come her way and obviously intended to stay single until her twenty-first birthday to avoid giving over her fortune. You should thank me for my work, because now you are the owner of her fortune."

Something inside my chest turns liquid hot. I keep my voice controlled, however. "Who, exactly, sold the horse? Fetch them for me at once."

A manservant named Charles is summoned. I question him until I have all the information I need. Once he leaves, I take the will and shift it closer to Agatha. She looks at it only long enough for her eyelids to shutter.

"I found some interesting things in this will." I flip past the first page to the second. "This estate, the building and all the grounds, are included in Katherine's fortune."

If it is possible, Agatha goes even paler.

"This house does not belong to you or your daughters anymore. You will move out by the end of the week."

"The end of the week?" she exclaims, pressing a hand to her heart. "But we have nowhere to go! Katherine wouldn't want us to be turned out on the streets! Does she know you are doing this?"

I cock my head. "Nowhere to go? Then what have you done with the bride price I paid for Katherine? Have you spent it all already? That was a very handsome sum, more than sufficient for a new home."

She clamps her mouth shut, her jaws working in tension.

"You have until the end of the week," I repeat. "You will take your clothes, your accessories, and your particular belongings, but you shall leave everything else. The furniture, the staff, the decorations. Everything will be left as it is or I shall take you to the royal court for thievery. Because, as we've established, everything here belongs to *me* now, so if you steal, you steal from me." I catch her eye, emphasizing the words so she knows *just* how serious I am. "I am not kind toward those who steal what is mine."

Agatha pushes to her feet. "You have made yourself completely clear, Lord Rahk. Now, do you have any other claims against me you must make? Or is the house and everything in it enough for today?"

I stay seated as I regard her slowly. Then I rise to my full height, looking down at where she tries to posture herself as threatening. "Yes, there is one other thing."

She visibly braces herself.

"I know about Lord Boreham."

Her lips part.

"I know he's your son," I continue, keeping my tone measured despite the way my gut twists in fury. "I know you sold Katherine's horse to force her into marriage with him. I know all of this was about trying to rob your own daughter—"

"Katherine isn't my daughter!"

My lips pull back in a snarl. "You might have succeeded in your plan if you'd had the dignity to accept her as such."

Her teeth flash. "Katherine was never interested in being my daughter. She was willful, difficult, self-absorbed, and cared nothing for the feelings of others."

"In that case," I say, picking up the will and tucking it under my arm as I stride toward the door, "you should be glad you no longer have to deal with her willfulness, difficulty, and selfishness. Instead, you will have to deal with me. And unfortunately, I think you will find a broken-hearted orphan is much easier to control."

I leave before this woman wastes any more of my time. I've got a horse to locate.

CHAPTER 43

KAT

"A BROWN MARE, yes, with a white splotch near her eye and four white stockings on her legs. What did you do with her?" I cannot keep the desperation out of my voice as I speak to the man Charles said he sold Bartholomew to.

The market is busy, and several people are lined up behind me to speak to this same man at his stall. Behind the stall is a pen of horses. I already searched there for Bartholomew, despite knowing there wasn't a chance she would still be there.

"I don't know, ma'am," the man says with an impatient huff. He looks beyond me to the people who wish to do business with him. "We buy and sell a lot of horses."

My throat almost collapses on itself. "Yes, yes, I understand that, but you must have *something*. Something about when she was purchased, or who might have been interested based on the description—"

He sighs deeply and plants both hands on the wooden table of his stall, fixing me with his full attention. "Look, all I know is that we had someone buy a lot of horses the day after you said yours was sold. Your horse might have gone with them. Or someone else. I don't know.

It's something.

I take the address eagerly and give it to Clifford, who drives the carriage, and climb inside. If only I hadn't had to wait so long to find her!

When we arrive at the address, the sign out front makes my vision split in two. "Oh saints," I breathe, fighting the mounting panic as I rush out of the carriage before Clifford can give me a hand.

It is a large warehouse, rather rundown. It takes me a minute to find the door, only to be stopped by a burly man with a blood-smeared apron wiping his hands on a cloth.

"Can I help you, my lady?" he asks. "We don't usually have visitors here."

"I think my horse might have been sold to you by mistake," I blurt, failing to keep the fear out of my voice.

He shifts uncomfortably on one foot. "When was this?"

"About three weeks ago."

He winces. "I don't know what to tell you, little lady. We buy up the old horses from the market and turn 'em into sausage. If it has been that long . . ."

I stagger. Clifford suddenly appears at my side, catching me under the elbow. "You shouldn't be here, my lady. Please let me take you home."

All protest inside me dies. I let Clifford drag me away and help me back into the carriage. I stare out the window numbly. My Bartholomew. Gone. *Slaughtered.*

It's too much. My mind invents vivid pictures of her struggling, her frightened. And I can't stop it. I'm so sick by the time we reach Rahk's estate that I can barely move. Somehow, I find the strength to get out of that carriage, walk past Edvear who says, "The master is out, if you are looking for him," and head straight to my own servant's closet.

When the door is firmly shut behind me, the torrent of tears finally comes.

RAHK

"There was a young lady asking about the same horse not long ago. This is the address I sent her to. It's all I've got."

I glance down at the address he scrawls on a dirty scrap of paper. "Did you sell the horse to this person?"

"Couldn't tell you for sure. She said the horse was older. I don't get many buyers for old horses. Except the butcher."

I take the address and leave without another word. This horse better be alive. If I find anything else, heads are going to roll.

At the butcher's, I swing down from my horse and march inside. The stench is so potent I almost take a step back. Quickly, I grab my *ollea* from my pocket and smear a drop under my nose.

Carcasses hang from the ceiling. I stride past them toward a man at the far end of this dimly lit warehouse. I hope Kat did not step foot in this place. Dark energy stirs inside of me at the thought of just how distraught she would be by this.

"You, there!" I call toward the man, and then curl my lip at the way he cleans his knives. "I'm here for a horse."

He grunts. "It wouldn't happen to be the same horse a young lady was asking about an hour ago?"

"What did you tell her?"

"Oh, just that there's nothing I can do for her. We make 'em into sausage. If we bought the horse that long ago, there's really no—"

I cross my arms over my chest and enunciate my words carefully. "You are going to take me back to all the horses. Even the ones in line to be slaughtered. You are going to show me every single horse on this property, and you had better hope I find what I'm looking for."

The butcher's face pales. He seems to take in the rest of me then. His mouth opens. "You're a fae. You're—you're *that* fae."

I incline my head. "Yes. Someone sold my wife's horse without her permission. I will get it back."

The butcher lays down the knife he was cleaning and gets up, using a dirty rag to mop the sweat off his forehead. "Come this way. I will show you what we have."

We survey many, many horses. None of them match the detailed description of Kat's horse that I got from the Vandermore stable hand. The butcher takes me out to the pasture then.

"We don't keep many out here," he says, pushing open the wooden gate. "But there are a few."

Almost immediately, I catch sight of one particular horse, grazing beneath a tall tree. She's a beautiful mare, with a shiny copper coat and four white legs. I don't even need confirmation. There is something very . . . *Kat* about this horse. I smile. "That's her."

"That's her?" the butcher repeats, squinting at the horse. He shrugs. "My wife liked her so much she asked me to delay putting her on the line. She said she liked her spirit."

"Does your wife enjoy being married to a horse butcher?" I ask dryly.

"She manages it."

I reach into my coat pocket. "What is your price?"

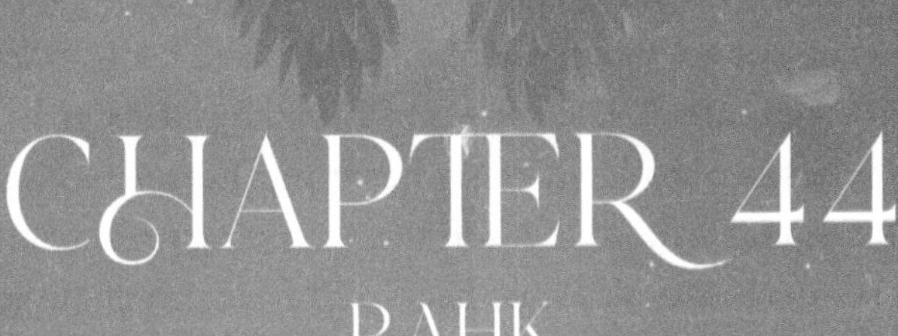

CHAPTER 44

RAHK

"KAT!" MARY RATTLES the locked knob of my room. "Kat! The master wishes to see you! He's outside waiting for you!"

I wipe my puffy eyes with my sleeve and smear my snotty nose on my pillow. "Can I speak with him another time? Please?"

"No, it has to be now." She sounds urgent. Urgently . . . *excited.* "Come at once! You will want to talk to him now. I promise you."

I delay a second longer. Then, with a groan, I drag myself out of bed and stumble to the door. My leg aches only a little bit, but enough to catch my notice when everything else feels miserable.

I drag my feet through the house toward the front door. Mary tries to get me to go faster, but I cannot think of what Rahk could possibly want to tell me that would make me glad for him to see me in this tear-streaked, red-faced, rumpled clothes, and matted hair . . . *situation.*

I certainly don't want to see *anyone* right now.

But it's not Rahk I see when Mary pushes me out the door into the courtyard.

It's four strong legs, with a glossy golden-brown coat, a thick mane, that characteristic white spot near her eye. She nickers and tosses her head.

"Bartholomew!" I shriek.

The tears are pouring free again. I rush forward and bury my wet face in her velvety neck. She immediately tries to eat my hair. I laugh, running my fingers over as much of her as I can. Then I survey her. "You're not any thinner than when you were taken! It looks like you've been well taken care of. Look at you! Oh, you beautiful girl!"

She tosses her head and blows her stinky horse breath into my face. Her ears cup forward, her soft nose nuzzling my cheek. I laugh as I hug her neck. She plops her heavy head over my shoulder.

She's just as happy to see me.

Then I remember Rahk.

I turn around. He's standing a few feet away, his arms crossed casually over his chest, his weight on one leg, as he watches me with a pair of twinkling eyes.

I don't care that Mary and the other servants have crowded around the doors and windows, watching my reunion with my horse. All I know is that the gratitude I feel for this man is too much to contain.

My legs carry me in a burst of speed straight to Rahk, and he barely has time to raise his eyebrows and untuck his arms before I barrel straight into him. I fling my arms around his waist and bury my head in his chest. In any other circumstance, I would be embarrassed by my out-of-control sobbing.

"Thank you!" I weep, embracing him as hard as I can. "Thank you, thank you, thank you, thank you!"

To my surprise, his arms wrap around me, holding me in return. I melt against him, breathing in his comforting scent, and all at once, become aware of how wonderful his embrace is. He brings his head down to mine and presses a kiss to the top of my wild hair. Lightning flashes through my gut and pins me in place.

"You're welcome," his low voice rumbles.

When I peel my face away from his chest enough to look up at his face, I find him smiling down at me.

It's suddenly too much. I withdraw my arms. He releases me and I step back, wiping my face with my sleeve to try to mop up the tears as I pull my composure back under control. Rahk's hand appears in my vision with a handkerchief. I accept the offering gratefully. In the tail of my eye, I catch him gesturing with his other hand that the watching servants give me privacy. They obey at once.

I return to Bartholomew, who prances her front legs in excitement as I scratch her nose. "How did you ever find her?" I manage to ask. "I was certain she was dead!"

"I just threatened life and limb and that did the trick," says Rahk with a little smirk.

I shoot a look at him, unsure if he is serious or not. He comes to my side and puts out a hand. To my surprise, Bartholomew nuzzles into it. Then she begins sniffing him, as though searching for something.

"Someone's wife thought she was exceptional and took good care of her in your absence. Now that I see the creature, I must agree. She is no young animal, but she is strong, well-spirited, and apparently a good judge of character."

I laugh. "She may like you without knowing you long, but I cannot call her judgment unflawed. She never liked Mary, which is obviously a strike against her. But that's alright. She makes up for it by being perfect in every other way. Aren't you, Bartholomew?"

Rahk chuckles and produces a package of carrots from his pocket. Bartholomew pulls her lips back from her teeth and tries to chomp them right out of his hand. He's faster, however, and grins as he hands them to me.

I usually only give her a few at a time, but this is a special occasion. I let her eat all of them with their leafy tops. Then I glance back at Rahk. "May I . . ."

He lifts a brow, waiting for me to finish.

It feels so ungrateful of me to not spend time with *him* after he's done me this great service, but I cannot help it. The request flies out of my mouth. "May I please take her for a ride?"

A smile stretches across his face. "Why do you ask me for permission? Do as you please."

I let out a high-pitched sound of excitement. I cast about for a stable hand—only to have Rahk call for him to aid me at once. As Bartholomew is being saddled, I cannot help but look back at the prince, with his usually severe manner so warm and pleased as he turns to go back into the house.

And then I'm running back toward him. He stops at the sound of gravel crunching beneath my shoes. His face is surprised, yet again, as I throw my arms around his neck and kiss his cheek.

His hand comes up at once, catching the side of my face and tilting it toward his. I haven't a second to be taken aback before his mouth claims mine in a searing kiss that shocks me to my core.

It's not a long kiss. In fact, it's very short. Just a firm press of warm lips—there and gone.

Rahk releases me, and his face is not amused anymore. Instead, he looks at me very intently. In that moment, as I stand there frozen, still on my toes, I don't know if he means to communicate something with that black-eyed gaze of his or if he is studying my face for a reaction.

I drop down to my heels. I cannot bear the intensity of his focus, so I swallow and retreat a step. My hand has found my hair, raking through it like that will somehow help me not drown in this moment.

"Thank you!" I blurt, meaning the horse.

I realize only as I turn and charge back to the stables that it sounded like I was thanking him for the kiss.

More than ever, I need the pounding of hooves beneath me, the wind tangling in my hair, the solid comfort of Bartholomew supporting me. Swinging into her saddle is like coming home. Together, we race out of the stables and into the grounds behind Rahk's estate.

It is like taking flight. I stand a little in my stirrups to stay out of her way, her movements full of power and yet so smooth. We soar across a green ocean of grass. Sharp wind drives tears from my eyes and into my hair. Bartholomew always loves when I let her gallop as fast as her heart wants, and that joy seeps from her muscles into mine. Rahk's kiss will be considered later. Right now, I'm *free*.

I missed her so much.

She wants to keep going, even when we reach the edge of Rahk's estate. I haven't the heart to stop her, so I let her take us toward the fields near Caphryl Wood.

We ride over the edge of the hill. I grin as we crest, savoring the sheer power of Bartholomew's body, when my grin is suddenly wiped away in puzzlement.

The valley below me, that leads into the forest, isn't empty as usual. There are . . . *people*.

Bartholomew comes to an unsteady halt at a word from me. I survey the scene before us.

The people look mostly poor, with tattered clothes and old, dented hoes and trowels. There are not many of them, perhaps a dozen in all. They are busy working in the part of the field that glitters at night. The part of the land that is now recovered from the forest.

In the midst of this work, I catch glimpses of fresh plants and though it's hard to tell from here, I could almost swear there is one the size of a small tree with enormous red fruit on it.

"Ymer will eat you all!" roars the troll's deep, rickety voice. "Get off Ymer's land!"

The troll is on his feet—the first time I've ever seen such a thing. He holds his club in one fist and stomps around the grass. People scatter at his approach, taking advantage of his slowness. Then, when he is distracted, others rush in behind him to keep working.

Bartholomew nickers beneath me, sensing my unease.

"What on earth?" I whisper.

I swing my leg over to dismount. Ymer continues railing at the people. They mostly give him a wide berth, but his face grows redder by the moment. If they miscalculate and get too close, he *will* kill them.

"Stay here, love," I say to Bartholomew, keeping her away from Ymer's gaze.

I grab my skirts and jog over to the nearest person. I never take my eye off of the troll. It is a middle-aged woman I reach. "What are you doing?" I hiss. "That troll will kill you!"

"Yes, yes," replies the woman eagerly, her face bright, "but this is a miracle! We plant the seeds, and the fruits ripen within *days*! They are bigger and sweeter than anything we've ever seen!"

The small tree with enormous red fruit, I realize in shock, is a tomato plant, with tomatoes bigger than a cantaloupe.

How am I going to continue my raids if there are people here? And what if Ymer actually starts killing people?

"Is that you, small elf?" roars the troll. "Ymer will skin you alive!"

My heart lurches. Everyone in my nearby vicinity scrambles to safety. I tear my gaze away from the strange plants, register Ymer's approach, and pump my legs into a run over the hilltop. I grab Bartholomew's reins and leap into her saddle, turning her around quickly.

"We need to go get Rahk!" I tell her.

We gallop back the way we came as fast as Bartholomew can handle.

CHAPTER 45

RAHK

RAHK!" I BURST into his study, gasping for air. He apparently heard me barreling through the hallways and is already getting up. "You must come at once!"

"What's wrong?" he demands, grabbing his cloak and striding after me.

I'm so winded I can barely get the words out. "Caphryl Wood—there are people—growing stuff—"

His hand lands on my back. "Are you hurt? Did someone threaten you? Frighten you?"

"What?" I look up at him. "No—no! It's not me. It's the land! It's magic! People are growing food that is strange! And there is a troll that wants to eat everyone!"

"People you don't know?"

"Never seen them in my life!"

"And it's your land?"

"Well, some of it, yes, but that's beside the point! You need to come and see what is happening. I ran Bartholomew back hard, so I shouldn't take her out again. We'll have to take two of your horses—"

I bolt toward the direction of the stables, only to be nearly yanked off my feet when he takes hold of my elbow to guide me in the opposite direction. "What are you—?"

There is a glint in Rahk's eye. A glint that makes him look wild—and very, very *fae*. "Horses are slow. There's a faster way to get there."

I look at him blankly. Unless he's trying to say that there are Paths in the human world as well, I have no idea what he means.

He pulls me after him around the back of the house, past the creek, beyond the view of any windows. Then he turns toward me. There is something in his expression, something in his wide-legged stance, that reminds me—as I'm so often forgetting—that he is a warrior who can tear me apart with his bare hands. That he is not just a tall human with long silver hair, but something entirely different. A being from a different world.

And then reality ripples behind him. The trees shiver like a droplet of water falling into the clear reflection of a still pond. I would have stumbled backward, tripped and fallen over the hem of my dress, if not for his grip on my arm.

Because right before my eyes, a great pair of jet-black wings spread from Rahk's back. They catch the sunlight, turning dark blue.

"You—you—" I stammer.

His mouth spreads in a slow smirk. He pulls me close to his chest, arching an eyebrow down at me. "You're going to have to hold on tight."

"I—what? No! Absolutely not!" I try to pull free, but he bends and wraps an iron-like arm around my ribcage, and another around my knees as he hoists me up against him. "This is *so* unsafe!"

He makes a sound at the back of his throat. "Katherine Vandermore, concerned about safety? No, I don't think that's true."

And with that, he launches into the sky.

I scream bloody murder as the ground shoots away from us. Wind pummels me from the force of his wings. I instinctively flail my legs and arms, fighting to get away from his hold on me. He tightens his grip, growling something at me that I cannot hear over the roar of air and the sound of my own knife-like terror.

We seem to even out, our direction shifting from up to parallel to the ground. I stop screaming long enough to glance down. Then my screaming renews even more violently.

There is nothing between me and the plunging fall of my death—nothing except Rahk's two arms which hold me tightly to his chest.

"Oh saints, oh saints, oh saints!" I shriek, only now realizing that I have a choking grip on his neck.

"I'm not going to drop you!" he shouts over the wind. "Just relax!"

"I'm going to die! I'm going to die!"

"You are *not* going to die."

"I don't believe you!"

"Don't look at the ground. Just hold on to me." He places his mouth against my ear so I can hear him. "I promise you; I will not let you fall. Trust me, Kat. I've got you."

He says it so gently that part of me relaxes. A whimper still escapes me as I squeeze my eyes shut and cling to him, as though to my own life. But then I notice just how solid his arms feel around me, how warm he is against the whipping wind.

I peel one eye open. He smirks at me again.

"You're embarrassing yourself at this point," he says.

"It is a crime that you never told me you had wings! Or could fly!" I protest, even though I *did* technically see his wings once before. It was dark, though!

"If it is a crime I have indeed committed, then please accept my apology."

"I'm sorry for lying to you! Now please don't kill me for vengeance!"

His long silver hair streams when he shakes his head and smiles. He pulls me closer so his lips touch my ear when he says, "How many times must I tell you I'm not going to kill you? Now look. See how beautiful the world is from the sky?"

I wrap my arms tighter around his neck and venture a peek below. From here, I can see the shadows of clouds playing across the fields, the spring green brilliant in its splendor. "Oh! It *is* beautiful!"

Pleasure radiates from him. His thumb on my ribs traces a soft caress. And then he nuzzles his nose into my hair. My gasp is swallowed by the wind as he says, "I've wanted to take you flying for so long. I wish you could feel what it is like to have wings."

I smile. "It is probably like riding a galloping horse—except this is far higher."

It's only a moment later that he tells me, "It's time to land. I will do it as gently as I can. Try not to scream, to avoid giving us away."

The words barely register in my mind before we swoop downward and leave my stomach high in the air above us. My shriek—not entirely made of fear this time—slams against my teeth, but I manage to perform the feat of the ages and keep it contained.

As suddenly as it began, everything is still. The wind has stopped. I peek open one eye and find Rahk watching me, his head tilted to one side. He holds me tightly, as if to convince me that he was never at risk of dropping me.

"We're done?" I squeak.

"For the moment."

When he sets me on my feet, my legs go boneless on me, and I flop to the ground, groaning as I fling my limbs out in all directions. "That was terrifying . . . and amazing."

Rahk shoots me a smile, but it is quick to vanish as he climbs the rise of the hill we landed on, keeping low so he isn't spotted as he peers over the edge. I'm still flopped on the ground, breathing hard, but I shield the sun from my eyes and watch him. His shoulders tense.

I moan low and then roll over, pushing up to my knees. My feet do *not* want to work, but my curiosity overpowers their weakness. I climb the rise and settle myself beside Rahk. It's as it was when I left—people planting haphazardly, while others pluck fully ripened fruit or vegetables off of enormous plants. They give Ymer and his cudgel a wide berth.

Rahk watches the tableau before us with a hardened brow. A quiet curse escapes him.

"It's from the magic?" I ask. "From the forest receding?"

He nods.

"Are you afraid Ymer will kill them?"

He shoots a look at me. "How do you know his name?"

"He has been screaming it at the top of his lungs," I say quickly, kicking myself for the slip. "Unless he is referring to someone else named Ymer."

Just then, the troll shouts: "Ymer will grind your bones into a fine dust and snort it up Ymer's nose!"

Rahk plants one hand on his thigh. "Yes, I am afraid he will kill them." He pushes away from the rise and gestures for me to follow him back down.

I scurry after him. "Aren't you going to talk to them? Or to the troll?"

"No." Rahk walks far enough away from the hill so we won't be seen. "No one in that field is going to listen to me. We're going to talk to the queen. At once."

"This is very bad?"

"It will get bloody soon if there is no intervention." He fixes his dark gaze on me. "And that's *your* land. If anyone ought to be profiting off it, it's *you*."

I wave a hand. "I'm not worried about the land or the money." *Just how on earth I'm supposed to get past them to get into the forest for my raids?*

He holds out his hand to me. The tall grass waves against our calves, my skirts blowing in the wind. The sky is bright blue above us, with only a few clouds.

"I will fly back with you on one condition," I say, not stepping close enough just yet.

"What is that?"

"That this is not the last time you take me flying."

The dark furrow of his brow is gone in an instant, and it is as though a light has been ignited inside his eyes. He pulls me straight to his chest, his eyes sweeping over my face once before he scoops me up into his arms.

"I wouldn't dare deprive you so cruelly," he murmurs into my ear—and then shoots into the sky.

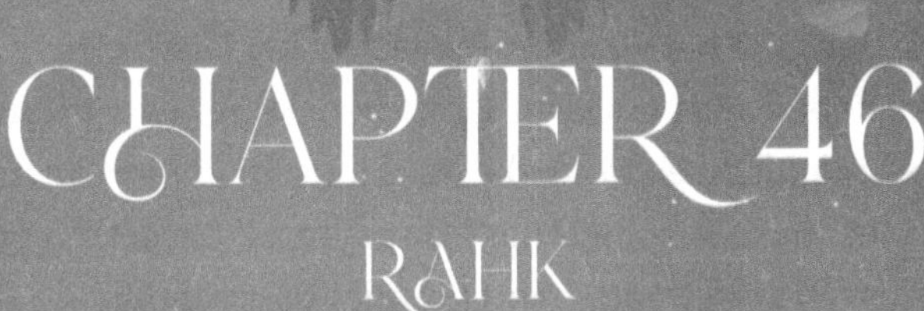

CHAPTER 46

RAHK

CAPHRYL WOOD. SHE called it by the fae name.

I must have called it by that name enough that it has slipped into her vocabulary. I shrug off the oddity as we each change into more presentable outfits to visit the queen.

"The queen doesn't take visitors without an appointment. Getting an appointment with her is a long process," Kat tells me as Mary runs after her and pins her flyaway hairs.

I button my cuffs as I stride into the courtyard where our carriage is waiting. "She will see us. It is urgent, and she is fascinated by us."

"Fascinated?" Kat hurries after me. I hand her into the carriage before stepping in after her and ducking my head beneath the low ceiling. It is late in the day and the shadows grow long. "Are you sure you're not just flattering yourself? I saw how cold she was to you at the luncheon."

I regard her evenly. "Queen Vivienne, for all her posturing and refusal to work with me to remove the troll, does find it vastly interesting that of all people, *you* seemingly chose to marry me. She wants the story. I saw it in her face at the wedding."

"Are you good at reading people?"

I lift one eyebrow. "Yes."

I expect her to lean forward and give a saucy reply, but instead she blinks and looks away. She scoots to the window and moves aside the curtain, watching the world move outside of our little box on wheels. I don't feign the same disinterest, and study her openly. I trace the line of her profile to her jaw, down her throat, to the hollow between her collarbones.

What does she not want me to read on her face?

I had hoped that once we'd gotten past her deception as my servant, she would open to me the way I long for her to. In some ways she has, but there is *something* I don't know. Something driving her—something she wants—and I cannot figure it out.

Have no fear, Kat. Your mind and motives remain a mystery to me.

Looking at her now, in her pale blue gown that compliments her dark hair and eyes well, with a simple silver chain around her long neck that someday I would very much like to kiss, I see two futures before us. One where we remain as friends, and our marriage a mutually beneficial agreement. I may not spend much time in the human lands long term, but she will remain provided for and comfortable all the days of her life. Not that she would need me to provide those things, situated as she is with her inheritance. Still, if she needed anything, she would have it.

The other future, however, sends my blood pounding.

No part of that future makes rational sense. She must stay here in the human world. I must go back to Faerie. She will live for decades more, and I will live for centuries. She will die, and I will take the throne of Nothril.

Something hot and frantic bubbles up in my gut at that thought. Even if I regularly returned to Ashbourne to visit Kat, I cannot stop her from growing old. I cannot prevent her death. When did my long life suddenly feel like the cruelest of curses?

"Is that why you came to the human lands?" Kat asks, breaking the silence unexpectedly. "To remove the troll? Did you know he would be a problem?"

I have not been sworn to secrecy regarding the Ivy Mask. I could tell her. Every fiber of my being balks at the idea, however. What would she think of me if she knew I actively worked to destroy the very person who likely rescued her mother from the depths of Faerieland?

She would despise me.

"My High King—he is the friend I mentioned before, the one named Ash—knew the troll would become a problem and sent me to address it," I reply.

"Then . . . why didn't you address it? While we were back at the Long Lost Wood?"

I release a sigh. "Because Ymer is very old fashioned, and will not listen to anyone save the ruler of the land. Queen Vivienne must bid him leave, or else he will not leave."

"That sounds annoying."

"Very."

By the scent shift in the air, I know we have arrived at the palace gates. I lean forward, pull aside the curtains, and bark at the guards, "Lady Katherine and I come bearing urgent news of the Long Lost Wood's border."

The gates open. We proceed unhindered.

The first person to greet us, besides guards, appears to be some sort of steward. He has a very wide mouth, with very large lips, and he runs down the grand staircase the moment I help Kat out of the carriage, blathering, "You do not have an appointment! The queen will not see you."

"The queen *will* see us, at once," I reply firmly, taking Kat's hand as she feigns distraction with the colorful palace roses flanking the steps, and tuck it into my elbow. She looks anywhere but me, her face flushing bright pink from the contact. I hide my satisfied smirk.

She is the one, however, who reaches out and places a gentle hand on the steward's forearm. "Queen Vivienne told me I may visit her at any time, and we come on no small matter. Please let us through."

Then she smiles, and his open mouth slowly closes. "This way."

When we are inside, I lean down and whisper, "That was impressive. Perhaps I ought to have married you sooner."

She flushes a little, and opens her mouth to reply, her lips angled in that way when she's about to give a sassy retort. She doesn't get a chance, however, because the queen's voice echoes into the chamber we stand in.

"Who are these *persons* who demand to see me so vehemently that my stalwart Nelson is shaking in his boots?"

"It's Lord Rahk and Lady Katherine, Your Majesty."

Her tone sharpens at once. "Lord Rahk and Lady Katherine, is it? Send them in."

Queen Vivienne sits in a very green chamber. The ornate, patterned rug on the wood floor is green. Intricate scrollwork is carved into the dark wood trim of the room. The curtains, the straight-backed upholstered furniture, and even the jewelry around the queen's throat are all the exact same shade of green. So is the screen behind the queen's back, which conceals all but a few shadows beneath it—shadows from warrior boots. How many men does she have back there?

Enough in number and skill for her to feel comfortable inviting me into this enclosed space after I dispatched her assassins.

That tells me everything I need to know about how much this queen trusts me.

Her son is with her. He wears a green doublet, embroidered in silver, and at our entrance, the queen kisses the boy's forehead and bids him to step out for a minute. Then she turns to us, and all the warmth she saved for her son is swept away into her queenly mask.

"Lord Rahk," she says in a guarded tone. Her attention shifts to Kat next to me as she curtsies. Her voice shifts very slightly to interest. "You've brought your new bride."

"I'm afraid we come on urgent matters," I say, bowing.

Queen Vivienne arches one groomed eyebrow. "Surely this is not another request for me to come speak to the troll. I sent that letter. Have you not taken it to him?"

"I did take it. He could not read it, so he ate it instead. You will have to come in person."

She clenches her jaw. Her gaze goes to the door her son disappeared through.

"You would be protected," I add. "By me, or your own guards, as your comfort dictated."

"You claim it would be safe for me to approach this troll?"

I hesitate slightly. Kat's silent gaze is warm on the side of my face. "It would not be *safe,* but as I said, you would be protected."

I ignore the tea a manservant pours. Kat takes two sugars and eyes the dish long enough to tell me she's trying to decide between being polite or taking a third sugar. I lean forward and use the spoon to place the third sugar into her cup without taking my attention off Queen Vivienne, who dismisses the manservant.

It almost seems like the queen trusts me . . . *less* after marrying Kat. The glances she gives my wife are sharp, as though she means to communicate or signal something.

She is trying to ask Kat if she is safe.

I lean back on the bench, finally understanding the dynamics at play here. The queen has believed from the beginning that I have ulterior motives for being here. Motives as dark, perhaps, as desiring to take her throne. Faerieland is finally returning the land it stole from the humans, but it would make sense from her vantage point that individual fae like myself might hate the High King and Queen's plan to return the land—and decide to take matters into my own hands to reclaim it. The troll might be my ploy to get her away from her throne, her beloved heir, and the protection of her people. Kat, herself, might be a captive victim threatened behind closed doors to act like the happy young wife to make the queen and court trust me.

Well, this just became far more complicated.

"Even if you do not address the troll," I say, trying to make my tone as unthreatening as possible, "your own people are at the edge of the Wood and the troll puts them in danger."

Queen Vivienne cocks her head to one side. "My people? What are they doing at the edge of the Wood?"

"They are growing massive fruit and vegetables!" Kat blurts. "Tomatoes the size of my head! Or bigger!"

"They?"

"Commoners, mostly," I clarify. "They are farming the land—stealing it from its rightful owners, the people who suffered when the forest encroached, and risking their own lives in the process. The phenomenon will wear off eventually, but it may be weeks or months before it does. I do not think it will be much longer before there are casualties at the hand of the troll."

Vivienne nods, sipping her tea. "Have you a proposal for this problem?"

I consider her question. Kat watches me expectantly, and she seems unusually curious about what I will say next. I exhale slowly. "I leave the decision in your hands, Queen Vivienne. Ymer, the troll, will leave if you go out to order him to leave. The matter of how to handle the land is for you to decide. My recommendation would be that the land be restored to its rightful owners."

Queen Vivienne smiles. "Which, I suppose, means much of the land would go to you."

Ah. She thinks of me as coming to claim the missing pieces of Kat's inheritance. It is a silly thought, because if I were here to steal the Harbright throne, I would have no need to bother with land I could otherwise commandeer at my whim.

I see no point in insisting that I will not touch Kat's inheritance. It will only set the queen further in the advantage.

"Only a small portion of all the land swallowed up by the Long Lost Wood belongs to Lady Katherine," I reply coolly. "The graver matter is the issue of the lives at risk as long as the troll is allowed to stay."

Queen Vivienne leans forward slightly. "If you wish to prove your loyalty to myself and to your wife, you should get rid of the troll yourself."

I don't bother replying. I've explained why I cannot do that in the past, though the thought of just killing Ymer and letting Ash deal with the consequences grows more appealing by the day.

I get to my feet. "We have taken enough of your time. We have delivered our message. Send a reply if you decide you wish for me to accompany you and your men to visit Ymer."

I hold my hand out for Kat. She takes it, and I've only just drawn her up when Queen Vivienne speaks again.

"Since you are here, you must ease my curiosity."

We both turn toward her.

She has a fiendish fire in her eye, clearly bent on unraveling me and finding my weaknesses. "Lord Rahk, since your children will be half fae, half human, will you raise them here or will you take them back to Faerieland?"

I blink in surprise at the forthrightness. Kat chokes on thin air—a sound that seems to shock the manservant who has reentered the room more than it surprises either me or the queen. Her head whips toward me, a look of sheer terror overcoming her expression.

I place a hand on her back and reply easily, "They would be raised here, certainly. I'm afraid they would not be recognized as legitimate in Faerieland."

"Not considered legitimate?" The queen leans forward at that. "I heard my sister, who has been gone all these years in Faerieland, has a son. Is he not considered legitimate?"

Kat subtly wrings her hands in the folds of her skirts. I give her spine a subtle stroke, meant to comfort her and tell her I'll handle this. She leans into my touch.

My heart races in reply.

"The situation with your sister is not the same," I say. "I am from a different Court. Lord and Lady Nothril will not recognize any half-human children of mine, and I consider that a fortunate thing." Before she can ask another overly personal question, I repeat, "Since we have delivered our news, we shall leave you. Thank you for receiving us."

She waves impatiently. "You both had better be at the ball at the end of the week."

"Of course we will." I push Kat out of the room with light pressure between her shoulder blades. The moment the doors close behind us, she turns a look up at me as if to say, *"Can you believe that?"*

I chuckle as we make our escape. She lets out a great big exhalation when she settles into the carriage and throws her feet up on the opposite bench, next to where I sit. They are startlingly small and distract me from the frustration of this meeting.

"I could go a long while without seeing her again!" Kat announces once the sound of horse hooves on cobblestones drowns out any possibility of us being overheard. "Only she could ask a question like that and not suffer consequences."

"It seems she has suffered a steep consequence: the lack of your good grace."

She shoots me a glare. I fight a smile.

"We've been married for only two days," she continues, huffing irritably. "And already we must face questions such as these."

A thought slips into my mind. I am forced to turn my face away from her, so she doesn't see how much I fail to contain my amusement. At first, I consider letting the thought pass by without comment. Then I decide I cannot leave a perfect opportunity to tease Kat into a blush.

She scowls out the window at the world passing by. Several wisps of hair from her bun have come loose and dangle about her cheekbones. I train my features into solemnity and my voice into a casual tone. "I have just realized that our children might have wings."

Kat's jaw drops open as her face turns the brightest shade of red I've ever seen. My grin slips past my guard, and she cries, "You said that *just* to embarrass me!"

My laughter fills the carriage. She rips one of her shoes off and smashes it against my shoulder. I catch her wrist, preventing her from whacking me again. She struggles to yank free, which somehow amuses me even more. I consider kissing her again. Maybe she wouldn't be shocked this time. Maybe I could pull her to myself—

"Did you marry me with the intent to spawn a brood of half-fae winged monsters?" she demands, yanking hard on her wrist. I release her, and she goes tumbling against the back of the carriage. More of her hair escapes her bun, framing her face with short, wild strands.

"No," I confess, trying to rein in my grin and failing. "But the idea grows more appealing by the moment."

"You take far too much pleasure in tormenting me." Kat crosses her arms over her chest, her discarded shoe beside her on the bench. "Mercy, I plead!"

I laugh. Then, after weighing the possibilities in my head, I venture a bold request. "If I offer you mercy and a reprieve from the discussion of winged monster children, then will you offer me a kiss?"

I was wrong—*this* is the reddest I've ever seen her. Her dark eyes shoot to mine. There's fear in her irises, but not of me. Of something I still cannot place. Beyond the fear, however, is something else that flickers and dances in her pupils.

She blinks and shuts her mouth firmly. "That doesn't seem like a smart bargain."

I lift my eyebrows. "Oh?"

"Kisses are known to lead to winged monster children. I cannot risk it."

I laugh and settle into my side of the carriage, pleased enough with her reply to not be too disappointed at her rejection. Her eyes betrayed her—she wants to kiss me. That knowledge is enough for this moment. "In that case, you must permit one more comment on the subject."

Her brows slant low together. "Don't tell me they would have claws and fangs too."

I shake my head, smiling a little before letting it flatten. "You should know that I will not ask children of you. As I said to the queen, they will not be acknowledged in my land or by my people. They would not be my heirs. Thus, I leave the decision entirely to your desires and wishes."

The corner of her mouth tilts in curiosity. Her fingers tap along the embroidered cushion she sits on. "You have no desire for children? No desire aside from having an heir to your Nothril throne after you die?"

I shift slightly on my seat. "Do you remember the conversation we once had about why—until you—I had not married?"

She nods.

"Having a child would be to give others more power over me. I do not wish that upon myself—or the child. Great Kings, I have been soft toward my youngest sister, and that is enough for Lord and Lady Nothril to bind me to their will." I hesitate, wondering if I should be this honest with her. It is the sight of those tiny scars on her face that remind me just how much I can trust her. "I desire for her to be gone from Nothril, so she will not be caught in the crossfires of my parents' intrigues and power plays."

Something quickens in the air around her. "Gone from Nothril? How would you accomplish that?"

I give a dry snort. "*I* cannot accomplish such a thing. Not if I value my life."

"Lord and Lady Nothril—your parents—would kill you? If you took your sister out of Faerieland?"

"Me, and her both. And likely many others just for the spite of it." Pictures carry across my mind's eye, splattered in the blood I was called to shed. "Someone else would have to do it."

"Who could break a princess out of Nothril?"

Don't tell her, the Nothril part of me growls. But when I look at her face, at her upturned nose and those freckles, I don't feel very Nothril anymore.

"One called the Ivy Mask," I whisper.

A powerful jolt goes through her body. Her eyes immediately flee from mine.

I cock my head to one side. "You know of him. He freed your mother, didn't he?"

She doesn't reply, clenching her elbow in one hand, her knuckles turning white.

A pang hits my chest. "I—I shouldn't have mentioned your mother. I am sorry."

She sits upright and sucks in a breath through her teeth—pulling together her rattled composure. "No, no, it is fine. I just haven't . . . I did not think I would hear that name from you."

Does she know much about the Ivy Mask? All this time, could Kat have been the key to finding him?

An uncomfortable weight settles in my gut. If she knew I wanted the Ivy Mask for more than just a means of getting Pavi out of Faerie, she would hate me.

"You know him?" I ask tentatively.

Despite her attempts to stay cool, her rapidly tapping foot betrays how uncomfortable she is. "No, I never met him. But I heard the name. A long time ago."

So she won't be helpful after all. I should be disappointed, but instead, I am relieved. If I caught the Ivy Mask and killed him because of information Kat gave me, she would never forgive me.

"You want your sister to be free of Nothril?" she asks. "Or all Faerie?"

"All Faerie," I reply immediately. "Fae rulers cannot cross the border into the human lands. If she were here, in the human world, Lord and Lady Nothril could not pursue her."

She considers this for a moment. "You would have her come here, but you yourself would go back? I thought she was the reason you had to go back."

"She is the most pressing reason, but not the only one."

"Then what other reasons take you back?"

Is there something behind that question? Does she want me to stay? My heart quickens. "I have a throne to inherit."

"Are you the only person who can inherit it?"

"One of my sisters could. If something happened to me." I am not the only heir, and thus, I am, technically, disposable. And if I find myself *disposed*, then who will protect Pavi?

"So you don't *have* to return for your throne. Unless you wanted to. Do you want to?"

Her dark eyes pierce me with their intensity, making me forget to breathe momentarily. She leans forward, and there is that sharp cunning flashing in her face. She usually hides it so well.

"I don't believe you want your throne, Rahk," she says quietly, though her words strike like arrows. "There is something else taking you back to Faerieland. What is it?"

So this is what it feels to be on the other end of my interrogations. I do not like it. When Kat looks at me like that, it feels like there is nothing I can hide from her. No one can see through me like she does. Not even Ash. It is something I have come to both dread and desire.

"I have a dear friend," I say hesitantly. "If I left Nothril and abandoned my throne, I would be cast away from Faerie. I would never see him again."

She studies me intently. I try to make my face as unreadable as possible.

"That's not why," she says at last.

"Kat—"

"I am not saying that you do not care about your friend, or that you would not be devastated by his loss, but there is something else that pulls you back to Faerieland. What is it?"

Tension builds up inside my chest. There *is* something pulling me back—but until now, I did not realize it was something besides Pavi or Ash or my responsibilities as a prince of Nothril. The thought of never going back fills me with coldness, with a sense of true, permanent failure. I *cannot* give up. It would prove—it would prove—

Then, like the clouds parting to reveal the sun, I finally understand.

My voice comes out low and quiet, but it fills the carriage. "I have always feared that the longer I live in Nothril, the more I lose myself—and the more corrupt I become. Ash always said I would be the first ruler in many, many ages who could bring goodness back to Nothril, but I have always worried that by the time I ascended the throne, there would be nothing left of me. I would be another Lord and Lady Nothril."

Kat listens intently, her face softening the longer I speak, as though she understands. Part of me relaxes. Maybe she *does* understand. Maybe she won't despise me for all the things I have done.

Maybe she will someday understand that when I destroy the Ivy Mask to save Pavi's life, I destroy myself too.

"But I do not want that to be true of me," I say. A slight tremor has entered my hand, I slide it away from Kat's gaze. "I want to be strong enough to not buckle under the pressure. Which means that I cannot walk away."

"Because walking away means you've admitted defeat," Kat finishes for me.

I hold her gaze, which is full of the kindness I've been so starved for. I wish I could bottle up her goodness and hold it inside me like a light when the night comes to devour me.

Her hand lands on my knee. The warmth of that touch travels all the way to my marrow. She gives a gentle squeeze. I swallow hard.

She withdraws her hand, and we do not speak the rest of the drive home.

CHAPTER 47

KAT

"WHEN IS YOUR next raid?" Mary asks in a whisper as she works a sweet-smelling herbal hair growth serum into my scalp before bed. Rahk has been out all evening—doing what, I have no idea—and so we aren't at risk of being overheard. I have not stopped thinking about the conversation we had earlier. I had not realized how much I wanted him to say, *"Nothing takes me back to Nothril. I would rather stay here with you."* But I have always known he would go back.

Now I understand why.

I never expected him to mention the Ivy Mask. My memory flashes back to the tentacled monster, when he told me he needed my help to save his sister. The pitiful part of me wanted then to shout, *"I'm the Ivy Mask! I thought you wanted to destroy me—but you really just want my help? Of course I will help your sister!"*

But no matter how deeply I long to fully trust Rahk, the stronger, more determined side of me demands reason. I can still help his sister—but he can never know who I am. If he has not already received orders to kill me, then that will change the moment I rescue his sister, and he will know who I am and how to find me.

I pick hair out of the brush she was just using. "It's the day after the ball. I'm going to the Star City this time. Then it's only a week before the big Nothril raid."

Mary inhales slowly.

I lower my gaze to my lap. "I know I'm going to have to stop."

"You've done so much for those people, Kat."

"I know," I groan, flopping back on the bed when she is finished with my hair. "But it's never enough. There's so many more to be helped."

"You don't have to help them *all*."

"How can I stop at some? How can I walk away from it? Mary, I've known for some time that it can't go on forever—but I just cannot imagine trying to live with myself knowing that there are people out there. Suffering. Parted from their families. Wishing to be free."

She pulls a face. "But ultimately, *you* aren't responsible for them."

"Yes, I am!" I cry, surprising both of us with my vehemence. "I have the means to help them. So to stand by and do nothing is tantamount to imprisoning them myself."

Mary turns fierce. "No, it is *not*. And you *don't* have the means to help them anymore. Not without risking your life."

"I've risked my life from the beginning, Mary."

"Not like this." She turns pleading, taking my hand in both of hers. "Kat, you're all I have. You cannot count your life as cheap. Your parents would be heartbroken to see you so cavalierly—"

"Don't bring them into this."

She smacks the back of my head with the soft side of the brush. "They're the reason you're doing this. They're at the core of this. I cannot bring them into it any more than you have. You know I will help you in any way I can. You know I love you like my own sister. And as a sister, I am afraid for you. I'm afraid the work you do will never be enough—and that you will sacrifice your life needlessly. I just . . . I just want you to be at peace, Kat."

My shoulders collapse. I haven't the will to fight her anymore.

She seems to be trying to find the right thing to say as she changes the subject. "Lord Rahk is very kind to you."

"You don't even know the half of it," I say, sagging even further.

She regards me with concern. "I know you're being careful."

A growling sigh escapes me. "I'm trying!"

The unmistakable sound of the front door opening and closing, followed by booted footsteps, announces Rahk's arrival. Mary and I share a quick look. I fear what might be visible on my face.

Mary, ever practical, merely picks up the jar of fae salve and motions for me to hike my nightgown and give her my calf. I listen to the pattern of footsteps, trying to determine Rahk's destination as the they grow fainter, and then louder. They come down the hallway. Mary's hand freezes just before she sticks it into the salve. A knock sounds on the door.

I swallow hard. "Come in."

Rahk's silver head is the first thing I see. His black eyes fall almost immediately to the exposed wound on my calf. My mouth goes dry. I'm suddenly very conscious of how dark it is, the fact that I wear only a nightgown, and I wonder if this is the night he decides to spend with me instead of at his desk.

"Thank you, Mary. You may go," Rahk says with a nod.

Mary's eyes find mine for only a half of a second before she sets the open salve down on the quilt, curtsies, and leaves. Rahk shuts the door behind her.

"You've been gone," I say to fill the silence.

It takes him only three strides to stand in front of where I sit on the bed. He takes up Mary's spot, sitting beside me. With one hand, he picks up the container. With the other, he takes a creamy dollop and lightly dabs it across my scar. It tingles against my skin.

"I was at the edge of the Long Lost Wood again," he tells me. He sets down the container and places his palm over my kneecap, holding my leg still as he gently massages the salve into my scar with two fingers. The pressure, though light, is enough to sharpen the remnant of the pain. I brace against it. Rahk's eyes flick up to me briefly before returning to his work.

"What did you find?"

"The queen still refuses to meet with the troll. The forest continues to recede. I had to intervene to keep Ymer from killing someone who tripped in their efforts to escape him. I am also concerned by how close the humans get to the edge of the Wood. They've discovered that the closer they are to the source, the better and faster their crops grow. It would not be difficult for an accident to happen, and one of them to trip over the border. A few thieves have also appeared."

"This isn't good," I say, chewing the inside of my cheek to stay focused on his words and not his touch. As he nears the edge of the wound and the cream works its magic, the pain disappears, and all I'm left with is the sensation of his warm fingers working against my skin.

"No, it isn't." Rahk finishes his ministrations and wipes his hand on his trousers before screwing on the lid and returning the salve to its place on the vanity. He takes up his seat beside me again, so that we're both watching the candles flicker in front of the mirror.

I rack my brain for something else to say on the subject and come up short. Instead, I ask, "Are you tired?"

He sighs. "I am." Then he glances sidelong at me. "You must be too."

At this moment? I'm *wide* awake. "It was a very full day."

"I shall leave you to your rest, in that case."

I blink, surprised, as he stands. He's not staying? I expect relief, and all I find is disappointment. He pauses in front of where I sit.

Slowly, he leans down, planting his hands on the bed, flanking either side of me.

I stare up at him, wide-eyed, forgetting to breathe.

His gaze travels over my face, lingering on the faint scars on my temple, then my freckles, and then, finally, my lips. He brings his gaze back up to mine and pins me there with the force of his endless black eyes.

"Would you like a kiss goodnight?" he asks softly.

"I know you're being careful"—Mary's voice echoes into my thoughts, completely unbidden, reminding me exactly what reply I ought to give my husband in this moment.

"Yes," I breathe, hating myself for my weakness, hating myself for revealing so much to Rahk in one word.

His hand lands on my neck, his thumb stroking beneath my chin as his mouth presses against mine.

How can his lips be so soft? All thoughts scatter in the wake of that question, because when I assume his kiss will be short, it lengthens and slows. I don't breathe for a single second, terrified for the moment he pulls away. But he lingers, kissing me sweeter and longer.

When he does finally pull away, candlelight flickers across his bright eyes, highlighting the color in his cheeks, the intensity of his focus. His touch remains a moment longer. His fingers move slightly on the back of my neck, his thumb tracing my jaw.

"Goodnight." His voice is a low rasp as he withdraws.

My mouth has fallen open, and I only realize it when he releases my hand and strides out of the room.

He's gone. I catch my breath, pressing my hand to my heart and staring into the darkness. I wonder how much longer I can lie to myself. I wonder how I will ever be free of him, even after he returns to Nothril.

"I have a surprise for you," Rahk tells me several days later over breakfast.

I set down the bite I'm about to take. "A surprise?"

"We'll leave in an hour."

"Leave? Where are we going?"

He looks up, and even though his expression doesn't change, his amusement carries in his tone. "I said it was a surprise."

I look down at my breakfast. The morning light shines across my mostly eaten poached eggs, sausage, toast, and a fresh glass of orange juice. It is a delicious breakfast, but my attention is suddenly much too diverted. "Are we going riding? Is it something we're *doing,* or a gift? If it's a gift, you really have been giving me too many gifts! Or are we seeing a person? Are we seeing my cousin about the estate?"

His mouth twitches, but he doesn't reply.

"Rahk!"

Finally, a smirk ghosts across his face as he looks at me. "If you're *that* impatient, we could go now."

"Yes!" I shove back my chair and get to my feet. "Let's go!"

He smiles and follows me to the front of the house. As he hands me into the carriage he says, "I thought you might want to go straight there. It is why I waited until the end of breakfast to mention it."

My eyes widen just as I land on the cushion. "Did you not get to finish your breakfast? We can go back! I didn't mean to pull you away—"

He climbs in beside me—instead of across from me—chuckling as the footman closes the door. He stretches his legs across the space in the cab, lets out a sigh, and leans back. He casually drapes his arms over the back of the bench. I happen to be sitting upright when he does so, which then presents me with the option of sitting with a ramrod spine the entire drive . . . or leaning back into his arm. I prefer the latter option, with the exception that it feels very intentional. Leaning back is a statement.

So is staying upright.

I lean toward the window, avoiding either statement, and eagerly peer out of it. Then, when that doesn't give me clues as to the surprise, I turn toward Rahk. "Do I get a hint?"

One of his legs is stretched straight, and he draws the other one up so it's bent at the knee. He looks down at me. I'm very aware of how only six inches separate my arm from his side.

"Do you want a hint?" he asks.

I nod quickly.

"Well, let's see," he murmurs, shifting his gaze to the opposite side of the carriage. At the same time, he slides his arm and wraps it around my shoulders, drawing me against him.

My eyes nearly bug out of my head in surprise. His familiar scent fills my awareness, somehow both soothing and enlivening. I should resist this—I should resist *him*—just like I should have resisted the kiss he gave me a few nights ago that I have not stopped dreaming about since.

But I love how warm his side feels. I love that he wanted me here. I love the way his hand settles on my ribcage and makes me forget every reason I wanted to stay sitting upright.

"It is a place," he begins, "that was once stolen, but is now restored."

That distracts me enough that I make a face. "What is *that* supposed to mean?"

He lifts one eyebrow, trying not to smile as he looks down at me. He gives my ribs a soft stroke. "That's the only hint you get."

"I asked for a hint, not a riddle," I reply, sitting backward. "Are you taking me to the Long Lost Wood? What surprise would you have for me there? Dead bodies and a house-sized vegetable?"

A wave of frustration over that situation passes across his face. Then he pats me lightly. "You only need be patient for a few more minutes."

Those minutes last a lifetime. I'm not sure what to do with the rather intimate way he has his arm around me. It feels silly and strange to ask, *"Does this mean you have feelings for me and want our marriage to be more than an inconvenient arrangement? I suppose the kiss might have also indicated that, but you haven't been kissing me the last few nights, so I don't know if that was a one-time thing. And if you go back to Nothril, would you ever visit me?"* It occurs to me several minutes later that he has given me an opportunity to reciprocate in some way—to flirt back, to lean closer.

And I cannot deny that in other circumstances, I think I would do exactly that. Maybe he would kiss me then. Maybe he would stop sleeping in his study then.

But the more I think about it, the more upset I become. He doesn't know I'm the Ivy Mask. I've lied to him and deceived him. I know our marriage can never work. He doesn't know any of this—save that he will live in Nothril and I will live here. I have to be the one to keep the boundaries between us. As much as I loved that kiss, as much as

I want more and more and more, how can I accept his affection, knowing what I know—and knowing what he *doesn't* know?

The carriage comes to a halt. I've forgotten about the surprise. I should be excited for it, but I find myself dreading it instead. Rahk removes his arm from around me and climbs out of the carriage, turning to help me out after him. Then I forget everything of the past few minutes.

Because we are standing in front of Vandermore Manor, with its vibrant green lawn and the shrubs trimmed into a rearing stallion, and every familiar door and window.

I turn in confusion to Rahk. "What are we doing here? Are we meeting with Agatha?"

If we are, I did *not* mentally prepare myself. What a nasty surprise that would be!

"She isn't here," Rahk replies evenly as he marches toward the door.

I keep pace with him. "Is she out calling? Are we here to see Bridget and Edith? Bridget often calls on her friends in the morning, so it will probably only be Edith."

"None of them are here."

I stop in front of the door. Charles hurries to open it, and I barely remember to send him a warm smile in my confusion. "Then why? I don't understand."

"We are here," Rahk announces as we cross the threshold, "because this is your house now."

My feet root to the spot. My mind rejects every attempt at understanding this statement.

"It's part of your inheritance."

I turn incredulous eyes up at him as realization dawns. "Are you saying that you kicked Agatha, Bridget, and Edith out of this house?"

He is standing with his legs braced wide, arms crossed over his chest, surveying the parlor where my identity was discovered. "It wasn't their house."

A loud, unladylike chortle bursts from my throat. I stare at this man—this fae—in utter astonishment. "You—" Nothing coherent emerges from my mouth. I shake my head and try again. "But—but I don't need this house! I'm living with you."

"They didn't need it either," he replies. "They had more than enough money from your bride price to purchase their own living."

I should feel terrible. I should insist that the money Rahk gave them should be put toward Bridget and Edith's dowries. Instead, I start laughing and I cannot stop. Tears leak from my eyes as I whack his arm soundly. "You are utterly wicked!"

He cocks one eyebrow at me. "I *am* a Nothril prince."

"When did you do this?" I demand, going to Agatha's favorite sitting room. Everything is in its place. Even the harpsichord Edith abused so soundly sits in its corner. The sheet music, however, is all gone.

"A week ago." He goes to the mantel and drags his finger along the wood. His nose wrinkles slightly, and I don't know if it's because of the dust that comes away on his fingers, or whatever his keen fae nose smells. "Your stepmother was shocked."

"Am I a terrible person for wishing I had seen that?" I reply, wandering to the next room.

"No."

I come to the dining room where I ate so many meals with my stepfamily. Something about it pricks my heart, leaving a pulsing ache behind. I sigh and close the door, continuing down the hallway toward the spiral staircase to the second floor. "Sometimes I don't know what to think of them. They were never kind enough for me to be glad for their family joining mine. They were also never cruel enough for me to truly hate them."

"They sold Bartholomew," Rahk reminds me. "On purpose. Knowing it would hurt you."

"That's just what it seems like. Maybe she didn't mean—"

"I got her to admit it. When we discussed the house. Lady Duxbury Vandermore knew exactly what she was doing."

That hits me harder than I thought it would. I sit down on the stairs. My chest burns.

Rahk leans against the railing. "She threatened to beat you. She tried to break your mother's glass slippers. She tried to trick you into a marriage with her son. You're allowed to hate her."

"Those things were cruel," I admit. "But growing up, when I was a child, she didn't treat me like that. There were even some years that Edith and Bridget and I enjoyed spending time together. Not as sisters, perhaps, but as friends. Sometimes I think that my fortune is what ruined everything. If I had been like them, if Father had split the fortune among all of us, maybe we could have been a family together."

Rahk's mouth thins. "Your fortune did not create your stepmother's greed. It only brought it into the light."

"But it makes me feel like a fraud! An imposter! I did nothing to deserve this fortune." I gesture at the house. "I don't need two houses! Shall I live here by myself while you stay at your estate?"

"If that is what you desire."

"I *desire* to not feel guilty that I have so much—far more than I know what to do with it—when they have so little."

"They hardly have *so little*. From my research, the son has a fine estate from his father, and besides that your father did leave your stepfamily with a generous living. When paired with what I paid them, they are as far from paupers as you can get."

I crumple my dress in my fists. "It's just . . . my stepsisters' dowries. I had every eligible man in the entire kingdom pursuing my hand. They don't have that."

Rahk gives me a pointed look. "More options are not necessarily a good thing."

"Stop trying to reason away my guilt!" I cry, burying my head in my hands. The words tumble out, an echo of what I told Mary. "This mess is all my fault! If I have the means to fix something, then to stand by and do nothing makes me feel as though I'm the one committing the crime itself."

I'm not talking about the house anymore, and I'm afraid he will be able to sense it.

Suddenly, Rahk crouches before me, gently pulling my hands away from my face. "Kat, that is ridiculous. There are things in this life that are our responsibility, and there are things that *do not* belong to us. Meddling in the business of others does not make us their savior. Sometimes it makes us their curse."

I shake my head, finding myself squeezing his hand hard, holding onto it to keep from fracturing into tiny pieces. He's wrong. He means well. But he's wrong. "I just . . . I just wish my family wasn't this broken, ugly mess. I wish that we'd never lost my mother. But if we had to, I wish Agatha could have been my new mother."

Speaking the words out loud make me realize just how true they are—and how I've never acknowledged that was what I wanted all this time. Deeper than that, though, I wish losing my mother wasn't my fault. I wish Agatha hating me wasn't my fault.

"Kat," Rahk says quietly, still crouching in front of me, his face level with mine. His gaze holds mine, turning gentle and tender when I am tempted to look away. "Giving away all that you have will not repair what is broken. If you wish to give the entirety of your fortune to Agatha and her daughters, you can do that. But it will not restore the relationship with them." Then, even quieter than the last words, he murmurs, "It won't bring your mother back. The tragedy of your family is not your fault."

I yank my hands away from him, the words bursting from me with a force I cannot restrain. "But it *is* my fault! I should be dead. Me—not Mama and Father. *Me*."

The shift on Rahk's face is immediate. I turn away from him, hating what he will read in my expression, hating that I let those incriminating words out of my stupid mouth—hating how violently tears fight against my restraints.

"Kat," he says slowly, "what *really* happened on the edge of the Wood?"

I shake my head, my shoulders trembling.

He climbs to the step beside me and gathers me to his chest as the tears finally win. He holds me close with one arm and cradles my head with his other hand. I haven't the will to resist, so I lean against him and weep.

"You don't have to tell me what happened if you don't want to," Rahk whispers at last, "but whatever happened, it does not change that you are allowed to have good things. And your existence does not take away good things from those you love."

A loud keening rips straight from my chest. I press a hand over my mouth, biting down on my palm to keep from letting further sounds escape.

Your existence does not take away good things from those you love.

How can he say something like that? How can he just stab me straight through the heart with a few words?

Rahk tightens his hold on me, and his voice sounds almost choked. "You don't have to earn your right to live, Kat."

That only makes me cry harder. He can say that—but he doesn't know what happened.

He doesn't know that it was not Mama who was swallowed by the Long Lost Wood.

He doesn't know that it was me.

Eventually, I pull my composure back together. It is a monumental effort, but he lets me take my time. When I finally sit up, pulling away from him, and dry my eyes, he regards me with solemnity.

"What would you like to do?" he asks.

My blurry gaze drifts toward the edge of the harpsichord visible from where we sit. "I would like the address of my stepfamily's new arrangements. I think they left a few things behind that I don't have use of. Then I would like to go home."

Rahk's gaze darts to mine, his pupils dilating at my words. He offers his hand and draws me to my feet. "Then let us go home."

CHAPTER 48

KAT

THE BALL APPROACHES in a blink. In the past, balls have always been a source of anxiety as I prepared for the flood of fortune-hunters. The anxiety that follows me now is of a completely different variety. Aside from our sudden wedding, I have not been in society with Rahk—much less as his *wife.*

Mary senses my jitters, but nothing makes me stop fidgeting with the laced edges of my bodice. Not even the whack of a folded fan against my knuckles and Mary's glare. I cannot appreciate the beauty of the violet gown with its exquisite pearl detailing. It's a shame, truly, because Bridget would have killed to wear a gown like this.

Rahk's footsteps approach in the hallway beyond the closed door. Instead of knocking, he calls, "Are you ready?"

Mary struggles to pin back the wisps of hair coming free of my updo.

"Almost!" I call back, my voice pitched high.

Mary finishes her work, looks me up and down with her shrewd eye, and then purses her lips. She looks like she has something to say, but she keeps her mouth firmly closed and leaves the room.

I stand before the mirror. Mary has done well—as always. Her skills, however, cannot overcome just how uncomfortable I look in this mirror.

"May I come in?"

My heart leaps to my throat. I glance around desperately, though for what, I haven't a clue. I've never *tried* to be pretty for Rahk before. Not like this. It is strangely vulnerable. I don't like it. Not one bit.

I smooth my hands down the front of my bodice. "Y-yes."

The door creaks when he opens it. My breath catches slightly at the sight of him, immediately forgetting myself. His tailored suit, which I picked out for him, fits perfectly, his tied-back hair emphasizing the beautiful cut of his cheekbones. He is dashing and handsome and more perfect than I could have imagined.

Then I realize that he is likewise taking me in, his gaze slowly traveling over me as I try not to fidget where I stand.

"You'd better like how I look," I say before I can think better of it. "Because I'm afraid this is as good as it gets, unfortunately."

A twinkle of amusement enters his irises. "If you are asking whether I prefer you dressed as a woman or a young boy, I do prefer you dressed as a woman. I can admire your figure better this way."

I'm not sure he could have said anything more shocking to me in that moment. I sputter, unable to think of a reply, and a second shocking thing happens: I realize I am delighted by his statement. "Um . . . well . . . excellent," I babble. My hands scramble over the dresser, knocking aside the rouge Mary used on my cheeks, until I grab my reticule and slip the loop over my wrist. "Is the carriage ready? We should leave at once. The sun is about to set, and I don't want—"

He catches my hand as I try to swish past him. I turn around just as he lifts my hand to his lips and kisses it. It's not the first time he's done this, but there's something so forceful about the way he looks at me while his mouth presses against my knuckles that makes this moment feel far more intimate than anything else.

"You are beautiful, Kat. I've always thought so," he murmurs.

"From the beginning?" I blurt. "When I was a boy? You're lying."

That one eyebrow of his turns crooked. "If you were a fae and could smell lies, you would know I am not."

I swallow. "Oh. Well, as I'm not fae, that isn't verifiable, so . . ."

He smiles and pulls something from behind his back I didn't realize he was holding. It's a box.

"Is this another gift?" I protest. "Rahk, I cannot—"

"Hush. This is part of a game."

"A game?" I perk up immediately. The box at once reminds me of my slippers. Did he . . .?

"I will give you this on the condition that you *must* wear the contents to tonight's ball."

It *is* the slippers! My grin escapes my guard, and I nod. I shouldn't keep accepting his gifts, but my fingers shake to hold this remnant of my mother again.

He hands me the box. I take it and rip off the cover. There are Mama's slippers, shining and gleaming like new. It's like my whole body fills to the brim with something shining and rich. I pull them out of their wrappings, kick off my own slippers unceremoniously, and bend down to put them on. Rahk gets down on one knee, surprising me with his intention to place them on my feet himself. He stops my misbalanced, awkward attempts and instead gently grips my ankles one by one, sliding the beautiful slippers into place.

"They're perfect! Thank you!" I lift my skirts enough to show off the glittering glass that catches the evening light. It's not exactly a *modest* thing to do, but he's fae, and has proven that he is not easily scandalized.

He smiles as he surveys them, and then flicks his gaze up to mine. "They belonged to your mother, but they were made for you."

"I never would have thought they would fit me so perfectly." I take a few trial steps. They're even more comfortable than my previous slippers—which I never would have guessed from them being made of glass.

Rahk picks up the box I have left discarded on the bed and hands it back to me, nodding toward it when I look at him in confusion. "You agreed to wear everything in the box."

I blink. Then I search through the box once more—and find what I missed the first time. It's a small bracelet of thin silver with light pink and green roses the size of my fingernail arranged along its length. My lips part as I trace my finger across one of the small roses. "Oh, my. I usually don't care much about jewelry, but *this* is lovely."

He smiles, pleased, as I slip it onto my wrist.

"This is too many gifts!" I cry. "You're making me feel terrible that I didn't think to get you anything."

He takes my hand and tucks it into the crook of his elbow. "If you would like to return the favor, then play a game of Fool's Circle with me later."

I laugh. "Only if you're ready to be beaten."

"I'm ready and waiting," he replies with a wink as we set off for the ball.

"Lord and Lady Rahk Varadirth," cries the announcer as we step into the ballroom.

I've been dreading this moment. The moment when all the eyes in the ballroom swivel to me. To us—the curiosity of the year. I set my face with my best smile as we enter the glow of thousands of candles in chandeliers hung from the ceiling. Beside me, Rahk is a tall, imposing mountain. He has resumed his own mask—one of utterly unreadable blankness.

I greet everyone I know as we walk into the ballroom. My gaze is drawn almost immediately to Agatha, who regards me with all the warmth of a viper's sting. *She really does hate me.* Bridget is beside her, beautiful in pink and lace. She offers a timid smile and a tiny wave, but she cannot hold my eyes before she looks away. Edith peers over the top of Bridget's head, and seems more interested in Rahk than me. Perhaps she realizes he has a normal nose—and that it is quite handsome.

We pass them, and the rest of the onlookers, and go straight to where Queen Vivienne is seated on her dais. Rahk sketches a bow while I curtsy. The queen looks especially regal tonight in a gown of deep red, her head tipped back and decorated with a silver crown. Her hand strokes the light brown curls of young Prince Lionel beside her. She gives me that same look she gave me when we last visited her—an eyebrow lifted in query. I give her a subtle nod, as I did then, to try to convince her I am *fine* and am *not* Rahk's captive.

As we leave her and I mentally prepare to mingle with those around us, I happen to glance down at my bracelet. The chandelier light has turned the pink roses a purple-ish blue. It's even more beautiful than before. I try to hide my smile before Rahk sees it and demands to know what pleases me.

A servant brings us each a flute of champagne. We make our way to the wall where we can sip and quietly survey the colorful ballroom. No one approaches us, but everywhere I look, I find more pairs of watching eyeballs.

"Is this where I make your marriage to me worth it?" I whisper to Rahk. "Where I introduce you to all the important people of Harbright and convince them you're not a bloodthirsty warrior who will murder them in their sleep?"

He glances sidelong at me. "I think they're more concerned about me murdering *you* in your sleep."

I purse my lips. "In that case, I'd better get to work. Come along, dearie."

I take him to Lord Oliver's elderly mother. "Baroness! It's so good to see you. You must meet my new husband, Lord Rahk. Lord Rahk, Baroness Cranswick."

She surveys him up and down. "Now I can look at you up close! You were much too far away at the wedding and my spectacles are broken. I have such bad eyes that I just couldn't see a thing. But I see that it's true that the fae are very beautiful. I don't blame you much, Katherine."

"Blame me?" I say lightly, laughing to hide my uneasiness.

"Oh, don't look so innocent." She taps me on the shoulder with her fan. Her smile suggests we share a dirty little secret. "You must not be far along in the pregnancy if your waist is still so trim."

Rahk flinches beside me, and it's a miracle I keep my smile pasted on my face. Before he can reply or react, I wrap one arm around his elbow, leaning into him, and give a bright laugh. "Baroness! You must have information about myself that I am not privy to! Am I with child? That would be exciting news!"

A stroke of confusion crosses the baroness's wrinkled face as she sputters, "That was what I heard! Is it not true? Everyone assumed with the wedding being so sudden that a child was the reason. I wouldn't fault you if it was—he's very handsome, Katherine, and I am not so old fashioned as many here—and with your fortune, you can make mistakes that others wouldn't dare—"

The temperature emanating from Rahk reaches near boiling. He remains so placid, so immovable, but I am suddenly very certain that he might explode if one more indecent thing is said about me.

It's Lord Oliver who rescues us. "Lady Vandermore—er, Lady Varadirth, forgive me—I am glad to see you! You've been long gone from court and we have missed you. And Lord Rahk, it has been far too long since we last spoke!"

Lady Varadirth.

It sounds so vicious. So . . . dark and seething. In this particular moment, I love it.

"Lord Oliver," I say, "I see you have met my husband, Lord Rahk." I decide not to mention that I did observe them together at the queen's luncheon while I was still disguised as a servant boy.

"Indeed, I have! We have become best friends."

"Have you?" I grin up at Rahk, who looks very slightly uncomfortable at that proclamation.

"Lord Oliver has taken great pains to ensure I am comfortable at court," says Rahk. "I am grateful."

Oliver turns to me, giving me a friendly wink. "What did I tell you? You thought I was crazy for suggesting that the fae coming to town would want to marry you."

My replying laugh is only slightly uneasy. I wrap my hand around Rahk's arm, leaning into him to give the illusion of newlywed bliss. "You're right. I assumed all fae find our race repulsive. Apparently not!"

"I'm afraid that is a misconception that must be rectified." Rahk slips his hand around my waist. I suck in a fast breath and then disguise it with a smile up at him. "Our peoples are, fundamentally, not that different from each other. We have enough superficial differences to make the contrary seem true, but the more time I spend in both lands, the more I am convinced that we have a great deal in common. We both, for example, enjoy the company of the clever young lady I am honored to call my wife."

Of all the things I expected him to say, that was not one of them. I look up at him as he smiles down at me. A giggle that isn't wholly forced escapes me. I turn to Lord Oliver and say in a loud whisper, as if it's a secret, "I'm afraid I've fallen under the spell of his charms. Matrimony has been a fear of mine for as long as I can remember, but it has proved a delight so far."

Oliver's reply is all genuine kindness. "I am glad that you have found a man who treasures you as you deserve."

His comment touches me. I wish I could thank him for always treating me with respect and consideration, but an appropriate reply refuses to pass my lips.

Rahk steps in to my rescue, addressing the young lord. "You proved yourself worthy at swordsmanship. Have you ever practiced archery?"

Oliver's face lights up. "Very little, but if you would have an amateur, I would love to learn the art."

"You must come to my estate then. There are grounds aplenty for target practice. Bring your bow and we shall enjoy the fine weather."

Oliver's reply is an eager grin and an enthusiastic nod.

Rahk and Oliver bow to each other, and I offer a curtsy before I take Rahk's arm and follow him toward the table of refreshments. I happen to turn around and see the baroness's suspicious gaze. Immediately, my good humor is doused with cold water. I tighten my grip on Rahk's elbow and hiss under my breath: "The gall of that woman to *confront* me in a public place over something so patently false! She's probably the one behind that rumor! She doesn't care that it could ruin both of our reputations—and halt your work earning the queen's trust—if you seduced me and lured me into a marriage to steal my fortune. You would be the worst kind of rake!"

"You cannot fault her. She likely hasn't seen anything so interesting in several decades."

That earns a snort from me, but it isn't enough to right my sour mood.

My bracelet catches my attention suddenly. The glass roses have all turned brown—and it's as though they've *wilted* and curled in on themselves. Only their centers seem alive, with a deep orange glow. I gasp. "Rahk! I've somehow broken the beautiful bracelet you gave me!"

He glances down at me, then at it. He lifts my hand to look at the bracelet. At his casual touch on my skin, I flush. The roses immediately uncurl and darken to a deep red. Rahk's gaze flicks up to mine. There's a mischievous smirk playing at his lips. "It's not broken."

It transforms once more, mirroring my awe as it brightens, the red shifting to a luscious indigo. My mouth drops open. "This is from Faerieland. And it . . . changes with my emotions?"

"Look at you. Living up to the description I just gave Lord Oliver."

His teasing grin is dazzling. My bracelet returns to the color of my blush. He glances at it, the skin around his eyes crinkling even as his pupils dilate. I stuff my hand behind me, hiding the bracelet from his gaze. "If we weren't in public, I would whack you for pulling such a dirty trick on me."

"Don't let the onlookers stop you," he replies, and laughs at the face I give him. He takes both of my hands, even the one I try to hide from him, and eagerly pulls me toward the dance floor. "Come, make my long hours of dance practice worth it."

"I'm not sure you needed those hours. You're a natural at dancing."

He wraps his palm against my shoulder blade, mine resting on his arm while our hands meet. He glances at the blush pink of my rose bracelet before lifting his eyes to me. They are warm and full and soft. He pulls me closer—not enough to be scandalous, but still intimate. "I practiced for you. I didn't want to humiliate you at these balls."

The music rises to our ears. It's a waltz. We step into the dance.

"It's a relief to not have to purposefully sabotage dancing with you," I say. "I had to work hard to think of the man's part instead of relying on muscle memory."

"It was a good effort. I was not fooled, but I might have been, had the circumstances been different. Then again, if I hadn't known you were a woman, I would not have ordered you to practice with me."

I laugh. "I thought it was wildly strange. In fact, there were many things you did that I thought were strange, but I hadn't spent enough time around men or fae to know for sure."

He shakes his head in amused disbelief. "I was openly flirting with you, Kat. I don't know how you didn't realize it."

His bluntness is not what I expect.

I shrug, looking away as my bracelet brightens in color. "I assumed you would confront me if you knew the truth. So when you didn't confront me . . ."

He shakes his head again, then draws me closer. I try not to let my breath catch too audibly. But the force of his black eyes nearly trips up my practiced steps. "That was your mistake. I like to wait and see how things play out."

I do my best not to go stiff in his arms. *Does he know?* Was that his way of telling me he knows everything, and he is waiting for me to tell him I'm the Ivy Mask?

But the saints-cursed bracelet turns a boggy green. Rahk's head tilts slightly. "Why did my statement frighten you?"

My eyes widen. "Is that what the green means?"

His eyes narrow, but they narrow in softness, not suspicion. "Kat."

Blast this all. I don't want to lie to him. I'm sick of lying to him. I desperately want to tell him what I am. This secret between us—it is going to eat me alive. But no matter how much part of me insists that if I tell him I'm the Ivy Mask, we might be able to navigate the situation together, I know better than that. I have so many people relying on me completing these next two raids. I may want to put my future at risk, but I cannot be so cavalier with theirs.

Everything Rahk and I have will crumble when he finds out.

When, not *if*. Because he *will* find out.

I opt for as much honesty as I can afford. "I know you always tell me you're not going to hurt me—and I believe you. It's only that sometimes, that old fear of you fae returns. Your statement made me afraid that your kindness now is only a ruse. It's silly, I know."

His eyes don't leave mine, even when I cannot bear to return his gaze. "Your family was torn apart because of my people. I know it will take time for you to fully trust me, but I intend to show you every day that I want nothing except your happiness."

He is too good. Too good for me. Too good to be in this horrible situation he knows nothing of. He may not see it, but I do; Nothril can never corrupt this man.

He will be devastated when he finds out who I am.

The dance ends.

As we leave the dance floor, I notice all the people watching us carefully—Rahk, especially. It's as though by dancing with him, I've broken a spell of fear, and now several people rush forward to me, clearly desiring to be introduced.

"You should dance with as many people as you can tonight," I whisper to Rahk between introductions. "It'll greatly aid your efforts with the queen."

"I'd rather dance with you," he whispers back, but with a sigh he leaves my side and asks one of his new acquaintances if she would give him the honor of dancing. Her mouth falls open and she blushes mightily but quickly accepts. With her children grown, I don't often see her dancing. I smile as I watch him escort her to the dance floor.

The moment he is gone, a new presence takes up residence beside me. From my periphery, I can tell it's Sir Alsbee. The young man who tried to seduce me when I was barely sixteen. He sent a note from a private room, claiming to be one of my friends in need, and I went at once—only to be fortunate enough to pass by that friend reading quietly in the library. Instead of going into the room he summoned me to, I hid in the opposite room until I watched Alsbee finally give up and leave. I have hated him ever since.

So now, when he stands beside me, I pretend I don't notice him. My bracelet wilts and turns soot black.

"Lady Vandermore," he says in a syrupy tone. "Or should I say, Lady Varadirth."

"Sir Alsbee," I reply crisply.

"Will you honor me with a dance?"

I find Rahk in the crowd of dancers. It is not hard, since he is the tallest man in the room. He's looking at me. Ignoring his talkative partner. Can he read my emotions from this distance? Or can he see the color of my bracelet? I paste a smile on my face and turn to Sir Alsbee. "I'm afraid I cannot. My husband is a wonderful man, but he is very possessive. He made me promise that I send all requests for a dance to him first. So you will have to ask him if you'd like to dance with me."

"Blaming your dislike of me on your husband? That's not very kind of you." Sir Alsbee tsks his tongue and then takes my hand firmly, apparently counting on the element of surprise or my desire to not cause a scene being enough persuasion to go with him.

I yank my hand out of his at once, glaring at him. "I did not agree to dance with you, Sir Alsbee. I've told you what you must do if you wish to dance with me. I will not dance with you otherwise."

"Katherine, darling, it's only a dance." He takes my hand again, grinning with the attempt at appearing good-natured. "I don't even know why you've disliked me so much all these years. Let us make up for the ill will."

I dig my heels into the polished floor. I don't care how large and unseemly of a scene I must make: I am *not* dancing with Alsbee. My bracelet turns so black, it crumbles into dust and falls off my wrist.

Alsbee takes two steps, pulling me after him. On the third step, he suddenly releases me, pitching forward. He cartwheels his arms and whacks a nearby gentleman's drink out of his hand. His legs fly out from under him, and he falls hard on his back.

Cries of surprise and concern go up. My eyes widen. I take the opportunity to put distance between me and him. When I look up, Rahk is dancing only a few feet away, his attention on me. A familiar light gleams in his irises.

My mouth drops open in delighted astonishment. *What did you do?* I silently ask him. The corner of his mouth twitches, and then he's lost in the depths of the many dancing couples.

CHAPTER 49

KAT

"IT'S HARD TO keep track of you while you're wearing those glass slippers," Rahk tells me many hours later. I am catching up with a few acquaintances in a quieter room when he comes up behind me and almost startles me.

I'm so glad to see him after he's been busy doing exactly what I suggested—dancing with the ladies of the court. I'm exhausted after this long night, but a renewed rush of energy fills me at the sight of him. "What do you mean?"

My friends make their excuses and leave, making space for Rahk to sit down beside me on the settee. The room is quiet, now just the two of us and curtains drawn over half a dozen enormous windows.

Rahk rarely looks tired, but he does now. "Those slippers don't leave a scent behind like regular shoes. I had to search several rooms before I found you."

My mind immediately latches onto that statement. I'm glad my bracelet disintegrated now, for fear it would have given me away in this moment. I hold up my empty wrist for him. "Your gift is gone."

"You must have not liked that fellow. Only very strong hatred can destroy the spellcraft holding Faerie trinkets together."

"I have good reason," I say, before explaining the incident.

He listens quietly, nodding along. When I'm finished, he remains silent for a few minutes. Then, he says, "I ought to have made sure he cracked his head when he fell."

He says it so mildly I burst out in laughter and can barely stop. Sleepless delirium approaches the closer we get to dawn. I wipe tears from my eyes and lean back against the settee. The back of my head hits the polished wooden trim. It's not comfortable. I glance at my husband. He also leans back, his legs spread wide, one hand planted on his thigh as he surveys the room. I note every perfect line of his profile. Then I note just how comfortable his broad, strong shoulder looks.

Apparently, it has been one too many hours without sleep. I scoot over, lay my head against his shoulder, and close my eyes. He startles very slightly, and I can feel from the way he shifts that he is looking down at me. He settles back in his seat, deeper than before. His smell surrounds me, so comforting I might just fall asleep right here.

I yawn. "How did you do . . . whatever you did to him?"

"It wasn't much. I glamoured a little drop in the floor. He had poor balance—otherwise it would have been easy enough to right himself." His voice is close to the top of my head, and I enjoy the way his low voice vibrates through his chest and into me.

I chuckle softly. "He left right after that. He couldn't handle the humiliation of a wine-stained waistcoat and a sore backside."

"Good." He moves, slipping an arm around my waist and pulling me against his chest. I melt against him, too tired to resist. Too warm in his arms. Too soothed by his scent.

"You know what news I've just received?" I ask sleepily.

"Hmm?"

"Somehow rumor got out about what Lord Boreham and Lady Agatha were plotting. He went at once to his home in Commington and everyone says the embarrassment is so great he will never return to court."

Rahk's rumbled reply is deeply pleased. "Good."

I smile and let my eyes drift closed. We stay like this long enough for me to doze. A nearby door closing wakes me up. Rahk's hand on my waist slides up and down in gentle caresses. "Would you like to go home?"

I nod with a yawn.

"Shall I carry you out to the carriage?"

I blink against my blurry vision and the candles fighting for their last inch of life. I push myself upright, only to find that Rahk supports my forearm, lending me balance. "I must walk out myself. To be carried out of a ball is a great shame. At least, I've always thought so."

Rahk chuckles and helps me to my feet. He turns his attention to the skirt of my gown, bending down to straighten the wrinkles, and then to my hair—which has become slightly mussed. He reaches around me to the fake bun pinned to my scalp, a furrow appearing between his brows, and uses his long fingers to adjust the pins. His motions are slow and deliberate, almost too gentle. I chew on my lip as he moves to tuck a loose strand of hair behind my ear. I watch him, my body turning warm, and when his gaze returns to mine, I think of kissing him. I wish he would kiss me like he kissed me before.

The saints know I wouldn't resist it.

He stands so close to me. The muscles in his throat constrict as he runs his gaze over my face.

Then he looks toward the door, ducking his chin briefly, and loops his arm through mine. My stomach drops in disappointment—even though I know rationally that kissing Rahk is the last thing I should be doing. I still want it.

I'm in a sleepy fog when we visit the queen and pay our respects once more before we leave. Her son is nowhere to be seen.

"Lord Rahk," the queen says sharply after we bow.

"Yes, Majesty?" asks Rahk, straightening.

She lifts her nose into the air and arranges her features into lofty disinterest. "I will go to the troll. You will not accompany me, however. I will take my own men."

I barely restrain my gasp and the bright grin I want to turn up to Rahk. *It worked!*

He keeps a much calmer composure, but I can read the spark in his eyes. "Thank you."

I wait until we are outside before I grab Rahk's elbow in both of my hands and loud whisper to him, "You did it! We did it!"

A small, satisfied smile twinges at the corner of his mouth. "It is a relief."

The air is chilled, the moon a fat crescent above us, and I press closer to him for warmth. He places a warm hand on the back of my neck. It's as though he wraps me up in a cozy blanket with that one touch.

He hands me into the carriage before him. I arrange my skirts as Rahk slides onto the cushion next to me, the faint creak of leather mingling with the swish of fabric. He orders Clifford to drive, and draws the curtains shut.

Then he turns to me. His eyes seem to shine brighter in the darkness, his silver hair gleaming in long waves. This carriage feels simultaneously too small and yet vastly too large. Acting on impulse, I lean forward and touch his hair. I am reminded again just how soft it is. He sits quietly, holding still while I run my fingers through a silver lock, testing its silkiness against my thumb.

"You have beautiful hair," I say.

His fingers land on my cheek, sliding until they wrap around to the nape of my neck. He pulls me to him, his mouth pressing firmly against mine. My sigh escapes me even before my eyes flutter shut. His grip on my neck tightens in response. I fall into his kiss. It wraps around me like a cocoon, making me forget everything outside this carriage.

My limbs turn to warm wax as I melt against him. His mouth is soft, but it is not gentle. He tilts my head and deepens the kiss. My head explodes with lightness. His other hand lands on my shoulder, his fingers stroking along the column of my neck, tracing the line of my collarbone, dipping to the sensitive skin of my upper back. Everything is so warm—every inch of my body, his mouth, his touch. I open my eyes just long enough to see the deep furrow in his brow as he holds my face and molds my lips to his.

His whole body shifts closer to mine, his mouth moving to my cheek, my jaw. My hand reaches out for support and winds up gripping his knee. Breathing fast, he kisses my mouth again, wrapping an arm fully around my waist and pulling me against his chest. His hand slides into my hair, messing up Mary's careful pinning of the fake bun.

I should exercise restraint. I should pull away. I should not let this continue.

Instead, I wrap both my arms around Rahk's neck and close all distance between us. I kiss him hard, with the hope that my gusto and enthusiasm cover my lack of skill. He responds immediately, both of his hands wrapping against my ribs and holding me close to him as he chuckles.

He kisses me again, very deeply, very slowly, until I forget everything until the carriage grinds to a halt.

His gaze lifts from me, sharpening, as the footman's steps come toward the door. I reach up to touch my hair, my face, finding the fake bun hanging by a single pin. My gown is wrinkled and mussed. Rahk surveys me quickly, registering just how disheveled I look. His mouth twists in a wickedly satisfied smirk.

"Mary is going to know," I hiss.

He cocks one very Nothril eyebrow. "And why is that bad?"

Mary would kill me if she knew I was kissing Rahk—because I *shouldn't* be kissing Rahk. It's like cold water splashes over me from head to toe, dousing the warmth brought about by fatigue and darkness.

What have I done? I never should have—

Rahk seems to note my sudden distress. He catches my face suddenly between his hands. I am so startled, so suddenly torn between leaning into him or pulling away, that I turn to a statue in his hands. But he doesn't kiss me. Instead, he presses his forehead against mine, swiftly closing his eyes. My eyes remain open, so I catch the way his face contorts, either from strain or pain. Just as suddenly as he grabbed me, he releases me.

My head feels different. I reach up to touch, only to find my hair back perfectly in place. My dress, too, is perfectly smooth as it was at the beginning of the night. I open my mouth just as the carriage door swings wide.

"Glamour," Rahk mouths to me as the footman hands me out of the carriage.

I send him a grateful look over my shoulder. The heat hasn't left his gaze. I look away quickly. Sunrise is still a few hours away, mercifully. Maybe I can get some sleep, even if it's just a little.

After what just happened, though, I doubt I will be able to sleep at all. Instead, I will tangle in my sheets and wish the carriage had never arrived. Even now, I can hardly see the hallway I walk; I see the furrow between Rahk's brows as he kissed me. I feel his touch and his lips. The cold of this night cannot reach me.

Mary is waiting in the bedroom for me. Her eyelids droop, but she smiles when she sees me. "Did you have a good time?"

Rahk is right behind me. "Take your rest, Mary. I will help Kat as she needs."

I blink, suddenly alert. Mary glances at me, a question dancing across her irises. I nod quickly, too afraid of what my tone might betray if I speak.

She leaves at once.

Then we are alone once again.

I hurry toward the vanity. In the corner of my vision, Rahk flicks his wrist, and whatever glamours he placed on me disappears. I find myself staring back at the very disheveled version of myself. I set to work at once, pulling the askew pins out of my hair, freeing the bun, and brushing the tangled mess through.

Rahk kicks off his boots and slides them into his wardrobe. His back is to me, and I watch covertly through the reflection in my mirror as he shrugs off his overcoat. I swallow. Removing my gown is a task for two people. He's going to have to help me. I steal another glance his way as I remove my jewelry.

I bet he knew very well that he would have to help me.

A thread of helplessness washes over me. I don't know what to do anymore. I don't know how to not hurt him in this situation. If I act distant, that will hurt him. If I release my inhibitions and fall into his arms without a thought for the future, that will hurt him too.

It makes me want to run away as far as I can. I want to climb through that window, mount Bartholomew, and fly away where he can never find me.

But that will hurt him too.

"What's this sad face for?" Rahk plants his hands on the vanity, framing my body between his arms. His hair brushes mine—light and long against dark and short. He lowers his head, and his lips brush over my shoulder, sending a shiver all the way to my toes.

Now I must lie to him. Again. The thought brings the sensation of a knife driving into my chest. Sharp and intense and agonizing. I hang my head. "I don't know what to do, Rahk."

"About what?" His lips ghost across the top of my head. "Tell me what burdens you, and I will fix it for you." His hand slides from the table to my waist, making me suck in a breath.

I turn around. He leans his weight on his other hand still on the vanity, his face mere inches from mine as his thumb lightly caresses my ribs. His eyes travel over my face. Trying to read me. I'm so exhausted after this ball, barely clinging to the remnants of my will, I don't know how he doesn't see every secret I've kept from him written plain across my face.

"Are you afraid that I will touch you tonight when you are not ready?" he asks gently.

My lungs shudder as they fill and empty. He's unwittingly offered me an escape from my turmoil. It is not his touch I fear, but my conscience if I allow it. Still, my answer to his question remains the same. I nod, not meeting his eyes.

He moves his hands to my shoulders, squeezing lightly and kissing my brow. I could weep from the softness of it. "Would you like to play Fool's Circle?"

My head shoots up.

"I don't know about you, but as tired as I am, I could use something to soothe my mind," he says. "We can play until you fall asleep."

The words are out of me before I can help them. "Yes, please!"

The skin around his eyes crinkles slightly. "Then get into something more comfortable and we shall play as long as your heart desires." I must have pulled a face, because he adds, "You object to this plan?"

I cast a pleading look up at him, my cheeks going hot. "I need help. This bodice is fastened at the back, and I cannot reach it."

His attention flicks to the reflection of my back in the mirror, before returning to me. "Then turn around."

I obey, facing the mirror as Rahk's hands fall to the top of my spine. "There are hidden hooks."

He traces the fabric until he finds the carefully disguised hooks. He fidgets for a moment, his brow furrowing slightly. "Human clothing is so complicated," he mutters, ducking closer to the dress and squinting at it.

I find myself smirking. "Mary can do it in about thirty seconds, if you want me to call her in."

The scowl that Rahk gives me is so dark, I burst into full laughter.

"Hold still," he demands, but there's a twitch at the corner of his mouth. He undoes the top hook. "There we are."

He moves faster now, his fingers working the hooks and eyes, until he reaches the end of the bodice. His eyes flick up to meet mine in the mirror, as if silently asking what is next.

"Thank you." I hold the bodice with a hand on my midsection. "I can finish from here."

He steps away, returning to the opposite side of the room, his broad back set to me. He busies himself with something I cannot see. I retrieve a nightgown and slip into my old room. I change as quickly as I can—which isn't very quickly with all the layers of a ballgown—but when I emerge, I feel much lighter.

Rahk has changed too. He wears a loose black tunic and a pair of soft spun trousers. He's already sitting on the edge of the bed—*his* side, the covers pulled back and the Fool's Circle board set up in the center of the bed. When I enter, he looks up, swiftly rakes his eyes over me, and then returns to setting up the board. He has set up one lone candle on the windowsill nearby. The rest have been put out. "Lie down. We'll play until you fall asleep. I'll snuff the candle then."

"You're not going to go hide in your study tonight?" I say, with probably too much cheek.

He glowers at me. "You know perfectly well I have done that for the sole consideration of your comfort."

I know it's true, and yet I cannot think of a reply. I slide into my side of the bed, pulling the covers up to my chin and staring sideways at the set Fool's Circle board. "Who starts?"

"You."

"Don't be such a gentleman." I move my pieces. "It's disgusting."

That surprises a chuckle out of him. He slides beneath the covers on his side, propping himself up on one elbow as he studies the board. He makes his move.

I watch the way he moves. He is graceful down to the way he selects a piece between his two fingers.

"Have you killed many people?" I ask.

He pauses moving his last piece long enough to shoot a look at me. "Yes."

I chew my lip and take my turn.

"But," he adds a moment later, when it's his turn again, "I will not kill you."

I restrain my rueful snort. "Do you enjoy killing?"

He sighs. "No. I am good at it, though. I do like being good at it."

"I can see that. I think I would also like being good at it."

He looks at me, as though trying to discern if I am serious or making a morbid joke.

"I don't want to kill," I explain, "but I think it might be nice to know what to do if, say, an assassin had a knife to my head."

Pain flashes across Rahk's face.

"You're not still guilty over that!" I cry, shoving up to my elbow. "Please, I will not have you hating yourself for that!"

He shakes his head. Then he reaches across the board, and I don't breathe as he lightly touches my temple. "You must reconcile yourself to the fact that I will never forgive myself for these scars."

"They are basically invisible," I grumble.

His silent reply is loud in the room: *Not to me.*

"I am glad you have never had to kill," Rahk says, resuming play of our game. "The frightening part of it is how little you come to care."

"Care about what?"

"The life you are taking. The first kills are always the hardest. Maybe for some people, they view every kill like their first. That was not how it was for me. The more I killed, the easier it became. Now, I do not think about whether they have families, or whether they are afraid or in pain. I just kill."

He says it so simply. I study his face instead of the board. His jaw gives a tiny flex.

I lick my lips and say tentatively, "It seems like it would be a heavy burden to take every kill personally. You would probably go mad."

"I probably would," he replies ruefully. "Though sometimes I wonder if the callousness is madness itself."

I think of all the people in Faerieland I cannot rescue. Callousness almost seems like a reprieve from the yawning torment inside me. I change the direction of the conversation. "When was your first kill?"

He frowns, considering the board between us. "When I was ninety-nine, I hunted down an assassin who had come to kill Lord

Nothril. I brought him back and slaughtered him before my parents. I proved myself to them that day." He looks up to find me staring at him wide-eyed. "Time runs differently in Faerieland, and we mature much slower than humans. The equivalent human age would have been around thirteen."

"You must have been a bloodthirsty child," I say.

His laugh is low and rumbling. "Compared to your average human child. But Faerieland is not a tame place. While you humans like to play your games of societal expectations, we play ours in blood. The stakes are higher, but so is the reward."

"What is the reward, then?"

"Long life. Beauty. Power. Pleasure."

"But you only have one chance at obtaining those things? If you take a misstep, if you ally with the wrong force . . .?"

"You lose all of it."

Rahk plays an aggressive move that destroys the plan I was working toward. I'm forced to adjust my strategy. "You crave those things? Pleasure and power?" I ask.

"I am drawn to all of those things, yes."

That sentence hangs there long enough that I add, "But . . .?"

"But," he says, claiming one of the few spots surrounding the Fool, "those things come with a cost. I do not like the cost."

"What is the cost for you?"

His chest expands with his deep breath. "There is no true freedom in Faerieland. Even when I become Lord Nothril in many, many years, after my parents' lives come to an end, I still must answer to the High Throne of Faerie. I still must bear in mind the considerations of the people I rule. And I will always have enemies."

Several turns go by. I claim another spot adjacent to the Fool. He nods approvingly at my strategy.

I lick my lips. "May I ask you another question?"

He inclines his head, focused on the board.

"What is that tattoo on the back of your neck for?"

"I thought you might ask about that again," he says, reaching up one hand to touch it. "It is . . . a little hard to explain, but the essence of it is that it is a bargain. Lord and Lady Nothril gave me a task, and if I do not accomplish it my sister will die."

All at once, the pieces fit together. The task must be capturing the Ivy Mask. *Me.* That is why he is hunting me. Lord Nothril must have been particularly angry after I freed his slave girl. And that is why, when the assassins came, he was so grateful that I saved his life. Because if I hadn't, he would not have been able to fulfill his side of the bargain. His sister would have died.

So one of us will have to die.

My stomach turns over. I feel sick. The game becomes my refuge from the swirling thoughts in my mind.

"I wish I could take you to Faerieland," Rahk says after a long time. "You would find it fascinating."

"Oh?" I keep my gaze fixed on the board.

"Most humans don't do well there. The land isn't made for them. I think you, however, would be smart enough to survive the perils of it, if your Fool's Circle instinct is any indication."

His praise warms my chest while simultaneously making me want to cave into myself.

"But it can never be," he adds. "To bring you across the border as anything other than my wife would be to guarantee your death and sentence as a slave." He glances at me. "I'm sure you wouldn't want to come anyway, after what happened to your mother."

My awareness sharpens on him. A conversation from weeks ago resurfaces in my mind—Rahk telling me about fae bindings. I'd forgotten about it until now. So our marriage might not be acknowledged in Faerieland as it is? I keep my tone casual as I ask, "Why wouldn't you bring me as your wife?"

He looks startled by my question. I've never seen the way his lips very slightly open, then close. I've cornered him, and if I'm lucky, he won't realize I've done it on purpose. He must now admit that he has purposefully avoided marrying me in the more permanent fae way or lie to spare my feelings.

He makes his move. I bite my lip at how careless of a choice it is. "Faerieland doesn't acknowledge human weddings," he replies, dodging the question.

I don't intend to let him off so easily. I want his confirmation that he has withheld himself from me, that he has chosen to avoid binding himself permanently to me.

I need to know that I am not the only one holding back from this marriage.

"There was that princess of Aursailles." I claim the second-to-last spot next to the Fool. Rahk blinks at the board, realizing the mistake of his last move. "She married the High Prince, or whatever his title was. Does Faerieland not acknowledge their marriage?"

It is dangerously similar to what Queen Vivienne asked of him. I ask it as innocently as possible, yet Rahk's black eyes still pierce me like twin blades of obsidian.

"The fae do not usually acknowledge fae and human marriages," he says at last, giving in, "unless they married according to fae tradition. You and I are married according to the human tradition. Our union would not be acknowledged there."

"Does that mean we aren't truly married?"

He narrows his focus on me. "To what end do you ask these questions? What is it that you are afraid of?"

Many things. So many things. "You're going back to Faerieland."

The hard line of his mouth softens slightly. "I will stay as long as I have a reason to."

"But you will still leave."

He sighs. He reaches across the board and tucks away a strand of my hair. His fingers linger longer than necessary, tracing the line of my ear. I hold very still.

"It's for your own benefit that I do not marry you my people's way," he murmurs. "If I am forced to leave you, you will be free to remarry. If we seal our bond with magic, however, as long as we are both alive—no matter where in the worlds—that bond is very, very difficult to break."

The words are dull thuds against my heart. It all makes rational sense. It makes even more sense when I consider my own secrets.

My time with Rahk has an ending point. It always has. I've known this. It fueled my jealousy when he said he was marrying. It fuels my grief now.

"It's not fair that the only man good enough to not care about my fortune is a fae," I mutter bitterly.

Rahk flops onto his back, staring up at the ceiling as a great exhalation leaves him. His voice is a whisper of defeat. "I don't know what to do, Kat."

Those words hang in the air, an echo of my own feelings. I don't know what to do with this mess of a situation—with this mess of a marriage.

I curl beneath the blankets and study the board because there is nothing else to do. Then, to my surprise, I see the end of the game in just a few moves. I take my turn. "You're going to finish this game. That is what you're going to do."

He rolls to his side, dully staring at the pieces. A moment later, his eyes widen. I can almost see the calculations running in his brain—a last, desperate attempt to pull his usual win. Slowly, he lifts his gaze to mine. His mouth curves upward.

"Make your move," I say, jutting out my chin and trying to keep a straight face.

He shakes his head, smiling, as he does the best he can. We take our last moves, but he can only delay my victory by a mere turn. When, at long last, I claim the fourth and final spot surrounding the Fool, my saucy grin breaks free. "There. I win."

And just for one moment, the demons and worries flee Rahk's face entirely. With one swift motion, he swipes away the board, scattering the pieces. I read the look in his eye and say, "No, don't you dare!" as I try to rip aside the covers and flee.

But he grabs me, grinning when I holler in protest, and pulls me to him. He tickles my ribs until I'm almost screaming with tortured laughter. He pauses once, letting me catch my breath, and warns me in a low whisper, with a conspiratorial smirk, "Careful about how loud you are. You'll worry Mary."

"You devil!" I cry, just before he pins my arms above my head so I am defenseless against his attacks. I roll and kick and writhe, trying to free myself as I laugh hysterically.

He finally stops, pulling me into his arms and holding me close as he buries his face in my shoulder. He chuckles as I reclaim my lost breath.

"That was not fair," I grumble.

He holds me tightly, no longer playing, and I find myself relaxing against him.

"I do not know what we are going to do," Rahk murmurs against my skin. "But I am not going to abandon you, Kat. I swear it."

I cannot find my voice to reply, so I just nod and close my eyes.

CHAPTER 50

KAT

I WAKE TO the smell of wind and open skies. I breathe deeply and sigh.

"You're awake," Rahk rumbles. His voice is very, very close.

I open my eyes and find my vision completely full of a thick neck and silver hair glistening in the sunlight. My nose is tucked beneath his Adam's apple, and my lips rest against the hollow of his throat.

Then I become aware of the rest of my . . . *situation*. My head rests on his shoulder. I'm lying pressed up against him, my hands curled up to his chest, my leg tossed over his hip as though I am a squirrel clinging to a branch. One of his hands rests just above my knee, while the other presses lightly into my low back.

"Did you sleep well?" Rahk asks, nuzzling into my hair.

"I . . . did," I reply hesitantly. I'm very, very warm—too warm. I should scramble out of his arms, straighten my nightgown, and reclaim my dignity.

But I don't *want* to.

"Did you sleep well?" I ask, sliding my leg back down to the bed where it's supposed to be. He lets go of my knee.

He rasps a low chuckle. "I didn't sleep much . . . but it was a pleasant night anyway."

I refuse to acknowledge what he means by that and practically hurl myself from the bed. "Well good!" I wince, covering my eye from the sun streaming in through the windows. "What time is it? It's got to be well into the afternoon!"

"It's not even noon."

I refuse to look back at him, but I can hear him sitting upright, followed by a rustle like he's running his fingers through his hair.

"That's unfortunate," I chatter, accidentally banging open the door to my wardrobe in an attempt to find some real clothes to wear. "I was hoping I got more sleep than that. Oh well! There's nothing to be done. If I take a nap this afternoon, I'll ruin my night of sleep. It's best that I stay busy. What are you doing today?"

"Apparently making you *very* uncomfortable," he replies dryly from right behind me.

I whirl, clutching the frock I've just selected to my chest in fright. "Rahk!"

"Kat." He leans around me and closes the wardrobe doors much gentler than I would have. Then he takes a seat on my side of the bed, tilting his head as he regards me. "Please. I do not wish you to be uncomfortable. I have made my regard for you obvious enough to get past even your stubborn refusal to acknowledge it."

I flush hot.

"You have also made your preference for me clear," he continues, even though I wish he wouldn't. "But I have also observed that, while you may care for me, there are clearly things that hold you back."

My fidgeting goes still. I look at his serious face, the way he sits with his knees wide and his hands clasped between them.

"I have no expectations for you." Rahk says the words very slowly, very deliberately. "I have been thinking hard the last few hours, and

I decided I want to make this marriage between us work—as unusual as it is, and as difficult as a marriage will be in our circumstances. I want it. I want to discover with you how we can forge a way forward. *But*." He draws a deep breath, his expression turning gentler. "If you don't want the same thing, or if you are not sure yet, or if you fear your mind will change, I will accept that. You owe me nothing—not your affection, your time, your fortune, your regard, none of it."

I cover my face with the frock, growling low in my throat. "Now I feel terrible. I'm not trying to—to—tease you and lead you on! I'm trying to be honest with you, but I don't know *how* to—"

He catches my forearms, tugging my hands and frock away from my face. "I know you care about me, Kat. I'm not suggesting that you are leading me on. I'm saying that you are allowed to need time."

I stare up at him. At his beautiful face, with all its hardened, chiseled edges. The same face I once thought was cold and ruthless. I swallow hard. I care too much about Rahk to not be honest about what I have the freedom to be. With a groan, I plop on the bed beside him. I open my mouth. The words are like knives, and it takes several tries before they finally leave my tongue. "I also want a way to make our marriage work. But it is not possible."

"It does seem that way—"

"You have to go back to Nothril!" I cry, my throat thickening. "I have to stay here."

"I can visit you."

"Can you?" I demand. "Lord and Lady Nothril would let you come back and forth from the human lands?"

Rahk purses his lips, looking away. "It would be challenging, and I would have to keep it a secret."

I press on, relentless. "What if you cannot get your sister out of Nothril? What if you visiting me puts her in danger if you are found out?"

"Kat—"

"I am a curse for you, Rahk," I say, choking slightly. "You are good and kind, no matter that you believe Faerieland is corrupting you, and so I cannot let you be hurt because of me."

His expression is stricken. He reaches out to me. "If anything happened, it would not be your fault. It would be mine and mine alone. You are no curse. You are my joy. From the beginning, that is what you have been to me."

He says it so earnestly, so pleadingly. I would not have believed it otherwise. But just because he believes it does not make it true.

Your existence does not take away good things from those you love.

He was wrong about that. And I won't have Rahk losing his sister or his life because of me. Neither will I have him bound to me as I age while he remains young and cultivates resentment against me.

He exhales slowly and pushes to his feet. "If your desires are my own, it would mean a great deal to me that you would consider my offer for a few days. I do not want to give up simply because it does not seem like it can work. Would you do that for me?"

I'm not sure what a few more days of consideration will do. I'm the Ivy Mask. This marriage was doomed from the beginning. Still, I nod.

He steps away. "I will send Mary in. I plan to watch the queen's visit of the troll from a distance this afternoon, to see if it goes well."

I watch him leave, my heart in my throat. I want to tear after him. He knows I care about him, but does he have a clue how deeply?

When Mary enters, I'm exactly where Rahk left me, holding my dress and staring at the door. Her eyes widen at the sight of me. She rushes to my side at once, supporting me as my knees buckle.

"Oh Mary, I'm in too deep," I cry as I collapse against her.

We end up on the floor, holding each other. She smooths my hair away from my face and kisses my brow. "I know."

"I need to tell him. I need to tell him. I must tell him!" I'm saying the words over the over again, barely a whisper for fear of being overheard. "I cannot keep going like this. I cannot keep this secret from him!"

"You cannot tell him," Mary replies, a growling edge to her words. "If you care about him, you cannot tell him. I see the way he looks at you. It would destroy him to have to hurt you. If everything you told me is true, he won't have any other option but to bring you to his Court for judgment, or kill you outright."

"That would be better than staying in this misery!"

"No, it would *not*." Her voice turns fierce. "Not for you, not for me, not for him, not for the people you save. Whatever happens, Kat, *you must stay alive*. Which means you *cannot* tell him. Even if it rips you in two."

"I feel like I am deceiving him no matter what I do! I lie to him when I don't tell him the truth. I lie to him when I give him affection. I lie to him when I keep my distance. *All* of it is a lie, and I cannot live with myself!"

Mary's face softens and hardens simultaneously. She takes me by the shoulders, peeling me back enough to look me in the eyes. "Do you love him, Kat?"

I nod miserably.

"Then you have to leave him."

Her statement shocks me out of my heartbreak long enough to stare at her in astonishment. "*Leave* him?"

She gets to her feet and motions for me to do the same. She rummages through my wardrobe until she has everything she needs to help me dress for the day. We move to the washroom, and she helps me into my clothes. "If you cannot live with him without betraying him or yourself, then you need to put distance between the two of you. Since he isn't going to take your fortune, you can return to Vandermore Manor and live there—away from him. You wouldn't need to divorce him unless you wanted to."

Divorce. Live at Vandermore Manor without him.

If I asked for such things, he would honor them. I'd break his heart in the process—but he would honor my wishes.

The thought makes me so sick I nearly throw up.

"Neither of you intended to get stuck in this situation," Mary says as she fixes my hair. "You've done the best you can for as long as you can. For the first time, you have the freedom to do whatever you want with your life and go wherever you want to go. It's time to cut your losses and leave."

I don't want to leave Rahk. Do I have any other option, though?

"I need a couple of days," I whisper. "Tonight is my last raid before Nothril, and I need time to tell him that I want to leave."

Mary finishes my hair and squeezes my shoulders. "You can do this."

I do not fear being unable to walk away from Rahk. I fear the rest of my life after I've walked away from him.

CHAPTER 51

RAHK

I PORE OVER the lists on my desk. Anything to distract me from the plunging despair. Anything to keep from trying to reason away Kat's concerns—even though I knew from the start that she was right. I cannot visit Harbright regularly. Lord and Lady Nothril would find out, and they would send Pelarusa to kill Kat. But part of me insists there must be *some* way to make it work.

I need to stop going around and around in my head over this. Just for a little bit.

So I search the lists of every person, from the greatest to the smallest, who was present in each Court recently infiltrated by the Ivy Mask. He has someone working with him. Someone who can access any of the Courts without raising suspicion. If my hunch is correct, I will find a name that is on each of these lists. The lists are extensive, however, and with how long it's been since I slept, my eyes start to glaze over.

Until I land on one name. My heart quickens.

It's not a name, but a title. One I am familiar with.

The Human Tailor of Valehaven.

He was there at the Nothril Court when the Ivy Mask last struck. I quickly scan the next list. *Human Tailor of Valehaven.* Then the next. And the next.

Every single one.

"There you are." I run my finger over the dried ink. The Ivy Mask's accomplice is the Valehaven tailor. The thrill of the discovery pulses through my blood, temporarily relieving my aching heart. I pen a quick message and get to my feet.

Now I won't only know when the Ivy Mask is in Caphryl Wood. I will know exactly what Court he is going to strike before he gets there. The chase hums in my bones. This is just the break I needed after . . . *everything*. This is something concrete and tangible. Something I can lay hold of and claim.

Something that will help me catch the Ivy Mask before Pelarusa is forced to join me.

"Edvear!" I call, leaving my cloak behind and strapping both of my broadswords over my back. I'd rather leave without Kat seeing me this way, so I wait until my steward slips into my study.

Edvear bows and shuts the door when he sees the look on my face. He glances between me and my blades. "What can I do for you, my lord?"

"Please tell Lady Katherine that I will be gone until late this evening." I must retrace my steps to every Court I have access to on this side of the Veil and give the notice to send an alert the moment the Valehaven tailor arrives.

"If she asks where you are, what shall I tell her?"

I shift my weight. "Tell her . . . that Lord Oliver invited me to join him fishing after checking on the troll."

It's not a lie—he *did* send an invitation to join him. One that I am refusing.

Edvear bows. "Yes, my lord."

I dismiss him with my thanks. To avoid running into Kat, I climb out the window. I draw stronger on my glamour magic to conceal me until I'm safely away from any prying eyes. It sends pain shooting through my shoulders, but I ignore it. Soon enough, I'll be back in my own world where such magic use won't be more than a mere thought.

It is easier to maintain a glamour this strong nearer the Wood. I keep myself completely invisible as I fly through the air and dive down past the hill.

The queen's men have already arrived. It is a large company of her most elite warriors. They fill the valley, arranging themselves between enormous ripening fruits and vegetables, and face Ymer. The troll sits where he usually is, his back hunched, his rotted teeth bared toward the warriors, his hand gripping his club. He does not look like much of a threat beyond his monstrous size, and he is slow, but few humans know just how strong one of his blows is.

The people usually here are nowhere to be found—thankfully. Perhaps they scattered when they heard the warriors were coming.

As I watch, the queen arrives on a beautiful white horse. She wears a gown of rich green, with a train that covers the rump of the horse, and a tall crown of gold rests atop her head. Another twenty of her elite surround her as she approaches the troll.

She better not be attacking the troll instead of bidding him peacefully to leave.

I brace myself, drawing my sword silently. *Don't make me intervene.*

Queen Vivienne rides her horse toward Ymer, who snarls at her approach. He gets to his feet, rising to his full height, and flexes his grip on his club.

"Who goes over yonder?" he booms. "Ymer will make cakes out of your teeth and eat them for dessert!"

The queen draws her horse to a halt. Fear flickers across her expression when she sees just how large and powerful this troll is.

Do not back down, I want to growl at her. I wish it was Kat who had this responsibility instead of the queen. She would not falter. She also would not have dragged this out so long.

The queen lifts her voice and calls across the field: "As the ruler of this land, I come to bid you, troll of Faerieland, to leave immediately!"

"Eh?" Ymer calls back. "Ymer hears not small woman on hornless unicorn!"

His voice carries where hers did not. I rake a hand down my face. This is going just about as well as I expected.

The queen, after a moment of hesitation, firms her brow and marches forward. At last, she is close enough to be heard—but not close enough that the troll's club can find its mark.

"As the ruler of this land," the queen shouts again, "I come to bid you, troll of Faerieland, to leave immediately!"

Ymer visibly stiffens at the disrespectful address. His ears flap at the flies buzzing around his head. He takes one step toward the queen. She pulls her horse back, her warriors rushing to create a barrier between her and the troll.

The troll gives a long sniff. Then his lumpy eyebrows draw together in a furious line. "Small woman on hornless unicorn tries to *trick* Ymer the Indefatigable? Small woman on hornless unicorn *lies* to Ymer the Indefatigable? Ymer knows you are not the ruler of this land! Only the true ruler of this land can bid Ymer to leave!"

I curse under my breath. Queen Vivienne is not the true ruler—she is the regent. I did not think that distinction mattered. Apparently, it does, and Ymer's connection to the land he has been squatting on tells him the truth. Only the young Prince Lionel can bid Ymer to leave.

Ymer makes a lunge toward the queen, but she is already retreating. Her face is a mask of fury, and I can almost see her thinking, *"I knew that fae was trying to trick me to get me killed!"*

There is no circumstance now where she will trust me enough to bring her only son out here.

The company of men amass around the queen. Ymer roars at her, but does not pursue as they turn and make their quick getaway. I flex my grip on my sword's hilt. If the rest of the queen's forces attack Ymer, I will be forced to intervene. No matter how much I'd rather foist the fallout of this on Ash instead of dealing with it myself.

To my great relief, they do not attack. The warriors move in defensive patterns, covering the queen's route of escape. I wait until they are all gone. His back to me, Ymer plops onto the ground with a force that makes the entire valley shiver.

My shoulders relax. I sheathe my sword and stride toward the Wood for my second task of the day. A stray thought occurs to me: *If I am quick, will I be able to return to Kat before she goes to sleep tonight?* I shouldn't get my hopes up, but it does quicken my step.

I expect to spend many hours traveling from Court to Court, but when I reach the Star City, with its great spires that pierce the purple skies, my plans are cut short by news better than I could have hoped for.

"The Valehaven tailor arrived this morning," the city steward tells me at the entrance to the palace.

"This morning?" I repeat.

"Indeed. He is delivering an order for the Starborn Prince."

I nod, hardly believing my good fortune. Still, part of me sinks. I won't be back tonight to see Kat. "In that case, I'll stay awhile."

CHAPTER 52

KAT

"YOU'RE SURE IT isn't too dangerous?" whispers Mary as I dress in my usual Ivy Mask uniform.

"Rahk is gone, and Edvear said he's with Lord Oliver until late. I couldn't have asked for better fortune." I finish stuffing the last things I need into my satchel. I smear the bottom of my boots with *ollea*. Only a few drops remain. Not enough for the rest of this raid *and* the Nothril raid, but I'm cooking up an alternative. "Since I don't know when he'll be back, you'll need to be ready to help me change as quickly as possible."

She balances the small basket on her hip with everything we will need to transform me back into Lady Katherine, including night clothes, perfumed lotion to hide any scent of Faerieland, and a hidden wound kit in case things go wrong again. She tries not to let her worry show on her face. "I'll be in the kitchen waiting."

I kiss her on the cheek before scrambling out of the window. My leg is fully healed by now except for a white, puckered scar. Rahk's salve was truly magic. Now more than ever, I'm grateful to not bear the weight of an injury.

And this time, I have Bartholomew too.

I thought long and hard about whether I should risk taking such an identifying animal. In the end, I decide that the speed she will lend me is worth it. I sneak into the stable while Clifford is eating dinner and hurry to Bartholomew's stall. She nickers happily and flicks her tail when she sees me.

"You ready for an adventure, pretty girl?" I whisper to her. She nibbles my cloak in reply as I apply *ollea* to each of her shoes.

Once we're riding together through the fields out to Caphryl Wood, I let myself acknowledge the fears I refused to in front of Mary. There is no chance that Rahk is with Oliver. He is out trying to catch me again—I can feel it in my gut.

"I cannot let him catch me until after the Nothril raid," I tell myself under my breath, the pounding of Bartholomew's hooves beneath me both a comfort and a thrill. Whatever I do, even if that means I get there and am forced to turn around and come right back, I cannot let Rahk catch me. Not tonight.

I arrive at the crest of the hill before the edge of the Wood. I dismount and give Bartholomew a chance to recover as I pull my hood low and peer over the edge of the rise.

Torches illuminate the darkness below me. People have settled back into the valley and work tirelessly below, hoeing the ground, planting seeds, harvesting giant crops. Borders made of rope have been erected, and even as I watch, a fight breaks out over one of those borders. I have to get past them somehow. And there's no way to access my cart.

A growling roar rips my attention to one side.

"You cannot be serious," I groan.

Ymer is still here. Still swinging his club at the people who come too close to him. He was supposed to be gone! The queen was supposed to tell him to leave!

"Good thing I prepared for this," I mutter.

I open my satchel and pull out the triple-wrapped chicken carcass. I mount Bartholomew and urge her closer toward the troll. Most people steer clear of Ymer, so when I go straight to him, we avoid those who might get a closer look at me.

"Small elf?" Ymer calls to me. A different note is in his tone this time. A note that, if I did not know better, I would think was *interest*.

"I brought you a present, Ymer the Indefatigable!" I toss the chicken to him.

He grabs it eagerly, using his fingernails to slice through the kerchiefs. "Ymer is very hungry," he says by way of thanks. Did his hand shake as he lifted one delicate rib to his giant mouth? "Small elf nice to Ymer."

Suddenly, I feel terrible for this troll. He really is hungry, and everyone is making him the enemy. He is just as much a victim of the Wood's shifting borders as many of us.

Though he *could* choose to leave if he wasn't so stubborn.

My concern evaporates. *Mostly*. I urge Bartholomew into a gallop and Ymer waves happily as we go and calls, "Ymer will repay!"

I keep my hood low as I find the right Path. As I step one foot onto it, my vision flickers with vibrant skies and glowing stars. *That's the one*. Together, Bartholomew and I plunge onward.

The Star City is more beautiful than I could have imagined. The sky is a deep violet, hung with large, low stars and a sliver of a crescent moon. The city is vast, full of slender spires of intricate architecture that seem so tall they reach the moon. I stand at the edge of Caphryl Wood, looking down into the city. There are paved roads lined with beautiful glowing lights. It makes the entire city look like a valley full of stars.

But I have no time to gawk at the beauty. I have three targets to find.

After tying Bartholomew, giving her a few carrots, and applying one last dose to her hooves in case we must make a fast escape, I follow the scrawled instructions Tailor gave me the last time I was at

Nothril, diving into the depths of the city on foot. I move fast and avoid the many lights.

At last, I reach the palace. Tailor's directions take me to a servant's entrance. The meeting place is a boiler room, usually checked only once an hour at this time of day. Smoke and heat blast me the second I open the door. The only light comes from the glow of coals and flames licking fresh wood in the furnace.

No one is here.

I yank the scrap of paper out of my pocket, straining my eyes to read it again, retracing my steps in my head. No, I'm in the right place. So why is no one here? Did Tailor not reach them? Do I need to go find them?

I wait a few more minutes, bouncing on the balls of my feet, sweat pouring down my face and back. I'm going to have to use extra *ollea* to combat the strength of my own scent now.

It is supposed to be a young boy and girl, and an adult woman. Even when I poke my head back into the hallway, there is not even a single approaching footstep.

Rahk is always fast on my trail. I cannot stay here much longer.

The door creaks open. I whirl.

A woman, with drooping almond eyes and a mane of thick, curly black hair, slips inside. She startles slightly at the sight of me with my mask and cloak.

"There you are!" I whisper. "Where are the others? A boy and a girl?"

"Jack and Mavis?" the woman asks. "I have not seen them all day."

She trembles in the darkness, her arms wrapped around her middle. She glances at the door every two or three seconds.

"Have you seen the Tailor?" I hiss. "Where is he?"

She shivers. "I saw him a few hours ago. He said everything was proceeding as planned."

I curse inwardly and pace two more lengths of the small, scalding room. Then I turn to the woman once more. "I need you to get to the edge of the city. I don't want anything happening to you if we are delayed. Can you see Paths in the Wood?"

Firelight catches on unshed tears. She shakes her head.

I purse my lips. She is going to fall to pieces if I show too much of my own anxiety. "That is fine," I say as calmly as I can. "If you can just get to the edge of the city, to the road that leads into the Wood, you will be safe. I will come get you as quickly as I can, and we will leave. Take this and smear it on the bottoms of your shoes." I show her how, using my second to last drop. Then I hand the bottle to her.

She places the last drop of *ollea* on her shoes. I try not to panic that my source is gone. I try not to let the tightness in my chest cut off my air as I wonder how I am going to get the last two targets out while Rahk is invariably right behind me.

We part ways, her to leave the palace, me to dive deeper into it.

These servants' hallways are well lit, to my dismay. I am just about to remove my mask and hood to give the illusion that I am not, in fact, breaking into a fae palace, when a shadow rounds the corner ahead of me. I glance around frantically for a place to hide. Nothing.

A small boy rounds the corner, only around nine years old. He must be the boy—Jack. His round little eyes go even rounder when he sees me. "Are you the Ivy Mask?"

"Yes!" I bend down to his level, and my heart could break that one so young would be a slave. Did he end up here because he was at Caphryl Wood's edge when the border expanded? "What's the matter? Are you Jack?"

He nods. A whimper escapes his lips. "My sister! I cannot get her out!"

I flex my jaw. "Take me to her at once."

CHAPTER 53
RAHK

THE TAILOR WASN'T hard to find. He smells of dry chalk and lingering traces of indigo dye and woad—a distinctive scent that allowed me an easy trail to follow through the mingling throngs of people. I track him through the lower levels of the palace to a staircase that leads to the upper floors.

But, as I expected, I don't get far before someone stops me.

A flash of purple robes draws my attention to the top of the staircase. There, with a cold lifted chin and luxurious robes, the *lumiral* light catching on his yellow hair, is the Starborn Prince.

"Caspar," I say, inclining my head.

He frowns at me, descending one stair toward me. "Rahk of the Nothril Court. I cannot say I was pleased when I heard you had come. Are you here to claim my city?"

I lift both of my hands. "My presence is not a declaration of war."

He takes his time coming down the stairs, never once taking his eyes off me. He's not as tall as I am, nor as broad, but there's a sharp cunning in his gaze as he looks me up and down. "Then what are you here for?"

"I follow the trail of the Ivy Mask. It has led me here."

"The vigilante who frees the human slaves?" His mouth twists. "I do not know why he would come here. We have few human slaves. His time would be better spent at your Court."

"Have you detected any signs of his presence?"

"Beyond the Valehaven tailor being here?" He chuckles. "Nothing."

I'm impressed. How long has he known about the tailor?

"You're surprised I know about the Ivy Mask's accomplice. I have my sources who keep me informed. It's not difficult to put the pieces together, as you've clearly done yourself."

I acquiesce a nod.

Caspar strides past me, tossing over his shoulder. "I have work to return to. Send a servant to me if you need anything. But please don't kill or capture the tailor while in my city. He's the best on this side of the Veil, and you will put me out considerably if you destroy him."

I shake my head. "I won't touch him. He's not my current quarry."

"Good."

I take the stairs two at a time, following my nose, threading through scents like unraveling a tapestry, until I find the tailor on the twelfth floor of the palace. The entire floor appears to be Caspar's private rooms, surrounded by a balcony that overlooks the city on all sides. The tailor is in the prince's large wardrobe room, bent over a maroon coat of exquisite make. He does not notice me, quiet as I am.

I slide the only door shut and press my hand to the lock. My mouth moves, my voice the barest murmur, and then the seal flares to deep blue before fading back into the wood.

"Who is there?" The tailor's muted voice permeates through the door. His footsteps are hurried. The doorknob turns, catches, jiggles. Then a fist bangs against the door. "The Tailor of Valehaven is in here! You must let me out!"

I turn on my heel and stride back the way I came.

"I am getting you tonight, Ivy Mask," I growl under my breath.

KAT

The boy takes me up several flights of stairs to a small antechamber attached to a fae woman's quarters. When he cautiously pushes open the door—while I watch for sign of anyone approaching—he cries, "She was right here! She couldn't leave because of her mistress. But now she's gone!"

I grit my teeth, casting about wildly for any sign of where the girl could have gone.

Instead of finding the girl, I see the beginning of a shadow appearing at the end of the hallway from where we came. There is a head, and the hilt of two swords rising above either shoulder.

My awareness turns white with panic.

I grab Jack's arm and yank him into the antechamber. I kick the door shut with my heel. "Where does this lead?" I point to the door at the other end of the chamber.

"The servants' hallway, and then to the library!"

"Perfect."

I launch into motion, dragging the boy after me. We hurry into yet another well-lit servants' hallway that is almost nice enough to be any regular hallway. Jack points, and we take a door that leads into the library.

The room we careen into would have stolen my breath at any other moment in my life. The soaring ceiling is stained glass, illuminating the most luxurious space I have ever seen in my life with jeweled shades of color. Jack twists free of my grip and dives behind an enormous tapestry along one wall. I start to follow, only to find the design of the wall itself creates small pockets only a child can squeeze into without being detected.

I search around, then dart into the stacks. Watching, waiting, as a shadow that might be Rahk's appears beneath the door. And then disappears.

Gasping breath escapes me. I slide out of the stacks, about to return to the boy, when something grabs my wrist. I choke on my swallowed scream. Then suddenly, I'm slammed backward against the wall. Both my arms pinned as though with iron vices against the tapestry. But nothing is there. I yank as hard as I can, curling my fingers into fists, but whatever invisible force pins me to the wall is relentless.

A silhouette emerges from the stacks, one shelf over from where I hid. He comes into the multicolored starlight that mingles with the low glow of fae orbs along the wall. His hands are tucked into his pockets as he strides casually toward me. A book is tucked under one arm. His head is canted to one side. Long purple robes swish with each step. He appears to be a young man, though I've interacted with fae long enough to know he could be thousands of years old. As all fae are, he is beautiful, with fine features and bright eyes.

I go still, refusing to glance at the place where the boy is hiding. I wait silently as he approaches. His chin jerks in one direction slightly—and then my mask is ripped from my face. It lands softly against the reflective floor. I blink and look between my fallen mask and the approaching fae.

The Starborn Prince.

I should be counting down my last seconds of life. Instead, I'm wondering: *how did he just do that?*

He stops two paces in front of me, his brow creasing as he regards me. "What are you doing?"

I swallow. "Robbing you, sir."

He inclines his head in a nod. "I appreciate the honesty. You are unassuming for the infamous Ivy Mask. What are you—a girl of eighteen?"

"I will be twenty-one tomorrow," I say between my teeth. "Are you going to kill me?"

He does not seem particularly violent or set upon my death. Instead, viewing me as a fascinating little curiosity. It is another fae game. *The human provides an interesting diversion, and the fae does not immediately slaughter them.*

He seems intrigued by our version of this game. Perhaps he loves games.

Just like Rahk.

A cunning light flashes in his eyes. "And keep you from facing your due penalty for your crimes? Certainly not. I believe in justice."

Justice? He is a fae who imprisons witless humans—and my rescue of them is perverting justice? I keep my mouth shut, trying to remember Mary's exhortations to not drive those who have power over me to further anger.

He smiles. It is cold and unamused as he takes his book, flips it open, and turns the pages until he is satisfied. Then he looks up. "I am a fae who enslaves innocent humans and so who am I to speak of justice? You're a human in a fae world. You ought to learn to keep your face from expressing your thoughts so plainly."

"I usually wear a mask," I grumble between my teeth.

"What else are we supposed to do with humans who break the treaty between our peoples? The treaty that is there to ensure our lands do not become consumed in war? Rulers like me cannot step foot in your world, and yet you are allowed to enter ours with no repercussions? No, that is the price you pay to not have your world overrun by us. You agree that once you step foot in our land, you become our property. And, when you consider it, what we do is a mercy. The alternative is to let them wander through Caphryl Wood with no Path to guide them to safety, no indication of the passage of time, nothing but the endless Wood in every direction, until they are swallowed whole by monsters or drained bit by bit by the Wood itself. Without a Path, humans go mad in the Wood."

His words bring horrible memories resurfacing. Holding my mother's hand as she rocked in her rocking chair, staring vacantly at the wall while I sang to her. Begging her to talk to me, to look at me, to not hate me.

The Starborn Prince studies me like I am a page full of text. I suddenly wonder what my face has betrayed this time. He slams his book shut. "There is someone here who has come for you."

"Prince Rahk of the Nothril Court," I reply, my fear rising at the thought of him walking through that library door. Seeing me pinned to the wall by nothing, my mask at my feet.

"You know him? Should I tell him that you are here?"

The words burst from me. "No, please!"

"Why not? He doesn't even know you're a woman yet. The Nothril prince is well known as a skilled hunter. You've evaded him a long time. It is impressive."

"I can evade him longer if you let me go."

He shakes his head. "I'm afraid that isn't how this works. I cannot simply *let you go*. But I can bargain with you. If you can give me something that will give me power over the Nothril prince this moment, I will let you go."

"Power?"

Rahk's words about fae craving power return to me, bringing heat to my lungs.

"This city of mine rests in a precarious situation, not belonging to any Court," says the Starborn Prince. "I intend to fight for its independence as long as I live. The Nothril Court has already tried to claim this city. But *you* have evaded the Nothril prince long enough to have figured out a thing or two of his weaknesses. We all know his fondness for his youngest sister and how he will do anything and sacrifice anyone to keep her safe. Give me one weakness I don't already know, and I will let you go."

I turn this over in my mind. It seems like my only option, but I cannot give him something that could truly put Rahk in a vulnerable position. "I will tell you a weakness of Prince Rahk's—"

"One that I don't already know."

"One that you don't already know," I repeat, sucking an impatient breath through my nose. "And in exchange, you will help me escape your city with the human slaves I came to free."

His smile curves in ice. He shakes his head. "Once you tell me a weakness of Prince Rahk's, I will release you and will not hinder your mission. Nor will I tell Prince Rahk of your presence—unless he asks if I've seen you. Then I have no choice but to tell the truth."

I do not like it, but it's better than my alternative. "Deal."

"Let it be so," he says.

My first bargain with a fae. A searing pain burns against the palm of my hand. I turn it over to find the tattoo of two swords, crossed at the middle. *Rahk's swords.* I hope I don't come to regret this foolhardy decision.

"Give me his weakness," demands the Starborn Prince.

I swallow hard. "I'm his wife."

True, pure shock overcomes his features. The invisible shackles fall off my wrist. I grab my mask—my tattoo already gone from my palm now that both of our ends of the bargain are fulfilled—and bolt for the door. I grab the boy from his hiding place and run.

We're halfway out before Jack pulls me to a stop, tears streaming down his face. "I cannot leave without my sister!"

I cast a desperate look down the hallway, wishing the girl would simply materialize. Wishing I had time. Wishing Rahk wasn't here.

Wishing—

"We must go," I tell him, my voice cracking, my heart shattering into a hundred pieces. "We've got to get out of here. I can try to come back later—"

"Not without my sister!"

That shadow reappears at the end of the hallway. Rahk's two swords, paired with his almost silent stride.

He is coming this way.

I grab the boy by the shoulders and hiss under my breath: "You have a choice. You can come with me now and I will *try* to come back for your sister another time. Or you can stay here."

A hardness that should never be in the face of a child overtakes his features. "I won't leave until she does."

With that, he breaks free of my arm and dives back into the library. I stare at him for only a second, feeling as though I've just been pummeled in the gut. Then I grit my teeth and sprint in the opposite direction, away from Rahk.

I navigate the servants' hallways and staircases blindly, operating on a mix of memory and instinct. Inexplicably, I make it out of the palace with my head still attached to my shoulders, my mask gripped tightly in my palm. The glowing fae lights along the street seem to scream my presence as I sprint to the place I told the woman to meet me.

The road that leads to the Wood is eerily empty. I search in every direction, turning on my booted heel, panting hard.

The woman is not here.

Was she found? Did she run away? I search frantically, looking for any sign of her. Maybe she found Bartholomew and stayed with her. I race toward my horse's hiding spot. There's Bartholomew, hidden from view of the city by the Wood, her ears back and her tail twitching uneasily. But no sign of the woman.

When I turn back toward the city, there is Rahk. Fully illuminated by the streetlights. Coming this way. My *ollea* must have worn off. It's impossible to tell if he has seen me yet. My hood came off while I ran. I quickly pull it low again and yank my mask back in place.

Cursing, I spring into Bartholomew's saddle and kick her into a gallop. I can barely see the slight speckled glow of the Path through the sheen of my tears. In all the years I've been running these raids, I've never had a failure like this one. I can already feel the weight of those three souls settling onto my heart. A burden I will never be able to cast off.

And if I can't get back home before Rahk catches me, I won't have a chance to redeem myself with my Nothril raid.

My *last* raid.

I push Bartholomew as hard as she can go through the Paths, straight through the people filling the edge of the border, crushing oversized fruit and vegetables in my wake. People scream, but I cannot look. Even a second will cost me everything.

I gallop as close to Rahk's estate as I dare, then leap off and take Bartholmew's lead, guiding her to the stables—which are still empty, as they should be. Normally I'd brush her down, but I barely have time to toss a bucket of alfalfa in front of her before I sprint to the kitchen.

Mary is there, alone, mending by candlelight. I barrel inside, streaked with sweat, grime, and tears. "He's behind me. I don't know how close."

Mary lets out a violent curse like nothing I've heard from her before. She drags me to the pantry and we frantically peel off my clothes. She has the small basket of everything we need sitting there by the door, and next to it is a soapy bucket of water—long gone cold. I scrub myself as fast as I can, my heart pounding a syncopated rhythm. Mary has a hair oil that she rakes into my scalp with almost enough force to break my neck. Next is the lotion I slather all over myself while she ties up my hair in a clean linen. My hands tremble so hard I can barely pull on my nightgown, so Mary yanks it into place.

A loud bang from the opposite end of the house sends both of us jumping an inch out of our skin.

"He's here," I whimper. "I cannot get back to the bedroom in time!"

The bellow, so thunderous and powerful, carries clearly across the hallways and doors and empty rooms between us, sending Mary and I into twin panicked states of paralysis.

"Where is Kat? Where is my wife?"

CHAPTER 54

RAHK

THE FRIGHTENED WOMAN with the curly black hair doesn't see me before I've crept up behind her. She hides just off the lit road, clinging to the shadows. In one swift motion, I have one hand around her upper arm and the other smothering her scream.

"Tell me where the Ivy Mask is, and I will spare you," I growl into her ear.

She trembles violently in my grip. I let go of her mouth.

"I don't know," she replies, the words coming out in shakes and stutters. "She went to find the others."

She.

All this time, and I've never realized my quarry was a woman. Kat springs to mind at once. The memory of how she felt curled up against me this morning, her lips pressed against my throat in a long, unintentional kiss, returns to me unbidden with a painful ache. I sweep all thoughts of her aside immediately.

"The other slaves?" I demand.

She nods. The motion makes her hair fall into her face. I take stock of her quickly, and my entire body responds with pulsating shock when I see a familiar object clutched tight in her hand.

An ollea jar.

She doesn't fight when I take it. Without releasing her, I hold the jar up to the light. Not a single drop remains. So *this* is how the Ivy Mask has been evading me so long. I never realized *ollea* could be used like this.

I think of the girl I found in my Nothril quarters so long ago. The mute slave who shouldn't have been in my room. The one I considered was working for the Ivy Mask.

She wasn't working for the Ivy Mask. She *was* the Ivy mask.

And she was in my room stealing this.

I picture the girl. She was slender, wearing an oversized uniform, with bits of black hair visible between patches of gauze covering her face. I think of her brown eyes, her straight nose. Again, Kat assaults my thoughts.

She has a similar build and height to the Ivy Mask.

Stop thinking about Kat, I tell myself. *You've got to focus.*

I cast around, looking for what I need. I drag the woman after me, away from her hiding spot, until I find a loose stone on the edge of the road. I lift it, testing its weight in my palm. A spell like this is only effective if created outside the Wood. I run my fingers over its smooth surface, muttering under my breath. *"Alathar illutrum o pomith sylithica pir bonrus."*

The stone begins glowing a soft purple. I hand it to the woman, who glances between me and it uncertainly.

"Take that and follow it through the forest—purple means you are heading in the right direction, red means you have turned the wrong way. It will lead you safely to the human lands. You will not be lost in the Wood."

"I can—I can leave? You're not going to kill me?" asks the woman, her hands in a knot at her throat.

"Not if you move fast and leave at once," I reply darkly. She obeys, tripping in her haste to run away. I retrace my steps to where I found her. Is the Ivy Mask nearby?

That is when I catch movement near the edge of the forest. Up the slope, just on the edge of the Wood, is a rider mounted on a horse. A *horse*.

That is her. That is the Ivy Mask.

Her cloak billows behind her, her mask of green ivy tightly against her face. She looks back at me. It gives me a full view of the sad face on her mask. Her clothes are dark, nondescript, and her form is slender.

But what else I see turns my blood to ice.

The Ivy Mask's hair flies out behind her just before she pulls her hood to cover it.

Dark and cropped short.

Suddenly, it is not the nameless Ivy Mask that rides that horse—the horse that I strain and fail to get a clear glimpse of in the shadows—but Kat. My wife.

Great Kings, please let it be anyone else. I have never prayed in my life, but I pray now. Desperately. *Please don't let it be her.* My whole body shakes as I release the glamours of my wings and soar through the air to the edge of the forest. I curse that I cannot fly through the Wood without losing my Path, tuck my wings in close, and run harder than I've ever run before.

It's not Kat. It's not Kat. It's not Kat.

I pound my way through the Wood, nearly running off the Path several times in my haste. At long last, I burst across the border into Harbright. I ignore the screams of the busy farming people. I ignore the troll bellows and the clang of violence. I leap into the air and let my wings carry me as fast as I can across the fields.

My estate looms before me as I fly low to the ground and drop out of the air, landing in a crouch. I don't go for the door but run straight for the window of our bedroom.

She's going to be there, I tell myself frantically. *She's going to be asleep in bed and you're going to feel terrible for waking her up. You'll laugh at the idiocy of your own suspicion.*

None of those assurances calm me down. I shove open the window and leap inside, feet first.

The bed is empty. The sheets on her side are mussed, but I don't see her. A quick sniff of the room, and I know she's not here. Still, I march to her old servant's room and throw open the door. Nothing. I check the washroom.

Nothing.

My blood boils. My hands tremble violently. I throw open the bedroom door. It smashes into the wall, the handle going straight through the plaster.

"Where is Kat?" I bellow. I don't care if it's late and everyone is asleep. I need answers. *Now.* "Where is my wife?"

I storm down the hallway, throwing open every door I come to. Every room is empty. The dining room. My study. The guest quarters that we've never used except when Kat was hurt. The parlor. The library. All the other rooms. With each empty room, my panic builds.

"Katherine Vandermore!" I roar into the emptiness as I throw open the door to the kitchen.

And there she is.

Her eyes are wide with fright, her hair wrapped up in a cloth like she recently bathed, a soft white nightgown clinging to her form. The pleasant perfume of her scent fills my awareness. She has a broken mug in one hand, and a puddle of what smells like hot chocolate dripping over the edge of the counter. Mary sits across from her, clutching her own mug, staring at me with Kat's mirrored fright. Their gazes shift from me to the swords strapped to my back.

"Rahk!" Kat cries, her voice shaking as she gets up. "What's the matter? You frightened me near to death!"

Mary sets to work cleaning up the mess of the spilled drink. Kat immediately goes to help her. I'm still staring at her, dumbfounded.

My mind tries to make sense of what I saw and what I see now. The scent of her is so unmistakably fresh and feminine—not at all what she should smell like if she'd just ridden across miles of field and forest.

"Why aren't you in bed?" I demand. I grab either side of the doorframe, leaning forward and back for any sign of a clock. There is one in the kitchen. "It's well after midnight!"

"Do I have a curfew?" Kat shoots back, frustration and irritation overtaking her fright. "I couldn't sleep! Mary made us hot chocolate and we've been sitting here talking."

Charity, Mrs. Banks, and Cliffored barrel into the kitchen just then, in an array of nightcaps and candles and nightclothes.

"What is wrong?" demands Mrs. Banks. "What has happened?"

I look between them and Kat. Kat, who clearly *wasn't* just invading the Fae realm at her whims. Kat, who *isn't* the Ivy Mask. I let out a deep exhalation, running my shaking hand down my face. I could collapse onto the floor in relief. "Nothing has happened. I returned late and found my bedroom empty. I thought something had happened to Kat and I panicked. Please accept my apologies for waking you all up."

Everyone disperses. Kat's hand trembles as a mirror of my own as she disposes of the broken mug. I curse myself for scaring her so badly. It just looked *so much* like her. I know her so well by now—her personality, her form, her face.

But it *wasn't her.*

It wasn't her.

I turn around, trying to pull myself together. I am usually not so easily shaken.

One way or another, this woman will be my undoing.

I breathe deeply into my gut until I am composed enough to speak. Still, I don't turn around. The sounds of her and Mary bustling around the kitchen have gone quiet, as though they stand waiting for me. "Kat," I say at last. "Please come to bed."

I leave before she gives an answer, marching to our room.

CHAPTER 55

KAT

"DON'T GO TO his room," Mary silently pleads with me. "We can leave now. We can go to Vandermore Manor tonight."

"He believed me. I saw it in his face. I'm perfectly safe," I mouth back.

She gives me such a look of pain I almost give in right then, just to see the worry leave her eyes. Then I think of the people I failed tonight. Jack, his sister, and that poor woman. My resolve hardens.

"I'm going to be fine. He isn't going to hurt me."

Not yet.

Before she can protest any more, I grab the shawl at the bottom of the basket we'd prepared. The basket that saved my life. I didn't have time to put on the shawl before he burst into the kitchen. I take it now and wrap it around my shoulders like a shield as I make my way to our bedroom.

Rahk is washing his face when I enter. He looks up, and between the long, wet strands of his hair, there is a fierceness in his eyes I have not seen before. He's discarded his clothes in favor of the same soft trousers he wore last night and a loose black shirt with laces he hasn't bothered tying, leaving his torso partially exposed.

I tug my shawl closer around my shoulders and would have marched straight to my side of the bed, pulled the covers over my head, and frozen him out for scaring all of us so much. Instead, he prowls across the room, intercepting me.

My back hits the wall as he snatches my jaw, forcing me to look up at him while his gaze burns into my face. "What are you doing?" I demand. "You haven't had enough of frightening the daylights out of me today?"

His voice is shaking with anger. "I thought I'd lost you."

Be clueless. Be confused.

Lie, lie, lie.

"Why would you have lost me?" I laugh uneasily. Now I'm shaking too. "I was just in the kitchen. Why did this spook you so much? You're not yourself."

Rahk's hands slide to hold my head, his fingers touching the short, dark strands of my hair. His voice comes out in a growl. "I was in Faerieland. I saw someone there. A woman on a horse. She looked just like you."

Everything inside me plunges to the floor. I try to think fast, to react how I would if I didn't know exactly what he meant. "Edvear said you were with Lord Oliver!"

"I deceived you," he admits. His forehead comes to rest against mine, his breath panting against my mouth. "I'm sorry. I didn't want you to worry. I return to Faerieland often. There is business for me there. But when I saw that woman, it scared me to death. When I came back, and you weren't here—"

"Rahk. It's alright." I try to say it gently as I reach up and cup his face. He leans into my touch, closing his eyes, releasing a shudder. "I'm here. I'm safe."

He swallows hard. "I'm sorry. I just—I thought I lost you, Kat."

His words drive knives into my gut. I fight the knot rising in my throat. My voice cracks. "You know we will lose each other, one way or another."

"I know," he growls.

Then his lips are on mine, his weight pressing into me. Rahk is always collected, controlled, and rational. But this kiss is scribed in desperation. He holds me like I might crumble through his fingers and be carried away in the wind. I kiss him back, wrapping my arms around his neck and pulling him to me with my own equal measure of desperation. I love him and I hate that I love him but there is no stopping it. I love him—my hunter and my husband. He will destroy me as I destroy him.

And if my death must come at the hands of a fae, then I long for it to be Rahk's.

His touch is comfort I do not deserve after leaving those three people behind. Still, I lean into it, holding tight to his embrace, letting myself be swallowed up in his bigness. This is the only place I feel safe, and it kills me to know that this safety will be gone sooner than I expect.

Tell him you are leaving. Tell him, Kat.

I cannot. I cling tighter to him instead.

"You make me want to give up everything and stay in these cursed human lands with you," Rahk snarls softly in my ear, "even if it shortens my lifespan."

I stiffen in his arms. "Shortens your life span?"

"You didn't know?" Rahk breathes softly onto my forehead. "It is not our blood that gives us long life. It is the magic in the air. The less I breathe that air, the shorter my life is."

I pull back in alarm. "Has your life already been shortened by the weeks you have spent here?"

He shrugs, then draws me back to himself with a soft groan. "Maybe. A few years—a decade at most."

As if a decade is nothing. As if I am not actively sucking away his lifeforce right this moment.

"You must go back to Faerieland immediately," I say, untangling myself from his arms even as he gives a small measure of resistance.

"You should stay there and only come here when you must! How can you be careless with your life?"

He lets me forcibly push him several steps toward the door. Then he plants his heels and refuses to go any further.

"Rahk!" I protest. "You've got to go back!"

He brings his face down to my level, his black eyes piercing through me, his hand catching my wrist. "Stop this, Katherine."

The knot in my throat thickens until I can hardly breathe. "I cannot have you suffering or dying. I won't allow it. And I will *not* be the reason for it."

He purses his lips. "I am afraid it is far too late for that, my darling."

He pulls me into a kiss, and for the first time, the way he holds my face and my waist, the way his mouth moves against mine, is possessive. He claims me with this kiss. Then my fire returns to me, and I claim him back. This is *my* husband. He may not be mine for much longer, but for this small moment, he belongs to me and no one else.

Breaking our kiss, he cups my cheeks so softly, his eyes running over every inch of my face. "Do you want me to go? Do you want me to return to Nothril?"

Tell him a lie.

Tears gather in my eyes. I shake my head miserably.

Something sparks to life in his expression. *Hope*. "Do you love me, Kat?"

My lips part, my tongue frozen. If I tell him that I do love him, he will find a way for us to be together—a way that will destroy his life, his heart, and his entire future. I cannot let him do that to himself. I thought I could take this one precious moment and keep it, but now I see that is selfish of me.

I must break him now, to save him. He will despise me. And maybe, when he finally hunts me down, that hatred will make it easier for him to kill me.

"I know you are holding back from me," he whispers softly. "I have known from the beginning. I do not know what it is, but I must. Once and for all. Deny it, Kat."

"Deny what?"

"Deny that you love me."

Pressure builds in my chest. This is not fair. I—

The heat of his lips brushes over my forehead. "Look me in the eye, Kat, and tell me that you don't love me. Lie to me, Kat. Lie to me. You've done it many times. So do it again. Tell me that when I catch you staring at me, it's not because you have feelings for me. Tell me that when I come close and your cheeks turn pink, it's not because my nearness affects you. Tell me that the tears you fight right now—tell me they are not because you care."

"I'm not answering that question," I growl, angry and defensive and too heartbroken to either admit the truth or lie again.

"Then you're a coward."

"Am I?" I push away from him, my voice rising. "Or maybe I just don't like the rules you've set up for this game. Would you believe me if I said no? Would you believe me if I said yes? Or would you just call me a liar and believe whatever you want to?"

Rahk throws up his hands, pacing away and then back, dragging his curled fingers through his hair. "I want the truth! I want you to be honest with me!"

I don't know what to do. I don't know what to do. I don't know what to do—

I close my eyes.

Giving up.

My voice shakes. "Do you truly want the truth?"

Rahk does not answer. I open my eyes to find that uneasiness has overtaken his features. But what am I to do? He demands I be honest with him. My heart demands the same thing.

So I manage to choke out: "I care deeply about you, Rahk."

Every part of his face suddenly lifts.

"But our marriage can *never* work," I finish. My vision goes blurry. I curse it.

The muscles of his throat contract and flex. "Why? Tell me a reason that is insurmountable."

My breath releases in a shudder. "There is an insurmountable reason. But I cannot tell you what it is."

"Why not?"

I can already feel him retreating from me. I can feel his regret already bubbling up inside him. The regret that tells him he should have listened to me when I told him I was a curse to him.

"Because it is a secret that belongs to others beyond me," I say. "I have longed, from the very beginning, to confide in you about it . . . but I cannot."

He turns his back to me, releasing a long, low exhalation. He rakes a hand through his long hair.

I hate this distance between us. This fear and the growing cavernous hole in my chest. I press the heel of my palm to my cheeks, trying to smear away the traitorous wetness.

The distance is good, I try to tell myself. *You need this. He needs this. It hurts, but this is the only way you can keep from destroying him completely.*

His shoulders rise and fall with his deep breath. "How long must you keep this secret?"

I stand where I am, longing for him to crush me to his chest, to tell me that it doesn't matter what the secret is, that he loves me and no obstacle is too great.

"How long, Kat? A month? A year? A decade? Longer?"

The tears come in earnest now. "I can never tell you."

Rahk's mouth flattens as his nostrils flare. "So you have a secret that you cannot tell me—ever—that will always come between us? Our entire marriage, when I have made my feelings clear to you repeatedly, you have always known that it will never work between us."

"I never wanted it to be this way," I insist. The knife carving out my heart hurts vastly more than I ever dreamed it could. "Please know that. If I were at liberty to explain, I would tell you everything."

He stares at me for several minutes. Then he goes to the bed and sits down. He rubs a hand down his neck, his jaw working. I want to go to him, to try to erase the lines between his brows, to soothe the tension from his arms and shoulders.

I want to take the pain from him. Mine already is unbearable, so what is more? I continue to be the curse to those who care about me. If I could ease his pain, I would.

"Well, I suppose I ought to say I have been keeping a secret of my own," Rahk says with a humorless chuckle. "You have done the noble thing to push me away while keeping yours. I'm afraid I have not been so noble. Perhaps this is my repayment of that selfish evil. You must forgive me."

He means the secret of him hunting the Ivy Mask. The Ivy Mask, who he believes I love for rescuing my mother. He must have assumed I would hate him if he told me.

I shrug, chewing mercilessly on the inside of my cheek. I do not trust my voice.

When Rahk speaks, he sounds like the distant, taciturn Nothril prince I first came to know. "Thank you for explaining. Now that we understand one another, we can move forward in a way that makes sense."

Maybe I should make myself cold like him. I can build a fortress around my heart to protect its tender wounds.

It's like losing Mama again, I think bitterly. *Your choices are to pretend you don't care, or be completely destroyed.*

Rahk gets to his feet. I expect him to storm out of the room, but instead he comes to where I stand by the vanity, my fingers knotting together, my breath a shuddery whisper. Oh so gently, he touches my chin, tilts my jaw up. He presses the softest of kisses to my forehead.

Then he leaves.

CHAPTER 56

RAHK

THE NIGHT IS thick around me as I pen a note to Edvear in my study. I try not to feel anything at all except a dull resignation. I did not come to the human lands to marry, much less to fall in love. I knew better the entire time. Princes of Nothril should not form attachments—I've always known this. Yet I loved Pavi. I loved Ash.

I loved Kat.

And now, just as I always knew it would, it has become my downfall.

It makes sense that there was something else holding her back. She loved me. Still loves me. It has been so plain across her face when I look at her. It's there in the small things—the way she cares so much about the length of my life. The tears she tried so hard to swallow.

I'm so relieved I never bonded with her in my people's way.

When I finish, I fold the letter, seal it with wax, and scrawl my steward's name on the back. Then I get my swords. Their familiar weight on my back reminds me of what I am. What I have always been. What I should never have been foolish enough to fight.

I leave my study. I crane my ears, listening for even a hint of Kat, but am met with silence. Every few minutes, however, when I turn my head just so, I can catch a whiff of her scent lingering on my clothes, in the air.

I make my way outside. The temptation to turn back, to search for a light in the bedroom window, is almost too strong. *Almost.*

I stretch out my wings, willing my heart to burn cold.

Then I shoot into the sky without a single backwards glance.

My glamours struggle the closer I get to the palace. I yank them around me harder. Pain bursts across my scalp, running down my spine. I grit my teeth and refuse to ease up on my magic use. When, at last, the flags flying in the palace turrets become visible in the night, I angle downward, tuck in my wings, and plunge over the walls.

I choose a shadowy rooftop to land. For a moment, I release my glamours. A gasp of relief nearly breaks free of my throat, but I keep it restrained. I keep my wings as close to my body as possible while I brace my boots against the clay tiles. Then I survey the palace complex around me. I note all the places I can see guards, and all the strategic places there might be guards that I cannot see. My glamours are so weak this far from Faerie that I cannot rely too heavily on them.

I do not know exactly where my target is, but it is not difficult to narrow down the possibilities. I consider my path, noting the guards, the sections where I must rely on stealth and the places where glamour is necessary.

Then I move.

My first guess proves right.

When I land silently on a window ledge and peer inside, I see just the evidence I wanted: a nursemaid fallen asleep in a rocking chair beside a closed door. I keep my breath even as I inspect the lock on the window. A small blade is all I need to slide the bolt and ease open the frame.

Though the moon is far from full, it casts my shadow in stark relief on the nursery floor. I slip into the shadows and approach the sleeping nursemaid. She does not stir until I place my hand over her face. Her eyes fly wide, but the words have already spilled out of my lips. She slumps back into the rocking chair as I brace against the slash of pain through my chest.

Young Prince Lionel slumbers soundly in his bed, holding a stuffed lion to his chest.

I place my hand over his face, and he does not stir as I use the same spell to deepen his sleep. Then I lift him into my arms, slip back to the window, and climb onto the sill.

I try to pull my glamours back in place, but after the second use of the sleeping spell, I cannot grab hold of the magic. I curse under my breath and grit my teeth.

But what use is the queen's trust to me now? Why not forever make an enemy of her? It is not as though I will be staying in Harbright. I have nothing to lose now. My loyalty is to the High King and Queen of Faerieland, and to Nothril. That was all that ever mattered.

So I do not use glamour as I launch into the night, holding the sleeping prince tight to my chest. Nothing shields me from the searching eyes of the guards on the ground and in the towers. I fly as quickly as I can, but the alarm goes up before I leave. I beat my wings as fast as I can and soon, I am beyond the palace.

We don't have much time now.

The flight to the edge of Caphryl Wood is excruciatingly long. I count the minutes, trying to estimate how far behind the queen's cavalry will be. Not as far as I would like.

We reach the rise before the dip into the valley at the edge of the Wood. There, I lay the boy on the ground. Ruckus and troll roars echo from below, but I focus on the prince. I place my hand over his face again, this time muttering a wake spell. It flows from me with relief this close to Faerie. The boy's eyes pop open. He startles immediately, sitting up and scooting backward to get away from me.

"What are you—" He stops, looks around. "Where are we?"

I do not get to my feet, lest he feel small compared to me. Instead, I put more space between us and stay on my knees. Anything to relax him even just a little bit. "We are here at the edge of the Long Lost Wood. You are the true ruler of Harbright, so there is something you must do to protect your people that no one else can do."

A serious light enters his young face. He straightens his shoulders, and he does not regard me with fear, but respect. He gets to his feet. "What must I do?"

My memory flashes back to when I was his age. I had the same attitude. The same innocent desire to serve my people. I turn away from him, a coldness entering my lungs. "Come this way."

He follows me to the edge of the rise. I point to the troll in the valley. He is his usual, lumbering mass, but to my horror, blood streams down his face. A body lies at his great, lumpy feet. A body that looks very like one of the thieves I saw trying to steal the farmers' hard work from them earlier.

I told the queen this would happen.

Prince Lionel gasps, covering his mouth. My instinct is to cover his eyes, too.

But he is the ruler of this land. He will one day be king. He should know the reality of his duty.

"That is Ymer the Indefatigable. He is one of the old trolls of Faerieland. Only you have the power to tell him to leave Harbright and return to Faerie."

The boy swallows. "If I tell him to leave, he will not kill any more people?"

"He will not," I reply.

"Will he eat me?"

I shake my head. "I will protect you. You do not have to go down there if you are afraid, but if you do not, more people will die."

The boy lifts his chin exactly the way Queen Vivienne always does. "I will go down there."

We walk down the rise together. The farming has not stopped, though a wide berth is given to Ymer. The boy's steps slow the closer we get to the massive troll in the midst of his bloody meal. He does not stop, however.

"Is that nice small elf with food for Ymer?" calls the troll toward us. Just as quickly, his face wrinkles. "Not nice small elf."

"What shall I say?" the boy whispers to me.

"You shall say, *'Great Ymer, the Indefatigable, as the ruler of this land, I command you to return to Faerieland.'*"

He nods. His cheeks turn pale. Still, he continues on until we stand before the troll.

"Great Ymer," begins Prince Lionel in his young, shaking voice, "the In—Inde—the Indefatable—the Inde—"

"Indefatigable," I mutter.

"Great Ymer the Indefat—igable," he manages.

He has accomplished the hardest part.

His voice grows clearer and stronger as he continues. "As the ruler of this land, I command you to return to Faerieland."

Ymer looks up from his meal. His attention glosses over me, coming to rest on the young boy at my side. Slowly, Ymer gets to his feet and pulls himself to his full height.

Prince Lionel takes a frightened step back. I place a hand between his shoulder blades and scoot him forward.

"Do not retreat," I order.

He seems to bite back a whimper.

"You are the ruler of this land," I remind him.

He clenches his jaw. Then he balls his fists and screams at the top of his lungs: "Great Ymer the Indefatigable, as the ruler of this land, I command you return to Faerieland! This *instant*!"

Ymer stares down at him from his towering height. Then he crashes to his knees, sending the entire ground shaking. "Ruler of this land!" Ymer bellows. "Ymer is honored to do as ruler commands! May ruler live forever!"

ANASTASIS BLYTHE

A slow, mirthless smile spreads across my mouth. Prince Lionel doesn't seem to have a clue what to do with a troll offering him obeisance. It does not matter, though, because only a moment later, Ymer the Indefatigable gets back to his feet, picks up the rest of his meal, and tromps into Caphryl Wood. Never to bother the human world again.

I smirk down at the boy. "Excellent work, King Lionel of Harbright."

He blushes.

The pounding of hooves yanks my attention back to the rise just as an entire army crests the hill. I curse under my breath.

I bend down to the boy. "They are here to rescue you, and kill me."

"Kill you?" cries the boy, immediately distraught.

If only he knew how many times his mother had plotted my demise. "If you want me to live, go back to them at once. It will give me a chance to escape."

Prince Lionel bursts into a run, screaming his name at the top of his lungs as he hurries toward the knights come to rescue him. I wait long enough to be sure that they will not charge their horses and run the boy over. Then, when he has been scooped up into the arms of a trusted warrior, I survey my options.

There are too many for me to fight. Far too many. I can use my glamours and fly back to my estate, but that will be the first place for the queen to send her forces. Kat could get caught in the crossfire.

No, the army must see me leave Harbright. For good.

I cast one last glance in the direction of my estate. Toward where Kat sleeps. A burst of pain, completely unrelated to magic use, slices through me. I ignore it.

The army of Harbright warriors charge into the valley.

I turn on my heel and sprint onto the Path to Nothril.

CHAPTER 57

KAT

I WAKE IN Rahk's bed. There is no sign of him in the empty room. Uneasiness crawls over me like dozens of small bugs. I throw off the covers, grab a robe, and hurry out of the room. I run into Mrs. Banks first, a basket of dirty laundry in her long fingers.

"Have you seen Rahk?" I ask.

"No, my lady," she replies curtly, skirting around me to return to her work.

I charge down the hallway and find Edvear returning from early morning market with a large canister of fresh milk and several packages of butter for Charity. "Where is Rahk?"

"Is he gone?" asks Edvear. His ears turn back. "He is usually in his study around this time or monitoring the situation with the Wood."

I did not check his study. I know instinctively, however, that he is not there. Still, I hurry there, clutching my robe at my chest, knowing exactly what I will find and yet terrified to find it.

The door is closed. It wails when I push it open. Morning sunlight streams through the window.

The same window those assassins tried to break into so many weeks ago.

It is empty.

Except . . .

Two notes lie on the desk, along with a wrapped package. One is addressed to Edvear. The other is addressed to me.

Edvear appears behind me. Wordlessly, I hold up his letter. He takes it, a knot forming in his brow as he breaks the seal and scans it quickly. Then he spits a dark curse.

"He has gone back to Faerieland," he growls. "For good."

I sink into Rahk's chair. I told him to leave. It is good that he is gone.

So why does every inch of my skin feel as though it is being ripped from my bones? Why do invisible knives carve into my chest? Why does it seem as though I will never take another breath into my hollow lungs again?

"What am I supposed to do with this?" Edvear cries, his own distress evident by his flattened ears and his wildly gesturing hand. "I kept asking him when we were leaving, but he never told me! How am I to dismiss all this staff with no certainty they will find other positions? Charity cannot easily find jobs that let her bring Becky with her. I would never forgive myself if I left them in a vulnerable position—all because Rahk demands we sell the estate as soon as possible and return to Faerieland at the drop of a hat!"

"He said to sell the estate?" I ask dully.

"As if that will happen quickly! What a mess! And Lady Duxbury Vandermore sent notice that she intended to call on you once they were settled in their new residence."

"Just let her call," I say with a shrug. No need to tell her no one will be here.

Edvear suddenly seems to pause, to realize I am sitting there, and his mouth falls open. "What are *you* going to do? Has he promised to visit you?"

He nods at the note I hold.

I have not opened it yet. Still, I swallow and say quietly, "He will not visit me."

Edvear stares at me. Then he storms out of the study, and maybe part of me softens when I realize he is furious at Rahk on my behalf. If only Edvear knew the truth.

I stare at the letter in my hand. At the precise, elegant flow of my full name scripted in ink. Do I want to read it? Am I brave enough?

I might not be brave enough, but I am definitely stupid enough. I break the seal and begin reading.

Dear Kat,

I had planned to celebrate your birthday with you by picnicking by the creek and playing a game of Fool's Circle in the sunshine. Then I was going to suggest you ride Bartholomew through the fields while I flew along beside you, so we could share our favorite things together. It was not much, but it seemed like what you would like.

I am sorry for leaving you. Even though you told me it was the only option, I know you did not want it. I fear that you will be miserable today, but I trust that it will pass soon enough. You have a large heart that loves easily. I am sure you will find someone who shares my preference for women who cannot keep their mouths shut even when their lives depend on it—and women who cook up schemes of dressing like young boys for dubious reasons. I am partial to Lord Oliver, as jealous as I am even writing that name, but I know you will have more than enough options. Stay clear of Boreham and Alsbee. I probably should have just relieved them of their heads before leaving Harbright, though I hear that is illegal.

This letter is getting too long. I meant only to apologize for missing your birthday and to assure you that, for a mixture of reasons I do and don't understand, my leaving is for the best. And to tell you that, even though I may live for thousands of years to come, as long as that life continues, I will never forget you, Kat. Neither do I regret meeting you.

Enjoy your present.

Rahk

I can barely read the swirling words on the page by the end. I sniffle, wiping my wet nose on my sleeve. He truly is gone. I asked him to leave, and he left. That forehead kiss was the last he will ever give me.

And I will never see him again.

My fingers are numb when I reach for the wrapped box. I peel away the paper to find a case of polished wood inlaid with pure gold leaf. I flip the latch and open the case to find a new Fool's Circle board. This one is full sized, like Rahk's, but the pieces of one side are made of solid gold, while the others are pure silver. The Fool itself is inlaid with diamonds, his hat covered in tiny emeralds, and his coat and shoes made of rubies. The board, with its spaces carved with lines of gold, is made of luminescent mother-of-pearl.

The whole thing is worth a fortune. A *true* fortune. This belongs in the queen's vault. Not my hands.

I shut my gaping mouth. He knows I will never use a board like this. He knows I prefer simpler things. But I think he did this on purpose—to give me something I will keep locked away. Something I will never lose, break, or be parted from.

For all that he speaks of me loving again, he is afraid I will forget him.

"Have no fear," I manage around my thick throat, "there is no chance of that happening."

Mary knocks on the study door a moment later. She doesn't have to say anything. She simply comes to my side and gives me a hug. Then she heads in the direction of the bedroom, and I know she means to begin packing.

I join her and get to work.

I focus on my busy hands. There is no room here for thoughts or, even worse, emotions. My entire existence is wrapped up in these bodices that I carefully arrange in a large trunk. Only when I pack my two Fool's Circle boards and strategy guide, does a scrap of longing make it past my defenses.

Mercifully, that longing is rudely interrupted by horses thundering down the estate's driveway. Mary and I exchange a look. I get to my feet and hurry to the window. "Warriors from the queen."

"Why did the queen send warriors here?" Mary asks cautiously.

I hurry out of the bedroom. Edvear meets me as I head out the front door. I bid him stay inside in case the sight of another fae complicates matters. The warriors pull their mounts to a halt and one leaps down.

"Lady Vandermore?" the knight asks.

Vandermore. Not Varadirth.

"Yes?" I pull my shawl around my shoulders. "What is the matter?"

"We have been sent by the queen to ensure your safety after what the fae did early this morning."

"I am safe," I answer quickly. "Did Rahk do something?"

"He kidnapped His Highness, the Prince of Harbright."

"What? You cannot be serious. Surely the prince is safe now?" My mind reels, trying to put the pieces together. This must have been about Ymer. Rahk must have taken him to tell the troll to leave—but Rahk never would have hurt the boy!

"We recovered him. He is safe, my lady."

Good.

I try to bite my tongue, but I cannot help asking: "Is the troll gone?"

"Um, well, it is impossible to know at this time if he is gone for good, but he appears to have left Harbright. For now."

I hide my small smile. Rahk did it after all. And I would bet my life that he was gentle with that prince in the process. "Well, in that case, please send my thanks to the queen for her generous care, and please tell her that I am perfectly safe." I pause, hesitating. Then I give up. The queen is going to find out—it might as well be from me. "You can also tell her that . . . that I am returning to Vandermore Manor and intend to dissolve my marriage with—" I cannot get the last word out. I blink quickly and force a smile. "It was not because he mistreated me or anything. He had to return to Faerieland for good. The marriage simply cannot work."

The knight shifts his weight, as though uncomfortable with this personal of a message to return to the queen.

I give him an earnest, "Thank you. Please ride safely on your return to the palace," to shake him out of his confusion. He nods quickly, bids me a good day, and hops on his horse.

I return to the house to continue helping Mary pack. After giving explanations to at least three people, of course, about what the knights wanted. I resume filling trunks.

At this rate, I'll survive until my Nothril raid. I might even survive beyond it, and if I'm living away from Rahk, then I might just be able to continue my work.

Who am I fooling? No matter where I am in the world, Rahk is still hunting me. He all but caught me last time. I glance at the small chest on the bookshelf—the chest where Rahk keeps his supply of *ollea*. It would be so easy to steal his last bottle. It would make the Nothril raid so much easier.

When Mary steps out for a moment, I get up, move toward the chest. I flip the lid.

Empty.

He took his last bottle before he left.

I sigh as I close it. This is for the best. If Edvear had taken his things back to him and a bottle of *ollea* was missing, it would look suspicious.

It'll be a miracle if I can succeed.

I think of the three people I did not get out of the Star City. I think of the frightened woman I met the last time I was at Nothril, breaking out Lord Nothril's slave girl. I think of my own mother, who endured horrible things because of me.

I will succeed at this raid. Even if it costs me my life.

CHAPTER 58

KAT

VIOLA, MATTHEW, CHARLES, and Beatrice are all waiting for me at Vandermore Manor when I arrive. I embrace each one of them. Seeing their familiar faces is a balm to my soul.

Now that Agatha is gone, I make my way up to her room. The room that once belonged to my mother.

The door whines softly when I push it open. I haven't been here often since Father remarried. White sheets drape the four-poster bed, the matching oak vanity, and wardrobe. The floor creaks beneath my weight. Mama kept the walls a shade of periwinkle, but Agatha changed the color to a dark green. I lift the white sheet over the vanity. There is no collection of cut glass perfume bottles. There are no precious jewels in elaborate settings of silver or gold in the drawers. Only when I check the back of the wardrobe do I find a single crumpled lavender sachet. From Agatha.

The room has been scraped so bare I struggle to find either woman here.

There is one thing, however, that remains from Mama.

The ceiling is covered in wallpaper. It shows a forest with a beautiful pool of water. Young forest creatures dance across the paper. Mama's paint color always brought out the color of the water, though Agatha's brings out the green of the forest. The wallpaper's beauty is clearly showcased by the fact that it is still here. Mama loved it because she said the big eyes of the white-spotted fawn reminded her of me.

I remember being a child, sitting here on the floor despite my parents' orders to leave the servants alone as they installed the paper.

I drag in a deep lungful of dust, mingled with faint traces of Agatha's perfume.

If I can just complete this Nothril raid in a week, I'll be at peace finally. I'll reunite these people with freedom, and I will call my work finished. Mary was right that I cannot free everyone. If my life was the only one on the line, I'd continue this work until I was inevitably caught and killed. But after the Star City, I can no longer deny how much danger I bring to the people I try to save. What even happened to that woman I gave my *ollea* to? I shudder.

This raid will be my last.

Maybe then, with my work finished and my fortune claimed, I will be able to focus on finding a proper human husband. Even if he is half as good as Rahk, I will be happy. For the first time since my mother's disappearance, I'll have a normal life.

"And you're going to *like* having a normal life," I growl into the silence of the room.

RAHK

"Yes, I am almost finished organizing the guard rotation for Mirror Tide. I will inform you the moment it is done," I tell the captain who has been hounding me the last several days since I returned to Nothril.

It would have taken me less time if his initial proposal had not been cobbled together so haphazardly.

I leave the captain and stride down the dark stone hallways. Only when I turn a corner does a surprising presence make me halt in my steps.

Ash throws up his hands, his crown knocked slightly askew. "Rahk! There you are! My sources informed me that Ymer was successfully on the right side of the border once more. I've come to thank you. You saved me the nightmare of a troll rebellion."

"No need to thank me," I reply.

Ash's eyebrow twitches. He looks me up and down. "What is the matter?"

Have I truly let my composure slip? I pull my shoulders back and straighten my features. "I still have not caught the Ivy Mask. Pavi's life is on the line, and I do not have long before Pelarusa becomes banished to the human lands to *aid the search*."

He winces. "That is ugly. I shudder to think of Pelarusa in the human lands." Then he peers closer at me. "But I do believe you just dodged a question, my old friend. You look like a ship with the wind gone from its sails. Why aren't you sniffing out the Ivy Mask right now?"

"She used *ollea* to disguise her scent. Only once I tracked a scent of hers, but I have never been able to catch it again."

"*She?* None of my intel knew the Ivy Mask was a woman."

"She is quick, clever in the human lands and clever in Faerieland. She has proven herself worthy of her reputation."

Ash folds his arms across his chest. He leans against the cave wall, only to stand upright when the cold bleeds into his back. "High praise coming from you. Are you certain you are not in love with her?"

"Very certain," I mutter.

Ash's brilliant complexion suddenly pales, his lips parting. I set into a quick stride and kick myself for what I've just revealed. My friend rushes after me, dropping his voice to a near-silent hiss. "You fell in love in the human lands, didn't you?"

"I have work to do."

"Rahk! What has happened? You must marry her. Bring her here—or go there. If you have found—"

I whirl on him. "I did marry her, Ash."

He comes to an abrupt halt.

"I am happy you were able to work a future out with Stella," I whisper, "but not all of us are so fortunate. We tried to find a way to make it work, but it just cannot. Now please, I truly do have many responsibilities, and I do not wish to discuss this any further. I am glad I was able to fix the troll problem before things got too messy."

With that, I leave him to find his way out of Nothril. I am determined to get to my own chambers for a few minutes of peace and quiet before I try to come up with some other trap to lay for the Ivy Mask—

"Let me know the *moment* the Valehaven tailor arrives with my gown. I want to be certain everything is in order for Mirror Tide."

That is Pelarusa's voice. It stops me dead in my tracks. I turn around, cut through a side hallway until I find Pelarusa speaking with one of the higher servants.

"Did you say the Valehaven tailor is coming?" I ask.

"It is rude to eavesdrop," she replies. "But yes, he is coming, and I am furious because he is not arriving until the morning of Mirror Tide. I asked him to come several days early, in case I needed any major changes to the dress, but he said he could not. Don't try to tell me I should use glamour on my outfit. It is far too tacky for a princess of Nothril."

Mirror Tide. If the Valehaven tailor will be here in just a few days . . .

Then so will the Ivy Mask.

I spare a thought for Kat, for how much she would hate me if she knew I was about to destroy her mother's savior. It truly is good that we parted ways. I refuse to keep letting people get tangled up in my affections.

I will not care when I catch the Ivy Mask. I will not think of Kat when I drag my quarry before Lord and Lady Nothril and slice open her throat.

CHAPTER 59

KAT

I'VE BECOME SO dependent on *ollea* that to no longer have it makes me feel as though I'm crippled.

I come up with an alternative plan. Mary purchased a new set of clothes for me and did her best to not touch them and get her own scent on them. I'll wear those along with a fresh pair of shoes to the border. Once I'm inside Caphryl Wood, I'll switch to my glass slippers. It won't be comfortable, but Rahk himself said the shoes didn't leave a scent.

I leave Bartholomew behind tonight, no matter how desperately I long to take her with me. I visit her before I leave, however, and give her an apple as a treat. "Not this time, my friend," I tell her while I scratch under her chin. "You've got to stay safe, and I cannot risk Rahk recognizing you."

The journey to the rise takes forever. The moon is full overhead, lighting my way. When I arrive, there is no troll threatening to eat me. It is good that Ymer is gone, but truly I would prefer him to the many lanterns filling the valley as people farm the magicked ground late into the night.

But I thought of this, and that is why I wrote to my cousin who manages my estate earlier this week.

I stay on the rise. And wait.

As I watch, a dozen torches light the darkness, approaching the valley to my right. It is not an army, but a hired band of mercenaries.

"We have come to claim the part of this land that belongs to the Vandermore Estate!" cries the leader of the mercenaries.

The people farming the ground look up. Some of their faces cast in flickering shades of concern, while others go back to work.

"Everyone must vacate the premises between these boundary lines!" calls the mercenary once more.

They're not looking in my direction.

Time to move.

I dive into the valley. It is like running through an orchard of vegetables. But even as I try to dodge around thick squash vines and hanging tomatoes the size of my head, I notice spots where the plants growing are much smaller and have not produced fruit yet. *The magic is wearing off.* It is such a relief that this strange situation will come to an end sooner than I imagined.

Yelling has started up between the mercenaries and farmers. A large group of people fall into my path. Quickly, I take refuge behind a massive pumpkin. It's so massive that its stem has snapped, and it lies there like a great orange wheel.

"We will take this by force if we must!" cry the mercenaries. "You have no weapons to defend yourselves! Take your lives and your produce and leave immediately!"

Judging by the volume of the exchanges, the situation is escalating perfectly.

Still, I cannot run all the way to the Wood without being stopped. I look around, then focus on the pumpkin. Maybe . . .

I almost reveal myself several times during the process of dislodging the pumpkin. It takes every ounce of my strength to shift it even an inch. Somehow, I manage. Then I get it rolling.

It rolls fast. I am nearly left in the dust, exposed to all eyes. I leap into motion, running alongside the rogue pumpkin and keeping my hand on it to avoid it falling and crushing me.

By the time it falls onto its head and cracks open, spilling seeds and its stringy guts everywhere, I have enough head start to bolt into the Wood and onto the right Path, before anyone can stop me.

The sentient eyes of the Wood fall upon me at once. The cool air wraps around me like a blanket. I wait for the voices to begin as they always do, but they remain silent. It is a thick, pregnant silence of interest.

This is the last time I will step into this Wood.

I pause, switch to my glass slippers, and nothing stops me as I move fast toward my final raid.

I know I have made it to Nothril by the wet scent that sinks into the Wood. I step off the Path quickly, so I do not run into the fae warriors who guard it, and head toward the dense, low foliage where Tailor and I always meet.

Thick eyebags hang beneath his spectacles. His shoulders are slightly hunched as he crouches behind the shrubbery. I slide into a crouch beside him and chirp, "Hullo! You look ready for an all-night raid."

He sighs and massages the bridge of his nose. "Princess Pelarusa is a nightmare to work for. I would refuse her if I could."

"I believe you," I reply. "Were you able to get the glamour?"

He fishes a small, translucent vial from his pocket and drops it into my open palms, along with a pocket watch. "It only lasts two hours, but it is a powerful glamour that will disguise you as a fae. It cost me my entire life savings to get my hands on it. Use it wisely. Your name is Ariselle, of Nothnim—one of the Nothril cities. Once you take the glamour, you have two hours to get everyone out. Remember, we have eleven targets tonight. Are you still sure we can get that many?"

My mind immediately returns to the Star City. I grit my teeth. "Yes." I tuck the vial into my breast pocket. "Give me all the information you've got."

Tailor and I work for several hours as the time of the celebration draws near. Between the two of us, we have slipped notes to all our targets except for one. It has gone so well that I am beginning to wonder if I will need the liquid glamour after all.

Until I track down the last person.

Well, save the one I haven't told Tailor about—*Pavi*.

It is the same woman who warned me and Lord Nothril's slave girl, Elizabeth, the last time I was here. She has not been released from Lady Nothril's service the entire time I have been here. I have no idea how I am going to let her know where to meet us.

I move carefully on my glass slippers through the servants' tunnels. I will need to leave and cross the hallway to get to the network of tunnels on the other side. Standing by the door, I peer through the grate, trying to ascertain if the coast is clear. This task proves challenging because silent guards are posted at the most inconvenient locations. I cannot always see them from the grate.

I wait, breathing through my nose as quietly as I can.

Then, a shadow falls across the opulent hallway. It is a shadow I know like my own name.

It is enormous against the pillars of carved ebony, the outline of his wings broad and tucked in close, the hilts of his twin swords rising above his shoulders.

Rahk.

I cover my mouth with my hand and press myself against the cold tunnel wall. Silently, I watch as he comes into view. He wears a long, dark blue tunic of exquisite make, an embroidered sleeveless overcoat that dusts the floor as he walks, and tall boots. Half of his silver hair is pulled back in a gold-banded braid, the rest falling in shining waves down his back. For a moment, I glimpse his sharp profile. He is painfully beautiful, and my eyes ache to look upon him again.

Footsteps behind me nearly send me leaping out of my slippers.

"Excuse me, lass," says an older man, carrying a tray of fragrant winged fish cooked in a purple sauce that brings out the iridescent tones of the scales and wings. The man's accent isn't from Harbright, instead reminding me of Algravia. I flatten myself against the wall and let him pass through the door to deliver his tray.

He's not one of the ones we're rescuing tonight.

How am I supposed to walk away from my unfinished work?

I look through the grate again. There is no sign of Rahk or anyone else. I cannot keep dallying. Guests will arrive soon for the celebration, and then it will be too late.

I dive into the hallway and slip into the opposite servants' tunnel. I shut the door behind me, breathing hard, and glance back through the grate to ensure no one is following me. *Good.*

Then I navigate to Lady Nothril's chamber. I have never come here before, but I've spent enough time scurrying like a rat through these tunnels that there are only a few places it can be. I find it within minutes.

What I find sends my stomach plummeting through the floor.

The peephole into the front of Lady Nothril's chambers reveals over a dozen servants standing at attention. It is a mix of fae and human, so I cannot risk slipping inside. Lady Nothril is not visible, but I can only imagine that she is beyond the grand door at the far side of the room, readying herself for the celebration. The longer I wait, I can hear drifted murmurs from that room that sound like Pavi. I spot my other target practically smack in the middle of all the servants.

She looks even paler than she was last time, the color gone from her cheeks. Her body has lost its softness, becoming gaunt with hard angles of elbows and shoulders. Even her hair has dulled to a gray in this lighting.

There is no way I can reach her here. She does not wear the usual drab gray uniform, but a sleek black dress, and I realize she might be one of those tasked with serving the guests tonight. I bite back my snarled curse.

I cannot reach Pavi either.

My hand goes to the pocket where my glamour rests. There is nothing for me to do except wait for the celebration to start. We cannot, after all, start smuggling slaves out until then for fear of discovery.

I creep away from Lady Nothril's chamber to find a better place to hide until the celebration begins.

I return to the laundry room and slip into the linen closet. I pull the small watch from the tailor out of my pocket and note the time. In that silence, the only sound filling the air is the soft *tick, tick, tick.* I stare at those two little hands on the watch face until, at last, it is time. I stick my hand into my pocket and find my mask missing. *Strange.* I know I brought it with me. Maybe it fell out of my pocket somewhere? Hopefully not where a fae will find it!

I will just have to keep my hood low once the glamour wears off.

I fish further into my pocket, find the vial, and toss its contents down my throat. I check the watch one more time. My two-hour countdown has begun.

I have until midnight. Time to move.

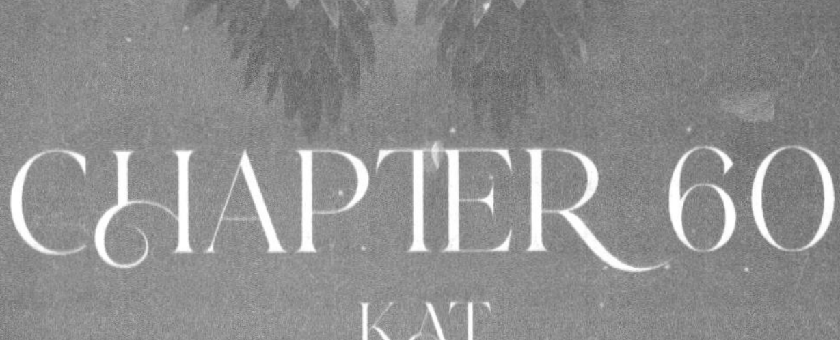

CHAPTER 60

KAT

MY GLAMOUR, AS I discover when I pass a window reflection, is not at all what I expect.

I look like I've been stretched out—I am about six inches taller, and my weight has not shifted to accommodate that. I am as thin as a reed, with arms the size of twigs, and a neck so long that if flexibility allowed, I could tie it in a knot. My gown, if it can even be called that, is a puffy array of gauzy black fabric draped and fastened at my shoulder and my hip, leaving one arm and one leg mostly bare. My glass slippers, thankfully, are hidden by the glamour, so it appears I wear a dainty pair of black vines that curl between my toes and up my ankles.

My face is long and angular, my skin a smooth, pale sheen unmarred by freckles or scars. My eyes are completely unrecognizable as a startling, catlike violet. I touch my hair briefly, which is a sleek, electric blue.

Well, one thing is for certain: there is not a *chance* I will be recognized.

It takes some finagling to unsuspiciously slip into the throng of fae proceeding deeper into the Nothril palace. The ground tilts downward, the cavern swallowing us whole. I try to keep my gaze focused forward to not look at those around me—wearing outfits as wild and black as mine—lest my eyes betray my trepidation. I place each step carefully for fear that my bumbling awkwardness will give me away as not belonging to the majestic, gliding fae surrounding me.

At last, our silent procession reaches a part of the cave that flattens and opens, revealing a great and terrible cavern by the black river. I am pulled along by the currents of the throng toward that river. As I watch, the fae before me kneel beside the water and mix it with soot to paint designs across their faces.

I do the same, stealing a covert glance at the gentle wave most fae draw on their foreheads. I copy them and then, to my relief, the fae begin dispersing across the shoreline. Tables of polished ebony have been erected, laden with abundant arrays of strange, colorful foods and tall glasses of drink.

Low horns blast through the cavern. I whip my head toward the entrance, away from the ripples the sound casts across the water.

The Nothril family has arrived.

Two princesses enter first. One is tall, with dark hair, her mouth twisted at a haughty angle. The other is much younger and shorter, her silver hair a match to Rahk's, her pink cheeks standing out like roses in this cave. Both wear gowns of deep blue—a contrast to all the black of the court. I watch the younger one—Pavi—and desperately wish she would separate herself from the group so I can reach her. She doesn't.

My heart catches when Rahk appears next. He wears a crown of stone, his tall, broad frame filling the entrance of the cavern. His face is carved as though from polished marble. Cold, unreadable, and harsh. It does not look like him at all. Instinctively, I withdraw a step, finding refuge in a slight overhang of stalactites. A drop of water lands on my bare shoulder, making me shiver.

He cannot see you. Remember the glamours you wear.

The low horns blast again.

This time, it is Lord and Lady Nothril who come through the entrance. My mouth goes dry. I thought Rahk was tall—but these two *must* both be over seven feet tall. They wear trailing robes of silver like stars, crowns of obsidian so towering they could brush the ceiling, and their beauty is incomparable.

They glide as one toward two great black thrones on a dais, allowing them full view of the celebration. Everyone falls to their knees as they walk past. I desperately want to keep my spine straight, stupid as it is, but I bow like everyone else.

"Rise." Lady Nothril's voice rings across the throng. "Eat, drink, and see what mysteries Mirror Tide will reveal to you."

That is the signal for the festivities to start. The deathlike silence becomes a steady hum of conversation, laughter, and arguments. The feasting and drinking begin. I pretend to be occupied with a silver goblet of saints-knows-what and hang back in my little nook. Fae pass me. Some give me strange looks, and I give them my best Nothril smirk.

I watch from my spot as Rahk approaches the river. Everyone pulls away, clearing the bank for him. I expect Pelarusa and Pavi to follow him, but they do not. Is it because Rahk is the heir?

He kneels on one knee at the bank. He takes his thumb and swirls it in the dark river before smearing it across his forehead in a fat line that drips onto his brow. Then he moves to the far wall of the celebration, leaning against it, with arms crossed over his chest and one knee bent. I follow his every movement, trying to read his thoughts beneath the coldness of his expression. I find nothing.

Except—the woman I am trying to reach brings a tray of delicacies to him. She keeps her head bowed, her hair bound up in a modest bun. My heart quickens. I must make it over to her. But to approach her is to approach Rahk.

I drag in a deep breath. There's nothing to it. He cannot see through my disguise. And I've got to get word to this woman of the plan.

I set down my goblet and get up. I have no idea if my effort to appear lazy and meandering works, but I manage to dodge the rowdiest groups of fae and make it to the servant's vicinity. Which is also Rahk's vicinity.

I sit down nearby and wait, counting the seconds. Then I lift my hand and say imperiously, "Slave! Give me one of those things immediately!"

She comes. Her head remains bowed, her eyes on the ground. She offers me the tray.

I sniff. "You think I shall sully my fingers to pick it up myself? Put it on the table for me."

She doesn't say a word, but hurries to obey. When she bends over to place the small flute of liquid beside me, I drop my voice to the barest whisper to avoid being overheard: "Get out of the palace as soon as you can. I'm freeing you tonight."

She looks up, her eyes meeting mine for the first time. Something swims inside those irises—*fear.* I offer the only encouragement I can: the tiniest of smiles.

She leaves.

A hush falls upon the gathering. Lord and Lady Nothril have risen from their thrones, and now stride down to the river's edge. She carries a large, shallow basin and stands on the bank. He swirls his fingers above the surface of the water before lifting them slowly. I watch in amazement as the water follows his fingers in a stream. He guides it into the basin and then releases it back into the river with a splash.

Lady Nothril lifts the full basin above her head. She closes her eyes, leaning back her head so her long, dark neck is exposed. She releases a string of incantations from full lips.

The contents of the basin begin to glow.

I should not be so enraptured, but I cannot tear my attention away as she lowers the bowl. The glow dissipates slowly. She carries the basin to a short, carved pillar. Then, as I watch, a black curtain seems to appear out of nowhere, surrounding the pillar and the bowl.

"See what mysteries of Mirror Tide reveal themselves to you," calls Lady Nothril. Her voice echoes through the cavern. "If you possess the courage to do so."

Immediately, several fae surge forward. The one who touches the curtain first steps inside, while the others draw back. He is gone for several minutes before he emerges again, his lips parted, a dazed look in his eye. The second goes after him.

My curiosity piqued, I sneak a glance at my pocket watch. I've got some time to spare. My target has already left the celebration, leaving only Pavi to contact. She gives no sign of leaving her mother's side, so I need to kill what time I have left in hopes she will move.

I've got time to look into that pool.

I wait a few minutes, not wanting to be one of the first to go, but the watch ticking in my pocket propels me forward faster than I am comfortable. I try not to seem hesitant as I approach the black veil.

The cloth itself feels as fine as dust as I move it aside.

The bowl itself is smooth black, the water crystal clear with no sign of the earlier glow. I stare down into it, canting my head to one side when nothing appears but the reflection of my own glamoured face.

Cautiously, I reach out and dip one finger in the water. Ripples fan out in every direction.

Light flares.

I wince against the brightness as the scene clarifies. It is a family sitting around a humble fireplace. A mother with her three children. I don't recognize any of them. Confused, I peer closer. The soothing timbre of the mother and the mischievous giggles of the young echo to meet me. Then a new figure enters the picture. A man in his thirties or forties. Something about him seems familiar though I cannot place him.

"Tell us again, Pa!" the children cry. The accents are from Aursailles. "Tell us the story of how you were saved from Faerieland!"

I go still with shock.

The father laughs, sitting down on the floor as his children begin climbing all over him. He looks very different from when I last saw him years ago, but now I can picture a young man from one of my first raids. "Again? I must have told you a hundred times!"

"Please!" the children cry at once.

The father lets out a sigh, a tiny grin breaking through his attempt at a serious face. "*Fine*. Go get your masks!"

Squeals erupt from the children, who rush out of the picture, only to return a moment later with little masks just like my own affixed to their tiny faces.

"Once upon a time, in a land far, far away," begins the father, just as the picture shifts. The next image is of a young woman with her hair pulled back, hard at work in a kitchen, offering a shy smile to a red-eared manservant as he balances a basket of potatoes on his shoulder. *Elizabeth*—the girl from my last Nothril raid. The image shifts to an elderly couple drinking tea on their front porch and watching the sunset. A couple I rescued from the Ildreer Court. It melts once more into a woman I recognize at once: the woman I left behind at the Star City. She bends over cloth, a needle in her hand, in what appears to be a very human shop.

"She got out?" I whisper, not believing my eyes. "How?"

The image changes to that very night, and I see the frightened woman on the edge of the Wood. I am not expecting to see Rahk there—holding out a glowing stone to the woman and pointing toward the Path.

He got her out.

For all that he is hunting me and trying to put an end to my work, *he cares too.* He always has. My chest nearly caves in.

The images keep moving, flipping through dozens upon dozens of human faces, in their own human world, living their lives, working, falling in love, raising families, making homes and beautiful things with their free hands, unbound by slavery. *Living.*

Because I got them out.

It's too overwhelming. I cover my mouth with my hand, my shoulders shaking with the tears I dare not cry. I blink furiously, not wanting to miss a single face, but it goes on and on, and every time I think we must have reached the end, it keeps going.

So many people.

I never kept count. I've always hoped they recovered from what they had been through, but I never had a way to find out where they are or how they are doing. I've always focused my attention on the next raid and the next and next.

I never stopped to look back at all the work I've accomplished.

I grip the edges of the bowl. This is my last raid. My last time to ever be in Faerieland. For the first time, that idea doesn't feel entirely wrong. I'm just one person—there's no way I can get *every single human* out of a world as vast and varied as Faerieland. But maybe, just maybe, the work I've done can be enough. Maybe these people, who now have their lives restored, are enough.

My sorrow and my death will give these people life.

The pool goes black.

I stay where I am, clinging to the edges of the bowl, my elbows stiff.

Then I remember that there are still more people. These last eleven. *I must finish this.*

I sweep aside the gauzy black veil to find Rahk waiting just outside.

His black eyes fall straight to me. I go stiff with fright. *He cannot see who you are,* I remind myself. I've got to act like a fae. And yet, how desperately I long to greet him as a friend. As far, far more than a friend.

Act like a fae.

I smile at him, giving him a pointed once-over and biting my lip as I wink. It makes my stomach curl, but he *is* my husband.

His gaze has already passed over me, focusing on his destination—*the pool.*

I should let him go. I've wasted enough time as it is.

But when he moves to walk past me, his scent wafts over me. Clear night skies and wind. It takes me back to what it felt like to be wrapped up in his strong embrace, to lose my head every time he kissed me. It takes me back to what it felt like to receive his many gifts, to be rewarded by his laughter when I said foolish things. He doesn't look like he has ever laughed, but I know better.

The letter he left me wasn't enough. Not *nearly* enough. This is the last time I'll ever see him. I cannot just let him go.

"I heard you've been to the human lands," I say, ignoring my better judgment.

He stops briefly but doesn't even look at me. "I have."

"What kingdom did you visit?"

The only show of his surprise is the flick of his gaze to mine. *Finally, he looks at me.*

"Are you familiar with the human kingdoms on the edge of Caphryl Wood?" he asks, almost suspiciously. And he's right to be suspicious—I would imagine that fae think of the human world much as the humans view the fae's: all one people, in one homogenous kingdom, speaking the same language, ruled by one king. Most fae wouldn't know to ask such a clarifying question.

"I collect tales of the humans in my spare time," I reply. "Once, I had the privilege of visiting. I miss it dearly."

His interest is immediately captured. "You've been to the human world? I have been both to Aursailles and Harbright, but I've spent more time in the latter."

"Truly?" I say brightly, drawing upon the persona I reserve for playing the noblewoman to give a pleased laugh. "Harbright was where I visited! It was ages ago, but the memories are so clear I think of it as yesterday."

"The smells too, I imagine," Rahk says, with just a tinge of that twinkle returning to his eye.

"The smells too!" I agree, hoping my enthusiasm covers my lack of experiential understanding. "The food was appalling."

Rahk smiles at that, and triumph thrills in my belly. "I found it to be unexpectedly pleasing, but I have never been particular about food."

"The white liquid drink was the most egregious crime."

"Milk?" His smile widens. "If the food was so appalling, what do you miss about the human lands?"

We've stepped aside from the veil, and someone slips past us to see what awaits them in the mirror's reflection.

"The scenery, for one. There is something beautiful in its simplicity."

Rahk nods in agreement.

"For another, those four-legged creatures that everyone rides or pulls their wheeled boxes on, with the long tails. Those creatures were beautiful."

That earns me a proper laugh. The sound draws the weighty gazes of Lord and Lady Nothril, and I try to shift slightly behind Rahk so they cannot look at me too closely. Rahk notices the dark and curious glares at once and steps into a secluded spot shielded by the arrangement of the cavern walls. I follow him, taking care not to trip and fall into the river from the force of my pounding heart.

"But mostly," I continue, before he can remember his duty and leave me, "I miss the stories the people would tell. Their lives are so short, and yet there is something so raw and real about their flaws, their death, their love. It captivates me."

Rahk's gaze shutters slightly. I can feel him drawing away from me, but not because I've bored him. Because I've brought to mind things he wishes to forget.

It hurts far more than I thought it would—to see him trying so hard to forget me. To see him withdrawing from anything that might make him think of me.

I cannot let him leave me on this note. Even though my heart cracks anew, as though freshly broken, I force a smile onto my face and ask, "What about you? Do you ever think of your time in the human worlds?"

He looks out across the dark river. He is silent for so long, I'd fear he wasn't going to respond at all—except I know him too well for that.

"Not a moment goes by that I do not think of the human realms." His voice is low, and far more honest than I would have expected. "Or what I left there."

The declaration makes my knees shake. I struggle to find my voice amid the rush of blood in my ears. "Someone? Or one of the box-on-wheels creatures?"

He doesn't smile at my joke, nor does he answer my question.

"Ah," I say with a little chuckle. "I see."

His eyes meet mine in question for a split second, before they shut in defense. "I doubt you do. Now, if you'll excuse me—"

No. I cannot let him go.

Will I ever be ready to let him go? No. But I need just one more moment.

"Did you bond with her then?" I ask quickly before he leaves.

His reply is gruff. "Of course not."

"But you loved her."

The muscles of his throat constrict as he takes one step away, putting distance between us. Then his attention returns to me. "What did you say your name was?"

The request is so abrupt that my mind momentarily goes blank. What did Tailor say my false name was? Why can I not remember it? *Ariselle.* Right. "Ariselle. Of Nothnim."

Rahk's black eyes dilate. He steps toward me, and when he gets very close, I retreat by instinct. He cannot see through my glamour—I still have time before it fails.

"That is an interesting trick you've just accomplished," Rahk says coolly, cornering me against the rocky wall of the cavern. His entire demeanor has changed in one instant. The face I look upon is cold, mixed with a strange sort of delight—that of a cat cornering a mouse.

"Prince Rahk," I say uneasily, telling myself repeatedly there is no way he could have seen past my glamour, "this is quite forward of you. We've only known each other for minutes."

I catch my mistake before the words have even finished leaving my mouth.

The next instant, a thin dagger is in Rahk's hand, the tip pressed against my throat. I go still.

"What a very human thing to say," he says, his eyes gleaming like I have never seen before. "Right after you tell a lie with no scent. *Ivy Mask.*"

I have played with fire. Now it is time to be devoured by it. I always knew it would come to this.

No, I growl inside my own head. *You do not give up.*

"Ooh, I like this," I laugh, reaching up to touch the tip of the blade. It's so sharp I barely feel the prick before I start bleeding. "Is this part of your wooing, Prince Rahk? If so, consider me *captivated.*"

His eyes seem to pierce into my soul, as though to strip the truth from the lies, trying to understand how I can be a human and yet wear glamours without a fae to maintain them.

I stand on my tiptoes, leaning into the dagger and embracing its sting. He reacts at once, lightening the pressure on the blade to not cut me too deeply. Because he wants me alive? Or because he is no longer sure?

My heart rages in my chest. He knows I am not a fae, which leads to the only assumption that I am the Ivy Mask—but he has been convinced that Kat is not the Ivy Mask. This leaves me with only one option.

An option that might be just as condemning as it could be convincing.

I dart forward and kiss him before he has time to guess what I'm about to do. It's a short kiss, because he pulls away immediately. But that contact is enough. Even glamoured, our lips know each other.

His eyes go wide as moons, a storm of horror overtaking the brief flash of delight. He grabs me by the shoulders, his grip almost painful. "Kat? What are you *doing* here? What—what is this glamour? Great Kings, how did you get here? Tell me what is happening! You're in grave danger!"

He instinctively takes up a protective stance, moving his body between me and the path that leads to the rest of the party.

It hits me then. He doesn't *want* me to be the Ivy Mask, so if I give him enough of a reason, enough excuse, he will believe me. Because he is too afraid of what it would mean if I am the person he hunts.

The Starborn Prince claimed I must be especially clever to evade a hunter as skilled as Rahk. That is hardly true. My cleverness only took me so far—his own willful refusal to see the truth has done the rest.

The lies spew out of my mouth, giving him that excuse, desperately trying to save the lives of the people I'm supposed to be getting out of here right now. I coat the lies with so much frantic truth that maybe, just maybe, the saints will forgive me. "I came to tell you that I love you. I just had to see you one more time. I had to tell you that I made a mistake. Please come back home, Rahk. Please be my husband again."

Hope flares across his handsome features. It quickly vanishes. He tightens his grip on my shoulders, his attention shooting to the celebration behind us every few seconds. His voice is laced with panic. "Where did you get this glamour? Tell me right now."

"I made a bargain with a fae, and he gave me this glamour—"

He spits a vile curse. His fingers dig into my collarbones as he brings his face close to mine. "What fae? What bargain? Tell me the exact wording of this bargain." When I hesitate, he snaps, "At once!"

"I—I don't know!" His panic is contagious. I check my pocket watch only to realize I have a measly *twenty minutes* before my glamour vanishes. How is that possible? I have only been here for half an hour at most! I need to get out of this celebration. Now. "It was just some creature I'd never seen before. He said he would take me to you and disguise me so I could see you."

"What did he want in exchange?" Rahk demands. "Tell me the exact words."

"He wanted me to lead the captives out of Nothril and into the human world, but he didn't say which ones. I figured he'd bring them to me or something when it was time to leave. Do you know what he was talking about?"

Can I fool him into thinking my life will only be spared if I get the captives out? Will he help me then?

Rahk's face twists in perplexity. "What would he get if you didn't fulfill this?"

I swallow. "My life."

"Katherine!" Rahk covers his face with his hands, releasing me. "You must remember the wording!"

"I just wanted to see you again."

"I wanted to see you too!" he snaps, rounding on me. "But I want you to be *alive,* you foolish girl! Tell me the wording of the bargain!"

I flinch at his tone, and it's entirely genuine. "I have to get out of this ball, Rahk, before my glamour vanishes."

"How long until it vanishes?"

"Eighteen minutes."

Rahk lets out a wordless growl of frustration. "Why didn't you say that at the beginning? I cannot believe someone as clever as you would do something as tremendously *stupid* as this is! Especially after your mother!"

I flinch again.

He gentles his tone very slightly. "Listen, this is what we're going to do. You are going to leave first. I will trail behind you. You are to go to the table of refreshments and pick up a drink—but don't you *dare* drink it—then you will slip out of the celebration. I will follow you and make sure you get out. Then we are going straight to my rooms to discuss how to fix this mess."

He places his hand on my low back and pushes me ahead of him down the path. Right before I step back around the bend, he leans down to my ear and whispers, "Pretend like you thought you were going to get a tryst and are disappointed after getting rebuffed."

"That won't be difficult," I reply darkly.

As I step into the throng again, my mind spins with how I'm going to get out of this one. I *knew better* than this. My own stupid heart might not just cost me my own life, but the lives of the people I'm trying to free.

If I cannot get them out of here, I will never forgive myself.

I give one last glance toward Pavi, who sits silently near her mother. I cannot get her out.

CHAPTER 61

RAHK

I HAVE ALWAYS known Kat to be impulsive, charmingly ridiculous, and inclined to act far less intelligent than she actually is, paired with a propensity toward trouble. But this is rashness, carelessness, and sheer *stupidity* that I cannot fathom her to be capable of.

Even as I watch her move through the mass of partygoers with movements that are undeniably Kat's, despite the strange glamours she wears, I stare in disbelief.

I'm furious with her. For risking her life, for saying the things I've dreamed of her saying at a time like this, for coming to Faerieland—which in and of itself is violation of the treaty between our peoples. She will end up enslaved by my parents. She's young and beautiful enough that Lord Nothril might decide she will be his next plaything. And for me to have to sit here, to have to be silent, because Pavi's life hangs in the balance, and watch as someone abuses my wife?

My hands shake. My heart feels like it is shaking inside my chest, ready to rupture at any moment.

"Infuriating females instead of doing what you came to do?"

The icy tickle of Lord Nothril's voice cuts through the roar of blood in my veins. Like a vault being locked, I bury everything inside me and pull my expression under my control. Lord Nothril wears floor-length robes of midnight blue, his skin almost translucent, his eyes twin daggers piercing into me.

"I am working," I reply coolly. "She had information for me. She tried to get a kiss in return for it—that's why she's frustrated. Someone associated with the Ivy Mask tried to get her to help him. She was smart to come to me with it."

"Take her to the dungeon and start removing her skin. That'll get any last pieces of information out of her."

He suggests it so casually, it almost destroys my composure. Thankfully, I have years of experience of hiding my true feelings. "Where else do you think I'm going?"

"Your means do not matter to me," Lord Nothril replies coldly. "So long as they produce results."

The cold lines of his threat hang in the air.

"You will have your criminal as sworn," I reply.

With a swish of his robes, he leaves me. I look up—and there is the tall, willowy, blue-haired Kat, keeping her stance steady as Lady Nothril towers over her, blocking her exit. I curse inwardly. How many minutes do we have left?

Of all the realizations to have right now, the wild and ridiculous one that climbs to the forefront of my awareness is that my wife is meeting her mother-in-law.

Kat starts to curtsy, then seems to realize that is a human thing, and tries to smoothly shift into a bow as she says, "Your Imperial Transcendence."

I could cover my face and groan.

"I do not remember seeing you before," Lady Nothril says in a disinterested croon.

Kat bows again. "It is my first time to this great palace for Mirror Tide, O Great One."

"Lady Nothril," I say, cutting in with a bow. I keep my attention fixed just beyond my mother and refuse to give Kat a single glance. "Ariselle has chanced upon information about the Ivy Mask. I am taking her to aid my investigation immediately. I anticipate the criminal being in your hands in a matter of hours, if less."

Lady Nothril is not fooled that I try to distract her from Kat. She runs her gaze in a sort of disinterested curiosity over my wife. Then she glides away, leaving me to stride quickly toward the door and Kat to race after me.

The moment we are out of the cavern and into the main hallway, I grab her forearm to keep her from vanishing and march toward my quarters. I try not to look at her even though we are alone. I still cannot *fathom* what would possess her to risk her life—and mine, and Pavi's!—to pull a stunt like this. She is many things, but plain *stupid* is not one of them.

I reach my quarters, unlock the door, and drag Kat inside before slamming the door behind us and renewing the lock. I turn on her just as her glamour melts away, leaving Kat as I remember her—and wearing trousers, a buttoned shirt, with her mother's glass slippers.

I stare down at her in bewilderment. What is she wearing? I shake my head. There will be time for questions later. "Tell me the wording of that bargain."

A loud cry from outside my quarters has me reacting—whirling toward the door and drawing one of my swords. Through the thick door, the repeated cry goes up.

"We've found the Ivy Mask!"

My eyes go wide. There are too many things happening at once. I must go investigate at once . . . but *Kat*.

I spin back toward her. She has gone pale and stares with parted lips at the door. Does she realize what I have been trying to do? Surely she pieced it together after hearing what I said to Lady Nothril.

I grab her by the shoulders. "Hide here until I get back. Whatever you do, don't leave this room. There is something urgent I must deal with. Then I will return, and we'll find a way to get you out of this mess."

The impulse to pull her into my arms, to press a kiss to the top of her head, nearly overwhelms me. But I cannot risk her human scent being detected by Lord and Lady Northril, and I cannot trust myself to glamour it right now.

I sheathe my sword, lock my door with Kat behind it, praying desperately that she will not become a casualty of this horrible night. Then I break into a run, following the sound of shouting, until I come upon the scene.

Two Nothril guards have a man on his knees, his face concealed by an ivy mask. His wrists are chained behind him, one of the guard's long blades resting against his neck.

"Prince Rahk!" cries one of the guards. "Is this not your quarry?"

I crouch before the man and rip his mask off. Beneath are a pair of round spectacles. He wears suspenders over a crisp white shirt. His expression is usually so blank, so focused, that to see him staring at me with some potent emotion in his gaze is startling. *The human tailor of Valehaven.*

This is not the Ivy Mask.

He's the distraction while the true Ivy Mask gets away with the Nothril captives. "Put him in the dungeon. I'll deal with him later," I order to the guards, shoving the mask into my pocket and getting to my feet.

I return at once to my quarters, shutting the doors behind me. "Kat, I need you to tell me the wording of that bargain and as best of a description of the fae that—"

The chambers are empty. Traces of her scent lingers, but not enough to indicate her presence.

"Kat!" I rush from room to room, but there is no sign of her. I grab the back of my neck, barely restraining my roar of her name. Did she leave? Or did someone take her?

There's no second scent. No sign of struggle.

I follow her scent to the servants' entrance. At once, my memory flashes back to the slave girl who I found crawling under my bed. I fling open the door. The damp chill carries the decaying scent of humanity.

There, halfway down what is visible of the tunnel, is a single glass slipper.

I shut my eyes, and it is like my entire life collapses on itself.

Because I finally see what has been staring at me for far too long.

I turn toward my weapon rack and grimly exchange my swords for a bow and a quiver of arrows. Then I duck my head and step into the tunnel. A few strides, and I've scooped up Kat's slipper. I bring it to my nose.

Glass does not hold scent well. But there is just enough still lingering that I pick up my trail.

I let out a deep exhale. I hope to the stars that I am wrong. "You'd better run fast, wife."

CHAPTER 62

KAT

"THEY TOOK THE tailor?" I demand. I whirl on my heel, looking back toward the Nothril palace I just escaped from. When someone shouted that they'd caught the Ivy Mask, I did not know what they could have meant. But now, as I check my pockets a third time for my mask, it hits me. Tailor slipped my mask from me when he gave me the glamour. Did he intend to get caught? All the slaves are here, waiting to flee. I want to go back, to try to save the tailor, but to do so would be to risk these people.

"If they put him in the dungeon, there is no getting him out," says one of the men. "We've got to leave, or we'll all be killed."

With a growl on my lips, I launch onto the Path. "Follow me very closely so you don't step off the Path!"

We start off at a fast pace. I wish we could sprint, but I cannot ask that of the entire group. The woman who was serving at Mirror Tide follows close at my heels. She speaks for the first time: "The Path is the glowing yellow thing we are on?"

My head whips to her. "You can see it?"

She nods hesitantly. In all my time, I've never had anyone who could see the Paths. I cannot see them well myself.

My mind starts working, turning over this development as we move fast. What if . . .?

This is my last raid. Rahk will pursue the moment he finds me gone from his chamber. There is only one thing I need to do left in my life, and that is get these eleven people out of Faerie.

I have the prickling sense that if I don't peel off from the group, we'll all be cornered.

I stop abruptly and point to the woman whose name I never learned. "Follow her on the Path until you reach the edge of Faerie. Nothing can hurt you so long as you stay on the Path. You will end up in a valley. If you cut across it and keep going, you will reach a city. In the city, there is a large cathedral. You cannot miss it. Someone is there with provisions for your journey. Now hurry!"

The woman grabs my elbow. "Why aren't you coming with us?"

"We don't have time. Go!"

The woman holds my gaze. Others have made to continue, but she delays.

"Go! The only thing you can do to help me is to *go!*"

At last, she goes. I watch as they leave, vanishing deeper into the Wood until, at last, it swallows them whole. I've got to lead Rahk away from them. I have no other option.

I've got to leave this Path and plunge into the Wood.

I lost one slipper at some point. I rip off the other one, kiss it with a quick, "Love you, Mama," and then place it off the Path—close enough that he'll see it, but far enough for him to know it's not a red herring. I'm truly diving into the wild fae Wood like a madwoman.

Then I take off running.

Immediately, the voices assault me.

"I know. I know it all."

"You poor dear—come to my warm embrace and sleep tenderly."

And then the one that has haunted me for years curls around my head, *"I know what you did, Katherine Vandermore. It catches up to you this day. You know it will."*

These voices never could truly touch me on the Path, but now they are like ice cold fingers clutching my heart. They pull at me like ropes tied to my limbs, and when my focus breaks, my feet actually turn toward them. I gasp and rip myself away.

They are going to catch me. They are all going to catch me.

I don't even know who *they* are, but I run faster. Sometimes the ground is a soft bed of pine needles beneath my bare feet, and other times it turns rocky and sends pains flaring up my legs.

I do not stop.

The half-light of the Wood swirls around me, the towering trees in every direction like prison bars. Slowly, I become aware of my shadow running alongside me. When I look at it, casting long across the ground, it waves back at me.

You know the Wood makes people go mad, I instruct myself sternly. *Don't fall for its tricks. You just have to—*

I come to a sudden stop. I look around.

What am I doing here? Where even am I?

The words spill out of my lips as alarm burns through my entire body. "Why am I here? I was doing something. Why—why am I here? Why am I here?"

I clutch my hair, my fingernails digging into my scalp. I came here for a reason. I know I did. But every time I reach out for that place in my mind, the place that knows, my fingers touch emptiness.

Something warm touches my ankle. I look down to find a vine twisted around my bare skin. My scream is locked too far behind my fright to be accessed. I try to yank my foot free, but instead the vine pulls hard. My back hits the ground with a force to knock the wind from me. It drags me toward a tree that suddenly *moves.* It cranes toward me, its massive trunk bending down as though to observe me as I wriggle and kick at the grip it has on me.

Branches come down. They touch my hair, run down my arm, fiddle with the collar of my shirt. The trunk of the tree morphs, until its bark arranges into a wide smile.

I finally scream.

The tree reels back as though I've struck it. It releases my leg. I leap to my feet, nearly falling in my haste, and sprint away. My shadow runs beside me. It points in one direction. I plunge the opposite way.

A living creature appears before me.

I come to a halt. It is a deer—an actual deer. Like those we have in the human lands. It grazes on a single patch of grass. I cover my mouth. I never thought the sight of a deer could bring so much relief. I step toward it, though I know not if I intend to touch it or just be closer to this piece of home. To my surprise, a bird appears in the air. A bluejay.

It is frozen midflight.

I glance back to the deer. Coldness washes over me. The deer isn't moving either.

I become aware of my own slowing heartbeat.

It's a trap.

I stumble backward, away from the frozen animals. I pick a random direction and burst into another run.

Then, abruptly, an oak appears in my vision.

I do not know why I am here or what I am doing, but I remember one certain truth: oaks are friendly to humans.

I collapse beneath it beside a clear stream I dare not drink from.

I pant hard, pressing my palm to my heaving chest.

There are two things that can happen now. I will wander for the rest of my life in this Wood, until I am driven mad, devoured by evil forces, or caught and enslaved by a fae. *Or* Rahk will find me and kill me.

The latter sounds far better, but I cannot give up too quickly. I have to give those people time to escape the forest.

I've got to give Rahk a good chase.

I remembered.

It hits me with the force of a thunderclap. I *remembered.* I know why I am here. I came here. To lead Rahk away from the people I am trying to rescue.

I notice the mud next to the stream. My mind returns to the story at the beginning of my Fool's Circle strategy book. I set to work grabbing handfuls of mud. Small grabby hands stick out of the pool, reaching for me. I move quickly to keep them from latching on. Then I smear the mud over my body and bare feet.

I get up, ready to pick a random direction and plunge deeper into the insanity.

But just then, a voice booms from behind me: "Stop where you are!"

I freeze. My hood is pulled low. *How* did he track me? Did I leave footprints behind?

Slowly, I peer over my shoulder beneath the shadow of my hood. Rahk stands a stone's throw away, an arrow notched in the bow he holds, pulled taut and ready to pierce my heart.

"Don't move," Rahk orders, as he begins approaching me.

He must know it's me. Running away after he explicitly told me to stay had to be condemning enough. So if he knows it's me, he won't shoot.

I burst into a sprint.

"Stop!" roars Rahk.

Absolutely not.

I slam my arm on some obstacle I didn't see. The pressure builds, yet I keep running.

I don't know if it is the mud, or the twining madness of the Wood, but eventually I look back. There is no sign of Rahk. I have no breath to spare for a sigh. I press my hand against a tree trunk. The second I do, I remember not to trust trees here. I yank my hand away. A piece of bark falls off.

The tree screams.

I cover my ears and burst into another run. Finally, when I am certain I am going to collapse, I find another oak tree.

Or is it the same one?

A clear pool lies just beside it with a muddy bank. There is no sign of me scraping mud away from it. I stare at the place suspiciously. Then, exhausted, I give up. I drop between the safe roots of the enormous tree.

I look down. The blood drains from my entire body.

A sharp stick has pierced straight into my left arm. At first, I think it is one of Rahk's arrows, but when I inspect it, there is no way it was an arrow. It is rough, crooked, and it has not cut all the way through my flesh. It must have just been a sharp branch I ran into while sprinting.

Blood drips down my muddy arm.

I stare at it, too shocked to fully comprehend what I am seeing.

I lean back against oak and let my eyes glaze as the pain roars to life.

I regard the throbbing injury again. At the thought of trying to pull the branch through my arm, I shudder. There's no way I'm getting it out—and that's probably for the best. I don't have anything to staunch the blood flow, and if the branch remains in place, I won't lose too much blood.

The pain seems to double, even triple, by the moment. It radiates down into my fingertips and up into my shoulder. I can barely move my arm without shooting pain.

"Curse you, stupid tree," I grit out between my clenched teeth.

My mouth is dry as sand. My limbs quake from hunger and the hours of endless exertion. I stare at the pool. It seems to call me, pulling—pulling—pulling—

I drag myself back just before I plunge face first into the water.

I turn my head into the oak tree, squeezing my eyes shut. I cannot be trusted to even *look* at that water. Who knows what dangers the water holds? Creatures could be lying in its depths, ready to drag me to my death. Or the water could be poisoned, or bring on endless sleep.

I don't know what to do. How much time has passed? Minutes, hours? Or years?

Maybe I've lost Rahk. Maybe he won't find me after all. I'll just die in this cursed Wood, slowly bleeding out from my wound. I get up, determined to leave behind this pool that calls to me even when I refuse to look at it. I stumble, and when I catch myself against the oak, agony nearly rips a scream from my throat. I stop where I am, breathing hard, my hood fallen low, my vision blurring in and out of focus.

Got to keep going. Got to keep going. Got to—

"Ivy Mask!"

My stomach pitches. He's found me.

I will my legs to run. I will every muscle in my body to propel me forward. But I don't move. Sinking dread fills me as the world swims around me. There's nothing left inside of me. Nothing left to give.

So this is the end.

No.

I can keep running. The longer I run, the higher the likelihood that those people will be free. I must keep running. I must—

I stop myself.

Rahk got that Star City woman out of Faerie. Rahk loves me. He would never hurt me, even if his life depended on it.

I need to stop hiding from him. I need to stop lying to him.

I need to, for once, truly trust him. With everything. With my life. With the lives of the people I have tried to save. I need to trust the Prince of Nothril.

It is time to stop running. From Rahk, from Agatha, from the fae, from what happened all those years ago. I'm *tired* of running.

I step out from behind the tree.

Sunlight cuts through the fog in the forest, illuminating the blanket of pine needles. And Rahk.

He stands with his legs braced wide, his arrow nocked in his bow, pointing it at my chest as he demands: "Take off your hood. Now!"

I'm already doing it. I almost smile. He still does not want to believe it's me. My wounded arm hangs limply at my side, my other shaking as I peel back the hood. I whisper, "It's me, Rahk."

Then there is nothing. No hoods, or masks, or cloaks, or lies. It is just me. It is just him.

His eyes meet mine and his whole body goes slack. I watch the hope vanish from his face. His voice comes out in a dreadful groan as he drops his bow and sinks to his knees. “Kat.”

CHAPTER 63

RAHK

I STUMBLE TO the back door of my human estate, holding an unconscious and injured Kat against my chest, and kick at the door. "Edvear!"

Edvear opens the door. "Master! I thought you weren't coming ba—" He stops, his mouth open mid-word as his yellow eyes fall to Kat's limp, filthy form.

"Send for a doctor, immediately!" I shove past him, careful not to jostle Kat's wound.

Mary appears in the hallway. Both of her hands go to her mouth, her eyes filling with tears. "Is she alive? Oh, I have been so worried! It's been *weeks* and I thought for certain she was dead! I came here out of desperation to see if—"

"Weeks?" I demand, dread coming over me. Caphryl morphs time as it pleases. I thought I'd ensured that we wouldn't be spit out far away from our timeline.

Mary's face is hollow. "She has been gone for fifteen days."

I whirl on Edvear. "How long ago did I leave?"

"A little over three weeks ago, my lord."

I curse. Then I whirl on Mary, fixing her with a black glare. "You knew everything."

She pales and doesn't reply.

My fury threatens to overcome my control. I move past Mary, heading to the room we once called ours.

"My lord!" says Edvear at my heels. "I must tell you—"

"Is that Kat?" a woman's voice calls from the parlor. "I have been *waiting* for hours now! I will not leave until I speak with her!"

My mind trips over itself. Lady Duxbury Vandermore is here? Why in all the—

"Kat will not speak to you!" returns an impassioned young man's voice. "You know you were cruel to her all those years and if she refuses to see you now, it is because you made yourself odious to her!"

Lord Oliver.

"My lord!" cries Edvear again as I barrel past the parlor, ignoring both uninvited guests. Kat is in a bad state, and I need to get to her at once.

I kick open the door to the bedroom. And immediately freeze.

Pelarusa lounges across my bed, her long hair splayed across my pillow, her gown draped over the covers. She sits up at the sight of me. "Great Kings, finally! I have been waiting here since dawn for you, and it has been an agony unlike anything else I've experienced. I can hardly *breathe* and my glamours are giving me a violent headache! Your incompetence is a cruelty! Wait, what is that?"

This situation gets worse by the moment. I am going to strangle every person in this house. I clench my jaw hard and stride past Pelarusa, heading toward the bathing chamber. I'll deal with my sister later.

"Rahk! What is that? Don't tell me *that* is the Ivy Mask!"

I use my toe to pry open the door and fling it wide. Mary is there a moment later, ladened with two full buckets of water. She dumps them in the tub.

"Is that the Ivy Mask?" Pelarusa's voice reaches a shrill note.

"Yes!" I snap, baring my teeth at her as I carefully place Kat on the floor, leaning her against the wall. "This is the Ivy Mask. Now leave!"

She draws back. "Don't tell me she's your mistress."

Edvear comes with another two buckets of water, followed by Charity. It's enough to fill the tub. Edvear takes Charity's empty buckets from her, and something about the way he gently touches her shoulder at a time like this rankles my ire. I dismiss everyone but Mary and throw a quick ward over the room so Pelarusa cannot barge in. Then I plunge one hand into the cold bath water, murmuring a spell under my lips. The water temperature rises, until it is warm.

"Did you do this?" Mary snarls at me, crouching over Kat like a mama bear protecting her cub.

I hold her gaze until she looks away. She should know that I would never hurt Kat.

She undoes the ties of Kat's filthy cloak. "You've got to protect her. She's your wife! You love her!"

"What I do with a criminal," I reply, "is none of your business."

Mary glares at me so furiously, I could expect her red hair to catch fire. "What you do with *my sister* is every inch my business."

I don't have the patience to deal with this. I get to my feet and point to the door. "Do you want to leave and let me tend Kat by myself?"

She shakes her head.

"Then work in silence."

She bites her tongue, but she isn't happy about it—and I don't care. I lift Kat and carefully place her into the bathtub. Mary spreads a large towel across the top and begins the slow process of wriggling off her clothes. The shirt we have to cut off to avoid jostling the wound. Mary and I work in silence, me keeping Kat upright with one hand while gripping just above her wound with the other, Mary scrubbing the mud from her skin.

We get her wrapped in a clean robe just as Edvear knocks, announcing the doctor's arrival. I don't trust my own wound tending skills at a moment like this. When I carry Kat back into the bedroom, Pelarusa is still there.

"Out!" I jerk my head toward the door. "We will discuss this in a few minutes."

She rolls her eyes and groans. "Why couldn't I have been the firstborn?"

"Pelarusa," I hiss.

With a huff, she storms out of the room. I lay Kat down on the bed, tilting her arm so the branch lies parallel to the bed instead of at an angle. The doctor comes to her side.

"What happened?" the doctor demands.

"That doesn't matter," I growl. "Just fix this. Mary, stay with her. Send for me if I'm needed."

She takes up residence beside Kat, holding her good hand while the doctor begins cleaning around the wound. I march out of the room and shut the door.

Pelarusa is waiting right outside, her arms crossed over her chest. "Why did you bring her back here? You should have taken her directly to Lord and Lady Nothril!"

"She was half dead," I reply coldly. "She wouldn't have survived until judgment."

"I don't *care* about judgment!" Pelarusa snaps back. "I care about not feeling like I'm constantly choking in this air! If you'd taken her directly there, I wouldn't have had to come."

I walk past her, not even realizing where I'm going until I end up in the parlor. Lord Oliver and Lady Duxbury Vandermore both shove to their feet. I immediately slam the door in their faces and march to the nearest unoccupied room. I pull a bench over to the empty fireplace and drop into it. "Well, that would have been a mercy for both of us, wouldn't it?"

Pelarusa crosses her arms over her chest. "I can't go back without her."

"You won't," I say dully. "We will move the Ivy Mask once she is well enough to be moved."

"Don't you *dare* try to find a way to get her free of justice! You know Pavi's life is on the line."

My fingers curl around the edge of the bench. "I will not allow Pavi to die. Tell Edvear you want a more comfortable room. He'll get you whatever you need."

"You have been insufferable ever since you received this post!" She slams the door behind her.

I listen to her footsteps as she leaves. Then, as the silence swarms and surrounds me, I bury my face in my hands and groan.

What am I going to do?

CHAPTER 64

KAT

ANXIOUS VOICES HOVER above me. I try to open my eyes, but they are sealed shut. Frustration burns inside my chest. It's like my ears are fogged too, and I cannot understand what is being said.

I fall back into blackness.

The next time my awareness surfaces, all is quiet. I breathe through my nose and wriggle my tongue. A familiar scent I cannot name caresses over me. A dull throb pulses from my arm. I try to touch it, but something restrains me. I pry my eyes open, blinking against the candlelight, and inspect what holds me in place.

I'm not expecting to see my wrist tied to the bedpost.

I try to move, only to realize all of my limbs are tied down. I thrash against the bonds, trying to find a weak spot, trying to find some give in the rope.

Nothing.

"Be still." Rahk's low voice comes from somewhere above me. "You'll rip open your stitches."

I follow the sound of his voice until I find him leaning against the wall beside the bed, his empty gaze fixed on the far wall, his arms crossed over his chest. No one else is in the room.

This is . . . Rahk's estate. Not mine.

I remember running through the Wood. I remember turning myself over to Rahk. Beyond that, I don't remember anything. He must have brought me here. But why? Why not take me back to the Nothril Court or kill me outright?

I would have had hope about that turn of events . . . if he hadn't tied me to this bed in a way that I cannot hope to escape.

"It all makes sense now."

Rahk's cold, emotionless rumble fills the quiet space with dreadful resignation.

I don't speak. Shame and sorrow fill me with equal measures, and I wish I could go back to the black oblivion I just came out of.

"All of it makes sense. The way you disguised yourself as a boy and came here—and why you never confided in me. Why you were always afraid of me killing you. Why I could never assuage your fears and make you fully trust me. How, even in our best moments, you always seemed to hold back from me. I attributed it to your mother's death. But your mother's death didn't hold you back from Faerieland; it propelled you into it. You became the Ivy Mask to ensure what happened to your mother never happened again."

I give a fruitless tug on my bonds. The walls of this room close in around me, suffocating me in my own lies and deceptions and the inevitable doom that has finally tracked me down.

"You knew I was sent to hunt you," Rahk continues, his voice growing quieter. "You knew the entire time—or most of it. You must have figured it out when I pursued you on that first raid. All my efforts to win your trust and affection, no matter how much you might have longed to give them, were for naught. None of it could change that I would someday catch you and kill you."

I give a few painful coughs to clear my throat. My words are scratchy and weak. "Now you know my temperamental nature is actually much more rational."

"I never thought you were *temperamental,*" Rahk growls back. "I knew you had reasons. Tell me: did you already know how to play Fool's Circle?"

I wince and nod, then try to push up on one elbow—and end up jerking my wounded arm. I hiss in pain. "I did know how to play, but not well. Gah, these ropes are biting into my skin. If I promise not to—"

Rahk plants two hands on the bed, leaning over me. My throat goes even drier than before. "But I cannot believe anything you say, Kat. You've lied to me. Countless times. I cannot allow you to run away again. I'm not untying you."

"I hated lying to you!" I cry, trying again to shoot up and only earning myself more pain. The burn inside my lungs turns to a roar. "Why do you think I panicked when we married? Why do you think I kept pushing you away? Why do you think I told you to go back to Faerieland? It was because I cared about you, and it was ripping me to pieces to have to keep this secret from you!"

"Then why didn't you leave?" Rahk demands, his voice shaking. "Why did you stay? In my house? As my servant? As my wife? Why did you wait so long?"

"Because I didn't have the power to leave!" I shoot back. "When I was your servant, I couldn't leave and work elsewhere without a reference!"

"I would have given you one!"

"But I still wouldn't have been hirable! I only worked for you for three weeks. I needed to have held a position for six months to be hirable elsewhere. When you found me out, I had no say in that marriage arrangement. What did you expect me to do? Run away again, with nowhere to go, abandoning my fortune, all while knowing that you would pursue me anyway? What would you have had me do, Rahk?"

He drops into a nearby chair, his shoulders dejected, his hand covering the back of his neck. "I would have had you tell me the truth."

That lights a fire inside me that sends words hurling out of my mouth. "You would have had me *abandon* the people who needed me? You would have had me turn myself over to you and say, *'Please chop off my head now, dear Rahk, I have nothing in this world I want or need save death at your hand'*?"

"I wanted you to tell me," Rahk seethes, piercing me with his black eyes, "so I could *save* you."

I stop. Then I bare my teeth at him. "You are berating me for lying to you, when you kept your own secret from me. You knew how deeply it would hurt me to know you were hunting for the Ivy Mask, so you refused to tell me. You admitted this—that you had no plans to ever tell me even though you gave me gifts and kisses and made me fall in love with you!"

He rakes his hands through his hair. "I know. I did not want to hurt you, just as you did not want to hurt me. What have we done, Kat? I am furious with you; I feel deeply betrayed and I hate being lied to, even though I know you have every right to feel the same things about me. There are just so many things I am confused about. How could you have gone after your mother into the Wood? How could you even have survived?"

I blink hard. "I did not go after my mother into the Wood. She went after me."

Rahk visibly flinches. "What?"

I draw in a fortifying breath, turning my face away. My hands fist in their bonds. "The Wood swallowed me when it expanded. We were having a picnic, as I said. My parents said to stay close, but I disregarded them. I went up to the Wood because it had always drawn me. I could hear it calling to me. Then, all of a sudden, it expanded. I was caught inside."

He waits in silence for the rest of the story.

"A fae found me. A great, tall fae with horns curling out of its head."

The blood drains from Rahk's face. "You were a slave? In Faerieland?"

"In Nothril."

He buries his head in his hands. When he lifts it again, his eyes are reddened. "You were a slave. In Nothril. As a child?" He looks away from me. Still, I catch the tear that slides down his cheek. It cuts me in half. The muscles in his throat flex. He seems to struggle pulling himself together before he croaks, "How long?"

"Not long," I whisper. "A few days. It was the Valehaven Tailor who had pity on me, and when he discovered I could see the edges of the Paths, he told me how to leave. I went back home . . . only to find Mama was gone. She'd come after me. No one knew what happened to her."

"So you went back," he whispers.

I nod.

"You knew how to find Paths," he continues, putting the pieces together. "So you tried different ones, searching for your mother. Was that how it began? You would go to different Courts and then you would show others how to get out?"

"It took me a while to be brave enough to go back. But once I started, I did not stop. I met the tailor again and we began coordinating rescues as I grew older."

"What ever happened to your mother?"

"I still don't know. My belief is that she wandered the Wood and against all chance, somehow found her way out. She was wearing the same clothes when she came out as she did going in. I did not find any evidence she had been a slave." I pause, hesitating. Then, "Rahk . . . I did not suffer much as a slave. The hardest part was losing Mama."

"But you felt like you *should* have suffered," Rahk says. "Because you were the reason your mother was lost—and because so many others had to stay a slave while you got out."

Emotion clogs my throat. I look away.

"It all makes sense," he says softly. Then, with earnest gentleness, "Do you truly think this changes how dear you are to me?"

I stare at him with more shock than if he'd sprouted two new heads. "Why, yes, I did think it changed things. I thought me being a criminal to the fae changed things very, very much."

"I never wanted to hurt you." He buries his head in his hands. "I don't know what to do now. I don't know how to protect you. If I don't take you back to Nothril, my sister will die."

My voice is dull with resignation. "Then take me back."

"If I take you back, they will make *me* enforce their judgment."

My own face crumples. "I'm so sorry."

He shoots to his feet, raking a hand through his hair as he paces across the floor. When he speaks, it sounds like there are tears in his voice again. They strike my heart like shards of glass. "I've known for some time it was you. I just so badly didn't want to believe it that I refused to even consider it. But I knew. I knew when I saw the injury on your leg."

I close my eyes, fighting the shuddering of my own lungs.

The slice of a knife through rope makes my eyes fly wide. Rahk cuts each of my bonds, until I am able to sit up and clutch the quilt to my chest.

"Whatever happens, there is something we must do." Rahk takes my hand, pressing it flat against his.

I have never seen this ritual, yet somehow I recognize it. I try to yank my hand back. "You cannot—you cannot bond with me! I'm about to die, Rahk!"

"You won't die if I have a say in things," he growls, tightening his grip on my hand. "I told you before. I cannot take you into Faerieland as anything other than my true, bonded wife. So if I take you to Nothril, then it will be as my wife."

I hardly breathe as he murmurs the words of a spell that feels so sacred, it should never be uttered on our magicless soil. Still, I do not protest when he tells me the words I must speak. He tells me his name, the name only he himself knows. I speak the words back, letting our names and souls twine together as one, fused by a drop of our blood. Our heartbeats pulse in tandem. A new, strange, and exhilarating sensation.

Then Rahk gets to his feet, his black eyes devouring me whole. "I don't know what to do yet, but I will. I am not letting them hurt you."

When he strides out, the air in the room feels thinner, stretched too tight. I clutch my palm to my chest, fingers pressing against the place where his presence lingers, where something irrevocable has settled into my bones. I don't call him back. But my lips part, just for a second, as if I might.

CHAPTER 65

RAHK

I SIT AT my desk, staring at the sad lines of the ivy mask in my hand. What am I supposed to do now? I cannot hand Kat over to Lord and Lady Nothril. That is certain. Our newly forged bonding pounds against my heart at the thought.

But I also cannot let Pavi die.

Despite what I told Kat, I have not a clue how I am to get out of this mess.

There is no way forward and no way out. I run the bargain over in my head, searching for any crack, any fissure I can exploit.

You will bring the Ivy Mask to us for rendered judgment within three moons, measured by the human lands.

My mouth drops open. There is the crack. It stares at me right now, gripped tightly in my fist.

If I bring the ivy mask *itself*, that will satisfy the bargain. Yes, it will start a war. Yes, I still might not be able to save both my sister and my wife—but it gives me a *chance*. We could delay long enough until we have a plan. Kat knows how to get people out of Faerieland,

and maybe we could even get Pavi out before I brought the mask to Lord and Lady Nothril and started the war.

It's dangerous. It will cost me everything.

But it might work.

"Kat!" I call, almost jubilant, getting to my feet and rushing toward her room. The rest of the estate feels oddly quiet after the arguments of Oliver and Agatha. I hope they left us to figure out this mess in peace. I throw open the door. "Kat—"

My voice dies abruptly.

The bed is empty.

The sheets are mostly on the floor, twisted as though from struggle. The window has been cleanly smashed. The air smells distinctly of Nothril. A burn flares at the back of my neck. I grab it, my fingers tracing over the disappearing lines of my tattoo. The blood oath is fulfilled, which means—

I stumble against the wall, catching myself as deep, soul-devouring dread consumes me.

Pelarusa took Kat.

CHAPTER 66

KAT

MY KNEES HIT the cold, unforgiving black slate floor. The force rattles my bones and yanks a muffled groan through my gag. The cold seeps into the light frock I'm wearing. My hands are bound behind me, greatly reducing my mobility.

Which really is the mildest of my problems, I decide as I lift my eyes.

Lord and Lady Nothril sit on their thrones, resplendent in both awe and terror. I thought their greatness overwhelmed me at Mirror Tide, but, bound at their feet, the instinct to keep my gaze from lifting to their towering beauty nearly overwhelms me.

Nearly, but not quite.

They look at me with such condescension. As though I am an insect beneath the heel of their shoe.

"Behold," Pelarusa announces, a smirk in her voice, "the Ivy Mask."

Lady Nothril does not reply. Her face is carved from ice, and I get the distinct sense of displeasure. Lord Nothril's mouth draws in a thin line. "Excellent job."

It hits me then: they are angry with Rahk. He should have been the one to bring me in.

When Lady Nothril drags her gaze to me, pure hatred flashes in their depths. I clench my jaw and hold her gaze. She may be great and terrible, and I may be nothing, but I will not shrink before her.

Pavi sits on a smaller throne to one side, one of three, and her shoulders cave in on themselves as our eyes lock.

"Where is Prince Rahk?" demands Lord Nothril. "Why is he not with you?"

"He succumbed to her charms and was dragging his feet about bringing her. But look! I have brought some slaves to replace the ones you lost."

My mind stutters. The grand doors behind us swing open. A rush of cold air and a familiar shriek assault me. I try to turn but Pelarusa grips my head and keeps me faced forward. Surely I didn't hear what I thought I—

"Let me *go* you monster!" cries Agatha. "I have done nothing! Nothing, I tell you!"

"If you don't hush, you are going to get us all killed!" hisses Lord Oliver.

My vision turns white with panic. What are Agatha and Oliver doing here? And why did Oliver say *all* of us—as though to imply there were others taken? Who was taken? What is happening?

I yank my neck free of Pelarusa's hold, taking advantage of the distraction, and whirl enough to catch a glimpse of a sight that sends my blood curdling.

Agatha is shoved to her knees behind me, her fine gown muddied and torn. Lord Oliver is next, his clothes in a similar state. He stares at me in shock and concern, but that concern quickly shifts to Mary, who is shoved hard to her knees beside him. Her red hair, always carefully pinned, sticks out in every direction.

Then, last of all, little Becky is added to the row.

That is it.

I thrash against my bonds, tearing into the gag with my teeth. I am going to *murder* Pelarusa. I am going to shred her to tiny pieces, and then I am going to burn this entire Court to the ground.

Lord Nothril glides past me, straight to the captives. I watch, helplessly, as he stops in front of Mary. Oliver's eyes widen, glancing between the two of them. Bound as he is, he scoots himself partially in front of her. As though he can defend her. As though Lord Nothril cannot wipe him out with half a thought.

Lord Nothril grabs Mary's chin. She does not look at him, not even when he tilts her face this way and that.

"I need a new slave girl," he muses. "I've certainly had worse than this one. She might be half decent after some work."

I am going to rip his fingers from the hand that touches my sister. I try to throw myself toward them, but Pelarusa drags me backward.

"Put the Ivy Mask in the dungeon," orders Lady Nothril. "If Prince Rahk has truly *succumbed*, then he will arrive shortly."

I try to shout through my gag. I try to fight. I try to swear via eye contact that I will get all four of them out of this.

But I am dragged away by a pair of guards, deep into the darkest part of the vast cave that is the Nothril palace.

They toss me in a frigid cell and slam the door shut. It echoes through what sounds like another large cavern. I give a frustrated, muffled scream and throw myself against the iron bars. If they touch Mary or Becky—if they hurt any of them—I am going to kill everything in this palace. I will destroy all of Faerie.

"Kat? Is that you?"

"Tailor!" I try to gasp through my gag.

"Come here," he urges, standing at the grate between our cells. "I'll remove your bonds."

Gratefully, I get to my feet and press my back against the grate. His fingers are cold as he works the rope at my wrists. It falls off. I sigh in relief and unknot my gag before spitting it out.

"Are you alright?" I ask, clasping his hands through the narrow space. I blink against the darkness, trying to see him, to discover if he is alright. I cannot see a thing.

"I'm fine. Did our targets make it?"

"Yes, they did." I say the words, believing that they are true even though I have no confirmation. "They made it out."

"What happened? Did Prince Rahk catch you?"

I summarize what happened as we sit down, back-to-back on either side of the grate. A distant drip is the only sound aside from our breathing and the occasional shifting on the floor.

"We're going to die, aren't we?" I ask.

I can feel him nodding. "We are. Though your friends may have their lives. As slaves."

Maybe this would all be easier to swallow if those people hadn't been dragged into this situation. My heart breaks thinking of Charity, who must be losing her mind with fright and grief. My worry extends even to Agatha. She would never survive long as a slave. And neither will Oliver if he continues standing up to the fae on behalf of others.

And Mary.

I never, ever wanted something so terrible to ever befall her.

I was so desperate to save those eleven, I got three of the best people I know destined for a fate worse than death. And Agatha too. The weight of guilt presses me into the ground.

"I hope I'll get to see Phillipa and Sunny again."

I tilt my head, craning my neck to look at him. "Who are they?"

"My wife and daughter."

I blink. "I didn't know you were married. Or that you had a child."

"I did. Once upon a time. They died at the hand of their fae master in Valehaven. I had been trying to get them out . . . but it was too late." He says it all very calmly.

"That's . . . awful," I say.

"It was tragic, yes. I found that life doesn't end when tragedy strikes. It keeps on going and going and going. You can either resist it, or embrace it. I've done my best to embrace it. Still, I want to be reunited with them. It has been a long separation."

"That was why you began your own work," I whisper.

He turns and smiles at me. "And why I took such a liking to you."

I lean my head back against the cold grate. "What do you think will happen to our work? Once we're gone?"

He doesn't hesitate. "It will continue. It won't be us anymore, but where there is a need, people rise to fill it. I believe that one day, this power struggle between our people and the fae will end. It may start as a whisper, but it will end in a flood."

"I don't know how that is possible," I reply.

"Not as our world is currently arranged," he agrees. "But you have heard of the Veil, have you not?"

"I have heard of it. I am not familiar with it, however."

"It is the great divider of the fae worlds. Only very, very strong magic can breach the Veil."

"You think we should create a new Veil. One between the human world and Faerieland."

"Someday, I think it will happen," he says softly.

The distant drip grows louder in the silence.

"If we're going to die," I whisper, "then I want to know your name. Your real name."

He lets out a sigh. "My name is Jacob Everfells."

"Jacob," I whisper. "I'm glad our paths crossed."

"I'm glad for it, too."

Heavy footsteps echo through the cavern. Guards—coming.

I stiffen. We each get to our feet. I look at him and see only the light of his eyes as he gives me a swift nod. *Goodbye.*

They go to his cell first and drag him out. I watch, horrified, clinging to the cold iron bars, until the sound of him being taken away dies into nothing. The memory of Agatha, Oliver, Mary, and Becky in that throne room returns with a frantic fervor that is no longer deadened by the tailor's calming presence.

He is going to die. They are all going to die. Because of me.

"Oh saints," I breathe, shoving my knuckles between my teeth and biting down hard as the panic settles in. Suddenly, I don't feel so resigned to death. I don't want Jacob to die, and I don't want to die either.

But I know in my twisted gut that this is the last time I'll see the tailor of Valehaven.

"You'll see Mama again," I whisper, trying to calm the frantic beat of my heart. "You'll see Father again. You'll see Jacob, too."

I won't see Mary. Or any of the house staff that is more like family to me. Or Bartholomew. How will Bartholomew ever be alright? She will keep expecting me to come to her. She won't understand.

I won't see Rahk either. And that feels like the greatest loss of all.

I've spent my life reacting to the great losses I've experienced, not realizing how much more I had to lose.

You've got to be brave, Kat, I tell myself, trying to fortify my spine. *You cannot shrink before these cursed fae.*

But now that I am alone in this dungeon, in the dreadful, unending silence, there is nothing to do but doubt that I have enough strength to meet a torturous end. My arm aches from the wound and its stitches. Still, the pain feels so minor compared to what I am about to face.

"I don't know what I am going to do," I whisper in the darkness. For all that my rage demands violence against Lord and Lady Nothril, I have no power over them. I am a prisoner in their dungeon. "This is all my fault. If I had just not gotten too close to the Wood. *None* of this would have happened."

All those years of trying to make up for the way I'd destroyed my own life by being a careless child—all those years of trying to free slaves as if that would ever absolve the guilt I bear that I ruined Mama and Father—they come crashing around me with a force that nearly sends my bones splintering. How could I have ever thought such a thing could make up for the curse I am to those who care about me?

Unbidden, faces flash before me from the Mirror. I think of those children with their own masks that mimicked mine. They never would have existed if not for what I did to free their father. But what are those children to me? Distant faces that might have been a lie in the Mirror. They are simply an idea. Now Mary is imprisoned because of me, and if I cannot get her out, she will be ruined like Elizabeth was.

But Elizabeth wasn't ruined, a tiny voice whispers.

I saw so little of her in the Mirror. She might have nightmares from her time in Faerie. She might be suffering endlessly from the abuse she bore.

Still, somehow, she landed on her feet.

I lean my head back against the cold grate. What if . . . what if all of this is so much bigger than me? What if Jacob was right, and the moment he and I are killed, others will rise up in our place? What if they are able to do more than I ever could? What if the little we did is just the beginning, and that after us, will truly come a flood? What if it is Mary, Becky, Oliver, and Agatha that start the new wave? What if they have their own story beyond being a captive here?

And if that is possibly true, what if my mistake of wandering too close to the Wood as a child . . . could lead to something? If I had not done that, I would not have become the Ivy Mask. And if I had never become the Ivy Mask, so many people would never have been free.

I never would have met Rahk.

Part of me softens as memories return, of our Fool's Circle games, of making him laugh, of dancing with him without a clue he knew I was a woman, of how good he was to me. Try as I might, I cannot regret knowing him. I cannot regret loving him.

You never would have met him if you had not wandered close to the Wood that day.

I close my eyes and warm tears stream down my cheeks. There are hundreds of things I can berate myself for. There are hundreds of people I can take responsibility for—those that I saved, those I didn't save, and those who were hurt because of me. I made every rescue and every failure about me. But I see it now.

All of this is so much bigger than just me. It always has been.

ANASTASIS BLYTHE

My part in this story has come to an end. A bitter, bitter end.

Now, it is time for me to let go. To fully surrender to forces and stories greater than me. I have done what I can. It is time to trust that, just as the suffering and adversity in my life made me stronger, it will do the same in others' lives. Even the lives of those I love most and wish most dearly to protect.

I have to let it all go.

In this cold, dark, empty part of the world, a strange calmness like I've never known falls around my shoulders. My burden is not gone, my fear for my friends has not left me--but for the first time, I feel strong enough to bear it.

A great clang followed by shuffling sounds from somewhere above me.

So, they have come for me.

I get to my feet and walk to the front of my cell.

I will not be afraid, I tell myself, forcing my wobbly legs to stand firm and not retreat as they open my cell. *I will not be afraid. I will not be afraid.*

The guards tower over me as they clamp iron grips on my arms and drag me out.

I will not be afraid, I think as they haul me into the strange low light of the palace. *I will not be afraid,* I think when they push open the throne room doors and drag me before Lord and Lady Nothril once again.

I will not be afraid.

The first person I notice in that throne room is not Lord or Lady Nothril, or Pelarusa, or anyone else. It is Pavi—who sits at Lady Nothril's feet in a gown of pale blue, her tear-streaked face turned away.

I will not be afraid.

My four friends kneel where I left them. Agatha shudders and shivers, a bruise blossoming on her face. Mary's face is hard like flint as she stares at the floor. Becky has scooted into Oliver, who has twisted his body to wrap what he can of his elbow around her small body. He whispers something to her that looks like, *"Keep your eyes closed."*

A dozen fae guards flank the thrones, ready to obliterate any opposition within seconds.

Pelarusa stands in the midst of the throne room. Her slender arm bears a long, wicked blade dripping with blood. And at her feet are the mangled, bloodied remains of Jacob Everfells. A pair of crushed spectacles lay nearby.

My crudely propped courage crumbles. My knees give out, and my guards have to hold me upright as they deposit me in a heap next to Jacob's corpse. I refuse to look, to imagine the pain he experienced—and that I will soon experience too. Rahk is not here to kill me quickly. Pelarusa will make me suffer.

And Mary and Becky will have to watch.

"So this is it," Lady Nothril declares with a grand sweep of her hand, indicating me. "*This* little thing is what caused all that trouble for all those years."

"And evaded Rahk for two moons?" spits Lord Nothril.

A chortle erupts from Pelarusa. She leans down to grab my hair and yank my head back to expose my neck. "He even *bonded* with her!"

It's Pavi's sweet, trembling voice that breaks the silence. "If he bonded with her, does that mean he loves her?"

"You spend too much time with your nose in tales of romance," Pelarusa chides her. "Love is irrelevant to the situation."

"Where is Rahk anyway?" Lord Nothril snarls. "I will have his head! He is no son of mine."

The throne room doors bang open.

"I am here."

I twist. There is Rahk, marching into the scene, arrayed in full armor, both of his long blades in his hands. His face is a thundercloud, and icy vengeance swirls around him.

"I have come for my wife. If anyone has laid a finger on her, I will raze this entire Court to dust."

CHAPTER 67

RAHK

KAT KNEELS, ONE hand braced on her leg, the other against the floor. Her hair is wild, her eyes ringed in white. Only two paces away are the remains of what appear to be the Valehaven Tailor.

I only barely made it in time.

I take in the rest of the room in a flash. The placement and identity of each guard, the arrangement of Pelarusa's additional four captives, my two sisters.

"You are back," growls Lord Nothril. "What a privilege to have you finally grace our presence!"

Lady Nothril strokes Pavi's head. Her calm, steady voice carries through the hall. "My dear son. I am troubled by the reports I have received of you."

It frightens me how strong the impulse is to sheathe my swords, clasp my hands behind my back, and fix my gaze above her throne as I've always done. To ask, without an ounce of emotion, what my sovereigns require of me.

But Lord and Lady Nothril have asked me for one too many deaths.

Kat is *mine*, and they cannot have her.

I do not care what it costs me. I have spent so much of my life trying to somehow be both, to be a Nothril prince but uncorrupted. I let Lord and Lady Nothril dictate everything in my life. I let them punish me for caring about my sister.

But I am done playing their games. I am done being their prince.

I have finally come to destroy the kingdom I spent my life building.

"I hear reports that you have been lazy in your search efforts, despite your own dear sister's life being on the line." Lady Nothril rakes her nails lightly across Pavi's scalp, even as the girl looks up at her, startled. Pavi did not know what a blood oath entailed. "I heard you bonded with a human woman, and the very criminal you sought. If I did not know better, I would think your loyalties had shifted."

I take in the room once more. I am confident I can get Kat and I out of this room alive. But the moment I did, Lady Nothril will slice her beloved daughter's throat—and order Mary, Oliver, Becky, and Agatha all slaughtered.

If I can delay the inevitable, it might buy me just enough time.

"There is one thing you can do to ensure your loyalties remain as they ought," Lady Nothril continues, a slow smile twisting her lips.

My focus narrows on Pelarusa. There is one thing I can do to protect Pavi's life.

Lady Nothril waves her hand, gesturing at Kat. "Execute the Ivy Mask as we instruct. You will be restored to your former position and glory as our heir. We will put all of this nonsense behind us."

She is out of her mind if she thinks I will seriously consider murdering my wife.

"What sentence would please you? She took your slave girl, after all. It is right that you should decide." Lady Nothril regards her husband.

"I have considered this," replies Lord Nothril, his pupils dilating and glittering. "She must be executed very slowly. A table will be brought forth and she will be pinned to it with a blade through her naval, her hands and legs pinned to the table with stakes. Then hot tongs will be used—"

"No!" cries Pavi.

I flinch at the sound of her throwing herself to the ground before Lord and Lady Nothril.

"Pavi!" Pelarusa cries, fear staining her voice.

"Please, don't make him do this to the woman he loves!" Pavi begs, and my world turns cold with dread. "She wasn't trying to hurt our people! She just wanted to help her own! She was being kind and brave. She shouldn't have to endure a horror like this!"

Pavi, no. No, no, no, no.

I just need you to stay alive for a few more minutes longer until—

The air turns deadly.

Stay out of this, I scream in my mind. *Let me handle this. Don't bring attention to yourself. Please, Pavi!*

But she cannot hear my frantic thoughts.

"I cannot bear to watch this!" Pavi is openly weeping now. "You always make me watch such horrible things and I can't do it! I can't do it!"

Pelarusa does what I cannot, and marches across the room to grab Pavi by the arm, to drag her back to her place, temporarily leaving Kat unattended. "Be silent!"

Pavi wrenches free. "I've been silent long enough!" She whirls on Lord and Lady Nothril, either not noticing the dark thrum of energy coming from the twin thrones, or not caring. "Mama, please! Papa! Don't do this horrible thing. Can you not see how this would destroy Rahk?"

"Pavi," Lady Nothril says with deceptive calm.

She looks up, hope filling her innocent face. Every muscle in my body braces. I scan the room for the hundredth time, trying to sort out exactly how to get us out of this mess.

"You can only interrupt someone's sentence if you are willing to take the punishment on behalf of the accused."

Pavi's face pales.

"Will you take the place of the accused?" Lord Nothril asks.

Pavi glances helplessly between me and the wide-eyed Kat beside me.

"You do not have to," Lady Nothril says with gentleness that I don't know if I've ever heard before, "but if you do not, then you cannot speak on these proceedings."

"You're saying I must *die* in order to say you shouldn't make a husband kill his wife?" Pavi asks, outrage turning her foolish. "That is ridiculous, and you know it!"

"Silence!" roars Lord Nothril. He grabs Pavi by her hair, yanking her to her feet as she screams. "You have refused to conform to the ways of Nothril for long enough. You will now choose between your tongue or your life."

He throws her to the floor. She lands hard, her fear palpable as she tries to scoot backward, toward me, away from the person she just called Papa. "What do you mean?"

He strides toward her, withdrawing a long, curved knife. "You will give me your traitorous tongue, or you will give me your life.

Kat uses the distraction to surge to her feet and dart to the four bound captives. Her fingers flying, she works the knot tying Oliver's hands behind his back. She mouths something to him I cannot read.

"Or," Lady Nothril's voice rings out against the cavern's walls. "If you wish to redeem yourself, Pavi, then you may perform the Ivy Mask's execution yourself."

At once, all eyes turn to where Kat should have been, then swivel to where she is. Pelarusa is across the room in a second, grabbing Kat by the arm and yanking her to the center of the room again. My blood turns to a lethal simmer. Still, I restrain myself. If I can just delay a few more minutes, I will have what I need to get Kat, Pavi, and her friends out of here alive.

"If everyone is too soft to kill the Ivy Mask, then I will!" Pelarusa throws Kat to the ground and lifts her sword. Kat desperately tries to scramble backward, throwing up her hands.

Everything inside me turns to ice. There is no time left.

I lunge.

Pelarusa freezes, choking.

I yank my sword out of her back. Her hand goes to the gaping wound in her chest, the blood streaming down her gown. Lord and Lady Nothril shoot to their feet as their daughter falls to the ground.

Dead.

"I said I would raze this Court if anyone laid a finger on my wife," I snarl.

I grab Kat and fling her behind me in the spare second of shock before all hell breaks loose. Then I hurl myself at the guards. They surge toward me as one—men I know, men who have been my comrades.

I cut them down with one thought: if they come for Kat, they die. Lord and Lady Nothril wanted me to be cold, cruel, unfeeling. They honed me into a lethal weapon. So that is what I become. It is my Nothril blood that makes my swords hit true. With Pelarusa dead, and my future as heir forever destroyed, Pavi is the only remaining heir. Lord and Lady Nothril will hesitate before slaughtering her as I slaughter their men.

A burst of light comes searing toward me. I barely manage to dodge Lord Nothril's death blow. It throws my balance off, just enough that the guard I fight slashes his blade across my chest. My breastplate shields me from most of the blow, but a gash cuts across my collar bone and into my arm. I throw myself forward, cutting under his guard to slide my blade beneath his armor, into his soft stomach.

A scream makes me whirl.

Kat throws herself at a guard, who raises his sword at Becky. The guard tosses the young girl aside and latches onto Kat. She manages to dodge one blow of the blade that comes for her heart—using one of the techniques I taught her. But she twists her feet in the process, falling onto her back. The guard pins her with his boot. Another runs to help him finish the job.

"Kat!" I scream. I drop one sword, throwing up my hand to shoot a bolt of pure magic at the guard. It destroys him, but the remaining guards have shifted their focus from me to Kat. In a single moment, she is surrounded. *"Kat!"*

A roar splits through the cacophony. Then, the walls of the cavern's entrance suddenly cave in. Stone flies in every direction as though from an explosion. We all turn as one to see a massive, rocky body smash through the wall with a club.

"Ymer the Indefatigable will eat any who hurt nice small elf!" bellows Ymer. And with that, he snatches up the surprised guards around Kat and smashes them into the stone wall with obliterative force. "No one hurts small elf!"

I cannot help my grin. *There* he is. Barely on time.

It did not take me long to put the pieces together that the *nice small elf* who brought Ymer food was Kat. It took me precious time after she was captured by Pelarusa to find him again in Caphryl Wood, and he took so long to come I hurried on ahead—only *hoping* he would arrive in time to make a difference.

It was not hard to convince Ymer that the nice small elf was in danger and if he wanted to thank her for the food, he should come protect her. Trolls are, after all, fastidiously loyal.

I don't see where Kat's four friends disappeared to, but I am just in time to watch her open some small servants' door and disappear through it. My breath comes easier as Ymer and I take down the rest of the guards.

"Stop this at once!" demands Lady Nothril.

"Rahk!"

It is the second voice—Pavi's high-pitched squeal—that stops me. I whirl. My breath catches. Lord Nothril has Pavi pinned against his chest, a ball of pure magic held just next to her head. Ready to destroy her in a flash.

"I am giving you a choice, Rahk," Lord Nothril seethes as Pavi whimpers. He pays no heed to Ymer tromping out of the throne room to either leave or go smash more of his palace. All the guards are dead by now. "You surrender now. Or I kill your beloved sister."

I shoot a glance toward Lady Nothril, who stands only a few paces away from him. Her jaw is tight, her eyes a roaring furnace as she regards me. Pavi cries softly, helplessly.

If I surrender, they will make me hunt Kat again. They will make me kill her.

I am not surrendering.

But neither will I let them kill my sister.

I drop my swords with a clatter. I know Lord and Lady Nothril, and I do not believe that they will kill every single one of their heirs. It is time to call their bluff. Even if it risks Pavi's life.

I stride toward Lord Nothril. Toward Pavi.

"Surrender!" cries Lord Nothril. "Or I *will* kill her!"

I summon an explosive flow of magic. It coalesces in a bright ball in my hand. I lift it, ready to hurl it straight at Lord Nothril's face. Even if I am not strong enough to kill a ruler of Faerie, he might flinch and give me the exact window I need to grab Pavi.

Instead, Lord Nothril turns his snarl from me to my sister. He wheels back his own magic-filled blow, his face contorting with strain as he rams it straight into her head.

"Pavi!" I scream. My blast fires wide and splits Lord Nothril's throne clean down the middle.

But Pavi is not the one who falls.

Lord Nothril crumples to the ground. Pavi stumbles away, unharmed. I search, bewildered, as Pavi barrels into my arms.

Lady Nothril stands behind Lord Nothril's fallen body, a bloodied, glowing knife in her hand. Her narrowed gaze, full of hatred, lands on me.

I see my death in those eyes. She will not let me get away with being the flame that set our family ablaze.

Still, I have space for one thought.

I am not the only one whose weakness for Pavi runs deep.

I brace myself, standing in front of Pavi, knowing Lady Nothril will cut me down without a thought. But I will still fight.

"Lady Nothril," I growl.

Suddenly, her eyes flutter shut. She slumps to the ground.

"Mama!" cries Pavi. I grab her arm before she can rush to her side.

My lips part as realization descends. Even as we watch, the dead body of our father begins to glow, and tendrils of magic snake toward our fallen mother. The ruling power of Faerie that was split between them reunites, collecting in Lady Nothril's body.

"Mama!" Pavi weeps again.

"She's not dead." I haul Pavi away, picking up my swords and breaking into a run. "We only have minutes before she is upon us."

"Then what happened?"

Tears stream down her rounded face, her cheeks and eyes reddened.

"They were bonded. She broke that bond when she killed Lord Nothril. It took all her strength." I look down at her. "To protect you. Now we've got to find Kat and get out of here before she rises again and kills us all."

CHAPTER 68

KAT

"I DON'T KNOW what is happening. I don't know what is happening. I don't know what is happening!" Agatha wails.

"Will you just *shut up*?" Mary spits. "If we have any hope of getting out of here, you cannot be announcing our location to every fae that wants our blood in the vicinity!"

"This way!" I call, diving deeper into the servants' tunnels. I hold Becky's hand tightly and, brave girl that she is, she runs beside me and does not make a sound.

"You are bleeding!" Oliver hisses at Mary. "Is that your leg? Do you need me to carry you?"

"I'm fine!" she replies. "No—really, I'm—Lord Oliver!"

I glance back just as he scoops an arm beneath her shoulders, supporting her weight. She looks up at him and purses her lip, but does not protest further. Agatha trails behind, her entire body trembling as her eyes dart about in terror. Then she looks at me and bursts: "I never should have sold your horse! I was a horrible stepmother to you! I am so sorry! I know this is my punishment!"

I shake my head. "It's fine. Just be quiet and keep up!"

"You know the way out of these tunnels?" Oliver asks me. "Is it because you were the . . . whatever they were calling you back there? The Ivy Mask? What even is that? I tried not to panic in there, but I have *no idea* what is going on!"

I reach a fork in the tunnel and stop, searching either direction. "Mary can tell you later. This way!"

We hurry down the tunnels, getting closer and closer to the exit. For the first time, my breath comes a little clear. We might actually make it. We might—

A door up ahead opens abruptly.

I skid to a halt as a very large, very fae body enters the tunnel, blocking our path. If that is a guard, we are all dead. I turn on my heels. "Back! Back! Back!"

"Kat!" Rahk cries. "It's me! And Pavi!"

I stop. My knees turn to liquid. "Rahk?"

His arm sweeps around my waist, supporting me before I collapse in relief. "We have a minute or two before Lady Nothril pursues us. We must be gone before then!"

"She killed Papa!" Pavi chokes a little on the words.

"This way gets us out. We're almost there!" I press forward, my energy renewed. Rahk's hand does not leave me, shifting from laying on my back to lightly holding my arm. As though he is afraid that, if he stops touching me, we will be separated forever.

"Are these the servants' tunnels?" Rahk glances around us as we run. He looks down at me again. "How well do you know them?"

"Like the back of my hand."

I'm so focused that it takes me a moment to realize he is staring down at me incredulously.

"How many times have you raided Nothril?"

I direct us all to veer down a sharp left turn. "This was my twelfth. Here, this door always slows me down because it's never unlocked. Give me a knife."

He pulls a knife from his boot and hands it to me, slightly skeptically. I press the tip into the pad of my thumb and press it to the door. It unlatches. I push it open and keep moving.

"What?" I demand, looking up to find Rahk staring at me, his jaw slack.

"You can bypass fae locks with human blood? How did I not know this?" He shakes his head. "I always knew you were clever. I never realized you were a genius."

His praise floods me with unexpected warmth. "I had to be, to evade you," I reply cheekily.

At once, we stumble out of the tunnels, spilling into gray foliage of the world adjacent to the Wood. I leap onto the Path. Rahk immediately divides our party into groups so no one accidentally falls off the Path. "Pavi, you take the lead with Becky. Kat, you, Mary, Oliver, and Agatha go next. I will take up the rear in case we are followed."

Thus grouped, we burst into full sprints. My vision blurs. The edges of the Path move and morph. I blink hard to get it to straighten. I end up following closer to Pavi and relying on her stronger view of the Path to keep from straying off it.

Then, abruptly, the entire Path shudders.

I stop. "What was that?"

Rahk glances in every direction. The Path shudders again. His eyes suddenly widen. "Lady Nothril is destroying the Path!"

"Rahk! The Path!" cries Pavi from the front—

—just before the entire thing vanishes.

Leaving us stranded in the middle of Caphryl Wood.

I whirl in place, looking for any sign of the Path, even though I know it's gone.

"Kat?" Mary asks uneasily. She still leans on Oliver, his grip tight on her waist. Blood soaks through her dirtied uniform, marking an injury somewhere on her calf.

"What is wrong?" Oliver demands.

"We are going to die!" wails Agatha.

"Are we truly going to die?" asks Becky softly.

My jaw flexes, fire erupting in my gut. "No one is going to die. We're going to figure out a way out of this. Rahk, how did you navigate the Wood when you were chasing me? You can navigate the Wood without a Path, right?"

Rahk's face is pale. "The Wood cannot be navigated without a Path. I used a spell. You take an object of the earth and place your destination inside it. It guides you through unnavigable places."

"That's perfect!" I cry, searching the ground. "What do you need? A stick? A rock? Are these pine needles enough?"

"You cannot set the spell inside the Wood."

I go still.

Rahk rakes a hand through his hair. "When I saw that you had gone into the Wood, I retraced my steps, worked the spell, and returned. That was how I could hunt for you and then get us both out."

I hold his gaze for a long moment. "So you are saying we cannot get out of the Wood."

He does not answer. Not even a small shake of the head.

Agatha's wails crescendo. I curse, pacing in the small clearing we stand in amid an endless death forest in every direction.

"Can we not just . . . pick a direction and head that way?" Oliver asks. "We can keep going the way we were heading. Surely we will find our way out somehow?"

"That is not how the Wood works," Pavi whispers quietly.

"My mother got out somehow," I say to Rahk. "Surely there is a way."

His voice is so low, a deep rumble in the curious silence of the Wood. "I do not know how anyone can navigate this place. You cannot control it. It decides where you go and what you encounter."

"So if the Wood wants us to go back to the very frightening queen who wants all of us dead, it will take us there?" asks Oliver.

"I should have known she would destroy the Path." Rahk clenches his fists. "I should have taken the precaution of making the spell. Then we wouldn't be in this mess."

"I never should have sold that horse!" wails Agatha. "If I hadn't, we never would be in this mess!"

That—is actually very true. Here I have been, blaming myself for all these woes, when other people have had equal responsibility in these crimes.

Kat. This way.

I turn toward the shocking familiarity of that voice. A voice I have not heard in so, so long. A voice that cracks my heart in two.

"Kat?" asks Rahk.

This way. I will take you home.

There. Between the trees about a stone's throw away, is a small, blue light. Hovering in midair.

"Do you see that?" I point to it.

Rahk tenses. "It is probably a lure for a spirit to trap you."

"Yes," I reply, even as I take a step closer. "But I *know* this voice."

It is a woman's voice. Soft. Tender. *I know the way out.*

My legs begin shaking. I take one step toward the glow, almost too terrified to say aloud the name I long to call.

You do not need to be afraid, my sweet. I came here to find you. Now I have found you, and I will take you home.

Even as I watch, the blue glow shifts. Her face appears, and the shadowy outlines of her body follow. The gentle lines of aging around her eyes crinkle into a smile. She lifts one arm, her finger pointed. Her voice is not afraid, not angry. *Let me show you the way.*

"Mama?" I choke. Then I stop myself, turning to Rahk. "It is a trap, isn't it? Oh, this cursed Wood!"

Rahk steps to my side. His hand lands on my back, but when I look up at him, his face is strangely . . . *awed*. "I do not think it is a trap."

Everyone in our group has gone silent.

Hope soars in my chest like never before. I turn back to the blue glow of my mother, floating at the edge of the clearing.

"I have never seen this," he murmurs. "It has always been said that Caphryl takes slips of spirit from everyone who enters it. I never thought that meant those same spirits could . . ." He trails off. Swallows. Then continues. "Somehow, your mother found a way out of Caphryl without a Path. This is the remnant of her spirit."

I look back at the glowing version of my mother, my voice utterly gone. She smiles, all liquid warmth and tenderness. *I have missed you so, so much. I am so glad to have found you. Please let me take you out of here so you can go home.*

I surge toward her. My legs cannot carry me fast enough. When I reach her, my hands go straight through her. A cry escapes my lips.

Do not be saddened, dear girl, whispers my mother softly. *I do not have a body with which to embrace you, but my heart is with you always.* She reaches out glowing tendrils of hands. They glide over my face, and when I close my eyes, I can feel the barest warmth at her touch. Everything inside me softens.

"You don't hate me," I breathe.

No. Mama smiles, as if the notion is silly. *I never have, and I never will. It was my love for you that guided me through this Wood back to you. Now please let me take you out of here. It is dangerous, and I could not bear it if anything happened to you.*

I swallow the gathering tears, the rock in my throat, and draw in a deep, clear breath. The last remnants of my fear, of my self-hatred, of my brokenness all evaporate. She loves me. She always did. She never hated me or blamed me or wished I had died that day instead of fallen into the Wood. She came after me, not out of guilt or a sense of responsibility, but because she *loved* me.

I grow lighter than air with relief.

Follow me, Kat, Mama calls. *This is the way home.*

I reach out and grip Becky's hand. "Let's get you back to your mother."

My mother turns and shows the way. We hurry after her. I never let my gaze stray from her form, drinking in the way her hair flows behind her and the bit of profile visible to me.

It seems like only moments before she stops and points. Toward the sun shining through the branches of the Wood. The *human sun*.

"We made it!" Pavi cries, running forward.

"I've got you. Just a little bit longer," Oliver says to Mary. He takes more of her weight as they disappear into the human world. Everyone in our party seems to rush forward, to throw themselves out of the Wood.

But I stop, turning around.

Mama hovers at my side, smiling down at me. All this time I hated her for abandoning me, when she was here. Always searching for me. Ready to help the moment she found me.

"Thank you," I whisper, my voice cracking. "I miss you. I don't want to leave without you."

She only comes to me and presses her formless lips to my forehead. Warmth fills my core, soothing the last ragged edge of my pain. *You aren't leaving without me,* she replies.

I memorize every inch of her face for the last time.

Then her glow winks out.

Instead of loss, a golden glow of peace fills the deepest parts of my heart and grows, until every part of me, down to my fingers and toes, is finally at rest.

I turn.

Rahk has stopped, too. The last one still in the Wood besides me. His neck twitches as he cranes his head to follow the trees to their towering tops. My heart goes out to him. I step to his side and slide my hand in his.

He looks down at me and squeezes my hand. A long, low sigh escapes him. Then his jaw sets in determination.

We step over the border of Faerieland for the last time.

CHAPTER 69

KAT

THE LAST THING I expect to find awaiting us on the border of Harbright is an army.

Armed soldiers are arrayed in three directions, surrounding us completely. I freeze, stepping backward against Rahk's chest. His hands come up, closing around my arms. His grip tightens, then he moves me behind him.

Agatha has already started running straight toward the army, shrieking for help at the top of her lungs.

"Agatha!" I cry, suddenly afraid she will be struck down.

But she makes it to the edge of the army. It swallows her up. Presumably without killing her.

"What is going on?" I whisper to Rahk.

"They might have been waiting for me in case I came back," he replies grimly. "Queen Vivienne requires my head now that I have kidnapped her son. No matter how brief or necessary the kidnapping, or how unharmed he was."

"I'm *fine,* Lord Oliver! Really—ahh!"

I turn toward Mary just as she crumples. Oliver, worn and ragged as he is, has never looked more determined than when he ignores her stubborn protests and scoops her up into his arms. "With all respect, my lady," he tells her, "quit being an idiot." He turns toward Rahk and I. "I can take her up the hill, right? They won't harm us?"

"You should all be fine," I reply. "Take Becky. I think Rahk, Pavi, and I are the only ones at risk."

Oliver nods, sweat streaking through the dirt caked across his face. He looks down at Mary in his arms, her red hair splayed across his shoulder. Becky scuttles to his side and he gives her a smile. "Ready to go home?"

"Are you alright, Mary?" I ask, before they leave. "I am so sorry that you got tangled up in this."

Mary's face is tight, but she offers me a smile. "I'm fine. I'm sure the leg is very treatable. I have a renewed respect for what you do. Also, I never would have let you go into Faerieland if I knew what you faced there. Oh yes, and I won't be letting you go back. Ever."

I give a mirthless chuckle. "Fair enough."

The three of them leave and safely make it to the army after picking their way across abandoned magicked farmland.

"What do we do?" Pavi asks.

"Do you think I can convince them to not kill you?" I ask Rahk, holding onto his broad elbow.

He studies the force against us. "I don't know, Kat. I do not want to risk anything happening to you."

"Last I checked, the queen still liked me. It is our only chance. I will approach and explain what happened. Maybe I can convince them to take you captive instead of killing you. Then I can meet with the queen and try to convince her to pardon you."

Suddenly, a pummeling force from behind us—from the Wood—drives all three of us to our knees in an instant. My hair blasts in my face, preventing me from seeing anything. The magic enhanced crops are swept away. Even the army buckles, retreating from the force of the rush. Screaming begins.

It is Rahk's voice that cuts through the din. "Get back! Get back!"

Somehow, I manage to turn around.

The giant form of Lady Nothril rises above the treetops of Caphryl Wood. Screaming from all around the valley reaches a crescendo. I fall backward in my attempt to scramble away. My heart nearly stops right then and there.

Lady Nothril is a fluid form that only seems to grow greater, more terrible, as she leans over the valley.

"Give back my daughter!" she screams in an unearthly voice that shakes the world at its foundations. "Or else I will destroy these lands!"

Blindly, I grab Pavi and drag her as fast as I can away from her reach.

Rahk draws his two swords, long and bloodied in each hand, as he braces against the wind and bellows: "No fae ruler may cross this border!"

Pavi and I scramble further back. Rahk, who has always looked like a mountain to me, now looks miniscule, standing as the lone figure between my entire world and a roaring fae queen filling the sky.

"You have a choice, son of mine," roars Lady Nothril. "Give me back my daughter, and I will spare your wife. If you do not, you will be forever banished from all of Faerieland."

Rahk stands his ground.

Lady Nothril drags one taloned hand through the trees and screams: "You will never see your homeland again. You will never see your friend the High King again. You will lose your throne. You will lose your long life. Would you give up a thousand more years for a mere hundred?"

Rahk grits his teeth against the force barreling into him. "You cannot set foot in this realm!"

"Will you give up everything—for that?" Lady Nothril's massive eyeballs swivel to me, pinning me in place. "A tiny, puny creature who will live a few more decades, at most?"

Rahk's answer carries over the wind. "Yes."

My hair whips across my face. A dagger stabs into my heart. I don't want him to give up everything for me. I don't want him to give up his only friend, his long life, his throne, his chance to do good in Faerieland.

Rahk looks back at me, holding my gaze as he repeats, "Yes."

I stop breathing. There is no regret in his gaze. Not a single piece of resentment.

He wants to spend the rest of his life with me. Here, in the human lands. No matter what it costs him.

Over everything, he chooses me.

Torn between laughing and crying and also running for my life from Lady Nothril, I end up just standing there stupidly, my mouth gaping open.

Lady Nothril's expression contorts in genuine shock, and I almost pity her. Her fingers curl into a fist that she smashes into the ground. Even on the other side of the border, the entire valley shudders. Then she plunges forward.

"Rahk!" I scream.

Lady Nothril's attention latches onto Pavi. "My daughter! Come back to me!" Her hand whips out—to reach across the border and grab Pavi.

A soul-splitting scream almost seems to tear the worlds in half. I crumple to the ground in a fetal position, covering my ears from the searing pain. When I look up, Lady Nothril waves a burning hand in the air, clutching her wrist and shrieking.

"You cannot come into this land!" Rahk yells back.

"Pavi!" screams Lady Nothril.

Tears stream down Pavi's face. She whips back and forth between looking at Rahk and her mother. That is when I realize it.

Pavi still does not know the monster that Lady Nothril is. She thinks that because Lady Nothril protected her from Lord Nothril, it means that she is less evil.

Rahk sends me a panicked look as he realizes the same thing. Then he looks at his sister. I watch the shift come over his expression. My lungs tighten.

He beckons Pavi to his side. She goes at once. He gets down on one knee before her, taking her hands in his.

"You are safe here in the human lands," he tells her. "You are not safe in Nothril, and you are not safe with Lady Nothril. But you are old enough to choose what you want. You can stay with me and Kat. Or you can go back." He draws a deep breath. "You must choose for yourself."

She looks up at him, looks at me, and then back at the towering visage of her terrifying mother. Her brow hardens. Her voice is quiet, but the swirling wind carries her answer to my ears. "I do not want to leave Nothril like this."

Rahk's eyes shutter. He tightens his grip on her hands. "You know that I cannot protect you if you go back. I will not see you again."

Tears well up in her eyes. She throws her arms around his neck, and he holds her tightly.

"I love you, Pavi," he chokes. "Do not let Nothril change your sweet heart."

She nods, clinging harder as she sobs. Then she pushes back and starts toward the Wood.

I block her path with my arm. "Not yet."

I step closer to where Lady Nothril towers over the Wood. I lift my voice and cry: "We will return your daughter in exchange for the release of every human slave in all of Nothril. Only then can you have her back."

Lady Nothril sneers down at me, my ripped dress flying around my ankles, my hair in my face. Then she dives back into the Wood.

The wind goes still.

The whole world goes still.

I glance at the rise to see the tops of soldier helmets peering over the edge. Then I turn back to the border. Rahk steps to my side, lacing his fingers with mine.

Neither of us breathes in that moment.

Then a lone figure emerges from the Wood. A human. I recognize him immediately as one of the slaves I encountered during the raid.

Several more people begin stumbling out after him. Bewilderment casts across their face as they look upon the human world.

They keep coming. Dozens—hundreds. Men, women, even young children.

Lady Nothril let them go.

It is the first man who finally releases a great, "Hurrah! We are free!"

I watch them come, tears leaking out of my eyes. "Jacob, if you could only see this."

It starts as a whisper but ends in a flood.

A squeeze on my hand tears my attention away. Pavi smiles at me, and though there is fear in her gaze, there is also a steely determination. "Thank you," she whispers.

"For what?"

She just smiles and lets go. She runs to Rahk one more time, hugging him desperately. He kisses the top of her head. Then she releases him and walks toward the Wood.

Rahk watches her go. She stops at the border. Turns around one last time. Waves.

Then she vanishes.

The wind whips Rahk's white hair around his face. He releases a great sigh. I watch his lips move briefly. Then he turns away.

Forever letting his little sister go.

Suddenly, a cry goes up.

"Hail Lord Protector of Harbright!"

I look around, confused, until I realize they are referring to Rahk. He also doesn't seem to realize they are calling to him. He has come to my side, but looks up in bewilderment. Then his eyes go wide as he hears what the soldiers and the rescued slaves alike are crying out to him.

They surround him, falling to their knees to thank him.

For a fae prince, he doesn't seem to have a clue what to do with all of this praise.

"What are you—?" he demands, stumbling backward, only to be met with more warriors thanking him for protecting Harbright. My tears turn to laughter.

Rahk looks over the heads of the people surrounding him. He searches the crowd, his eyes scanning fast, his face twisted in concern—until his gaze lands on me. He visibly sags in relief.

Then he shoves aside the people coming to him. He breaks into a run, and I've hardly a moment to breathe before he's caught me up in his arms, holding the back of my head and kissing me desperately. I grab hold of the top of his breastplate, pulling him deeper into the kiss and pouring every piece of my heart into his lips.

"There are no more secrets," I gasp between kisses. "I promise, I promise, I promise."

He smiles and kisses my nose. "I know."

"One benefit to having your mother nearly invade our land," I add with a gesture toward the empty fields, "is that I doubt people will have any interest in farming carriage-sized pumpkins."

He laughs. That beautiful laugh that only I have been able to earn. It makes me happy as he replies, "I daresay your assessment will prove correct."

EPILOGUE

KAT

I WAKE SURROUNDED by warmth. I stretch my limbs, only to find them very firmly trapped. I open my eyes.

Rahk sleeps soundly beside me, his arms banded around me, his hair tickling my nose. I smile and nuzzle closer to him. His hand skates up my back, a sleepy grunt escaping his throat. Sunshine pours through the window, but neither of us make a move to get up. Rahk's hand moves a little more intentionally, making me realize he has awakened.

"Morning," I murmur.

He grunts in reply and then, eyes still closed, kisses my face in search of my lips.

A knock sounds at the door. It is Mary. "Kat? My lord? I am so sorry—but I think the queen's carriage just parked in front of Vandermore Manor?"

I sit bolt upright. Rahk pulls me back down and calls in his sleep-deepened voice: "Tell her to come back tomorrow."

"Rahk!" I chastise.

He grins.

I grab a robe as I get up. "Do you know what she might want?"

"She did not bring an army, so I don't think she intends to arrest or kill Lord Rahk."

Rahk leans back, his hands tucked behind his head as he says, "A fruitless endeavor."

I shake my head at him, and he just flashes that Nothril smirk back. "Well, she cannot do anything to hurt Rahk. Harbright would riot. Can you get her settled in the parlor with tea and Charity's finest culinary temptations while we get ready?"

"I will do my best," Mary replies.

"Wait, Mary—wasn't Lord Oliver coming this morning too?"

"If he isn't *late*," Mary grumbles in a grumble I know far too well. It's the grumble when she is trying to be angry but cannot.

I smile to myself. "We will be there soon!"

"Wrong," murmurs Rahk from behind me as he wraps me up in an embrace and kisses my shoulder. "You said yourself the queen cannot hurt me. We might as well let her enjoy the parlor in solitude."

"We need her to like us," I reply, trying to be stern, but it melts into giggles as he keeps kissing me. "Stop it! You are impossible!"

Somehow, we manage to keep the queen waiting only twenty minutes. I offer my brightest smile, and Rahk mostly keeps a straight face. *Mostly*. The very corner of his lip tilts just slightly up.

"What an honor, Your Majesty," I say, curtsying deeply.

Queen Vivienne wears a smart red dress, elegant but fit for more practical wear. She still carries her chin with that haughty tilt. She has not touched the tea, but two of Charity's biscuits are suspiciously absent from the plate.

"I have come at the very particular request of my son," Queen Vivienne says abruptly. "He requires Lord Rahk's tutelage in the matters of fencing. He says he will take lessons from no other, despite my best coaxing."

I blink. Is that her way of saying we are back in her good graces? Does she trust us now?

"You will be supervised at all times, of course," the queen says, not waiting for Rahk's answer. "Also, a diplomat from Aursailles has come with concerns of their receding border. I have promised to send you, Lord Rahk, to aid my father in these matters. I anticipate other kingdoms will have similar requests, so I expect you will stay as busy as you like in the coming years."

Rahk's miniscule smirk widens slightly. He bows. "As you wish, my liege."

"That is all," Queen Vivienne announces, getting to her feet. "Prince Lionel will have your service begin tomorrow. My steward will send the details."

With that, she sweeps out of the room. Rahk leans back against the doorway, listening until Edvear sees the queen out and the front door shuts behind her. He arches an eyebrow at me. "That could have been a letter."

I grin up at him. "You, my husband, are *officially* back in Harbright society."

"I missed it dearly."

I shake my head, trying not to give him the satisfaction of a smile. The rattle of approaching carriage wheels draws my attention to the window. I peer out as Lord Oliver's carriage arrives, driving past the trimmed hedge that once displayed a rearing stallion, but now is in the shape of a humble man with a needle and thread.

Mary is already out the door, and I can almost hear her telling him he is late again as he hops down from the box. He flashes a charming grin at her, replying something as he stops just a smidge too close. His gaze is wholly fixed on her as she gestures with her hands and tells him something. His cheeks turn pinker by the second. Then, abruptly, he darts forward and kisses her on the lips.

I gasp, then cover my mouth. I'm about to look away, to give them privacy, when she smacks him away and makes to storm off. He grabs her hand and pulls her back, laughing, and for all her protests, she leans into him just slightly. I smirk. Oliver says something to her, clear enough that I can read his lips. *"Mary, you know I'm going to marry you, right?"*

I step away from the window to avoid nosing any further into their privacy, lifting my eyebrows at Rahk. "I think Lord Oliver might be in love."

"You are just now realizing this?"

Mary marches inside the house then and comes straight to the parlor. Her face is as red as a beet. "Well! I had better clear these dishes now that the queen is gone!"

Rahk and I share a smile and step out of the parlor. Edvear meets us with a bright smile and erect ears. "Lady Katherine! News from your cousin has come. All the land at the edge of the Long Lost Wood has been restored to their rightful owners, yourself included. Though he expressed some concern over the speed with which the liquid part of your fortune was being spent."

"Ah yes, that. Tell him not to worry about it."

"That's it? He just should not worry about it?"

"Not at all. It is all going to a good cause."

The cause, of course, being helping to get all the freed Nothril slaves on their feet. Five hundred and thirty-seven people found freedom unexpectedly that day, and as it turns out, ensuring they all have a roof over their heads, food in their belly, clothes on their back, and enough to go where they want in the world, can make a rather significant dent even in a fortune as vast as mine.

"You seem particularly chipper this morning," Rahk observes of our steward.

Edvear's smile broadens. He ducks his head, clasping and unclasping his hands in front of him. "Well, I have received good news."

"Oh?" I ask.

"Well . . . Mrs. Finch has given me an answer. To a question I asked her."

Rahk's eyebrows shoot up. "Truly?"

"What question?" I demand, looking between the two of them.

"She agreed to marry me!" Edvear bursts, color blooming across his happy face.

Just then, the door at the end of the hallway bursts open and Becky runs out. "I'm going to have a papa again!" she cries, barreling into Edvear's arms and hugging him tight.

"A very good papa," Charity says, appearing in the doorway, a kitchen towel tossed over her shoulder.

"That is wonderful news!" I rush to embrace her as Rahk claps Edvear on the back.

"I knew you had ulterior motive for always asking when we were leaving the human lands," Rahk says.

Edvear's ears twitch. "It was stressful not knowing if I would all of a sudden never see them again, and never know if they were taken care of!" He glances at Charity, then down at Becky, who clings to his waist. "I am glad we are never leaving now."

Rahk and I leave them to have their moment, stepping outside into the warm sunshine. Bartholomew nickers happily in her stall. I greet her with kisses and she tries to chomp my hair.

"What do you say?" Rahk says from behind me. I turn to find his wings fully extended as he holds Bartholomew's saddle. "I think it is time for a belated birthday celebration."

"Wait one minute!" I cry, racing back into the house. When I return, Rahk has Bartholomew saddled and ready to go. I cannot help but admire his beautiful wings in the sunshine. He turns when he hears my steps. The look he gives me is so warm and full of love.

I hold up my wildly expensive—and heavy—birthday present. "We cannot forget Fool's Circle."

He leans down to kiss me. "No, we cannot."

Then we are flying through the fields at breakneck speed, me on horseback and Rahk low in the air. The wind rushes past us and we share a grin as the thrill fills our blood.

WANT TO READ A DELETED ASH AND STELLA SCENE?

DOWNLOAD THE SCENE HERE:

AnastasisBlythe.com/Stella

COMING SOON:

BRIDE OF THE STARBORN PRINCE

An orphaned lady-in-waiting searching for her past.
A fae prince desperate to protect his city.
Will their forbidden attraction destroy everything they are trying to save?

MORE FROM ANASTASIS BLYTHE

THE ZHENINGHAI CHRONICLES

Maiden of Candlelight and Lotuses
Guardian of Talons and Snares
Warrior of Blade and Dusk
Princess of Shadows and Starlight
Captive of Twilight and Treachery
Daughter of Darkness and Dreams

THE KING AND THE ASSASSIN

The Assassin Bride
The Neverseen King
The Nightmare Queen

BRIDES OF THE FAE

Bride of the Fae Prince
Bride of the Midnight Prince

ABOUT THE AUTHOR

Anastasis Blythe makes her home in central Texas with her husband. When she's not writing, she gardens, accompanies local bands and choirs on piano, rescues feral cats, and tries to keep up with the laundry. She loves exploring the world through reading, walks in nature, and thoughtful conversations.

To stay connected with her, be sure to sign up for her newsletter at AnastasisBlythe.com/Rahk.

Connect with Anastasis online at:

Website - AnastasisBlythe.com

Instagram - @AnastasisBlythe

Facebook - Anastasis Blythe

Goodreads - Anastasis Blythe

www.ingramcontent.com/pod-product-compliance
Lightning Source LLC
Chambersburg PA
CBHW020344310726
48979CB00015B/2496/J

* 9 7 8 1 9 6 0 6 0 6 1 2 9 *